T0221984

# Dead Things Are Closer Than They Appear

# Dead Things Are Closer Than They Appear

ROBIN WASLEY

SIMON & SCHUSTER BFYR

NEW YORK LONDON TORONTO SYDNEY NEW DELHI

SIMON & SCHUSTER BFYR

An imprint of Simon & Schuster Children's Publishing Division
1230 Avenue of the Americas, New York, New York 10020

SIMON & SCHUSTER BOOKS FOR YOUNG READERS
and related marks are trademarks of Simon & Schuster, LLC.
Simon & Schuster: Celebrating 100 Years of Publishing in 2024
For information about special discounts for bulk purchases, please contact Simon & Schuster
Special Sales at 1-866-506-1949 or business@simonandschuster.com.
The Simon & Schuster Speakers Bureau can bring authors to your live event.
For more information or to book an event, contact the Simon & Schuster Speakers Bureau at
1-866-248-3049 or visit our website at www.simonspeakers.com.
Interior design by Hilary Zarycky
The text for this book was set in Perpetua Std.
Manufactured in the United States of America

2   4   6   8   10   9   7   5   3
Library of Congress Cataloging-in-Publication Data
Names: Wasley, Robin, author.
Title: Dead things are closer than they appear / Robin Wasley.
Description: First edition. | New York : Simon & Schuster Books for Young Readers, [2024] |
Audience: Ages 14+. | Audience: Grades 10–12. |
Summary: Seventeen-year-old Sid lives in a tourist town where magic lies buried beneath the
earth, but other than that, has a completely ordinary existence, until one day her brother goes
missing and the ground opens up, unleashing the magic and zombies within.
Identifiers: LCCN 2022052486 (print) | LCCN 2022052487 (ebook) |
ISBN 9781665914604 (hardcover) | ISBN 9781665914628 (ebook) |
Subjects: CYAC: Magic—Fiction. | Zombies—Fiction. | End of the
world—Fiction. | Sibling—Fiction. | LCGFT: Zombie fiction. | Novels.
Classification: LCC PZ7.1.W388 De 2023  (print) | LCC PZ7.1.W388  (ebook) |
DDC [Fic]—dc23
LC record available at https://lccn.loc.gov/2022052486
LC ebook record available at https://lccn.loc.gov/2022052487

*This was my tenth book. It took me twenty years to get here.*
*I can't say I never gave up. Sometimes life happens. Sometimes you think*
*you've lost the part of yourself that dreamed big.*
*What I can say is sometimes quitting isn't forever.*
*And sometimes you do the things you thought you couldn't.*
*I dedicate this book to myself.*

# CHAPTER 1

*W*hen it rains in Wellsie, you can see the ghosts.

That's what we call these remnants of a thing long past, laid to rest in the ground with all other dead things. Magic *was* here once. And it left its toenail clippings for you to find.

The thing is, we're a tourist town. They want to sell this.

It's the same deal for any place sitting on a fault line, though the lingering energy manifests differently. In Siberia, people get vertigo. The temperature drops, all their body hair stands on end, and they fall over like one of those baby goats. I've seen GIFs. In Alaska, steam jets from the earth every time the earth rumbles, a natural sauna smelling of molasses or roses or woodsmoke depending on who's sniffing it. The point is, for those who want to stand where magic lies sealed beneath the earth, there are dozens of places to go.

They come to Llewellyn—Wellsie—because our "ghosts" look like rainbows. Plus, we have mountains and whatnot.

This is relevant because our reputation as a top vacation destination directly affects my physical and emotional well-being.

Like when Wellsie decides to have a deluge of apocalyptic proportions.

Fault-line tours run in the rain, obviously. But with none of the usual hiking, camping, or kayaking going on, everyone else just hangs out in coffee shops all day. Which means I do hard labor.

Wrapping a rag around the steam wand, a gush of hot mist wafts upward, fogging my glasses and multiplying the frizzies around my face. In the movies, people are always polishing their glasses while staring off into the middle distance and having deep thoughts. In reality, it's something people do when they realize they've made the wrong drink and are weighing the pros and cons of handing it to the customer anyway.

Through the haze of steam, people crowd around every table; some hover at the window, wiping the condensation away to watch the rain. Lulu's is not a large place, going from cozy to cramped in seconds. The customer line extends all the way back to the door, where umbrellas are stacked in a haphazard heap. It takes everything in me not to scream "Squirrel!" and clear the place in five seconds. It's the college kids' fault for feeding them all these years. Now they're a menace to society, afraid of nothing, crawling up a pant leg to wrestle the bagel straight from your hand.

Lulu's Café has been packed every day since Sugar, Sugar closed. We serve decent coffee, but Sugar, Sugar was far superior in the baked goods department. Sugar, Sugar cared about their customers. They had actual name badges. I have *a* name badge, but it does not say, SID SPENCER. It says, HELLO, MY NAME IS HERE'S YOUR COFFEE, PLEASE GO. We stand behind the counter, stare into space, do next to nothing, and scowl any time the bell on the door jingles. I'm pretty sure Joe specifically hires people who embrace mediocrity. Just this morning, when I was blearily drinking the coffee my mother (a morning person) made, I asked her how she got it so perfect—strong, yet not too strong. And she replied, "I measure it."

Whatever. I'm not a morning person, which means I become

competent at life an hour before bedtime. Some people jump out of bed, eager to face the day. Some people wake up and sob, "I wish I knew how to quit you" into their pillows. My ex-best friend Nell once said, "If you aren't getting quality sleep, how can you be your best self?" Maybe I don't have a *best* self. Maybe I have *one* self with no qualifier, a self that takes the last nacho everyone else is too polite to take.

As the orders multiply next to me, I work halfheartedly on latteing through them. It involves a lot of yawning and sprinkling the wrong spices on top of foam.

Our crowd-control needs increase by a factor of ten when spring and summer roll around and the town is at its rainiest. Losing even one of the ten million coffee shops in Wellsie means we'll be infested. We *need* Sugar, Sugar. The tourists need to go somewhere to demand oat milk. The college students need to go somewhere to buy one small coffee and camp out with their laptops all day.

A warped reflection of my face appears, all red and sweaty, hair literally everywhere, in the chrome of the espresso machine. I'm reminded of all the times I've looked in the mirror without my glasses. Soft around the edges, round in the face, doughy in the body—exactly like a cream puff. And when I put my glasses on, same.

Enough people in books gaze at themselves in mirrors to convince me it's something everyone does and I shouldn't feel weird about it. But girls in books do it to see that they are white and possess a beauty of which they are wholly unaware. In my personal experience, I stare at my reflection to see that I'm Korean and that I could maybe pass as a semifunctional human being if I wasn't too lazy to shower. You have two choices with curly hair: 1.) Wash it, brush it when it's wet (NEVER DRY), spend two hours lying on the floor with it fanned out to air-dry, and refuse to expose it to the elements ever again; 2.) Don't wash it and throw it into a nest on top of your head.

I chose the latter option today so that's where I'm at, emotionally.

"Sara!" I shout, as a tremor ripples through the floor, jiggling the cup I've placed on the pickup counter. Bracing it with one hand, I wait for the quivers to subside. You can instantly tell the tourists from the locals based on who stops midsentence and gapes and who bites unperturbed into their biscotti so all we hear is open-mouthed crunching.

A woman wearing a WELLSIE: WHERE THE MAGIC HAPPENS T-SHIRT—Sara, I assume—clutches the counter with both hands for balance. An extremely extra-looking camera hangs around her neck. When the earth rumble fades, she stares at me, wide-eyed. "Does that happen often?"

I shrug. "Often enough. It happens on every fault line. You'll get used to it."

Oblivious to the customers giving me death glares as the crowd expands by the second, she whispers ominously, "Is the magic trying to get out?

"It *can't* get out," I say as patiently as seventeen years of this allow. "What you see, what you hear, they're just echoes—"

"*Guardians* still have magic, though," she rushes to say, and I realize engaging at all was the wrong move. "They could unlock the fault lines." She leans in closer, watching me without blinking. "Have you ever . . . met one?"

"I've met a lot of con artists," I say, trying to figure out if she's one of the conspiracy theorists who come through here convinced the whole town has superpowers and we're just covering it up.

Her eager smile fades.

"Well, it must be wonderful to grow up here," she muses, not making any move to leave. "To remember that magic used to be everywhere once."

It was, and people abused it, and it had to be locked in the ground forever, but whatever.

Joe, the café manager, who treats customers like crap in a way I've always admired, pauses next to me, glowering at Sara. Joe is even less pleased everyone's coming to Lulu's. "You got your coffee," he barks at her. "Please leave."

Occasionally, people think he's being funny, which never leads anywhere good. Luckily, Sara looks properly offended and backs away, muttering that she'll go to a better-mannered fault-line town next time.

"The one in Iowa is top-notch," Joe, unfazed, says to her retreating back before giving the never-ending queue of cups next to me a significant glance. He's never been to Iowa because no one goes to Iowa unless they've been kidnapped and brought there in the trunk of a car. Still, he promotes it to everyone, hoping they'll never come back.

The bell above the door jingles again. Two more people wedge themselves inside.

I freeze for a moment, a deer in headlights, not knowing what to do with myself.

He shakes his head, droplets flying everywhere, as she shields her face and laughs, a musical laugh I can hear over the din of conversation.

*It must be wonderful to grow up here. To remember that magic used to be everywhere once.*

But most of us are not Guardians. We don't possess powers. We aren't chosen to protect Keys of sacrificed bone. We just exist here, unextraordinary, and all we see are the remnants left behind. Memories of what we lost.

My body restarts. Instantly, I'm back to packing espresso into the brew head.

I thought they wouldn't come.

I grind more coffee and pretend I'm grinding bones, watch espresso dribble into shot glasses like black blood, and foam milk until it resembles the froth oozing from someone's mouth when they've been poisoned. My hearts in the foam look like lumpy teardrops.

Neither of them orders a latte; I won't have to call their names.

Nell's hair is getting long and remains perfectly straight and silky. "Look, I have frizz too," she said once.

"That's static," I said back. "It's not the same."

She'd tilted her head wistfully and said, "I wish I had hair like Blackpink."

"You can't have hair like theirs unless you have a legion of stylists following you around." It wasn't what I'd wanted to say. I'd wanted to say I wished I did too. That in a town like this, a Korean girl has to be Blackpink or she's no one and there is no in between.

Finn's hair is longer, too, the same blond as hers. He has green eyes rather than her blue, but they look like matching Gap models. I read an article once saying couples tend to look alike and they choose partners with similar levels of attractiveness. The article didn't specify how one measured this.

A touch of pink tinges her cheeks as she ducks her head. Finn reaches across the table to brush a lock of hair out of her face, smiling like she's the most precious thing in the world.

I focus on the amber-colored beams overhead and on the chalk menu on the wall, reading the names, the prices. A local artist is displaying a whole lot of naked fairy art.

And then I'm staring at a name on the coffee cup in my hand, and my breath suspends in my lungs for a moment—Adam O'Brien. Of course he's here. "Adam? I have a latte for Adam?" Shaky, sounding like a question. Like I'm afraid.

A hulking red-haired figure approaches the counter. It's not fair we're the same age, yet he has this much extraneous height. He always complains I make the lattes too hot. He doesn't dare complain to Joe or he'll get ice-cold milk with a few coffee grounds floating on top.

When he doesn't move away immediately, I force myself to give him what I hope is a dark, forbidding stare that probably comes off as constipated, while he gives me *that* look, the look someone gives you when they *want* you to know they know something about you. His gaze is a spotlight and I'm exposed, not just to him, but to everyone. He makes a show of turning the cup around to where his name is scrawled.

"Checking for a confession of eternal love," he says. "I hear that's your thing."

Adam once shot at the fault line. The bullet ricocheted, and now he has no ear. He really doesn't get to mock anyone for their decisions.

Maybe I'll ask if he remembers our last conversation, after he asked Nell out. How I also know something he'd rather I didn't.

The truth is, there are two types of girls in this world: those who get asked out and those who reject people for their friends. The first boy I rejected for Nell was Dave Wrenn—my first crush, second grade. He wasn't the last. I never told her, not any of the times. It's the kind of secret you keep from beautiful people. Rejecting Adam was easy, though, the way it is when that person rolls freshmen down the stairs in trash cans. I still told him gently. It didn't matter. He'll never forget *I* was the one who embarrassed him, not Nell.

His lips curl, not a smile. "That letter you gave Warren entertained us for weeks. On the bright side, at least people know you exist now."

Because before that, I was "Nell's friend." That's what he means, and the sting brings tears to my eyes. Triumph widens his smile.

"Joe," I say, a distinct hitch to my voice. "Adam O'Brien doesn't like his coffee."

Joe turns off the coffee grinder and faces him, clenching a spoon in his fist. A spoon is not a particularly threatening object, but the fist holding it is rapidly turning red. Joe takes coffee complaints seriously. The amusement fades from Adam's eyes.

"Something wrong with your coffee?" Joe growls.

Adam stares at him sullenly but says nothing.

Joe's eyes narrow. "That's what I thought. Get out."

Adam strolls away, but not without a mean snicker that travels back to me.

It's accurate what they say about high school and gossip. Once you become "that girl," it follows you. There are worse things to be known for, obviously. I could be that guy who got an erection during his eighth grade China presentation. Spontaneous erections are a thing, and in my mind, they could happen to anyone. If I had a penis, it would absolutely happen to me, because of course. The point is, fair or unfair, he never lived that down. I am the girl who wrote a six-page love letter to Finn Warren and that's all I'll ever be.

I feel Nell's gaze even before our eyes meet. She doesn't smile. Something flickers over her face, but it vanishes so quickly, I can't decipher it. She says something to him, to Finn. As his head turns, I'm already looking away, and there's a lump in my throat I can't swallow.

Maybe she misses me.

"I'm sorry you're upset," she'd said at the time, in her quiet way. *Not* an apology. Except she was teary-eyed and afraid to look at me. "People can't help who they like."

Nell is the kind of quiet that comes off like she'll only notice you if you're worth her time. If she likes you, you believe you've proven something, and therefore you like yourself more. It's a psychological thing. I've had years of studying it. Maybe I'm an example.

Meanwhile, if you're average, you're approachable; people like you well enough, and you're the one they talk to. Even if you aren't the one they want.

She knew him because of me. She barely said a word to him for months.

I sneak another glance at their table by the windows. They've gone, though the weight of their presence lingers. I have to wipe their table, stand where he rested his guitar case. They left their coffee mugs on the table rather than bringing them to the dish bin. It's okay to hate people who do that, right?

Do I miss Nell? That's not really a question when you meet someone in the first grade and you've been together ever since. A decade.

I pick up her empty mug. Vanilla-flavored coffee with cinnamon sprinkled on top.

I met Finn Warren when he played an open mic in this very café, when we talked all night. I was his first friend in town.

"I feel like I can tell you anything," he'd said at the time.

I'd thought the same about him, though half a year later, a letter seemed easier.

Easier until his whole basketball team knew. Until everyone knew.

And when he asked Nell out, she knew too.

The thing about Nell no one else ever saw is that she's not cold or aloof, just painfully shy. Her deepest fear is embarrassment—walking around with her shirt inside out the whole day.

Or having everyone stare at her and laugh.

Finn did that to me.

I miss Nell. I miss her all the time. But she chose.

• • •

There's no sign of my brother, Matty, outside the café, though his shift at Hunt and Hike ends the same time as mine.

Wellsie's a small town, but ever since the sexual assault at Hampton College last year, my mother doesn't want me walking alone at night. It doesn't help that she recently watched the news and found out the KKK capital of the state is forty minutes from here, thus my white mother is now afraid of all white people. This would be fine except Wellsie is really friggin' white. So this is my life now.

Under the portico, shielded from the rain, I check my texts on the off chance my sister, Ella, decided to pick us up. The last text is a drooling emoji in response to me saying I have the book she wanted from the library. With a quick glance down the street toward Hunt and Hike I decide to walk before the rain gets worse. Matty can catch up with me.

As I turn, there's a split second of darkness before I slam straight into a stone wall appearing out of nowhere. With my face.

White lights blink against the black. Pain bursts its way through the shock.

This is what death feels like.

My nose is obliterated. Not even a graze, but a full-on face smash. Tears fill my eyes, blurring whatever vision I have left.

A hand grabs my upper arm to keep me from toppling backward, and the other catches my glasses before they slide off my nose. *Walls don't have hands.*

"Sorry," I mutter, checking my nose for protruding bones.

It takes a second to get over the blow, apparently caused by a chest. In my defense, all tall people are walls when their chests are on level with your face.

He probably hits his head on a lot of doorframes, and, like, trees.

Through tears, I register a rangy white dude with a Sugar, Sugar T-shirt beneath his hoodie. I'm wearing a Lulu's Café T-shirt. We're rivals. Maybe I should challenge him to a dance-off.

I brush the moisture from my eyes to see Brian Aster looking down at me, his brown hair plastered to his forehead and dripping with rain. Sometimes faces are difficult to describe because they're nondescript. Brian's face is hard to describe because it's not. His face is all lines and angles. Like his nose, sharp and triangular. Like the brows, all perfectly horizontal. Plus, he's looking *directly at me*. It's only when faced with this unnerving blue stare, a dark blue I can't see past, that I realize no one does that, looks *directly* at you. Except maybe Paddington Bear. Paddington Bear is always going around giving people hard stares.

The SUGAR, SUGAR in curly script across his chest is a little incongruous with the whole tattooed, I-clearly-cut-my-own-hair vibe he has going on.

That's when I remember.

*It's Brian Aster. I'll have to say something.*

Everyone knows what happened. We organized clothing drives, put out collection cans, and sent flowers and cards.

When Matty graduated from Mountain Ridge Academy, the fancy school I most definitely do not attend, Brian was a year below him. I don't know Brian or his stepsisters, aside from seeing them around town.

I was mentally complaining about Sugar, Sugar closing earlier, because I'm the worst.

I have never spoken to Brian. Unless you count me ordering sticky buns every Saturday. And I've definitely never talked to anyone experiencing a tragedy. The options are limited and terrible: it gets better, everything happens for a reason, what doesn't kill you makes you stronger. Sometimes there isn't an upside. Sometimes what doesn't kill you maims you for life.

Brian has never spoken to me either. Unless you count him silently handing me every sticky bun they have with no judgment whatsoever. So it isn't really fair when I don't say anything nice, and instead snap, "You should watch where you're going."

One eyebrow lifts. "Sorry."

Right . . . I crashed into him. But he was the one lurking over here in the shadows. I tuck a stray curl behind my ear for lack of something better to do, and it pops out anyway.

He bends to sweep up the phone and book I dropped during the crash.

*Oh my God.*

Both his eyebrows lift as he looks at the cover of *A Vampire Felt Me Up Last Night*, then back at me.

Obviously, I need to move across state lines. That is the only option at this point. "Thanks," I say, snatching them out of his hands.

"So," Brian says, as though nothing happened. "I was just at Hunt and Hike. Matt wanted me to tell you not to walk home alone. He had to stay late to finish up with a customer, but your sister is on her way and will meet you both here."

I glance at Hunt and Hike two blocks down. "My family is terrified rapists or white supremacists will approach me in the night."

Brian's expression doesn't change.

I didn't really mean to insinuate he's one or the other, but here we are.

He eyes me standing with my arms crossed. "According to Matt, you once went sledding on the mountain in a no-trespassing area," he says casually. "A ranger on a snowmobile came by, but instead of running into the woods with the others, you dropped to the ground and pretended you were dead. As you don't appear to be lying prone on the sidewalk, I assume you don't feel threatened."

"I don't feel threatened," I say, peeved Matty would tell *anyone* that story, much less Brian Aster. "Thanks for letting me know." I slide down the wall under the café window where the sidewalk is dry. Instead of taking off, he sinks his long, lean form to the ground a few feet away.

*Okay . . .*

In the silence, I drum my hands on my knees. "I don't need you to wait here," I blurt out. "I'm not helpless. My family is overprotective. I tried to become a runner a few years ago, but my mom made me wear glow-in-the-dark ceiling stars taped to my shirt until she could pick up a reflective vest. It was so embarrassing, I stopped running."

Brian pins me with that direct stare. "I don't think you're helpless. Maybe I don't have anywhere I need to be right now."

"Okay." I force my hands to stop their awkward rhythm. "I didn't realize you and Matty were friends. Were you buying weed off him or something?"

He frowns. "Yeah, Spencer, because I do all my drug deals at Hunt and Hike."

"I thought . . ." I sneak him a dubious glance. "I'm sorry, you don't seem like you hunt. Or hike."

"Maybe I hunt and hike all the time," he says. "You don't know me."

He's right. I know he's a musician and people in town say he was a child prodigy. I know his father owned Sugar, Sugar. I know his parents died three months ago.

"I'm sorry," I say again, softly.

"I don't hunt or hike," he admits.

I'm unable to make out his expression as he stares straight ahead.

Even in the dark, the fault-line ghosts are visible because of the rain. Wisps, translucent as heat waves, yet iridescent like floating gasoline, rise through the pavement unhindered. Rainbows made of smoke. Objectively, I can see they're beautiful. I understand why the tourists come here.

The silence hovers around us like the humidity in the air. Thick, slightly uncomfortable.

His arms rest on his knees. A tattoo peeks out from his sleeve on the underside of his wrist where it meets his hand: f-holes like those on a violin. Faint oven burns dot both his hands. He used to work at Sugar, Sugar. With his dad.

Tourists think the remnants in Wellsie are proof magic never really left us. But if it *is* here, and the world is this hard, then it's good for nothing.

"Um," I try. "Are you . . . okay?"

He faces me with a closed expression, waiting for me to continue, but not in the normal way people wait, neither polite nor impatient. One shoulder inches toward his ear. Like he's bracing himself.

Because he knows what I'm going to say next. It must have happened to him countless times in the last few months. Strangers talking to him for the first time, in the worst moment of his life.

*He wants to talk about literally anything else.*

"If you were a Guardian, what superpower would you want?" I blurt out, because it's easy, not heavy, and something we've all thought about at some point. What if we had individual abilities, unique to us, the way they do? The way everyone did once. When magic was free.

His eyes close, lashes nearly kissing his cheekbones. He pauses for a long moment, his head resting back against the wall. "Is it weird to say I've never wanted one? That all I want out of life is to play violin and live in reasonable comfort?" He doesn't wait for me to respond. "Or were you expecting me to say: the ability to bring people back from the dead?"

This didn't go the way I planned. "No," I say too quickly. "I expected . . . like . . . maybe you'd want the power to put pockets in all women's clothing. Or the ability to turn horses into unicorns."

"Unicorns are just horses with horns on their faces."

"Right, they're murder horses. Who wouldn't want a murder horse?"

He says nothing, but one corner of his mouth lifts, so I know he'd want one if given the opportunity.

"Do you want a peanut butter cup?" I say.

His eyes are open again, treating me to a direct stare that makes me want to pull my hood up. But his shoulders relax. For the first time, I notice the blue-purple circles beneath his eyes. "Yeah, I'll have one," he says.

He waits silently while I dig a bag of peanut butter cups out of my raincoat pocket.

When I hand him a foil-wrapped chocolate, he doesn't look like such a hard person—he looks like a dude holding a peanut butter cup. I wonder if he measures his eyelashes with a ruler so he can brag about them to everyone he knows.

He eats it while we wait, watching the rain hit the puddles in the street. The air is made of mist tonight, giving the streetlamps a soft, orb-like glow—the light doesn't stream; it floats.

A couple minutes later, I place another one beside him. He eats that one too.

"What do you think of white chocolate?" I ask him.

"I think it's not chocolate," he says.

I take his hand and pour about six into his palm.

When Ella pulls up in her white jeep, honking five cheerful, jarring times and earning a glare from both of us, Brian pushes himself to his feet. He glances down at me and reaches out a hand, palm up. I stare at it, uncertain, and give him a low five.

He coughs, more like a rusty laugh, bending to take hold of my wrist and tug me to my feet in one easy motion.

*Oh.*

"Thanks," I say, feeling ridiculous.

Though his hand falls away immediately, the heat of his grip lingers, fingerprints cooling in degrees. A shiver ripples between my shoulder blades, and I realize for the first time how chilly the night is.

He's still standing there looking at me when Matty jogs up through the rain, slicking strands of wet multicolored hair back from his forehead. "Sorry, I got held up going through every single brand of camping stove. I'm one hundred percent sure Chester Graves is a doomsday prepper—he basically admitted he has a bunker in his backyard . . . " He pauses, his gaze darting to Brian, to me, then back to Brian. "Hey."

Brian nods at him. "Hey."

"Um, do you need a ride anywhere?" I ask Brian.

"No, I'm fine," Brian says at the exact moment Matty says, "No, he's fine."

I blink at Matty and we have a silent yet easily readable why-are-you-like-this? conversation.

Unperturbed, Brian says, "I'll see you later, man." He gives me a brief nod and steps out from under the portico and into the rain.

"That was rude," I tell Matty under my breath.

"You don't need to be hanging out with him."

As he's never been *that kind* of older brother, I bristle. "Why?"

"He's a good guy," Matty says quickly, though something dark and foreign crosses his face. "But you don't want any part of that situation."

Before I can ask more, Matty tosses me a foil-wrapped cylinder I recognize instantly as my favorite burrito, otherwise known as the Mighty Bean, and then he's three steps away, hauling open the car door, conversation over. It's a classic diversion. 1) Make me catch something, instantly sending me into panic mode. 2) FOOD.

But as I watch Brian stride off down the street, his shoulders hunched, head bowed against the spray, I wonder what Matty meant.

# CHAPTER 2

*M*atty lets me have the front seat.

"I got your book," I mutter to Ella, tossing *A Vampire Felt Me Up Last Night* into her lap. "Out of curiosity, does each book in the series feature a sexy beast reaching a different base?"

Ella is checking her makeup in the rearview mirror, smoothing one fingertip under one cat-shaped blue eye. Her blond hair remains in a sleek high ponytail, despite the rain. "One can only hope," she says. "They're funny. The heroine is blond and sassy. Like me."

"In that case, is the next book *A Werewolf Snuck Out My Bedroom Window and Climbed Down a Drainpipe and Got Caught by My Father?*"

"No, because that's way too long." She glares at me. "And it was a trellis—get your facts straight."

When Dad removed the trellis on the side of the house, brutally murdering Mom's roses, at the time I thought he didn't like bees. Turns out he didn't like boys.

Ella peels out into the road, straight through a shimmering wall of rainbows. "Wheeeeee!" she cries, legit the only person in Wellsie who hasn't lost her sense of wonder.

As we careen down Main Street, I decide to save my burrito for when I'm less at risk of losing it to the floor and pretend not to hold on for dear life while pumping an imaginary brake. When her daughter, Zora, is in the car, Ella drives like an old lady, but when Zora is not in the car, she drives like a bat out of hell. In the next month, tourists will fill the town's bed-and-breakfasts for fault-line tours and camping excursions on Mount Hemsworth. Town Center, stuffed with sporting goods stores, restaurants, gift shops, and, yes, cafés, will be crawling with people. We urge Ella not to drive through Town Center in the summer. She works the front desk at a spa in East Wellsie and technically doesn't have to drive down Main Street at all.

Eventually, we'll steal her car and pretend we had nothing to do with it.

I turn to look at Matty in the back seat, still annoyed. He's gathering his dyed rainbow mane into his usual man-bun. Matty's hair doesn't react to the weather. It's the hair people always assume Asians have—all straight and shiny. I don't have it. We're both Korean, but not blood related. People here assume all Asians are related, so no one has ever noticed we don't look alike.

"Brian Aster cuts his own hair," I say to Matty. "And he has a thing for peanut butter cups."

"I thought he looked striking and intense," Ella adds.

Matty frowns, clearly having not considered any of these things before asking Brian to come meet me. "Brian is a good person," he reiterates. "He counts his items before getting into the express lane at the supermarket. I've seen him do it."

"I don't think he has friends," I say. "Everyone needs friends."

Matty rolls his eyes. "Like Finn Warren?"

"What do you know about Finn Warren?"

"Ella told me everything." Ella shoots him a murderous look in the rearview mirror that he ignores. "Also, since you and Nell aren't friends anymore, Mom's afraid you'll start making bombs in the basement."

I scowl at him, and he smiles in return. I'm not like Matty, a flame drawing moths. He has new friends at Hampton, plus his old friends from Mountain Ridge—a special K–12 school for that portion of the population that scores well on tests or has some impressive talent like Brian Aster. I go to Llewellyn High like a normal person.

"You didn't have to make him wait with me," I say.

Matty glances at me. "I didn't ask him to wait with you. I told him to tell you I was with a customer." He frowns before grumbling, "How come you never carry the stun gun I got you?"

I frown back. He bought me an electroshock weapon the size of a cell phone last year—a strange gift coming from the same person who got me a plastic moose that poops jellybeans. He explained the moose with "It reminded me of you." He never explained the stun gun.

"I'm not sure I have it in me to taser anyone," I say.

"It's not a taser—it doesn't shoot probes. You would use it if some dude was uncomfortably close. I thought you'd rather do that than stick your thumbs in his eyes."

That is accurate.

"I have one," Ella says breezily. "And I'd use it in a heartbeat."

"On who?" I ask, dubious.

"The father of my child."

Ella is six years older than Matty, eight years older than me. We often joke that our parents adopted her as a test kid. When she turned out weird, they adopted two spares out of desperation. It was strange when she became a mom. She had a baby, *a tiny human*, and yet she's still that person who threw my Bear Bear off the deck during a vacation, never to be seen or heard from again.

"The awkward meetup is tonight, isn't it?" I say quietly.

Ella's face is blank, but her fingers tighten around the steering wheel. "It's that time of month again." The time of month when my parents and Zach's parents drag Ella and Zach to dinner to maintain some semblance of a relationship between him and Zora. I'm pretty sure Zach goes so that his parents will continue to pay his child support. And Ella goes because she doesn't want Zora to grow up and wonder, the way she does, the way Matty does . . . the way I sometimes do.

"I'm staying at home tonight—you don't have to drive me to my apartment," Matty says to Ella.

That's weird. It's Saturday night. Doesn't he have anything better to do?

I get why Matty doesn't live at home, though Hampton College is basically down the street. No one wants to live with their parents during college, and his apartment in South Wellsie costs less per year than Hampton room and board. But considering how often he stays at home, I'm not sure it evens out in the end.

Then again, Matty is an insomniac who shares a tiny apartment with an extremely chatty Libertarian, and I, too, would need a break from nearly twenty-four hours of that special hell. Here, he can read all his books twice, play every video game to the end, learn to knit and pick locks and make cheese and all the other things I've caught him doing to pass the long hours of the night. No wonder he's always gotten straight A's. If I didn't need ten to twelve hours of sleep, maybe I'd go to a special school and get an early acceptance to Hampton. I'm not insecure or anything.

"Staying over again?" I ask him. "Why?"

"To hang out with my annoying sister who will either force me to watch *Train to Busan* for the millionth time or some K-drama she says is cute but will absolutely fucking wreck me by the end," he mutters. None of this sounds suspect. Except he's staring out the window with that same dark and foreign expression as before.

My sister scowls ahead through the rivers of water the wipers aren't quite managing to push aside. "Scenario: when I came out of the bathroom this morning, Zora was lying facedown on the stairs."

"As one does," Matty says.

"At these dinners, I'm supposed to provide updates on how Zora is doing—is this something I have to mention or should I pretend she's normal?"

"Say nothing," I say. "How long has this behavior been going on?"

Something about Ella's pause, and the narrowing of her eyes during that pause, makes me uneasy. "Oh, I don't know," she says in a singsong voice. "She's been upset since her evil nemesis, Madeline, caught her with a bag of rotting chicken bones at school and then the teacher took them away. According to Mrs. Hammer, Zora explained her possession of said bones with, and I quote, 'My *aunt* told me that if I want to unlock the fault line, I have to cut off my hand and make a key out of the bones.'"

"Oh God." I close my eyes. "You have to understand, I thought that would be a deterrent! I specifically said that was how the *OG* Guardians did it, that she would need to find a Guardian to give her a Key if she wanted to be one now."

"You've met my daughter, so I don't know why you thought she wouldn't instantly fixate on performing a blood sacrifice. You are so lucky she didn't amputate an appendage."

A suspicious snort emanates from the back seat, and I turn to glare at Matty as he guffaws into his sleeve.

"It's not funny," Ella fumes. "The confiscation of bones was not even the worst part. The worst part was Madeline telling Zora she wasn't a *real* Guardian and my five-year-old child replying with, 'Well, you're a fucking asshole.'"

I open my mouth, then close it, hiding my face in my seat belt.

Matty lets loose an explosion of laughter as he sprawls across the back seat.

"I get to have a parent-teacher conference on Monday. I didn't know they had those for kindergartners."

Still silently laughing, I manage to say, "Where did she learn to swear? Dad?"

"It was probably me," Ella says, swallowing. "Because I'm the worst mother."

An ache settles in my chest. She can't possibly believe that. I glance back at Matty. "Who is the worst Spencer in this car, raise your hand?" Except all three of us do.

My sister huffs, and in that moment, she looks exactly like Zora. Same hair, same forehead, same eyes . . . same pointy elf ears. I wonder how it's not weird for people when they look like someone else. I never have. Neither has Matty. Neither did Ella until she had Zora. When Zora grows up, she'll steal Ella's identity and commit crimes in her name.

"You are *not* the worst one, Siddy," Ella mutters.

"I'm pretty sure I'm the one who says, 'I'll be right back,' before heading to the basement to fix the electricity in a movie called *A Summer to Die*," I say.

Matty leans forward again. "Listen, I'm the one Dad picked up from the police station in the middle of the night."

"I had a child out of wedlock—I win," Ella says. "Matty is the smart one. Siddy is the one who tries the hardest—Mom always says that."

She does say that. I *try*. She said that upon receipt of my SAT results. Ella doesn't need to know that, or to know hearing it knocks the wind out of me.

Ella takes a shortcut through Hampton College. I roll down the window to help with the fogged windshield, and the campus smells of everything green: new leaves, fresh-cut grass, and dirt, which isn't green but smells green. Apple trees line both sides of the street, but the rain has washed the blossoms away early. A carpet of wet flowers covers the road. Ella pulls to a screeching halt to avoid hitting five students, flinging her arm across my chest to stop me from pitching forward. It's unconscious, the mom-arming.

"You're a good mother," I murmur.

She sits in profile, but a blue eye with a golden-brown rim around the pupil rolls toward me.

"You are," I insist. "I want to be like you when I grow up."

The blue-gold eye rolls back, flutter-blinking. She doesn't know that's always been true. I grew up thinking I'd be beautiful and charismatic and confident. I'm still waiting. When she gazes at herself in the mirror in the morning, I wonder if she sees what she is.

"You're raising a kid alone," Matty says softly. "If there's a super-hero in this town, it's you, magic or not."

Ella sniffs again. "Well, I suppose if anyone tried to hurt my kid, I would destroy them." She pauses. "It's probably wrong to take down a five-year-old named Madeline, though."

"Madeline could be a changeling demon child," I say.

We drive in silence for the rest of the way as we all contemplate ways to disappear someone without being caught. I've got nothing. All my nemeses are alive and well.

But when Ella pulls to a stop in the driveway, I hesitate before getting out of the car, facing Matty again. "You made a face when you mentioned Finn Warren. Why?" *Because he's the worst, right?* Maybe I want Matty to say that.

"At an open mic, he played a Nirvana song in a major key," Matty says. "That can't ever be forgiven."

Ella glances at me, a rueful smile curving her lips. "Listen, I know what it's like when a boy doesn't choose you. But that doesn't determine your worth." She presses on the horn five cheerful, jarring times.

I look at my hands. People say these things when others have flocked to them their entire lives. When it's always been easy. Zach was the only guy who ever left Ella, but he left her with a tiny human, so I will never say that to her.

There's a tenderness in Ella's eyes as she watches our mother come out onto the porch, carrying Zora under the armpits while she hangs there like a dead body. "One day you'll look outside yourself, at all the people you do have, and you'll see who you really are."

"It's like the magic," Matty says so softly I almost don't hear him. When he sees my quizzical look, he shrugs. "They say magic shows you who you are. Maybe love does that too."

It's uncharacteristically sentimental of him, but he doesn't elaborate, just leaps out of the car.

With a sigh, Ella gets out to clomp across the driveway in high-heeled boots to fetch her daughter, clad in a pink rhinestone-covered dress, hair in an identical high blond ponytail. As Ella waddles back with Zora in her arms, I round the car to help with the door.

But the moment Ella sets her down, Zora looks up at her, then at me, before calmly lying facedown on the driveway.

My sister observes her motionless child for a moment before

squeezing her eyes closed and tipping her face to the sky, letting the rain pelt her.

I exchange a glance with Matty, who leans against the car, amusement dancing around his lips. "Zo? I like your dress," I say.

My niece does not respond. She lets out a sigh, sounding like a motor in the puddle beneath her face.

Ella bends down. "Guardian or not, you're my favorite person," she says to her quietly.

As both of us peer at the side of Zora's face, one blue eye with a golden-brown rim around the pupil rolls toward us, narrows, and rolls back to stare at the wet pavement.

Ella hauls her daughter's limp body from the ground and plops her into the car seat.

"Thanks for the ride," I say to her. "I'll see you tomorrow, and I'll watch your child for exactly one hour."

She turns to beam her wide Ella smile, all perfect teeth and sparkling blue eyes. "I love you," she says.

"I love powdered orange cheese," Matty says, as he gives Zora a silly smile she does not return.

"I hate assholes," Zora says.

I doze during *Train to Busan*, curled in the corner of the couch under one of my mom's wool blankets. We've seen this movie so many times, I know it by heart.

The scent of the kimchi pajeon we burned and ate anyway lingers in the air.

When Matty's phone vibrates a soft, buzzing rattle on the coffee table, I'm instantly alert. For my first months in this country, I slept all day and cried all night. I blame prolonged jet lag for the fact I'm not a morning person and also why I sleep on a hair trigger.

That he flails for his phone to pick up on the first ring is annoying considering how many times he's sent me straight to voice mail.

"Yo," he says under his breath. "Hold on."

A silence follows. The hairs on my neck stand up the way they always do when someone's hovering over me like a giant creep. Out of instinct, I keep my breathing deep and even.

The cushion depresses slowly and Matty's weight lifts. When he moves, the floorboards creak, though he walks on the balls of his feet, tiptoeing, trying not to wake me. He doesn't turn the movie off.

I sit up in the dark, peering over the back of the couch. The bright light of the television splays across his retreating form. He holds his phone to his ear, but the movie is too loud for me to hear him.

And too loud for him to hear me.

Honestly, I'm worried he's into something foolish. Matty will say yes to most things, like streaking down Main Street in the dead of winter, slipping on ice, then requiring ten stitches.

Inch by inch, gritting my teeth every time the floor squeaks beneath my feet, I creep toward the living room and press my body to the wall beside the door.

"Why are you calling me?" Matty says in a low voice. "Aren't we meeting later? Why would you use one of those dancing-tooth post-cards the dentist mails to remind me of a six-month cleaning . . . at eleven p.m. . . . in the middle of nowhere? My mom thought it was a mistake and threw it out. You know I don't live at home anymore, right?"

Is Matty part of some college secret society that receives coded invites to meet in the dead of night? He's not even white—how is this possible?

"Slow down, Shandy. What happened? What did Josh say, exactly?" Urgency punctuates his words.

*Who's Josh? Shandy? Shandy Ohno?* He's a senior at Wellsie High, so it can't be a college group. I know Shandy; everyone knows Shandy. He high-fives every single person he passes in the school hallway. Also, he's beautiful, with eyelashes that curl up, whereas mine spike straight down, which strikes me as horribly unfair.

*Shandy* . . . so Matty is in a secret Asian club? There are only, like, four Asians in Wellsie. If I'm not invited, they can't even play proper mah-jongg.

I peek around the corner, but Matty's back faces me. He stands completely still, shoulders tensed.

"It's probably nothing," Matty says, but his voice wavers. "I'm closest. I'll go meet him and Parker. Call the others—tell them I'm on my way. Get there as soon as you can." Slowly, the hand holding his phone falls to his side. For a moment, he stands there, staring into the darkness of the living room.

I move away from the doorframe, back flat against the wall. Something on the edges of his voice sticks in my mind. It's the same something flickering over his face the moment he strides back into the kitchen. He sees me and freezes. Eyes wide, a deer in headlights. In the next instant, he rearranges his face, or attempts to.

"'Sup," I say.

"What the fuck, Siddy?" He brushes a wisp of rainbow hair off his damp forehead.

Ignoring that, I say, "I didn't know you knew Shandy Ohno."

"I know everyone." He's already grabbing the keys to Mom's car off the hook on the wall.

"Where are you going at this hour?"

"I . . . nowhere." But he inhales and lets it out slowly. "Look, a friend of mine is in trouble. I have to go get him, okay?" He's moved into the front hall and opened the coat closet.

"What kind of trouble?" My eyes bore into his. They're the same color as mine, so dark you can barely see the pupil.

Matty pauses in the middle of shrugging on a raincoat, his face half-cast in shadow. "It's nothing, okay?"

*It's not nothing.*

"Matty, what's going on?" I can hear how my voice has risen in pitch, bordering on panic. "Why are you being so weird?"

Suddenly he's in front of me, hugging my head hard. "I'm not into anything bad, Siddy, I swear," he says in that soft way he reserves for me. "You don't have to worry."

But I'll always worry about him. Once upon a time I had no brother. Or sister. Or parents. My brother and I don't share blood. We don't look alike. We are strangers brought together by chance. When we were kids, he used to run away to the end of the driveway every time he got mad at our parents. It never had anything to do with me, but I'd pack a small duffel bag and go with him. We'd discuss branching out from the driveway, going to stay in the bunker we were sure Mr. Graves had. I would have done that, too. Because when you get a family by luck, when you know love is not guaranteed, you hold on to it with both hands.

"I'll come with you to help your friend," I say. "Remember that time I said I'd go with you if you ever wanted to visit Korea?"

His voice is scratchy when he says, "Remember that time you drunk-texted me 'the shuttle tonk long so I peed in a bush' and I had to come pick you up from a party except you were wandering around on a street corner? I have that text screenshotted, printed, and framed on my desk. But my real question is, would you have wanted me to bring someone in that situation?"

"That happened *one* time," I mutter. "So it's a designated driver situation?" His conversation hadn't sounded like that at all.

"We'll talk when I get back, okay?"

"Okay." I let him pull back, his steps quickening to a trot as he heads toward the door.

When his hand is on the knob, he stares for a moment at the deadbolt. He glances back once and smiles, but it doesn't look like his smile. "Be back soon. Lock the door behind me."

He closes the door gently.

But moments later tires squeal as he backs out of the driveway too fast, accelerating down the street. I notice my heart then, the thud of it inside my chest, like a drum, like a warning.

Behind me, the movie plays; someone screams onscreen.

*I should have gone with him. I should have insisted.*

Because Matty's dark and foreign expression, the scratch and quiver in his voice—it had been fear.

I jerk awake, blinking into the darkness, tense, listening. Raindrops pummel the skylight overhead. But the house itself is silent.

Wedged between two couch cushions, the blanket tangled around my body, I dig for the phone in my pocket, squinting through cloudy contacts. 11:23 p.m., it says. I stare at it, uncomprehending, reading the numbers several times.

*I fell asleep.*

I would have woken up if Matty had come home. Come to think of it, I would have woken up if my parents had come home. But they're not here. Scrambling out of my blanket cocoon, I propel myself off the couch, already calling Matty as I fumble with the light switch.

The phone rings . . . and rings . . . and rings again. Voice mail. He didn't silence the call. He never lets it ring.

Listening to his voice-mail greeting, I make my way to the front door to peer out at the street. Our neighborhood is graveyard silent but for the rain, a light sprinkle against the glow of the streetlamp.

I call again, stepping out onto the porch.

The streetlamp flickers.

It's soft at first, the earth trembling. Like the rumbles we know, but then—

The porch shifts beneath me. My feet scrape nothing but air. And I'm on my hands and knees, phone clattering against the wood. It's a faraway impact, the pain scattered at the edges of my mind. My phone doesn't stop rattling even as my hand covers it, tries to pin it down.

Thunder.

One crack, single, but so loud and shattering, I feel it rather than hear it. But it isn't air exploding overhead. It's from below, and it echoes, coming from everywhere at once.

It takes a second. My breath catches in my chest.

*The fault line.*

A groan spreads through the earth, through the foundations of the house, vibrations tearing through my body all the way into my jaw.

Terror jams in my rib cage, a rock between the bones, mingling with the trapped air I can't release.

Heat travels up from the ground, through the floor, burning my palms. I concentrate on the hard, solid wood beneath my knees, the rainwater bleeding into the fabric. My gaze rises toward the dark shadow of Mount Hemsworth in the distance, looming over our town.

I know what this is. I grew up here.

*But we've never had a breach. We have Guardians. They'll stop it. With their Keys of bone. Any second.*

When the ground ruptures inside that black forest on the mountain, it's beautiful. If I live to be a hundred, I'll never see anything like it again.

A lightning bolt of gold stretches across the ground, zigzagging a bright, shining path through the trees. Down the mountain the bolt travels, down . . . to us.

*They'll stop it. They're the only ones who can.*

*They're the only ones who can release it in the first place . . .*

The sounds of breaking earth are far away, but the echoes travel. The ground shakes beneath me, screaming in my bones. And it doesn't stop.

Panels of gold radiate into the sky, illuminating all of Wellsie with magic.

And rising from the still-glowing gash, an iridescent fog lifts to cloud the air. The pale rainbows we've lived with our whole lives evaporate in the light, swallowed back into the magic that left them behind.

I stare at the sky, shivering uncontrollably, as the light explodes into powder—mist—but paler, translucent, both here and not here.

*Magic used to be everywhere once.*

The splotch hovers there for a second before spreading outward, like ink spilling over paper. Outward toward the edges of town.

The ground shudders and stills, and the only tremors are those running through my body, but thin gold tendrils bleed through the trees, snaking closer, too close.

My phone is ringing, a burst of BTS's "Fire." It's Ella's ringtone. *Ella.*

"Siddy," Ella says immediately, her panicked voice too loud. "Siddy? Siddy, can you hear me? Hello?"

"They opened it," I say numbly—a calm voice, an alien voice. "Ella, they opened the fault line."

"I know. We're stopped on the highway. Everyone got out to look. We can see it from here. It's like . . . like a bomb went off. Are you at home?"

I nod, though she can't see me. My parents are shouting in the background.

A shimmering wisp unfurls at the end of the driveway.

"Ella, I can see the magic. It's coming . . ."

I reach out a hand as a bright strand stretches toward me, curling around my wrist—

Something impossibly hot, but not painful, hits me full in the chest and bowls me onto my back. A burn grows there, radiating outward, sinking into every organ, every limb. When I open my eyes, my body is lit with white fire as the golden threads course down my arms to my fingertips.

I can't feel the cold, hard floor beneath me anymore.

Ella's voice grows distant as my hand holding the phone falls away.

"Are you there? Listen to me, okay? We're a half hour away. We'll be there as soon as we can. Stay where you are. Stay with Matty. Hold on—"

The line goes dead.

Out past the driveway, the streetlamp flickers once more, and goes out.


When you're young, they tell you magic used to be everywhere once, that it reflected our souls and enhanced the very best in us.

When you're older, they tell you magic showed us who we were, for better or worse. You could make anything happen with enough power. And because you've experienced a bit of the world by then, you know this power would have ended us eventually, had it remained.

But they sealed the magic, locking it away with whatever we did, whatever we *made*, when we had the ability to do anything. They—the initial Guardians of each fault line—kept us safe from ourselves.

For a while.

When I open my eyes after a second, a minute, an hour, I'm still on the porch floor. A damp chill washes over me. Only a hint of light remains in the sky, dissipating in degrees, black chasing away the gold. The burn has faded. My hand finds my chest, rubbing at the center where pinpricks linger here and there. My skin is warm to the touch despite the cold.

I haul myself to my feet, grasping my phone in stiff fingers.

When I call Ella, the ring never comes. I call Matty . . .

There's nothing on the line, just silence.

My phone has no bars. **No service**, it says.

*When did Matty leave, around ten?* He should be back by now. He promised me.

In the distance, police sirens pierce the night. Panic digs its way through the blanket of numbness, and I stumble back into the dark house. In the kitchen, I flip the light switch in the kitchen up, down, up, down.

When I was little, my sister made me watch a documentary that ominously predicted human extinction at the hands of the big four: climate change, pandemic, nuclear war, or fault-line breach. Realizing we'd be in the first wave for that fourth option, Ella and I practiced drills in the middle of the night. I was supposed to collect the cat. Ella would rouse our parents. Matty would fend for himself.

"The time to prepare is now," Morgan Freeman had informed us gravely. "While we still can."

Our plan was to follow protocol, go to the shelter in the basement of Town Hall. We learned later they stored file boxes there because no one ever expected it to be used.

After all, how do you prepare for the unknown? It's been so many centuries since the initial blood sacrifice that no one knows what's actually true. Only theories remain. Rumors.

*What do I do now? Breathe. Everyone will know what happened. Matty will try the shelter or the police station—*

Except the fault line runs straight through Town Center and God knows what's going to come out besides magic.

No, Matty would come here first. My parents and Ella are on their way. I just have to wait for them. We can hunker down together. The whole world will know what happened in Wellsie. They'll send the National Guard. They'll evacuate us. We'll be okay.

I hear something crack right before the floor ripples beneath my feet, a groan of wood not meant to bend. The sound comes from everywhere at once, a chain of multiple fractures. Outside, and close. The floor tilts again.

I grip the counter, and vibrations rattle every bone. It's too close to be an aftershock. Fear slides down my back, seizing my spine at the base.

The house, the whole house, lurches.

I let go of the counter, fear spurring me into the hall as the house lists to the other side. More cracking, snapping, splintering wood. A scream rises in my chest, but I swallow it. I need all the air I have.

A mewing at my feet almost makes me lose it. It's our cat, Chad. Just a fluffy white cat who is as terrified as I am. I sweep her up—immediate mistake—as she yowls and leaves a long scratch down my forearm for my trouble. I fling her over my shoulder anyway, and she claws my back.

I stumble at the next hard shake that rolls like a wave beneath me. In the guest bedroom, also my father's office, I trace the edges of the large wooden desk and crawl beneath it as the next shake comes. Chad struggles out of my arms and I let her go.

Curling my knees to my chest, I wrap my arms over my head. Chad's nails raised thin welts on the back of my neck. I breathe, in through the nose, out through the mouth, eyes squeezed shut. *Breathe. Just breathe. Call Mom. Dad. Matty. Ella.*

I pull out my phone again. I squint at the bars. **No service**, it says.

I don't know how long I sit there under the desk, hearing the sounds of pavement caving in, of metal squealing, of things crashing down. The muscles in my upper arms tremble. I huddle there, counting each second in my head.

One minute. Ten minutes. Fifteen minutes. Twenty.

Until I can't hear the pounding in my chest anymore. Just a terrible silence.

The floor slants, but it appears sturdy enough when I crawl out from under the desk. Feeling along the walls, I make my way through the dark.

On my tiptoes, I reach into the front hall closet to grab one of the flashlights, but it takes a minute to force myself to open the front door.

Sending a beam of light out over the yard, I step out into the rain, edging carefully until my feet hang over the first porch step.

They slide in the grass as I walk farther, lifting my flashlight higher toward a giant shadow ahead.

My toe catches on something hard. I go down, knees, then stomach. Lying there, gasping, on the cold, wet ground next to the garden,

I stretch out one hand and touch a sharp edge. The driveway. Broken into large slabs of asphalt.

For long moments I lie there, holding the edge, my chest hitching, until I can bring myself to lift my head, to shine my light on the driveway, or what remains of it.

A giant root splits through its center, forking into smaller roots. With frozen fingers, I follow the twisting wood, my palms skimming over rough bark as bits of crumbled driveway dig into my knees. I'm in the road, fumbling over more roots, knocking my shoulders into . . . poles? Except they have a slight give. The flashlight illuminates the grotesque shape of a tree, a massive tree. I think it's a banyan, with a trunk ten people with joined hands couldn't span. The poles are dozens of fibrous roots, falling from branches overhead. Banyans don't grow in Wellsie. They don't grow in the middle of streets.

I look back at my house, my normal gray house, and I barely see it. A forest has sprouted—trees everywhere, roots everywhere. I shift the light from one tree to another and another—evergreens, birches, maples, oaks . . . one of them grows straight through my neighbor's roof.

And I am alone.

"Oh my God. Oh my God . . ." My fingers tighten around the base of the flashlight.

The branches provide shelter, but I can't stop shivering. The spasms hurt.

A forest popping out of nowhere should have woken the whole neighborhood, but no one is out here. No one but me.

Except, between the trees, I sense movement, a shadow rounding the corner of my house, the shape of a person stumbling over roots the same way I did.

*A person. Someone.* I lift the light.

It's definitely a person, a boy, slowly crossing our front yard, soaked to the skin.

I struggle to my feet. "Wait! Please wait." I rush toward him, my progress slowed by roots.

When he turns, I recognize the stocky figure clad in a polo shirt and a backward baseball hat.

"Sid Spencer?"

It's Dustin, Dustin Miller from next door—he goes to school with me. The shivering loses some of its violence as my body relaxes. "Dustin, thank God. Are your parents home?"

"No. When the earthquake stopped, my parents, a lot of the neighbors, we were all running toward the emergency shelter. We didn't know what else to do. The phones weren't working." He gestures around, eyes wide, terrified, body trembling. "Halfway there, the quakes started again, and this . . . this *forest* was growing everywhere. We got separated." His eyes dart back and forth as he scans the woods behind him. "I tried to keep heading toward Town Center, but I kept . . . I don't know, I kept sensing something was following me and doubled back, trying to lose it."

I squint through tree trunks, sweeping my flashlight from side to side. For a second, I see a shadow, a hint of movement. Dustin is already stepping toward it, over the driveway, winding through vines. "Who's there?" he shouts, pushing past branches.

"Wait, Dustin, let's go back inside." I trip after him, grasping at the back of his coat.

But when he stops, I crash into him.

"What the hell *is* that?" he whispers.

I can't see past his torso, but the quiver in his voice has me backing away, terror suspending my lungs. Dustin spins back toward me and I catch his face, frozen in the beam from my flashlight, and in his eyes, a warning.

Fingers, dirty, white, mottled with purple, inch over his shoulder.

*Magic had consequences once.*

*Dustin* . . . My lips form his name, but no sound emerges.

Teeth, broken and yellow, rotting, clamp into the side of his neck from behind. Dustin's scream pierces straight through me as I dash forward and seize him around the waist, as the thing . . . *the thing* rips its head violently to the side, tearing flesh, stretching rubbery muscle from bone until it detaches.

Sobbing, I pull at Dustin with all my weight, though my mind begs me, shamelessly, to run. To leave him.

When I disconnect them, Dustin pitches sideways, and he's too heavy for me to catch. He falls into the brush. Blood spurts from the gaping wound at the juncture of his neck and shoulder. His wet gasps gurgle in his throat. I make myself look at his eyes—wide, pleading. *Help me.* But his face goes white and bloodless and I already know.

*He's dying.*

I yank at his arm, inhaling as deep as I can to keep from vomiting. But Dustin coughs once, twice . . . not a third time. *Oh God.* I still tug. *I can't. I can't . . .*

And the thing emerging from the bushes twists around, cocking its head at me, all while chewing, slowly chewing. Its limbs are spindly, the body starved and wasted, wearing something that might have been clothing once.

*Magic had consequences. They made things. Blurry images in our picture books we never named. We didn't know.*

The flashlight, lying among leaves at my feet, gleams enough that

I see his eyes—bloodshot, but blank—and his skin—pale and anemic, with dark splotches beneath his eyes, and shadows in the hollows of his cheeks. The shadows move.

Maggots eat away at a putrid wound.

*Oh my God.*

I drop Dustin's arm, and the thing moves in the stop-motion way people move under strobe lights. Slow, jerky, but sensing me somehow. I dart sideways across the jagged remains of the driveway. The shadowy structure of the porch looms in the darkness, a few steps away if I run, but fingers fumble at my wrist, slowing me. My free hand slams at his chest—warm, hard, like a living person.

When he launches at my neck, I scream.

## CHAPTER 3

Jaws clamp down on my shoulder.

My vision blurs for a moment, but the thick fabric of my sweatshirt shields my skin.

When I fall, he falls.

I hit the porch stairs, slamming my hip against a hard wood edge, and he's on top of me. I can't breathe, still grappling wildly at his face. But he doesn't budge. There is only a looming mouth full of sores, stinking of rotten meat. Another shriek bubbles up inside me. His neck strains.

*Click, click . . . click-click.*

A gaping maw opens and closes.

*He's too heavy. I can't move.*

I glimpse the beams of the porch ceiling above me. A last image. A slowly fading view.

Bile gathers at the base of my throat. My arms burn as I twist my face away, finding his collarbone, sturdy enough to push against with everything I have. A blast of hot breath, and teeth graze my cheek. He's *alive.*

"Please," I beg.

I use one hand to claw at his face, his eyes.

"MOM!" I cry, sobbing. "Dad!"

Bony hands close around my neck. A second of my air being cut and panic explodes. *He's going to kill me.*

The base of my palm connects with his nose in a sickening crunch. My stomach heaves, but the blow is enough to dislodge him, enough for me to move. My hand is wet, sticky with blood.

I crawl up the stairs, finding smooth cold tile—the front hall. Fingers encircle my ankle, dragging me back. The corner of something hard and sharp catches the side of my head with an explosion of pain. I swipe at the hot trickle down the side of my face. The doorstop—that's what I hit. *Solid cast iron.*

The creature inhales, makes a hideous grunt. His shadow surges closer to my wound, in a frenzy.

The metal is cold in my hands. With one swing, I slam it into the side of his skull. He topples sideways and I drop the heavy weight, cracking the tile, already lunging to my feet.

He is behind me somewhere. Still moving.

Something pale appears in front of me, and I barely bring my hands up before crashing into it. A wall. A door.

He is behind me. Somewhere.

I fumble at the knob. *The cellar? The cellar.* I thunder down the stairs, and he falls after me, crashing to the bottom. Bones snap. I hear them. He can't get up after that. Yet he does, limping now, leg dragging across the floor.

There is no light here, no windows, just stagnant air. My abdomen catches on my mom's sewing table. I stretch my hands in front of me.

Shuffling—I hear him shuffling. Close, but my breathing is too loud to know for sure. I force myself, without my sight, to remember the basement layout—if I trip, if I fall, I will die down here. But there's a path through the old furniture, the suitcases, the boxes of old photos. I just have to find it. I kick my foot in front of me.

*Box, table, box . . . empty space.*

The moment I find it, I move. Hands out to the side, skimming the boxes bordering the pathway.

It takes three tries to slide the latch on the cellar doors leading to the backyard.

There could be more out there, but the choice is between maybe and *definitely*.

I push the doors up and out, and light rain stings the side of my face. Blood gathers in the corner of my mouth. I drop the doors with a slam. *Now what? Lure him out of the house? What if he gets back in? Can he break a window?* The cellar has no windows. But these doors only lock from the inside.

My battered old bike leans against the backyard fence, secured with a cable combination lock. I don't know how many seconds I have left. The combination . . .

*It's Finn's birthday. Oh my God, Finn. And Nell. Nell is out there.*

I hold the lock close to my face, squinting to see the numbers, to push the dials into place: *0-2-2-0. Hurry. Oh God, hurry.*

The cellar doors lift, then thump back into place. He's here. I untangle the coil, yanking it desperately from the spokes of the wheel, and run, throwing my weight against the doors as they tent upward again. One blue eye appears through the crack.

As the doors rattle beneath my body, I thread the cable through the door handles, looping it as many times as I can. I click the lock into place and collapse on top of them. Just for a second. I can't feel the rain anymore.

*There could be more.*

I move, stumbling.

Around the side of the house.

Inside the front door.

I turn the bolt, resting my cheek on the wall next to the front door.

*Go.*

The basement door is a black gaping hole in front of me as I race toward it.

I stare down the stairs. Shuffling. Thumping. Below, boxes fall to the ground—years' worth of family photos my mom always meant to organize into albums. I slam the door, lock it, wedge a dining room chair beneath the knob. Trapped. He's trapped.

My back makes contact with the wall behind me and I slide to the floor, leaving a wet smear down the wallpaper. I wheeze, my breath high-pitched. There's a red handprint on the carpet next to me. Mine. My mother will kill me for locking a thing in our basement. Not a thing, a zombie.

She'll come home. My father will come home. He'll stand out in the rain, tall and imposing, and unafraid. With hands on his hips, he'll thunder about the state of his driveway. No zombie wants a piece of that.

*Zombies are supposed to be dead. He was warm.*

I shake the thought away.

Matty, Ella, and little Zora will breeze in after them. Matty will joke that I have rabies. Ella will joke that this is *not* the next story in the Sexy Beast series she's reading. Zora will hug me, tell me she missed me the way she does on the phone every day, even if I've just seen her.

"It's time to wake up." The words come out in a whisper. "It's time to wake up. It's time to wake up . . ."

Hugging my knees to my chest, I let out the first sob. There's no holding the rest back.


I wake up on the hallway floor to the dull pound of a body knocking repeatedly against the cellar door.

It's still raining.

My limbs are stiff, aching, when I get to my feet to make sure every window is locked, and every blind drawn. I don't look out, but I hear the rustling of a million leaves and branches, concealing things I don't want to see. Like Dustin's house across the yard. Like Dustin on the ground.

I light one of the votive candles from the dining room table.

My eyes are red and swollen when I peer at myself in the mirror. An open cut slashes my temple, rough with dried blood. Rusty stains smear my sweatshirt. I discard it and shove my T-shirt collar aside to look at my shoulder. The zombie left more of a bruise than a bite, but maybe I'll contract a fever in the next hour and my family will come home to a Sid who is alive but not Sid anymore.

What I do know is without magic sealing the fault line, a zombie climbed out. There will be more.

My dad has been saving a stack of wood planks in the garage to build a shed in the backyard. I make too much noise carrying them inside. Thaddeus throws himself against the cellar door. I named the zombie Thaddeus, though the reason eludes me now. I nail boards in an X across the door, across as many of the downstairs windows as I can until the boards run out, then push bookshelves and chairs and bureaus against the others.

The water works but comes out brown, which means the pipes

have been disrupted. We have a water cooler with at least two extra five-gallon jugs, along with a case of bottled water in the pantry; I'll be fine for a little while.

My mother's fleece robe hangs on the back of the bathroom door. It smells like her when I put it on.

*We're a half hour away,* Ella said.

*Be back soon,* Matty promised.

Someone will come to save us. There will be helicopters overhead. Trucks with loudspeakers telling everyone to stay inside until the threat has been eradicated. They're organizing their rescue teams now. It'll be a day at most.

Yet here in my boarded-up house, reality is a harsh overhead light revealing every flaw. Fault-line towns govern themselves independently, they always have. The lack of central oversight meant Guardians could never be controlled, their power never concentrated. I never thought much about what that might mean, the consequences, but now it runs through my brain on loop. Does it mean, if the worst happened, the rest of the world would cut us off to fend for ourselves?

*I saw someone die tonight.*

There's still no service, but I call everyone I know, even Nell, even Finn, but none of the calls connect.

The rain continues to fall. Its faint rhythm sounds more and more like the theme from *Halloween* the longer I listen to it. The ticking of the mantel clock is the only other sound, a reminder of how much time is passing.

Chad, her puffy white fur matted and saturated with rain, comes to sit by my side. Her green eyes glow in the dark. I forgot about the cat door in the laundry room. We tried to make her an indoor cat, but all our efforts to contain her failed. She'd been a barn cat before the owner died and Chad ended up at the shelter. We picked her because she walked straight to Ella, rubbed against her legs, and curled up in her lap, purring—then we brought her home, and she was like, 'Surprise, I'm a sociopath!' Exactly like the movie *Orphan*.

Chad would definitely eat me if I died. Matty is the one she likes, though he's allergic to her. I suspect she knows that.

She's left a dead mouse on the floor by my feet.

"For me? I'll have to polish this off today or it'll go bad."

When my cell phone dies, I keep staring at the blank screen.

*They're coming. They'll be here.*

Bouts of tremors come and go.

I upend a bag of dry food into Chad's bowl. It overflows and spills over the entire floor of the laundry room. That should be enough.

Much to her annoyance, I nail the cat door closed.

At some point, I climb into my parents' bed. I make a nest of blankets beside me for Chad.

"This green blanket is Matty's," I tell her. "I know he's your favorite."

Then I cry.

The gutters need to be cleaned. My father would want me to do that.

Instead, I sit at the counter, on the middle stool. The one on the end is my mother's. When I turn toward the empty space, she's there, looking all neat and put together without a blond hair out of place. No doubt she gazes into the mirror each morning, and thinks, *And everything looks up to par, as per usual.*

She gives me a quick once-over. "You look like you're dying on the vine—did you get enough sleep?"

"It could have gone better," I say. "I had a dream there was a spider on the wall. This bird came along and the spider ate it. Though the spider tried to expand to accommodate it, there were still all these bird parts poking out of its body. A beak here, a feather there. But the spider was still alive, skittering back and forth. Then I woke up. Anyway, I think I'm the spider . . . and the bird is life."

"You've got the most vivid imagination," she decides to say.

"You need to come home," I tell her. "It could get bad. I might freebase angel dust."

"Sure," she says. "But first, define 'freebase.'"

Walking by us, my father—as tall and bald as my mother is short and blond—wears lime-green pants with tiny blue whales on them and a navy-blue sweater. He has about six of the same sweater, like he's preparing for the day people no longer make clothes. I glance at the bottle of Windex he holds.

"A clean car runs better," he says to me.

"It's raining," I tell him. "The car will clean itself."

When he turns to stare at me, I know what he's thinking. He's failed. I am unprepared for the world.

I sit in the front hall, staring at the door.

*It's been too long. They were a half hour away.*

Nell will be okay. Nell lives in East Wellsie in a mansion made of glass, but she has a gate. She can hole up in her basement with its movie theater viewing room where we watched the PBS *Anne of Green Gables* at least once a month. Finn will find her. They'll joke about how their names both end with a double letter. He'll play the guitar and she'll sing in her perfect soprano, and they'll be safe together because I can't worry about her. I can't imagine her out there screaming.

I do anyway.

What if Adam O'Brien is dead?

"He laughed at me," I tell Chad.

Chad has no reaction to this. It's uncharacteristically tactful of her not to reveal she's had the powers of speech this whole time and say, "Who hasn't?"

Instead, she crawls into the lap of the girl sitting next to me, to knead the curtain of silky blond hair draped over her shoulder. Nell shrugs helplessly. "I don't know why she likes me. I didn't do anything."

"Typical," I say, rolling my eyes. "You act indifferent and she loves you." I narrow my eyes at Chad. "I don't care if you like me or not, okay?"

Chad lashes out with a paw and I barely jerk back in time.

Nell slips a protective hand in front of my face. "This cat has been lost to the darkness."

"Why are you so perfect?" I mutter, something I always say to her, only to see her flinch this time.

A memory surfaces—I'm walking down the hall in her house, voices floating toward me from the kitchen. "That dress is not forgiving," I hear Nell's mother say. "Why don't you go on a cleanse this week?" When Nell spots me hovering in the doorway, she wipes her expression clean, but not before I see the same stricken face she wears now.

I reach out a hand to her, finding nothing but empty space. "You're okay, right?"

But she doesn't answer.

Every kitchen knife, ordered from large to small, lies on the counter.

I palm the meat cleaver, but I have trouble gripping it with stiff, yet trembling fingers.

"I know this is not ideal," I say to Chad. "But maybe there are people left in the neighborhood. I need you to stay here and carry on the family name if anything should happen to me."

She sits in a magnanimous pouf.

I squat beside her. "If I'm not back in fifteen minutes, take my bike and head west. Leave this godforsaken hellhole and never come back."

Chad bats my face with her paw.

On the porch, I count to five and step into the rain. The drops have lightened considerably, but the air is thick with moisture, the scent mossy and fragrant, with death on the edges.

With each forced step, my feet sink several inches into the mud. I swing the cleaver, tentatively at first, then harder, as I come to terms with the climbing vines, roots, and low-hanging tree limbs surrounding the house. This is how the world used to look, how I imagine it will look when all humans disappear.

In the woods by my house—the normal woods, before this—a red birdhouse hangs from a tree. There's a blue one near Nell's house. She would put little notes in mine and I would put little notes in hers, so we could pretend we were children of warring families who could only communicate to each other in secret.

I think of this now as that distant red spot sways. I haven't checked it since . . . since I stopped knowing her.

At the faint movement in the trees, I freeze, both hands tightening around the cleaver.

A branch rustles. Wind, maybe. A squirrel. A zombie.

I must have run. I don't remember. But when I'm sitting inside my front hall, breathing too fast, sweating too much, I tell myself I tried. I clutch the bite bruise on my shoulder with one hand.

Ella would be out there. She's not like me. She would be hacking through forest. She would—

As I stare at the cleaver, my stomach bottoms out. What if my parents and Ella made it back to town, but they are trapped out there, surrounded by zombies?

What if I was here, just waiting, the whole time?

The knowledge is there, deep in the marrow of my bones: something is wrong. The outside world should have arrived in Wellsie.

My parents, Ella and Zora, Matty—they would do everything they could to come get me. If they're not here, it's because they can't get here.

I hate myself for not thinking of that, for only thinking my family would come take care of me as they always have. Instead, I left them to fend for themselves.

Nell's out there too. But I left her months ago, didn't I?

This time, I don't walk slowly across the yard, I run, heart racing in my ears, barely seeing anything. Blurs of trees, maybe zombies. Wet branches hit me full in the face, bushes scrape at my legs, but I make it. I hack at the frayed rope with the cleaver.

After I survive it, that one rescue mission, and I'm sitting with my back against the front door again, raincoat slick and covered with dead leaves, the red birdhouse sits beside me, stuffed with rolled scrolls of paper.

She kept writing messages. All this time.

Chad sits in the middle of the front hall, watching me.

"Chad," I whisper. "We need to find them."


I don't know where Matty went, but if he couldn't get back here, maybe he made it to his apartment in South Wellsie. Once I find him, I'll have a better idea of what it's like out there, where people could be, where my parents and Ella might be.

I'm trying on one of my father's tool belts that I can stuff with weapons, including the mini stun gun Matty gave me, when Chad growls deep in her throat.

Facing the kitchen, my cat bends low to the ground, ears twitching, tail flicking at the tip. A ridge of hair ripples down her spine.

My gaze shifts slowly toward the front door.

The doorknob turns—left, right, then rattles hard.

*They're home.*

In seconds, I'm dashing to the door, reaching for the bolt.

*They have house keys.*

I freeze, hand on the knob.

If they've lost them, they would use the secret key in the third hanging plant on the porch.

The doorknob stops turning.

I back away, in inches, as a shadow crosses one of the x-ed windows.

*It's a person.* My hand finds the bruise on my shoulder. Or is it? And if it is a person, should I open the door? It could be anyone. If they were harmless, they'd knock, wouldn't they?

Moving as silently as possible in my squeaking rain boots, I blow out the candles in the room, grab the first weapons I can find off the table, and press my back against the shelf with all the cookbooks. I make myself as small as I can, hunching inside the doorway of the kitchen.

Cupping my hand over my mouth, I breathe through my nose, blinking in the darkness.

Footsteps sound overhead, and I jerk my head toward the ceiling. Back and forth across the roof, someone is thumping around, skidding on the shingles. Not a zombie. Thaddeus wouldn't have been able to do that. They'll go away. They'll find all the windows locked and go away.

Chad's eyes narrow, gazing in the direction of the stairway, and she growls again.

Glass shatters.

Trembling, I sink down the shelf to the floor. Upstairs, two feet hit the carpet with a muffled thump.

Cold sweat drips down the side of my neck.

The footsteps cease for a moment at the top of the stairs. All the movement overhead has riled Thaddeus, and the cellar door shakes in its frame.

Each stair creaks as the intruder takes slow, careful steps down. Too coordinated to be a zombie, but ax murderers are probably quite spry. I peek my head a couple inches around the corner of the doorframe, long enough to glimpse a tall shadowy figure with what looks like two criss-crossed sword hilts sticking out from behind his shoulders.

I flatten myself against the wall again, heartbeat pulsing in my ears.

*Oh God. What do I do? What do I do?*

*You have the upper hand. He doesn't know you're here.*

His wet shoes squeak on the floor, closer than before.

Slowly, in inches, I turn my face toward the doorway next to me.

The instant the huge shadow passes through, I leap up from the floor.

"Holy shit!" he yells, jumping back as my arm slices an arc toward his middle, cleaver blade singing in the dark. He dodges the crowbar I aim at his shoulder.

With a lunge, he catches both my wrists, nearly lifting me off my feet as he barrels forward and pins me to the bookcase. The crowbar hits the ground with a jarring clang. The cleaver lands, blade lodged in the wood floor. Well, now my mother will kill him, and I won't have to. But the intruder is at least a foot taller, and I am caged in by arms and chest. A scream rises, but no one else is here. No one will hear me except Thaddeus.

Abruptly his hands fall away.

I don't think about why; I'm already snatching the stun gun from my tool belt. I catch a scent, like the forest outside but more heavily evergreen, before I jab the weapon against his stomach and squeeze the trigger.

"Son of a bitch," he bellows, crumbling to his knees and going down, twitching. Groaning, he rolls to his side, his body slightly curled.

All at once, I realize something.

Beyond the panic, the staccato of my heart, I . . . know that voice. I definitely know that voice. I know that shape lying there on the floor.

*Oh God.*

I scramble for the kitchen counter, feeling around for the flashlight I left there.

Shining the light tentatively at the dark figure, I kneel, poking at his shoulder. When he doesn't roll over, I shove him less gently onto his back, and aim the light down. First, I see a cap of rough-cut dark hair followed by a weary unshaven face of sharp angles and frowning brows. *Oh God.*

Guilt settles in my stomach like a brick. Slowly, I lower the flashlight, and sit back on my heels, watching his chest rise and fall with each labored breath.

*What is Brian Aster doing in my house?*

# CHAPTER 4

*W*hat the hell is on me?" Brian mumbles, batting at his chest with one hand. Chad perches there, a vibrating cloud, kneading biscuits in his T-shirt.

"My cat, Chad," I inform him from a safe distance away. "We couldn't think of a name for her for several weeks. Nothing suited her. Snowball. Marshmallow. We were brainstorming one day and my mom said, 'Let's list names for white things.' And I was like, 'Mayonnaise,' and Ella was like, 'Cottage Cheese,' and Matty just shouted, 'Chad!' Anyway, that one stuck." I don't know what I'm saying at this point, but it's been days without human interaction. "She hates everyone except for people who are allergic to her. Are you?"

Brian sneezes.

"I guess that answers that."

Brian sweeps the cat off him and sits up, blinking. "You're alive," he says, his eyes focusing on me. Something flickers over his face. Relief, maybe. But when I hold up my candle, it's gone. He glances around, brows inching together. "Why am I on the floor?"

I sit several yards away with my candle. The shadows playing over his face emphasize its hardness. "I hit you with my mini taser—Matty says it's called a stun gun."

Brian stares at me as my words sink in, and his hand skims over his stomach.

"You're a little disoriented," I add.

"Oh, *you think?*" he growls. Gripping the doorframe, he hauls himself to a standing position. His eyes dart downward. "Is that . . . a *meat cleaver?*" He fingers his camouflage raincoat, in which I see a slight snag from the blade, and when he looks back at me, I shrug defensively.

"You broke into my house and manhandled me. I had no other choice."

"You attacked me first! I heard thumping somewhere in the house. I wasn't going to announce myself." Glaring, Brian steadies himself using the wall, then takes a step toward me.

I take a step back.

Brian stops. "I'm not going to hurt you."

I take another step back. "You look exactly like Chad when she's about to attack, which I guess means you look like Chad on a normal day."

Chad is rubbing her head against his leg and purring, which Brian is most definitely not doing, but I ignore that.

He crosses his arms. "So you just assume I'm here to murder you and chop you into little pieces?"

"A of all, I didn't know it was you. B of all, even if I did, why should I trust you? Maybe I don't like you."

"Well, it's good to know you only attack people with meat cleavers if you don't like them." Brian turns away to remove the shoulder harness, which is carrying two long machetes, before shedding his wet coat—slowly, as though he's sore. He rubs at the back of his neck and I lift the candle higher. Three scrapes curve around the side of his jaw, nearly hidden in the stubble. I glance at the tattoo of a music measure along the outside edge of his forearm, marred with bruises. His knuckles—they're bruised too.

"I didn't know it was you," I say again. "And excuse me, but this is *my* house and you were a gigantic, silent intruder. Why are you here?"

His face is unreadable. "I'm looking for your brother."

*He's here for Matty?* "Matty isn't here," and it comes out in a whisper. "He got some mysterious call the night this happened, and he left. He never came back. My family was out of town—they were a half hour away, but they never . . ." I swallow because I don't really want to know the answer to my next question. "How long has it been?"

Brian closes his eyes, raking a hand through his hair in an agitated way. "Two days." When he drops his arms, his bangs settle back over his forehead in an uneven line. "I don't think the rest of your family made it into town. Or anyone else, for that matter."

"How do you know that?"

"Because no one came to rescue us," he says stiffly. "But it's never been clear if anyone would."

The same fear I've had over the last few days echoes in his words. "Do you think they'd leave us to die?"

He doesn't answer. He doesn't know. But his expression indicates it's possible. It's possible we're alone in this.

I can exhale in the knowledge that my parents and sister are likely still outside of Wellsie, but the relief doesn't last long. "Matty is in town somewhere."

The way his gaze gentles flares an intense rage inside.

"Don't look at me like that," I say. "Like he's dead."

He says nothing, just does exactly that.

My voice rises. "If I'm alive, and you're alive, then why not him? I will find him."

He doesn't speak for a long time, and I am having a hard time finding other places to look. He doesn't find it difficult to look directly at me.

"Okay," he says, softly. "Then you will."

I scowl at the floor. Maybe he's placating me. Also, my anger-fueled confidence is already gone. "A normal person would have knocked, especially given the circumstances. The last person in this house was Thaddeus and he tried to kill me."

Brian stills at my words. "Thaddeus tried to kill you? Did he hurt you? Who is Thaddeus?"

"A zombie thing. He bit me."

He lets out a whoosh of air and strides toward me. I don't back away this time. "Where?" he asks.

"Am . . . am I going to become a zombie too?" My hand moves to the bite on my shoulder.

Another long breath escapes him. "You won't become like him. It doesn't work that way."

*How does he know that? What is it like out there?*

That blue gaze scans my face. Not a pale or piercing blue, but deep. Instead of answering, he asks, "Did I hurt you when I grabbed you?" This, in a quiet voice, and he doesn't move as he waits for me to reply.

"No, you just . . . scared me. You shouldn't break into someone's home. And you shouldn't grab someone unless they're about to walk into oncoming traffic." I don't mention that he grabbed me to stop me from disemboweling him. Still his fault.

"Would that be Thaddeus in your basement?" Brian says, eyes

flicking to the thumping coming from the basement door that's become normal to me.

When I nod, his focus shifts to the wound at my temple. "Did Thaddeus do that?"

*Sort of.* My shoulders lift in a small shrug.

He takes the candle from my hand and holds it near my temple, each gesture careful. "Can I see?"

I tilt my face up and to the left, inhale, and hold it.

"Spencer."

I see where he's looking—at the bruises on my neck where Thaddeus choked me. I cover them quickly with my hands.

People have all kinds of micro-expressions they can't control— flickers of emotion, gone the moment you notice them. His are more subtle, but his brows inch together and his mouth softens in the same fleeting moment. Maybe he doesn't like seeing pain.

With surprising gentleness, he brushes my hair back to study the wound at my hairline. His breath feathers the baby curls there and I shiver without meaning to.

He jerks, his shoulders rippling, and the tiny flame of the candle flickers and almost goes out. He gives me a weird look, a definite weird look, and I inch back. Realizing he's still cupping my head, he hastily drops his hand and returns the candle. "You'll live," he says, rubbing his upper arms with both hands.

"I figured," I mutter.

Brian takes a few short strides into the kitchen, wearily rubbing his eyes. A fat drop of water hits his forehead and races down the side of his face. "Your skylight has a leak," he murmurs, glancing at the ceiling. He hasn't changed out of his Sugar, Sugar T-shirt, the same clothes he wore when I saw him outside Lulu's. Maybe the same clothes he was wearing the day a fire took everything he had.

He doesn't look like his dad at all, except for being tall and white, though not looking like one's dad is normal to me. I used to see Jack Aster at Sugar, Sugar all the time. He was a grinner, and exactly what the word "baker" would look like if the dictionary had pictures—round belly and face, with burn scars up his arms. I study Brian's profile, the individual shapes of his face, each one harder and sharper now that I search for a curve. His eyes, nose, and angular jaw must come from his biological mother.

I touch the curl by my ear, the perfect spiral. It's the one thing I've always wondered about, where my hair comes from.

We stand there awkwardly. I'm transported back to the last time I didn't know what to say to him. Under a portico in the rain.

"I'm sorry I scared you," Brian says then. "I wasn't sure what I would find here."

"Why *are* you looking for Matty?" I say as my brother's face, right before he headed out into the night, appears in sharp detail in my mind.

Brian faces me again, wearing the same expressionless expression that's become familiar to me. "Has anyone else been here?" he says instead of answering. "Anyone else looking for your brother?" There's an urgency hanging at the end of his sentence.

I shake my head. "No one. I've been . . ." I stop myself before saying *completely and utterly alone.*

He scans my face like he's reading something there. There is a strange stillness to his body, and it occurs to me people are only still in times of tension, like if they're standing on a cliff, trying not to sway. A person is only still if they aren't breathing. "Your brother has been missing since the night a portion of the fault line opened, right?"

*A portion?* "He was here, but he got a phone call. It was Shandy Ohno. One of their friends was in trouble."

Brian inhales, holding my gaze. "The friend was Josh Monroe. Josh thought he and Parker—Parker van der Kamp—had been made. Matt was closest, so he went to pick them up, to bring them to a safe house. They never arrived."

I blink during the pause. I have never heard these names in my life. Safe house? Brian seems to be waiting for a reaction. "Made into what?"

"Identified," he says grimly. "When we reached the meetup location, we found Josh dead in the woods—murdered. His Key was missing, the Key to the segment of the fault line that opened. Parker and Matt were MIA. The only thing we know is no other segments have opened, which means those two could be alive. They've either been taken or are on the run."

At some point as he was speaking, the world around me dimmed, Brian's face blurring into a shapeless mass. His mouth moved, so I know he said a whole lot of words, but they were distant, hazy, as though I heard them underwater. Taken? Why would anyone take Matty? Why would he be on the run? Something clicks. Brian used the words "Josh" and "Key" in the same sentence. Only Guardians have Keys. Didn't some part of me know a Guardian must have done this? Josh must be a Guardian. Correction: Josh *was* a Guardian. Josh is dead. Who the hell is Josh? "Matty is friends with Guardians?" I say blankly. "Are *you* friends with Guardians?"

Brian's direct stare doesn't waver, but his mouth softens. "I am a Guardian. So is your brother."

. . .

I think time passes before I speak, before Brian's face comes back into acute focus.

"I don't believe you." The voice sounds strange—hollow and detached—though it's mine. "Matty couldn't be a Guardian."

If . . . if Matty is a Guardian, he has a power and a Key made of bone. Someone would have had to *pass* the magic to him, trust him not to lose an enchanted object. He misplaces his earbuds on a daily basis.

"He doesn't have a superpower," I say. "I would know. He wouldn't . . . he wouldn't keep something like that from me. He would never—"

*Except before he left that night, you could see it in his face. There was something he wasn't telling you.*

"He's not," I insist anyway. "And *you*, you said you never wanted a power. You're either lying now or you lied before, which makes you a liar either way."

He's still subjecting me to that soft pity stare.

And a hush falls over the house.

The rhythm of the rain across the roof ceases all at once.

I'd gotten used to the constancy of it in the background, the ever-present drip, drip, drip from the skylight overhead. I can't hear individual raindrops anymore, just a dull roar from somewhere far away.

My breath halts and I am as still as Brian as he looks at the ceiling, at the leak . . . where a drop of rain remains suspended in air over his head, floating, glittering in the light.

*It's not possible.*

Brian holds out two shaking hands, trembling with effort, and moves them slowly, painstakingly upward.

And the droplet moves with them—up, up, a slow-motion rewind.

Some unseen force wrenches the embedded cleaver from the floor, lifting it until it's level with my face, where it hovers in the air, spinning languidly. On the counter, the line of knives rise in an unsteady row.

The kitchen table rattles. The walls groan as the wood bends inward. Something shatters—a glass inside a closed cupboard.

Brian's face has gone stark white, covered in a sheen of sweat. His jaw grinds as he fights for control, and then . . .

His hands fall limply to his sides.

The knives come crashing down. The table, the chairs. The corner of the cleaver digs another deep wound into my mother's precious hardwood floor.

Outside, rain pelts itself against the roof again. Inside, the leak hits the side of Brian's face with a quiet *pat, pat, pat*.

His eyes are closed, face ashen. He braces two hands on the counter.

"I didn't lie before," he says, almost inaudibly. "About not wanting a superpower. I just didn't say I had one anyway."

I say nothing. Because *clearly*. Because he moved objects with his mind. And if he's telling the truth about himself, he must be telling the truth about—

The locked front door bursts open, slamming against the wall with the force of the wind.

I leap back with a scream as two shadowy figures dash into my house.

Someone skids to a halt at the edge of the kitchen, ax poised.

Brian, still braced against the kitchen counter, glances over his shoulder. "I forgot to mention I'm not alone."

Candlelight falls over Shandy Ohno's face, all golden skin and cheekbones framed by shining black hair. He squints at me. "Sid Spencer? Is that you?"

In their defense, none of them said a word when I ran into the living room and huddled alone in the dark for an extended period of time.

There's a difference between knowing something and *knowing* something. Panic drifts on the outskirts of my mind, like a migraine waiting to barrel through.

People always focus on the superpower, but it's now hitting home how much power a Guardian truly holds. Even if Matty's Key is for one "segment" or whatever, it still contains a whole lot of magic. They keep themselves secret for a reason. Their Guardianships can be passed. Or they can be *stolen*.

And now Matty's missing.

Brian's earlier words come back to me, words I'm now processing. The Guardian—Josh—is dead. Someone must have killed him for his magic and used his Key to unlock his segment of the fault line. But if someone is murdering Guardians with this aim, Matty has to be alive. Only one portion has been opened.

*Matt and Parker were either taken or are on the run.*

These strangers know more about Matty than I do.

But that means they're my best chance at finding him.

While I'm tucked in the corner among a hoard of supplies I was getting ready to pack, hope eases the hitching in my chest, slows my breathing.

As my body calms, low voices filter in from the kitchen.

"How'd you get in here?" Brian is muttering. "I know that door was locked."

"The third hanging plant on the porch," a girl says in a solemn voice, a child's voice. "Lots of people hide keys in nearby plants if there isn't one under the mat." As if that's a totally normal thing for a kid to know.

"You used your power, so I thought something seriously bad was going down," someone says. Shandy. "What took you so long?"

"I was . . . waylaid," Brian says. "Matt isn't here. While we don't know who did this, at least no one has been here looking for him. They might not know anything. Morrissey should be done with his sweep of the town soon, but Hyacinth is about to drop from exhaustion and we can't travel in the dark."

Hyacinth Radcliffe-Aster, his stepsister. She's the one who found our hidden house key.

Something prickles at the back of my neck. And when I slowly unfold myself, lifting my head from my arms, I see her.

A young Black girl, maybe eleven or twelve, stands a few yards away in the middle of my living room. Dozens of tiny braids cascade over her shoulders, sparkling with raindrops. She's small, delicate, like a bird. A bird who was dragged out of bed in the middle of the night two days ago—slender hands with nails painted black peek out from pajamas with tiny white skulls on them.

I didn't hear her footsteps. That doesn't bode well for me when I'm out there trying to avoid zombies.

Hyacinth's face is tipped up to study the picture over our mantel, the one of my family during our Fourth of July barbecue last year. My father always edits the red-eye out of pictures which, in this case, resulted in me having twin pools of darkness. "Does Sid look a little . . . evil?" my mother had suggested casually when he unveiled his latest masterpiece. He'd stared at it and said, "What?

What's wrong? It looks just like her." So that's our mantel photo for all to see. I am the short, slightly plump demon in front.

I scowl at the picture. "Are you a Guardian too?"

Hyacinth turns to peer at me, solemn eyes in a small, triangular face. "No, but Brian and my sister Daisy are."

"Did you scream internally when you found out?"

Hyacinth tilts her head to the side. "No." She has the same direct stare as her brother, but deep brown. One thin shoulder lifts in a tiny shrug. "They have to be someone's sibling or parent or child."

I wonder what it's like to be logical. "How old are you?"

Her eyes narrow. "Eleven."

"Oh. I see what's going on here. You're precocious."

One eyebrow lifts. "I do have a very high IQ. Higher than Brian's. Not as high as Daisy's."

She's gifted. Like her siblings. They all go to Mountain Ridge. I guess these traits run in her family while a particular abhorrence of mayonnaise runs in mine. "I am totally mediocre in all things," I announce.

Hyacinth turns her attention back to our family photo. "Your family doesn't look alike," she says matter-of-factly.

"We aren't blood related." I shrug, looking down at myself. "Obviously."

"My family doesn't look alike, either." Hyacinth looks down at herself. "Obviously. It bothers Brian." She hastens to add, "Not because my half of the family is Black and his isn't. It bothers him that he doesn't look like his dad. Brian never looked like anyone except his biological mother and she's not around." That serious face with the serious eyes shifts back to me. "Does it bother you?"

In the picture, my father looms over everyone, especially me, with his hands on his hips. My mother's blond bob lies without a strand out of place. Ella and Zora with their matching elfin beauty both grin too widely for their faces. And Matty, all bronzed skin and mischievous eyes, smirks into the camera.

Through a sudden lump in my throat, I say, "Someone once told me about a study showing mothers could recognize their newborns by scent alone. When my parents met me for the first time, all they had was a picture. They were worried at first that they wouldn't recognize me, but it turned out I was the only baby with hair. A halo of curls. That's how they knew I was theirs." I look at the picture again, at the curls that have remained to this day. "It never bothered me that I didn't look like them because I thought that was a normal story to have. Then I went out into the world and people asked me if I thought my parents would have loved a 'real' kid more. I guess because of the baby-sniffing thing."

Hyacinth doesn't say anything in response. Usually when people ask me these questions, they ask them like we're some fascinating oddity. But Hyacinth asked because she gets it. That it's complicated sometimes. That the more I live, the more not looking like my family means more parts of my life they can't share. Some days it's hard. Some days I don't think about it at all. But every day, it's just the way my family is; to me, it's normal. In another universe, I'd be someone else. Maybe better. Maybe worse. Maybe just different. Whatever the case, I am who I am because it happened this way. I'm not sure that truly sank in before, not the way it has now when I'm looking at them on the wall, when they're gone.

She's still watching me when I finally look away from the picture. "You're like him," I say. "Brian. You make the same face."

Hyacinth's brows draw together. "What sort of face?"

"Um . . . your general at-rest expression. Anyway, my mom, Ella, and I have the same voice. My dad and Matty argue the same way. Blood is a means of getting you into this world, but it doesn't make you." I think of Jack Aster in his Sugar, Sugar T-shirt. He towers over me like his son does. "Brian and his dad are the same height," I say.

She looks down. "Were."

I realize, as we were talking about our families, both she and I had forgotten.

And I hate myself for the immediate thought crossing my mind. The hope that, for me, it will be different.

"My biological dad died when I was two," Hyacinth says, still focused on the floor. "He was hiking in the rain and he slipped at a steep spot. I don't remember him. Daisy does—she's the one who found him, in the woods by our house. Rain. Fire. The elements don't like our family."

*She has lost every parent she's ever known.*

She stares at me with huge eyes, and though her expression doesn't change, I sense that, like Brian, she doesn't want me to say anything—she just wants me to know.

"So . . . does Brian have an average IQ?" I say.

She scowls at me. "Brian is smarter than most people." Her tone is defensive. "He is a champion among men."

"Okay," I say, hands in the air.

Her shoulders relax. "My parents would have liked you." She does not feel it necessary to reveal if she does or not. But she waits. Silently, expectantly.

*I can't stay in here forever.*

Reluctantly, I shove myself to my feet to go with her.

In the kitchen, Brian and Shandy have lit more candles, casting a cheery glow over the room, though I see for the first time how dirty the floor is, covered in great smears of dried mud and blood. My mother would be humiliated. I look around at the paisley curtains, the walls she regularly cleans to keep them white and spotless, and it no longer feels the same—not without her.

Shandy turns, guzzling water, and his face brightens when he sees me. The thing about being popular is you can wear a silver belt buckle embossed with your last name and everyone just goes with it. He looks tired and bedraggled, but it's giving angel-that-fell-out-of-heaven-into-Japan vibes. Striding forward, he sweeps my unsuspecting self into a bear hug. Water drips from his drooping bangs onto my shoulder.

It takes a second to comprehend the fact that Shandy Ohno is hugging me and he smells like coconut and sunshine. Also, he's made of solid muscle.

"Sid Spencer, you're alive!" The long, sleepy eyes that tilt up at the corners crinkle with warmth. "That means, like, two of the four Asians in Wellsie are still alive!"

"You're forgetting to count Hampton College," I say.

"Oh, right, so two out of, like . . . five."

"Matty's alive," I say, but my voice shakes.

Shandy's eyes find Brian's, but he squeezes me again before letting go. "I know he is and we'll find him," he says gently. "Is it okay if we rest here for a beat?"

I nod. There's a deep sense of relief I'm not by myself anymore.

Brian steers Hyacinth over to the kitchen table, where she sits to remove her boots. She doesn't have a mark on her, though she looks exhausted. I eye Brian's knuckles again, then glance at Shandy, who lowers himself stiffly into a chair, wincing the whole way.

"Don't get too comfortable," Brian says, watching him relax in the chair. "There's a shell in the basement."

*Shell.*

Shandy sighs again and swipes a hand through his hair. "I need a second, okay? My whole body is a bruise."

"Aren't you a hockey player?" Brian says. "You get hit all the time."

Shandy sweeps one hand down his body. "Yeah, please understand that I pad all this."

"Is that why you took so long?" Hyacinth's eyes flick toward the thumping basement door. "There was a zombie in here?"

"Spencer came at me with a cleaver," Brian says, shrugging. "Then she tasered me."

Shandy looks back and forth between us. When he presses his lips closed, a laugh honks through his nose. He pretends it's a sneeze by pinching his nose, but it honks out his mouth.

Hyacinth's expression hardens. Out of nowhere, she produces a hatchet and makes sure I see it. In fact, I'm pretty sure she angles it so the light hits the blade.

I glance at Brian, who raises his hands in a *what can you do?* gesture.

"You hurt my brother?" Hyacinth doesn't blink once.

I make the same *what can you do?* gesture.

But Hyacinth is directing that stern glower in his direction now, which cements my conclusion they have one to three expressions they rotate between each other. "Did you do something to deserve being tasered?"

Brian puts his hands on his hips.

"He broke into my house and I didn't know who he was," I say before he can speak. "I was scared."

She looks me over, then she looks Brian over, pursing her lips as she reviews the information. "I can see how he might seem very tall to someone like you," she says seriously.

"Yes, it felt excessive and unnecessary," I say.

Brian sighs.

"He should have declared peaceful intentions," Hyacinth decides. "He was in the wrong." She lowers the hatchet. "Also, he owes you one favor."

"You would think getting tasered would be enough to make things even," Brian mutters, rubbing his belly.

"That's not how it works," Hyacinth says, her tone firm. "If you do something bad, you need to do something good. They never liked punishing us. Don't you remember?"

A shadow falls over Brian's face, but he tilts his head at me, hands still on his hips. "Fine, I owe you one favor, Spencer. Within reason."

That seems fair. "I require a coupon so you don't renege."

Brian tears a bright orange Post-it from its stack by the phone and makes a note on it. When he sticks it to my arm, it reads, *To Spencer. From Brian. COUPON for IOU. Terms and Conditions: Within reason.*

"There are a not insignificant number of knives on the counter," Shandy observes.

"Spencer was preparing to leave to find Matt," Brian says.

Suddenly all three pairs of eyes are trained on me.

I am wearing my mother's fly-fishing vest, a tool belt, and a neon-green fanny pack.

"That's . . . an interesting outfit," Brian says. "Hot date?"

"Listen, I have no idea what I'll be facing out there," I say, irritated. "Unlike you, I am completely in the dark." I can't keep the accusation out of my voice.

Brian and Shandy exchange another glance. "Let's deal with the shell," Brian says. "Then we'll talk, okay?"

*Shell. Like a shell of a person.*

"I couldn't kill him." I take a breath. "What's in the segment that opened? What *is* he?"

Brian hesitates for a second, perching on a kitchen stool, favoring his tasered side. "There are eight segments to the Wellsie fault line," he begins slowly. "Eight Guardians, eight Keys."

Like a spine with eight vertebrae.

"Josh's segment was what we called the Undying."

Suddenly it's harder to block out the thumping. I remember why I named him. "Thaddeus was a person once, wasn't he?"

"Yes," Shandy says quietly. "Magic is meant to be ephemeral, flitting from person to person. But if it's used too often for too long, it'll fuse to the soul, become a part of you. There would be less of it freely available. So if someone tried to take more for themselves, from a person it had merged to . . ." His lips twist into a grimace. "You can't rip out the magic without ripping out the soul along with it."

"But he's . . . alive."

"They were alive when it happened—it wasn't a clean severing." Brian looks off toward one of the boarded windows. "The magic splintered, leaving pieces still tied to them. They are technically alive. They'll get injured. Their bodies will starve, their muscles will waste, but . . . they won't feel anything, or speak, or laugh. They'll still be compelled to move, hungering for the very thing the magic needs to truly work."

*Hungering for the souls they lost.* People tried to take magic from others and they made them into monsters. This is one of the things they did that proved none of us could be trusted with power. "Can they be killed?"

"The head," Shandy says wearily. "Destroy the brain and the fragments disperse back to the magic. Trial and error."

They've been battling for two days now.

Shandy rests for three seconds more, then launches himself to his feet, but not without effort. "Let's do this." He walks off toward the front door where their packs lie and returns a moment later with a trekking pole.

They approach the cellar door in the hallway outside the kitchen. I follow after, knotting my hands together.

"If he gets past us," Brian says, but he doesn't finish the sentence. I see who he's looking at.

Hyacinth stands by her chair, clutching her hatchet. *Protect her.* I nod at him.

Brian retrieves the crowbar from the floor and, without hesitation, goes to work on my barrier of wooden planks. The thumping intensifies from the other side.

Shandy keeps one hand braced against it as Brian tears each board away. When he's finished, he hands the metal bar to me. I clutch it against my chest, backing up so I stand in the space between them and Hyacinth.

Shandy twists the lock on the knob. They exchange a brief, silent look, then Brian flings the door open.

Thaddeus falls forward into the hallway, groping the air, reaching for them. In the light he's more grotesque, all pale tangled limbs. The spot where I hit him with the doorstopper is bruised purple, caked with congealed blood. My brain screams at me to run. But I can't. I promised.

Brian has Thaddeus by the collar of his threadbare shirt, pinning him to the wall by his neck. Shandy spears him straight through his eye. His *eye*. If I'd eaten anything today, it would be on the floor.

Thaddeus's flailing ceases; he hangs on the pole, blood trailing thin ribbons down his cheek. And he does not move again.

With a grunt, Shandy yanks the weapon out. Taking deep gulps of air, he lets it fall to the ground.

I can't stop staring at the open cellar door and at the dark splotch on the wall.

Brian approaches, reaches out a hand to brush my cheek, and draws it back, a tear glistening on his thumb. His face, when I look, is drained of color. Gently, he pries the crowbar from my frozen fingers and sets it aside.

"I hit him in the head w-with a doorstop, but he kept moving." I blink back more tears. "I should have tried harder."

"You survived," he says quietly. "That's enough."

I follow, blurry-eyed, as they drag the motionless body through the kitchen.

Now that he's not moving, Thaddeus is a collection of bones barely held together. He doesn't weigh much. They heft him easily down the porch steps to lay him in the garden. I flinch when he lands softly in the soil. My mother's daffodils will be particularly vibrant this year.

Shandy strides back into the house, digging both hands into his hair.

Brian stands by the garden, head bent, shoulders slouched.

They stabbed something in the eye. Guardian or not, this is hard for everyone.

The lawn is a swamp beneath the grass, mud squishing around my boots as I come up next to Brian.

A few yards past us, somewhere in the grass, lies Dustin Miller. I squeeze my eyes closed, but it doesn't help. I'll never forget how he looked, how he screamed. And a few yards past him, there might be more of Thaddeus's kind, lurking in the trees. As long as the fault line remains open, they're going to keep coming.

*Please let Matty be okay.*

It's still raining, the spray barely visible in the weak glimmer of moonlight through the clouds, faint but cold on my cheeks.

A shadow overhead blots out the light for an instant. Something drops to the ground behind us, a soft squelch. I whirl, panicking, swinging a fist at the shape lurking over me.

*Contact.* Pain explodes in my hand, radiating all the way up my arm. Brian grabs hold of my shoulders to keep me from going down in the muck.

"Jesus fucking Christ," someone sputters, stumbling back two steps. "Why the *face?*"

Doubling over, clutching my throbbing hand, I register the words first. A slim figure in a sodden wool coat comes into focus through the smarting tears. He gingerly cups his cheekbone, scowling at me.

Brian rubs a hand through his badly chopped hair and gives the newcomer his direct, hard stare.

"Morrissey," Brian says.

"Brian," Morrissey says.

# CHAPTER 5

*W*hen I come downstairs, the house feels warmer, though the weather hasn't changed. My brother's face flashes through my mind every minute, but the edge of my anxiety has been filed down a bit.

Brian, Morrissey, and Shandy are gathered in the kitchen. They've lit a Sterno can and set it beneath one of the metal burners from the stove. Brian toasts bread over the small fire while Shandy chops tomatoes and garlic by the sink. Morrissey sits alone at the kitchen table with a bottle of Scotch and a crystal glass about a third full. Apparently, he found the liquor cabinet. I am going to have to fill that with apple juice later and hope my parents think it was Ella.

All I know about William James Morrissey III is he's the sort of person who flies and he's not the first of his name.

One cashmere-socked ankle rests across his knee as he leans back in his chair, swirling his drink. He's in his early twenties, slender and white, and not particularly handsome, though his chestnut hair is pretty perfect—thick, with hints of red, curling a bit at the ends. His skin is paler under candlelight, making the bluish smudges beneath his eyes much more pronounced, like a character in a period drama who comes back from the war but dies of consumption so his betrothed can marry another. He probably has excellent penmanship and seals all his letters with wax.

In the corner, Chad has taken a liking to the wool overcoat Morrissey threw down with the declaration that it's soiled and he'll never need it again. The shoes by the door are part loafer, part slipper, with GUCCI stamped into the leather at the heel. I let Chad make a nest of the coat with zero guilt.

I hover in the hall outside the kitchen, wondering if they're going to say anything Guardian-ish they haven't told me. Morrissey stares down at the blue sweater he wears—my dad's—with shadowed eyes. "Never did I imagine my life would come to this."

I decide not to apologize for hitting him.

Leaning forward, he peers down at the cover of a book on the table, a book Ella told me I could read first—*oh God*.

"Are vampires a thing?" he murmurs, a slight frown creasing his brow.

"Yeah," Brian says. "I googled it a couple days ago. Apparently, they glitter."

"I'm into that," Shandy says. I peek around the doorframe to see him piling tomatoes on top of toasted bread. That he's using chopsticks to do this is amazing to me as the kind of Asian who uses one chopstick to stab food and eat it like a kebab.

"Is this glitter effect magic or is there some physiological reason?" Morrissey asks, all dubious, AS IF THE THREE OF THEM ARE NOT GUARDIANS WITH SUPERPOWERS.

Brian shrugs. "Maybe they rub themselves down with oil."

"That's shiny, not glittery," Morrissey points out.

Brian stares at him. "Sorry, maybe they dip themselves in egg and roll around in tinsel."

"Okay, do none of you know how glitter works?" Shandy exclaims. "If a vampire gets into some glitter, either on purpose or by accident, it will literally be on him forever."

These are the people with the fate of the world in their hands. Brian said there were eight. So far, I know of these three, Hyacinth's sister, Daisy, dead Josh, the missing Parker, and the missing Matty.

Hyacinth emerges from the guest bathroom and sees me lurking in the hallway. I gave her a sweatshirt and some old sweatpants that hang on her thin frame. She doesn't ask what I'm doing. Then again, she isn't a Guardian, either, so I bet she's eavesdropped before.

"So many dudes," I murmur as she approaches.

She nods solemnly. "We're all gonna die."

I can't disagree.

Together, we move into the kitchen.

Shandy wears one of Matty's waffle shirts and a pair of sweatpants. Brian wears his own jeans, but the white T-shirt and black hoodie are Matty's. Pain flares in my chest, but I bury it deep. I take a seat at the counter next to Brian.

His dark hair lies flat, and jagged, and way too short. With my own hair washed, it occurs to me social norms are the only reason I bother to clean myself at all.

Shandy glances at me. "Look at your hair!" he says, smiling. "It's so curly." His wet hair swoops in perfect jet-black waves over his head.

"Yeah." I resist the urge to stuff mine into a bun.

Brian is looking at the spot by my ear where one of my curls hangs in a tight ringlet. Only the one curl does what it's supposed to do— the rest are hit or miss.

Shandy drizzles olive oil over the toasted bread and layers on tomatoes and garlic and a chiffonade of basil over the top. A drizzle of balsamic vinegar finishes it off. He sets the plate in front of me.

"Did you eat anything today?" Brian asks.

I shake my head. "I don't know if I can eat."

"Sid Spencer, you know you have to take food from an Asian when it's offered," Shandy says sternly. "Otherwise we'll pretty much hate you forever."

I dutifully take a bite. Everyone appears to be watching me, which means a tomato decides to launch itself directly into my lap. "Really good," I say to Shandy. And it is. My body wakes as soon as the food hits my belly.

"We have to take care of ourselves," Shandy says firmly. "Have a spoonful of peanut butter or something—you need protein."

Brian puts five heaping spoons full of sugar into what appears to be lukewarm instant coffee.

"Your grandma owns Obasaan, right?" I ask Shandy, mouth full.

"Best Japanese restaurant in Wellsie," Shandy says. "Where do you think I learned my hard-core knife skills? They make my grandma slightly less embarrassed about passing on the family name to someone with abysmal Japanese."

"My Korean is nonexistent, so . . ." We take that moment to high-five across the counter.

Obasaan is the *only* Japanese restaurant in Wellsie, but I don't mention that. He and his grandmother live in the apartment above it. "Is your grandma . . . okay?"

"She went out of town the Friday before this happened." He takes a deep breath and the knife stills in his hand. "She's probably worried sick, but at least she's not in Wellsie."

He says she's not here like that means she's safe, the way Brian implied that about my parents and Ella.

"The outside world must know what's happened," I say abruptly. "It's been days."

Behind me, a chair scoots back, and I glance over my shoulder as Morrissey gets to his feet, taking a gulp of his drink. "They didn't leave us," he says flatly, answering my unspoken question. "There's a barrier around the town. No one can get out. No one can get in."

It takes a second for that to sink in before fear jump-starts in my stomach.

Brian rakes a hand through his hair. "What did you see?"

Morrissey stands at the counter, and the hand holding his crystal glass trembles a bit. "I've spent two days in the sky on the lookout for anyone who might have done this. But between the rain, the shells, and the forest, I saw nothing. Nothing except for a shimmering gold wall right before the bridge out of town, light as air, but solid to the touch." He lifts his gaze to Brian's. "It's the magic. Only Josh—or only the person who took his Key—could've made it do that. It's why there's no electricity, no cell service. Nothing is getting in or out. No one's coming to save us."

The bruschetta tips in my limp fingers, tomatoes showering onto the plate.

"But you're Guardians," I say slowly. "You know what to do, right? You have a plan."

They don't look at me.

"We have no idea what we're doing, Spencer," Brian says softly. "We get some information from our predecessors, but our histories are oral. We couldn't even be sure what we had was accurate. And the whole Guardian network is decentralized, so it's not like we can ask any of the others."

The rest of us know even less.

In the silence that follows, when my panic is touch and go, Hyacinth hands me a small, framed picture from my dad's desk in the guest bedroom. It's a picture of our family on a trip to Florida a few years ago. We climbed a banyan tree, much like the one at the foot of the driveway, and we're all sitting among the massive limbs. My eyes pause on Matty's smiling face. His hair is green here, not rainbow.

*It's up to us*, Hyacinth's dark eyes say—they're a warmer brown than mine, solemn but hopeful. She's trying to motivate me. Her sister is out there too.

I turn the frame over and pry up the back to remove the picture. To bring with me. "Tell me everything you do know, then."

There's a stack of maps sitting at the far side of the counter. Brian unfolds the one they give to tourists and spreads it out, leaning over it. "That's about where the fault line opened—it's maybe half a mile long and ten yards wide."

Hyacinth takes a black marker from its spot by the phone and follows the path of his finger, drawing a jagged line down Mount Hemsworth that ends after Town Center.

Wellsie's new canyon that's a gateway for living dead people that want to eat us.

"This is . . . was . . . Josh's segment," Brian continues, the slashes of his brows inching together into one line. "The rest of the fault line remains sealed."

Hyacinth spies the sugar bowl by the sink and spoons a thin line of glittering crystals around the map's border, the magic barrier.

But I remember something. "Whoever made the wall didn't use all the magic. When it was first released, it *spread*. Some of it hit me."

At my words, Brian looks instantly at Hyacinth, who rubs at her chest. "The same thing happened to Hyacinth."

"But if the magic is traveling around," Hyacinth says uncertainly. "That means whoever made the wall isn't controlling the rest of it right now. It should be affecting all of us, right?"

*Magic is meant to be ephemeral, flitting from person to person.*

Her eyes lower. "I haven't been able to do anything."

"Same," I say. It's not outside the realm of possibility that I have nothing the magic felt should be enhanced.

"You haven't been able to do anything *yet*," Morrissey says. Ominously.

"So half of the magic was used to make the wall and the remaining half is scattered," Shandy mutters, as Hyacinth showers the map's surface with sugar.

"But it doesn't make any sense," Morrissey says, shaking his head. "Whoever stole Josh's Key made the wall and left the rest? Why wouldn't they use all of it?"

"Maybe Matt and Parker stopped them before they could," Brian says slowly.

Matty and Parker who are MIA.

Brian surveys the map, the furrow between his brows deepening. "The only thing we know for sure is someone wanted to prevent anyone from entering or exiting Wellsie." His lips tighten grimly. "They're looking for us. My guess is they want all the Keys so they can open the entire fault line."

We all take a moment to absorb that. More magic for whomever it is. More chaos for the rest of us. Those segments could contain anything.

"And none of you can release the wall or close the fault line, can you?" I say.

Slowly, they shake their heads.

None of them are the Guardians of that section. None of them own the Key that did it.

Fighting back tears, I point to the northwest corner of the map. "We are here." I trace a line eastward with my finger. "And you've been through there? Have you seen any people?"

"Yes," Brian says, watching Hyacinth scatter red pepper flakes over Main Street to represent shells. "Town Center is overrun. We told the survivors to barricade themselves inside with as much food and water as they could." He doesn't elaborate further. How many did he see? How much did he tell them?

"The forest has completely engulfed the northern side of town as well," Brian adds, as Hyacinth creates it out of leftover basil.

Main Street is a death trap. My finger has stopped on East Wellsie. "You haven't been here, though?"

Shandy shakes his head.

But I can't look away from that spot under my finger, the spot where Nell lives.

"If Matty thought someone was after him, he wouldn't come here," I say softly. "He knew . . . he knew I was here. He wouldn't risk leading them to me. He might be holed up in his apartment." I point briefly to the general area of Matty's place so Hyacinth can drop a cube of potato from Shandy's home fries prep.

"We'll need to go there, no matter what," Shandy says, drawing all eyes to him. "Matt didn't carry his Key—it's probably somewhere in there."

I picture Matty's disaster area of a bedroom and I think setting the whole thing on fire might be the way to go. When everything is in ashes, the Key will remain.

"Daisy is his buddy," Brian says, and Hyacinth perks up at the mention of their sister. "She would have tried to track him first, and then come looking for us. If she's still—" He doesn't finish that sentence.

"Daisy is alive," Hyacinth says with absolute certainty as he looks away. "She will find us."

Shandy points at Hampton. "Eleni is my buddy. She lives in the dorms on campus." But he chews his lip as he frowns at the map. "She won't know what happened, but she'll know *something* did. She'll know I'd come for her." His thick bangs droop into eyes when he says, "But I, uh, don't have her room number. Or her dorm."

Hyacinth sighs loudly and places a potato cube in the center of Hampton College.

Searching every dorm on campus will take forever and also suck a lot. I scowl at Shandy, who crosses his arms in a defensive stance. "Listen, I have lots of good qualities. I'm charming, I'm a badass hockey player, I have really good hair, and"—he looks down at his torso—"I have rock-hard abs."

"We have to go to campus," Brian decides, ignoring him. "We need everyone together. Josh was Parker's buddy, so we don't have a lead on her. Morrissey is my buddy—"

"So clearly we are the only ones who did this right," Morrissey says.

"Having all the Guardians together means someone could take you out all at once," I point out.

"People are stronger together," Hyacinth says, and we all look down at the five potato cubes huddled together in the corner of northeast Wellsie, where my house is. "Separate, we're easier to kill." She says this matter-of-factly, but she fixates on the square in her palm, toying with it anxiously. It has no known placement on the map. Her sister.

Even paler, Morrissey sifts his fingers through the sugar border. If only it were that easy to get out. Chad leaps onto the counter to sit in a voluminous white mass in the center of town, destroying Hyacinth's map. I watch Chad bat the potato cube that represents Matty.

"Question," I say to Hyacinth. "Do you use food visual aids for everyone, or just people who are most likely to freak out?"

Hyacinth's brows knit together as she gives me a once-over. "I adapt to the situation," she decides to say.

That's fair. I scoot my stool back. "I need . . . I need to pack," I say abruptly, ignoring the four people plus one cat who watch me go.

I need to be alone for a moment, is more like it.

But when I'm standing in the dark living room, in the middle of all the supplies I collected with no idea what I'd need, I inhale several shaky times. Even if I'd been preparing to leave, it's too real now.

*I don't have a choice.*

I transfer Nell's notes, all written on scraps of notebook paper, from the birdhouse to a plastic bag and stuff it inside the front pocket of a backpack. In case I want to read them. In case I don't come back.

Behind me, the glow of a candle approaches.

"We dragged our packs in here." Brian's voice floats down from overhead. "It seemed to be where you store everything you own."

"You start with everything you own, then you slowly narrow it down," I say, glancing over my shoulder. "Isn't that how everyone packs?"

Brian lifts a bottle, brows raised. "Whiskey?"

"In case my foot gets caught under a boulder and I have to saw off my leg and disinfect my bloody stump."

As he wanders among the piles, picking items up, he glances at me with expressions I can't decipher, then puts them down. I feel

attacked. Like he has any right to make judgments on what's important in these trying times. I reach for my pillow and hug it defensively
against my middle.

"Is that a pillow?"

"Yes. I can't sleep on anything else. When I was younger, I always
thought if I loved my pillow enough, it would become a real pillow.
Like how the Velveteen Rabbit became a real rabbit."

He turns his face away, but not before I see his lips twitch. "Far be
it from me to deny your pillow the chance to frolic through the fields
with all the other real pillows," he says solemnly.

I quickly wad my pillow up and cram it into the backpack.

He lifts a flat wooden paddle from the coffee table and shoots me
a questioning look.

"That's my dad's frat paddle."

"I see that. What's it for?"

"Spanking zombies."

"Okay," Brian says. "Here's what appears to be a handheld tape
recorder."

"That is my audio diary."

"So what's this?"

"That is my written diary." My eyes narrow on the thick volume,
tied closed with a leather string. "I haven't written in it since I was a kid."

Casually, he flips it open. "June first," he begins. "Dear Diary, I
think I have a wax buildup in my left ear. Finn says I'm talking louder
because of it—"

"That is private," I shriek, lunging forward to slam the diary
closed and pull it from his hands. I toss it amid the camping equip-
ment, looking anywhere but at him.

"Why do you have two diaries?" Brian asks.

"I have a lot of feelings, okay?"

"Who's Finn? Finn Warren?"

"Why are you being so nosy? Let's go look through your stuff and see how you like it." I lift the harness to which the two machete sheaths are attached. "Another stop at Hunt and Hike?" I survey the ax and collection of sheathed hunting knives and avoid touching the trekking pole Shandy used earlier. "Did you loot all this?"

Brian shrugs.

Everything of theirs is neatly tucked into two camping packs. He has no personal items, nothing to which I can say something snarky. They burned to the ground with his house and his . . . well, that snuffs my indignation right out. I lift one of the machetes, turn it over in my hands. I don't have any weapons like this.

"I can attach the sheaths to two belts—one for you and one for me," Brian says.

"Hyacinth can have my stun gun," I say in a small voice. The one Matty gave me. When he left the house that night, he didn't have any weapons. "W-what power does Matty have?"

Brian shoves his hands in his pockets. "Matt never gets tired."

*Magic shows you who you are*, Matty once said.

It all clicks into place. The insomnia. The time he ran a marathon with no training. But even when he was young, he could never sit still, was always doing a million tasks at once. So many of his childhood pictures are slightly blurred—a body in motion.

That power won't protect him from physical violence.

"If he doesn't need to sleep, he'll always be one step ahead," Brian says softly, seeming to read my mind. "He'll always be on the move."

Matty could have transferred the Guardianship at any time, but he didn't. Now, someone could kill him for it. I know him. If he was told to protect the magic, he'd take that seriously. He'd never back down.

The knife of anxiety in my back wedges deeper. Even though they're magical, they're just people, and people can die. There used to be eight of them. Now there are seven.

"You're like BTS," I say.

He blinks. "Yes, exactly like BTS. No difference whatsoever."

I eye him thoughtfully. "You're the Yoongi of the group."

"Is that good or bad?"

"I won't dignify that with an answer."

His brows lift. "Then who are you in this scenario?"

"Normally I'm the person who stands near them with a tiny fan or blow dryer to cool them down when they're sweaty, but in this particular case I'm Hobi's sister."

"Okay."

There's an enormous part of me, ninety-five percent, that wants to give up and die here.

"If I travel with you, I'm bringing my cat. If she runs, she runs, but I can't leave her here. If we meet people out on the road, I won't steal food from them or kill them for batteries. And I'm definitely not going to chain people and eat them a little bit at a time."

Brian's hands are on his hips as he steps closer. "If I chain and eat people, feel free to stab me in the face."

Maybe it's not in me to stab anyone in the face, not even a shell. I close my eyes. "Do you believe it's possible something could be there without you knowing it? You can't always feel the things you have, right? Like your hair. Or your gall bladder. Or—or your courage."

"Yes," he says softly, the sound tickling the hairs on the back of my neck. "I do believe that, Isidora."

My eyes snap open. How did——? "No one ever calls me that." Ariella, Matthias, and Isidora: the fancy names our mother gave us that even she doesn't use.

He shrugs one shoulder. "It's your name, isn't it?"

"Yes."

"Okay, then. I'm Brian."

"I know that."

Brian takes another step forward. "Then imagine you know me. Imagine I'm your friend. And if you can imagine that, imagine you're not alone."

I look at his eyes, softer now. Softer, because the light of the candle flickers in their depths. Softer, because I do know him. "After we find Matty, I have to go to East Wellsie," I blurt out. I didn't know those words were there, lurking beneath the surface. "There's someone there I have to find."

He doesn't ask who. "I will help you," is all he says.

"Thank you," I whisper.

He lowers his head in a nod.

The picture of my family is still in my hand. *I am who I am because it happened this way.* I can only hope that whoever I am without them is strong enough.

Either way, it's up to me to find Matty.


I can't sleep. Lying in the middle of my parents' bed, I fluff my pillow, punch it, trying to make a comfortable hollow. Nothing works. I flop onto my back, staring at the ceiling.

The house is silent but for the rain against the windows, like I'm alone again.

I should check one more time that the front door is locked. *Lock the door behind me,* Matty said, the same Matty who gave me a taser. Because he knew then what I know now: Wellsie isn't safe.

With a lit votive, I pad barefoot down the hallway.

When I pass the guest room, a small body lies curled in the center of the bed. Hyacinth.

In the living room, Brian is sprawled under a blanket on the couch with Shandy scrunched in the loveseat opposite him. They could have used an actual bed in one of the upstairs bedrooms like Morrissey has, but then I see the machete and ax on the floor between them. Just in case.

A pair of slitted eyes glow near Brian's head as Chad stands protectively over him. A warning growl emanates from her chest.

I scowl at her.

Brian sneezes in his sleep.

I creep closer, edging around the piles of all my semi-useless supplies to get her so he won't wake up with puffy eyes.

When I'm about a yard away, Brian speaks.

"Don't."

I freeze. "What?" I say, a squeak, holding the light up. He has one arm thrown over his face. His knees are bent so he can fit on the couch, and he looks smaller that way.

He mumbles something, his breath hitching.

I blow the candle out.

Suddenly he thrashes onto his side, curling tighter.

Chad peers at me with an impatient expression, as though I'm supposed to do something about this.

Everyone expects something from me all of a sudden.

I should leave and pretend like this isn't happening.

A sob escapes him, harsh and dry.

I take a step forward. And another.

He weeps into the throw pillow under his cheek, and his hands curl into fists against it.

Something gathers in my chest, a knot. No, it's a sob. I've sobbed enough times in my life to know what it feels like. I can't watch people cry without wanting to throw up and die. I'll cry because he's crying.

I kneel beside the couch, wringing my hands at first. I reach out, but he moves, and I snatch my hand back.

"Brian," I whisper.

He throws an arm out, nearly hitting the coffee table.

I catch it, hold his wrist that is thicker than I thought, then his fist that is larger than I thought. I've never held a boy's hand before.

The floor trembles beneath my knees, faint, and the windows rattle. At first, I think it's another earthquake, until I feel the heat of his skin under my fingers.

*It's him.*

I tighten my hand around his. The whole house hums with movement. I remember what happened when he moved the raindrops, how he struggled. In his sleep, he can't control it, and it scares me. How much could he do if he tried? He could destroy things.

But he has bruises all over his knuckles.

"You're going to hurt yourself," I say softly.

"Don't leave me alone here," he says. "Please don't leave me alone."

An ache settles in my throat, the ache that always precedes the tears. *Don't leave me alone here.* It's what I've silently begged of my family for days. It's what he's said to his parents for three months. Ignoring the vibrations coming through the floor, the sound of glass shaking violently against wood, I say, "You're not alone."

He flops onto his back again, breathing raggedly. The rattling slows.

"Okay . . . that's better. That's much better." I hold his hand, pry the fingers open. Calluses cover each of his fingertips.

Nell used to make me take yoga classes with her sometimes. I remember the breathing. In through the nose, out through the mouth. They tell you to exhale or sigh it out.

He smells like a forest. Like evergreen, like winter, and something else, something very *boy* I can't describe.

"It's probably your soap," I say to him.

He lets out a deep sigh. The floor stills beneath me.

I imagine snow, because the slow drift of white is always calming for me. A cabin, too, nestled among pine trees, with woodsmoke coming out of the chimney. There is a certain peace when the world is *that* quiet, and nothing else moves, including you, except for snow, weighed down by nothing.

Chad settles herself like a loaf on the arm of the couch, watching over him.

Though he doesn't speak or move again, it takes a while for his body to fully uncramp. Eventually his breathing deepens and slows.

I nearly fall asleep curled against the side of the couch. As my head nods, I jerk myself awake. The house is silent again. Nothing moves.

Slowly, so as not to wake him, I extricate my hand from his and stand, my knees creaking a bit. I look down on him for a long moment to make sure he's okay and turn to go, but Shandy's head shifts on his pillow.

His eyes are open, watching me—I can see their wet shine in the dark.

"Thanks," he whispers. "That's been going on for days."

Or longer. Embarrassed, I duck my face. Without saying a word, I return to bed as quickly as my tiptoes allow. And I dream of snow.

# CHAPTER 6

Shandy wakes me some point before dawn. I suspect he never slept.

The rain grew heavier overnight. I opt for contacts instead of my glasses, yoga pants that will dry quickly if wet, a pair of waterproof hiking boots I've never used, and my mother's brown raincoat. The others wear the camouflage raingear they stole from Hunt and Hike. *We can't be seen*, Brian had said. I think shells will sense us no matter what, but he meant *people*.

They stand at the front door, packs on, waiting for me. Shandy holds his trekking pole, but he's stuck the ax through a loop on the side of his pack. They say nothing as I leave one of my father's two-way radios on the counter with a note.

*Matty, radio me on channel 2 if you come home. Love, Siddy.*

There's no way to stall now. It's time.

I hear the forest before I see it. I've been listening to the wind and rain for days, but they've become traffic sounds, there in the background, normal. As I open the door, the sounds reach a crescendo. I've always imagined nature as quiet until now. I breathe in, like inhaling the vapor from the humidifier, like drowning while breathing. But instead of tasting nothing, I taste . . . kale.

"It smells like that algae-colored smoothie you spilled in my car," Morrissey mutters to Shandy.

"The car you tried to make me keep because it was 'soiled'?" Shandy snorts.

Morrissey shrugs. "Well. It's not like I don't have other cars."

The sky is that strange in-between shade of soft dark, a blue that is almost black. My eyes detect no light, and yet they adjust the way they wouldn't if it was full night.

Across my mother's flooded garden, the swamp of the front yard, and what used to be our driveway, the banyan's shadow lurks as large as the garage. And beyond it, a forest. Trees, all types of trees with vines hanging from their branches. I glimpse rooftops jutting through the canopy, some as solid as ever, others not so much.

Not a single candle flickers anywhere.

"The shells and the forest are hella concentrated around Town Center," Shandy says, pointing toward the banyan. "There are less of them here, but we have no way of knowing how fast they'll travel."

I scan the neighborhood to the west. Morrissey had said large stretches of the road remain intact in that direction. The trees are much sparser—almost normal. But that way doubles the distance.

Chad's ears twitch, changing direction with every sound. Abruptly, she struggles out of my arms and bounds down the porch steps. The white ball of fluff darts off toward the west, disappearing into the neighbor's bushes. I tried.

"When I was a kid, I put a harness and leash on her to take her for a walk so she wouldn't keep trying to escape the house," I say. "She wouldn't let me near her afterward. It was Matty who got it off her. Sometimes I wonder if that's why she likes him and not me."

"Something tells me that cat survives," Brian says. *Even if we don't* are his unspoken words.

I don't look at Thaddeus's body lying in the grass. Or Dustin's. Both are still, no threat. But in the trees, there are too many creeping shadows, too many shapes. A twig snaps somewhere.

"Let's move," Brian says, and steps off the porch into the grass.

We follow, one by one.

Wind blows my raincoat hood off my head, and I give up trying to keep it there after the third time of tugging it back. The rain slants sideways, needles pelting the side of my face. I remain close to Brian, nearly stepping on his heels, Hyacinth at my side. Shandy and Morrissey bring up the rear.

Brian leads us into the swamp of the front yard. High grass that was never there before skims my thighs. Leaves conceal pits of mud that submerge my boots and are reluctant to let them go without a struggle.

Morrissey trips on a root, stumbling into Shandy and almost going down before grabbing his arm.

As he tugs Morrissey up, Shandy pauses, tense, squinting at the forest, head cocked. In the next instant, he shoves Morrissey onto his hands and knees.

"What the hell," Morrissey utters just as my ears catch a faint whizzing sound.

Shandy snatches something out of the air inches from his face. I wouldn't have known anything was there had I not glimpsed the blur of his hand.

Brian stands frozen in his tracks, looking over his shoulder at Shandy, who opens his fist. A dart with a feathered tuft lies in his palm.

In the dark, Shandy's face shines stark white. "Run."

A scream bursts through the silence, bloodcurdling, a warning, before it cuts off abruptly. In the aftermath, booted feet crunch through leaves.

Brian turns back to face the trees. "Parker," he whispers.

Shandy dashes forward to yank Hyacinth to his side, narrowly rescuing her from another dart. "Run," he says again, voice hoarse. *"Now."*

I spin right, left, but those footsteps, those footsteps seem to surround us. Run where?

A single pop echoes in the dark.

Behind me, something blasts through the porch window, blowing a jagged hole in the glass.

It takes a second. To comprehend.

*Gun shot. Not darts now. Bullets.*

"Everybody down!" Brian shouts, dropping the pack from his back.

I am aware of Shandy's arms around me, dragging me, dragging Hyacinth, to the ground. Just as the first wave comes.

But Morrissey screams, clutching his lower leg as a dark rose blooms through the fabric of his pants.

There's no time to feel anything.

*This is real.*

With a roar, Brian flings his arms out.

Bullets hit wood—the house, the trees—and pepper the puddles. One after another after another, so much louder in real life. Not like a car backfiring the way I'd always thought, but the sound of a heart exploding from a chest, punctuated with a scream—my scream.

But nothing hits us.

Between shots, Brian's breath heaves. Lashing out wildly, Brian moves the bullets, left, right, up. Right. Left. Up. There are too many shots to be one gun. He can't stop them all.

Beside me, Shandy's heaved his body over Hyacinth, but she jerks with every sound.

"It was not a good call to stay here," Shandy gasps.

"OH, YOU THINK?" Morrissey lies on his side, pain etched into his forehead, as he hugs his knee to his chest and tries to staunch the bleeding from his calf with both hands.

Cold sweat trickles down the side of my neck.

I want to close my eyes. I can't. I can't even blink.

My cheek hurts, pressed into a pebble. Tall blades of grass poke my ears and neck as I inhale the scent of earth, the rotten odor of stagnant water. The dirt doesn't smell half bad, actually. Something about moldy, decaying leaves reminds me of fall. I could live here. That's an option.

*I miss Nell.* The thought comes, unsolicited. I picture her, lying next to me in the mud, blond hair shoved neatly under her hood. "If you're looking to get murdered, you are one hundred percent playing your cards right," she says to me.

Except she isn't here. Maybe she's dead.

Several yards away, Brian dives to the ground, landing on his side. He crawls toward us, painstakingly, a distant strain in his eyes, face ghost-white and wet with rain or sweat. Or blood. A bullet has nicked his ear.

"Hello?" A man's voice calls out. Pleasant, friendly. *Close.*

Beyond the yard, at the tree line, shadows move.

Heavy boots clomp through the brush.

Beside me, Shandy lifts his head, eyes darting anxiously around the yard, then toward the west where the forest is thin. If we run, will they shoot us in the back?

Brian is trembling as he struggles to his knees. He breathes in quick, short breaths, but I don't see him release any of them, no puffs of mist when hot air meets cold. "Stay where you are," he shouts, lifting his hands in warning. But his arms wobble. He's tired.

Flashlights flicker in the darkness, trained on us like spotlights. Behind them, beyond the glare, a shadow emerges from the woods.

The man's rain-slicked hair bears a silvery-blond color, longer on top than on the sides, and combed neatly. He wears all gray, from his open overcoat to his three-piece suit, and it washes out his already white skin. Expensive clothes, but they don't fit him the way they would a rich person. The way my nice dresses never fit the way Nell's clothes do, because mine aren't tailored for me.

The face, not handsome, not unhandsome, is one I won't be able to describe later. Though I memorize every detail, there's no defining feature.

He could be anyone.

But I know instantly he's not from here. The eyes, staring straight at Brian, carry that same gleam the eager tourist at Lulu's had. His gaze fixes on Brian's trembling hands, brightening with wonder. And hunger. That's what I'll remember later.

*He's here for the magic.*

The man smiles, then, like a normal person in his thirties, like there isn't a line of men with semiautomatic rifles behind him.

There are ten, their shapes bulky and square. Visors cover each face—riot gear.

"I'm Paul Ford," the man calls out. "You must be Brian Aster?"

Brian's shoulders stiffen, but he says nothing, even as the men push someone out in front of them. A chill seeps into my chest, filling it all the way to the edges, because for an instant, I see a bun in the shadows. *Matty?*

But it's a woman, pale and shivering, her blond bun tangled with bits of dead leaves. Mud smears one cheek. She looks . . . she looks the way Nell will look in ten years.

Shandy pushes himself to his knees, shielding Hyacinth with his body. "Parker," he murmurs.

And though she's gagged, hands bound, and a gun jabs into her back, her chin lifts in defiance.

"It's an honor to meet a Guardian," the man, Paul Ford, continues smoothly, directing his words to Brian. "But we're all just people at the end of the day, Guardian or not." At the jerk of his head, the men lower their weapons. "I am willing to stand down. Call it a gesture of goodwill to pave the way for negotiations. So you'll remember I want a solution that works for everyone."

Except they were the ones that started shooting.

"I'm sure you know why I'm here," Ford says. "You have something very important to me. And vice versa. I would like to propose a trade."

Parker's gaze shifts to Brian, and though Brian doesn't move a muscle, her lips tighten into a stubborn line. Two men stand on either side of her, each with a hand clamped on her shoulder. She gives an almost imperceptible shake of her head. *Don't trade anything for me.*

Paul Ford cocks his head, smiling the smile of someone who obsessively whitens his teeth. "You understand I had no choice but to fire off a couple warning shots. You had to know what I'm capable of. But I don't want to hurt anyone unless I have to. Why don't we chat?"

Brian cocks his head, mimicking him. "Go fuck yourself," he says softly.

And Parker goes limp, slipping from her captors' grasp as she drops to the ground.

Brian has a clear path.

With one savage blow, he throws Paul Ford backward with a surge of power that topples the entire line of men. A few wild shots are discharged, but none make impact. Bodies hit trees with agonized screams. The cracking could be branches or bones, but Brian doesn't stop. He forces them farther, creating as much distance as he can.

Before collapsing on his belly in the dirt.

In the silence, I feel my limbs, all pins and needles, and the heartbeat in my chest again. Wind washes over me, a deep, wet cold. Brian crawls over to the curled-up ball that is Hyacinth. Without saying a word, she flings her arms around his neck. He presses his cheek into her hair as he hugs her, taking in deep gulps of air. Someone takes hold of my arm, and I lurch to my feet, stumbling under the weight of my backpack. Dazed, I stare up into the light drizzle. *Is it still raining?* It is, barely. A tickling spray.

The sky has lightened to a dark navy, in small degrees I didn't notice until now.

"Sid, the ropes," someone says. Shandy. He nods toward Parker as he crouches down by Morrissey.

"Do you have to put all your weight on my gaping wound?" Morrissey roars.

"Yes," Shandy snaps.

Numbly, I unsheathe my machete and saw at the ropes binding Parker's wrists. Wide blue eyes stare at me impatiently, and for the first time I notice how bloodshot and puffy they are. From crying. She moves her arms back and forth in an attempt to speed the process. The instant her hands are free, she's tugging at the rag tied over her mouth.

"We have no time," she gasps, in a voice that sounds like it's been dragged over broken glass. In seconds, she's by Morrissey's side as

Shandy pulls a bandanna from his pack to wrap the leg. "You're lucky it's a graze. Those kinds of guns are built to destroy."

"Yes, super lucky, just excruciating pain, no big deal," Morrissey grinds out through clenched teeth. His hands are slick with blood, oily black in the dim light.

"Reinforcements are coming," Parker says, looking at Brian who still clings to Hyacinth. "Our advantage right now is he only brought maybe thirty armed men. You took out ten, but the second group is stationed about a quarter mile away, and the third group is set up in a perimeter around this whole area."

"I don't understand." Shandy holds pressure on Morrissey's leg. "How is facing thirty men with guns an advantage? I can see the bullets coming but you can't."

"The alternative is fighting people with magic," she says sharply. "He came here to find Matt; he didn't bring any heavy hitters. He sent the people who got the strongest powers to search specifically for Brian and Eleni."

*Matty.* "Matty's alive?" I cry, and the fog of numbness lifts. My body comes back to life.

"Yes," Parker says. "Or he was the last time I saw him." Her eyes dart, panicked, to the tree line. "Ford will be back here any moment. If he's radioed his men for backup, we need to be long gone before any of them manage to get here."

"But Brian threw him," Shandy says, eyes on the trees again. "That Ford guy is probably . . ." *Probably dead.*

"No," Parker says, pale. "He isn't."

"Is he a Guardian now?" Morrissey asks, face tight with pain. "Did he open the fault line?"

"It's . . . it's complicated," Parker says in a rush. "Ford has Josh's

Key, but Josh was able to transfer the Guardianship to Matt before he—" She swallows with difficulty but can't seem to finish that sentence. "Matt is the actual Guardian of that Key now. Ford can't use it. But if Matt doesn't have it, he can't use it, either."

"If Ford was never a Guardian, who—?" Morrissey tries.

"There's no time to explain," Parker says, her voice rising in pitch. "He is coming. We can't beat him. Brian, *you* can't beat him. We have to go. NOW."

Her terror finally makes impact.

Shandy hauls Morrissey to his feet. "Can you put weight on that leg?"

Morrissey shakes his head, jaw set in a rigid line. "I can't go on foot."

Brian drags Hyacinth to her feet, bending to cup her face in his hands. Her dark eyes glisten as he kisses her head. "I need you to do something for me," he says thickly, while fishing in his coat pocket. When he peels his fingers open, a glowing ivory key rests in his palm, so bright I shield my eyes. He grabs her trembling hand, wrapping her fingers around it. The light abruptly dies. "You need to hold on to this for me, okay?" He glances at Morrissey, Shandy, then Parker. "It's not safe to carry our Keys. This way, no one will be able to take them, no matter what happens to us."

"My Key is in my grandmother's backyard," Parker says. "There's a small knothole in a tree. I wouldn't tell them. That's the only reason I'm alive."

Shandy and Morrissey exchange a grim look. But their fists become twin balls of white flame, and they drop their Keys into Hyacinth's hand. Hyacinth tucks them all into her bag, though her lips tremble.

"I need to get Josh's Key back from that man," Brian says to his sister. "Without it, Matt has no chance of closing the fault line. You're going to fly with Morrissey, get as far as the West Bridge."

The West Bridge over the Llewellyn River is the wrong direction, the long way around, but we have no choice.

Hyacinth meets his stare, just as direct, but her chin trembles. "No."

"I'll meet you there. But if . . ." His gaze shifts away. "If it's been a while, and I'm not there, you'll go find Daisy, okay?"

She shakes her head violently. "I won't leave you."

"Yes, you will," he says, as he hugs her again like it's the last time. "Take her. *Go.*"

I don't know who he's speaking to at first, until Morrissey limps forward, wrapping his arms around her middle.

Hyacinth's eyes widen, but he's already launched into flight, lifting her with him into the air, and up—

"No! Brian, no!" Her scream carries for a moment before it's gone. Before they're both gone, a dot against the charcoal sky, then nothing at all.

Brian hunches, hands on knees. "Get out of here," he says roughly. He lifts his head, eyes falling on me. "You'll be safe with them."

"You're drained, Brian," Shandy says quietly. "You can barely stand. You can't fight him alone."

"I am the only one of us who can," Brian says. "There isn't a choice."

Parker isn't listening to them. Instead, she's looking at me, the blood draining from her face. "Shell," she says, strained. "Behind you."

I whirl around. At first, I see only my machete blade in sharp focus.

Nothing else, until one of the blurred shapes beyond it moves.

The shell wanders around the edge of the house, bushes snagging the threadbare shreds of fabric stuck to her body like they've become part of her skin. Lank brown hair falls across a bruised face. One arm hangs limply from her shoulder socket. The other stretches toward me. She moves on rubbery legs, sensing me without seeing me.

Her head lifts. Cracked lips pull apart to reveal rows of broken teeth. Her jaws open and close, open and close.

Shandy is rushing toward the other side of the house, where three more shells emerge. He's lifting his ax, swinging, and I look away. Impact. A watermelon being cleaved open.

But the second the distant *pop pop pop* splits the air, I don't remember what I'm supposed to do.

*Gunshots. Not again. Please.*

Brian's head whips toward the woods.

Parker's quivering voice finds its way through the rushing in my ears. "They're on their way."

I flinch at the next shot, but my feet are frozen. Guns in one direction, shells in another.

Brian looks back at me and I see his eyes like they were by candlelight, so dark a blue they're like the sky right now, before the sunrise. I can hear the marching in the woods, getting louder, closer.

He turns, taking a few unsteady steps toward the tree line, lifting his hands. "Run," he says hoarsely.

*No.* Hyacinth's scream echoes in my ears.

But Parker is at my side, propelling me toward the left side of the house, toward the shell. She's shouting in my ear, but I only hear bits and pieces. "We need—take out—shells—" But she has no weapons on her—it's up to me.

*Merriweather*, I name her. She's moving faster. Yards away. Feet away.

I jab the machete forward, but it slides off her jaw, leaving a red line behind. Off balance, her sliced face lurches forward, sagging lips catching the fabric of Parker's sleeve. In my mind, I see Dustin Miller, the blood pooling at the base of his throat. Thaddeus's hands are around my neck as his jaws snap toward my face—

Parker screams as those jagged teeth pierce her skin.

With a cry, I sink the blade into Merriweather's skull with all my strength. The force of it radiates into my clenched hands, my wrists and elbows, everywhere the joints hinge. Something hot sprinkles my face.

She's sinking, and the machete is stuck in her head, pulling the handle from my stiff hands. And I don't look. But I can smell her. Not vomiting is one of the greatest achievements of my life.

Shandy rushes up next to us, hacking down a shell I didn't notice. He doesn't stop. Hack, withdraw. Hack, withdraw, almost graceful, like a hockey player, like someone who never misses. "This way," he shouts.

Parker helps me wrench the machete free, and I hear a wet, sucking sound. Red smears the blade. In the corner of my eye, there are more blurred figures, but at the back of my mind, through the panic, there's the image of Brian facing the trees, the image of him crying in his sleep. *Don't leave me alone in this*, he said. I can't leave him.

"We have to be alive to help him," comes Parker's voice in my ear.

We run, tripping over a couple thick roots, going down, leaping back up. Shouts echo behind us, the running footsteps about to reach the edge of the woods. Out of the corner of my eye, flashlights blink on in the darkness, beams of light shining out from the trees and crisscrossing over the ground. They're searching for us.

Suddenly there's the familiar, slippery feel of neatly cut grass beneath my boots. Solid ground.

A leafy branch hits me full in the mouth, then drags along my cheek, leaving the taste of earth behind.

Parker drags me to my belly behind the neighbor's bushes, wedged against the lattice running beneath their porch. Curls of paint spring off the wood.

A nudge on my ankle spurs me to shimmy forward on my belly, wincing as the splintery mulch digs into my skin. "Okay. Okay, let's Shawshank Redemption this business," I whisper, but a sob escapes my chest. "I'm sorry, I don't . . . I don't think I'm okay."

But Parker is behind me. "Sid." Her quiet voice finds me in my panic. "You're Sid, right? Matt's sister? You have to keep going."

*Keep going.*

I slide forward, breathe in the pungent scent of soil mixed with the sharpness of evergreen, and slide forward again. But underneath the rustling of branches, the low-level whistle of the wind, the birds waking and chattering, feet squeak in the wet grass. An urgent grip on my ankle halts me.

Several pairs of boots approach, mere feet from my head.

I take a deep breath and hold it.

"I think they went this way," a man murmurs.

"They'll escape west," another says. "Let's go."

Their steps quicken. Two men jog past our bushes.

I count a whole minute, straining my ears the entire time for footsteps, but all I hear are the gentle pats of drops hitting the leaves overhead. Parker touches my ankle again.

My hands fist in the dirt, dragging my body forward. The lattice is broken in patches, large holes hidden by the bushes, probably entranceways for raccoons, or let's be real, dead bodies in garbage bags. These neighbors always gave out homemade treats for Halloween, which meant they were probably poisoned, and my mother never let us eat them. Parker wordlessly directs me to go through the largest hole and crawl under the porch.

I have to remove my bag and flatten myself completely to fit in the shallow space.

I can't see anything in the dank darkness, but spiderwebs cling to my cheeks. The top of my bun catches on the boards above, but the pain is distant, separate from me. One action followed by another action. *Keep going.*

When I've crawled enough for Parker to fit in behind me, I sit back against the house's foundation. I can't see anything, but I definitely don't want to. It smells like something died under here. Then Parker is beside me, our gasping breaths the only sound. She sits next to the hole in the lattice, peering out.

There's blood on my face and the scent of rotting flesh in my hair, on my skin. I killed something. I stabbed a head. I don't have this in me.

As I breathe fiercely through my nostrils, tears leak from the corners of my eyes.

Parker's hand is on my shoulder, gentle, but firm. "Remember, your brother is alive," she whispers. Her own breath keeps hitching. In the dark, I catch a glimpse of shining eyes, filled with moisture. Like mine. "Breathe deeply, slowly. I'll tell you what I know, but I need you to not freak out."

I rest my head back against the house, hands knotted to keep them from shaking. *Matty.*

After a moment her hand falls away.

"We should wait here for a couple minutes," she says in a low voice. "I don't have a weapon on me and you need to save your strength. It'll be to our advantage if Ford thinks we all left."

She must have been so scared when she was with those men, expecting to die at any moment. She wanted to run the instant she was free and yet she's here to help Brian.

When I turn my head to look at her, she's brushing wisps of blond hair off her forehead and for a second, she looks so much like Nell I want to cry. It takes me a second to speak through the lump in my throat.

"I need to know what happened to Matty," I say. "Please."

Parker lets out a long exhale. "That man, Paul Ford, he knows everything about the Guardians—who we are, what we can do. Josh told him. I don't know how Ford found him, but he knew enough to go for Josh first. He was their plan. Or rather, I was."

"What do you mean?"

She hesitates a moment, but there's a look in her eyes I've seen before. In Brian. In Hyacinth. I didn't define it as loss until now. "Josh and I were dating. Ford thought if he threatened me, he could force Josh to do whatever he wanted. I was on my way to the meetup when they took me. One Key, one segment of the fault line—that was never the plan. He wants to open the whole thing."

The other Guardians had surmised as much, but . . .

"Why did they need Josh?"

"The power he had." Her lips twist. "If he gave you a command, you'd have to follow it. They knew this—they wore headphones the whole time. They planned to keep him alive until they had the rest of us."

"Ford wanted him to command the Guardians to transfer their Keys," I say slowly, realization dawning. "*Josh* was the one to open his segment of the fault line. *He* was the one who created the barrier. To save you . . ." But as soon as the words are out, I regret them. Because what would I do in that situation? If it were Matty.

Parker's gaze hardens. "You never know what you'll do," she says coolly. "You can think you are a good, honorable person, but no one knows who they are until the moment presents itself."

That's why Brian sent the Keys off with Hyacinth, to prevent the Guardians from surrendering them. "What did Matty do?"

"Matt had one advantage: he's from here, they aren't. They don't know this town the way we do. You know the hilltop house? That was our monthly meeting spot."

Everyone knows the old, vacant mansion on Highland Point. People used to throw parties there until someone fell through some rotten floorboards.

"The house is down the street from Highland Point Adventure Park," she says.

Matty worked the zip line there one summer.

"There's a ropes course in the surrounding woods. He was in the trees. They didn't know he was up there. Everyone thinks about the magic, but no one thinks about what else is down there. Matt knew what would happen if the fault line opened; he knew about the shells. They didn't."

A house flashes before my eyes—a crumbling Victorian that used to be white but is now yellowed, like the pages of an old book. I imagine Ford bringing his men into the woods, where the fault line begins. Josh driving that Key into ground that nothing else could penetrate. And the magic answering, drawing a thin jagged line of gold headed away from him, down the mountain.

I felt it when the earth cleaved open, like stitches ripping, saw that bright golden light, like panels of sunlight streaming from below and illuminating the sky.

Ford and his men weren't prepared for the spindly fingers clawing at the hard rock edge of the abyss.

"When it happened, Ford abandoned the plan, took Josh's Key," Parker says, voice quivering. "Shot him in the chest. But Matt jumped down from the trees, touched Josh before Ford could, so Josh's magic would transfer to him instead. Matt's the Guardian of two segments now."

*But Ford has the Key to Josh's.*

"Ford got magic from the fault line anyway," she continues. "Like you all probably did. I saw Matt shoot a crossbow straight at Ford's chest and the arrow ricocheted off like he was made of rubber."

I imagine my brother standing there, buffeted by wind and rain, shock fusing his feet to the ground. And this blond man all in gray smooths a hand over the hole in his coat, a hole where no blood blooms . . . and he smiles.

She doesn't have to tell me what happened next. Matty made the choice to run, to protect Wellsie, even if it meant leaving Parker behind. Because he knew what would happen if Ford killed him and took the power to use that Key.

Over Parker's shoulder, the dim hint of an impending sunrise peeks through the lattice.

"I think he rode the zip line down the mountain," Parker says wearily. "But they'll be searching this town high and low for him."

*Matty's smart, though. He eluded them once, he can do it again. He's going to be okay.* I close my eyes and the tension in my neck, my fear that he died days ago, releases.

"*Psst,*" Parker whispers, beckoning to someone as she peers out from beneath the porch, sweeping aside the branches for Shandy to crawl through and squat beside the hole in the lattice. He breathes harshly, forehead dripping with sweat.

"There you are, thank God. Ford's men are going house to house," he says wearily. "The shells are fairly spread out in this direction. Did you get bit?"

"I'm fine," she says, though she clutches her arm to her chest and a dark splotch bleeds through the fabric. "Brian wants to get Josh's Key back from Ford, but let's be real, I breathe underwater and you can only protect yourself. We have to cut and run. Leave the Key. Get him out."

"I have an idea," Shandy says, and both of us stare at him. His mouth goes slack and he swipes the hair out of his eyes. "You know, people look at *all this* and assume I have no useful skills, but I went through a dark period once where I learned how to hotwire cars." Before we can ask if he stole cars regularly, he says, "The point is, the road west is relatively unbroken. Go get Brian while I find a ticket out of here. It's the long route, but we have no choice."

"And how do we stop Ford from killing Brian in the meantime?" Parker says, spreading her hands wide.

"Create a diversion." Shandy maneuvers his pack off his back and unzips it. Inside, there are a dozen bottles, all filled with liquid, rags hanging from the tops. My bag is full of pillow and handwritten notes from my ex–best friend, so I didn't get the memo. Shandy digs out a couple lighters and we both take one.

Shandy looks at her for a long moment. "I'm sorry about Josh."

She draws in an unsteady breath, but says nothing.

Shandy bows his head. "Stay alive until I get here. Be ready. Look to the west."

He leaves us, holed up under a porch with bottle bombs. He can't possibly believe we have any control over who lives or dies anymore.

"We can't be seen," Parker says. "Wait for my signal before you throw any bottles. Stay on the lookout for shells, too. Are you ready?"

"No."

"Me neither." She launches herself out from under the porch and through the bushes. I allow myself three seconds to breathe alone in the shadows. And I follow her.

# CHAPTER 7

*B*rian kneels in the swampy clearing in front of my house. A pale fog rises from the ground. He faces the forest and a line of five men standing at the tree line. The rest of the second wave searches for Shandy, for Parker. For me.

But Brian isn't looking at them, tilting his face toward the sprinkle of rain instead.

This is the first time I've seen a sunrise—a dark blue dome with fire at the edge.

Four of Ford's soldiers wear riot gear, but they don't have visors. They have faces. They wear the same expression he does. Mild. Calm. They look like people I'd see on the street, in the grocery store, at the diner. One of them has a weak chin. Murderers probably only look like murderers once you know they are.

Ford stands in the center, hands in his pockets. If not for the mud and bits of brush, you'd never know he was thrown through a forest. There's not a single drop of blood marring his clothes, no bruising, no limbs hanging at wrong angles.

*Matty's arrow bounced off him.*

No one moves—Brian isn't letting them, even as he shakes with effort. He went into this without a plan. He must've known this would happen. So why did he stay?

*To hold them off. So we could get away.*

Well, that didn't happen. Huddled as small as possible, I conceal myself in the shadow of the house. I hug three bottles to my chest, two in each raincoat pocket. In my aching fist, I hold the lighter too tightly.

Parker is somewhere on the other side and I have no idea what we're supposed to do.

But watching Brian wobble on his knees as the men test his strength every couple of seconds, pushing against his power, my heart rises in my throat.

*He can't hold them forever. I need to aim for them. Can I set people on fire?*

I look at the bottle. There's no way I'm going to hit anything, anyway.

"Hitting a series of trees at significant velocity is as excruciating as you might imagine," Ford says casually, like they're friends, rubbing one hand along the back of his unbroken neck, rotating his shoulders. It's not a good sign he can move at all when Brian is trying to hold them in place. "No hard feelings, though."

Ford waits for Brian to react but receives stony silence in return.

"You're very impressive," he says softly. "Extraordinary. Your parents never got to see your power. They transferred to you the night before they died, right? They would have been proud."

Brian flinches. I see it. Ford sees it.

"I'd like you to speak freely, Brian. This conversation feels very one-sided. And as I was saying before you tried to inflict serious bodily harm, I was hoping we could strike a deal. All you and the other Guardians need to do is transfer your Keys to me and you can walk away from this."

"You'll have to kill me first," Brian says through gritted teeth.

Ford's eyes harden to steel. "I will if you want to make this difficult."

Tension falls thick over the clearing.

There's something wedged between my shoulder blades, an invisible knife I can't reach. And my muscles contract around it. I concentrate on the spongy texture of the wet ground beneath my knees, the water bleeding into the fabric. I stare at the texture of rain hitting a puddle. *Listen. Breathe. Wait for your moment.*

"Do you think *this* is the hardest thing I've ever done?" Brian says suddenly, every word a burst of effort, as he raises his chin to look directly at him. "The hardest thing I've ever done is tell my sisters our parents were dead. My stepmother had premonitions, but you know that, don't you? She and my father transferred their Keys the night before they died. The fire—it was you. You killed them."

An image bursts to life in my mind. Of Jack and Rose Aster. Burning. Screaming. Pounding on a closed window. Brian must imagine that all the time, in different scenarios. Maybe scenarios where he saves them, gets there just in time. It wasn't a gas leak. It wasn't an accident.

My fingers tighten around a bottle neck.

"They were dead before the fire," Ford says calmly. "I'm not without mercy."

At those words, Brian falters. It's only a moment—a shift of his weight, of his focus—and Ford takes one step forward.

Though Brian manages to hold him, he struggles more visibly this time, one hand braced in the mud to remain upright.

"Some part of me has been searching for Guardians my whole life," Ford says softly. "As a child, I collected newspaper clippings about fault-line towns. Later on, I researched people who seemed . . .

extraordinary. Do you know how easy the Wellsie Guardians made it? Did your father think enchanted baked goods would stay off the radar forever? He won awards. He was in magazines. What did one article say? 'Jack Aster's pastries are so good, he must use magic.'"

I squeeze my eyes closed, remembering the intense high of those buttery sticky buns that lasted for hours. It's so obvious, but I didn't know. Brian didn't know. We weren't looking. But someone reading every article between the lines did. We've always been one cookie away from danger. Maybe the miraculous thing about fault-line towns isn't the Guardians, it's the system lasting this long.

"Your father gave you up," Ford says. "We held a gun to your step-mother's head and that's all it took. He told us everything. Who you were. Where you met. What powers you had. He gave up everyone, including his own children."

"No." Brian shakes his head, keeps shaking it. "He wouldn't do that. He would never do that." The trees rustle, bending, moving with his pain. He's losing concentration.

"Are you sure?" Ford says. "He was only human. You are all only human. Eight humans, like everyone else." He pauses. "Sorry, you *were* eight. You're less now, aren't you?" As he speaks, his voice rises. "There's magic loose for the rest of us, but we're limited until we open all the segments. And if you think about it, really think about it, Brian, you'll realize how unfair that is."

Behind the cool gray of his eyes, the jealousy is there, barely suppressed.

It takes Brian two tries to get to his feet, but he straightens to his full height. "My sister will find you. She will hunt you down."

Though Ford's face remains tight, a muscle ticks in his cheek, and when he speaks again, his voice is lower, composed. "The little one?"

But then his brows rise—perfect, symmetrical, definitely plucked. "Ahh, you mean Daisy. There are zombies afoot—what makes you think she's not already dead?"

"She's not," Brian says, quiet but firm. "And she'll kill you."

A gentle laugh escapes him. "No, Brian, she won't. No one can."

Behind him, his four minions move, stiffly, against the fractures in Brian's hold.

*Shandy, where are you?*

"Are you tired, Brian?" Ford murmurs. "Because I feel right as rain."

With a grunt, Brian jerks his hands toward his body, wrenching the weapons from the four men who hold them, and sending them sailing onto the roof of the house. And then he breaks, falling to his hands and knees.

*It's time. We don't have a choice.*

Parker's first bottle explodes at Ford's feet.

Flames spread up Ford's trousers. Two of the men dive at him, slapping wildly, extinguishing flames with their bodies.

Parker dashes into the yard from the other side of the house, hurtling bottle after bottle at Ford and the two men who cover him protectively. Glass explodes in every direction.

Ford's muffled voice emerges from beneath them as he struggles to shove them off. "I am *fine. Get off me.* I can't be hurt. Get the woman. *Get her.*"

The two men who didn't dive on top of him swivel toward Parker. She's out of bottles. She whirls, sprinting back behind the house as the men give chase.

I light one bottle. As the flame bursts to life, the two men struggling to help Ford to his feet see me at the corner of the house. Praying, I throw.

The bottle hits the ground at their feet. They leap back. The ground is too wet; the misting rain keeps the fire from spreading.

Eyes stinging, heat burning along the crests of my cheeks, my legs propel me forward, and I throw another bottle. Tears run warm along the side of my face, off my jaw.

One of them turns to me, eyes meeting mine. A smile touches his lips.

And then he's jogging across the flooded yard, water splashing up off the ground.

I have five seconds. I clench a bottle neck, panic tensing every muscle.

Heart thundering, I bend at the last moment.

A cry escapes him as he trips over my balled-up form, but he's already rolling, struggling to rise. I shatter an unlit bottle bomb over his head. As he slumps to the ground, blood dripping down the side of his face, the other man charges toward me.

My next bottle misses. One left. He dodges. He's steps away, hands reaching out, face twisting with malice. I brace for impact.

Still on his hands and knees, Brian lets out a roar and sends him skidding back. The man catches himself on a tree branch at the edge of the yard, holding on for one second before sailing back with a scream that abruptly cuts off.

Brian lurches to his feet, collapses, and starts to crawl toward me.

I sprint toward him, falling to my knees beside him. "Brian, get up," I beg.

"Spencer," Brian says through labored breaths. His face is leached of color except for those faint purple-blue smudges beneath his eyes. "Do you think I killed them? Those men?"

His eyes are glassy as I cup his face, but horror lurks in their depths. "We won't hurt anyone unless they try to hurt us," I say.

He swallows. "You have to run."

I fling one of his arms over my shoulders, heaving him up with everything I have, silently willing him to walk. As his hand clamps down on my shoulder, some of the strain pinching his forehead dissolves. He takes a deep breath and rises fully, though we barely maintain our balance.

And we face him—Ford, walking toward us, unhurried. His scorched clothing hangs off him in places, but otherwise he's completely unharmed. Pausing, he bends down to pull a pistol from a holster at his ankle.

Brian lifts his head, veins popping out of his forehead, teeth clenched, attempting to stop him. He extends his arms, pushing me behind him, as though anyone can shield me from this.

We're at a standstill. For a moment, but no more than that. I feel the tremors running through Brian's body. He's got nothing left.

"It's over," Ford murmurs. "Give up."

I close my eyes. Exhaustion drags at my limbs, fighting against the adrenaline. Dried mud crusts my cheek, tightening the skin. Every ache and sting is magnified. And I want to. I want to give up.

An engine revs.

Tires squeal at the edge of the yard.

I open my eyes, blinking as my flooded yard, the trees, the rising sun appear through a lifting fog. Ford turns to face the jeep careening through the mud, sending sprays of water in its wake. He fires once, twice, into the windshield, before Shandy smashes into him.

I turn my face away but hear the crash of metal against flesh, the thud of a body hitting the ground close to the tree line.

Brian's weight grows heavy against my shoulder as he passes out completely, and I sag, struggling to hold him. Shandy leaps out of the car, sprinting over to us. We each support one of Brian's arms as we drag him through the mud. We reach the car, and Shandy takes most of Brian's weight as I fumble with the door of the back seat, tossing my bag in first.

I glance anxiously across the yard where Ford rolls onto his belly, pushing to his knees.

Rounding the house at a sprint, Parker, filthy and covered in leaves, dives on top of him. He rolls, easily tossing her off, but she tackles him again, clawing at his shirt collar as he grapples at her face, her hair, fingers twisting in her bun to wrench her off.

Yet as she pitches to the side, she tears something from his throat.

I don't understand. Not until he roars, an inhuman sound of rage, and she's on her feet, running. A long scratch curves down the side of her face. Water drips off her chin—sweat, or tears. Something's clenched tight in her fist, something slender and white attached to a broken chain. I've seen one before, three of them, when they were glowing. This one doesn't light up in her hand. It didn't light up around Ford's neck, lying against whatever heart he has. *Josh's Key. The one only Matty can use now.*

Behind her, a gray figure closes the distance.

Parker leaps over a root, her strides lengthening.

*She's not going to make it.*

I let go of Brian as Shandy shouts my name, still struggling to maneuver him into the car. No thought goes into this. I'm crossing the yard as she's reaching out to me—no, she's going to throw it—

I reach out my hands, pray I'll catch it.

One bang.

Parker sags to her knees.

My broken gasp cuts through the echo of that single shot.

She drops, facedown, a ragdoll in the grass.

Those blond strands, so much like Nell's, are saturated with blood. Littered with bits of bone.

Beyond my blurred vision, the man in the burned gray suit holds a smoking gun.

The whistling in my ears is breath, not the wind. But through it all, I hear the clomping of feet. His reinforcements are moving in.

But there, lying in the grass between us, a few inches from Parker's dead hand, lies the sliver of pale bone.

I'm closer than he is, a few steps.

"Don't even think about it," Ford says.

Slowly, I lift my gaze from the Key on the ground. I'm staring down the barrel of the pistol. Everything slows. My limbs go cold and numb, frozen. Behind me, the motor of the car hums and I know Shandy should probably go. If I run to the car, Ford will shoot me in the back. Like he did with her.

He walks toward me slowly, gun leveled at my chest. Fear crushes my heart in a fist. There's no rain or wind anymore. Just us.

His eyes are paler up close, watery, and red rimmed as though he hasn't slept in days. I'll remember those eyes in that unmemorable face. But no one will ask me to describe him later. I'll be dead.

Ford studies me a moment, too, confusion passing over his face as he tries to place me. "Who are you?" he asks.

Nothing comes out at first. And when a voice does emerge, it doesn't sound like mine. "I'm just . . . a random girl." I swallow, but my tongue is sandpaper. "Forget I was ever here."

Something flickers in his gaze. "It's interesting you would say that," he says softly. "You have a name. If you tell me, I'll remember it. I'll remember you."

Maybe he thinks his words are comforting, but honestly they're creepy AF.

It takes a second to identify that look in his eyes while the gun's still pointed at my heart. Recognition. Like he's seen me before. Like he knows me.

"You think you don't matter," he continues, taking another step closer to Parker's lifeless body. "That you're an anonymous face in the crowd. Because you know what it's like to be speaking to someone, to have their gaze shift past you, searching for someone better. You know what it's like when people don't see you."

His words seep past the wall I built, finding a sore spot. *Nell.* But her image fades, replaced with wide staring eyes and blond hair painted with blood. An older version of her, dead.

I edge back, but can't bring myself to spin around and run. Slowly I turn my head to see Shandy, frozen by the open car door, his eyes moving from the gun to me in silent dread. Brian lies across the back seat, unconscious.

"It's some magnified form of hand-eye coordination, right?" Ford says to Shandy as he squats, casually laying his gun on his knee to lift the spindly Key from the ground. He turns it over in his hands, admiring it from every angle. "You may be able to dodge a bullet, hit every target you aim for, but she can't." Ford languidly polishes the Key on his burned coat. "If you move, I will kill her and you know that."

*Will I die immediately? Will I feel it?*

"So much magic for so few people." Ford looks down at Parker, his eyes falling on her limp hand, resting in a puddle. "Have you ever wondered why some people are chosen to be extraordinary and others will never be? Or did you simply accept it could never be you?"

Bitter words echo in my mind. *I wanted to be chosen. Just once. But it'll always be you.* Words I said to Nell while tears spilled down her cheeks. "Am I . . . am I supposed to answer?" I say, struggling to extinguish the memory.

"I'm saying I know what it's like to feel lesser," Ford says in a gentle way, taking in my flinch. "To crave being seen. But what if you could *make* people notice you?"

*What if I could be extraordinary? What if a part of me hungers for it?* "You're k-killing people." It comes out a whisper.

His expression hardens. "Sometimes sacrifices need to be made. You have magic now. I gave you that." He gestures widely at my new yard—a swamp surrounded by jungle—and the dozen more men with guns who emerge from the trees.

It takes a second to pull a trigger, to pull a dozen triggers.

A flash of white moves in the corner of my eye. I go rigid, willing my face to stay composed, even as I blink rapidly, even as the matted animal, fur stained pink in several places, darts in front of me. A ridge of hair arches over her back as she hisses at him. She doesn't know what a gun is, or that he could shoot her.

Ford ignores her as she ventures closer to me, settling in a protective crouch for the first time in her life. "You could join me. Or you could die. Make your choice." Eyes locked with mine, burning silver with triumph, he takes hold of Parker's wrist.

I remember how the magic looked when it shot out of the ground. I remember it winding through the trees, stealing through the dark in bright gold wisps.

But as Parker's magic leaves her, it turns to ash, a blacker shade of black than the night sky, devouring any trace of light. The tendrils swirl around Ford's body like a tornado, wrapping close around his limbs, seeping into his skin and eyes and mouth. If he ever gets ahold of her Key, it'll recognize this magic in his blood, in his bone.

A laugh escapes him as he stretches his arms wide, the waves of magic nearly bowling him over. The gun slips from its perch on his knee, landing with a soft thud in the mud. In that moment, with the black magic sweeping around him, clouding his vision, his men along the border of the yard stare at him mesmerized, a wild yearning in their eyes.

They're not looking at us.

My hands find Chad, lifting her as I whip toward Shandy. The sound fades from the clearing, muted by a ringing in my ears. I hear nothing but that high-pitched tone—not my breath, not my feet moving faster than they've ever moved. Still, the yards stretch like miles between us.

But Shandy's already in the driver's seat, door closed. Through the window, he meets my gaze once, eyes wide and urgent, before flicking upward. He shouts something muffled by the glass—one word I can't make out. And he slams on the gas, tires spinning in the mud. Bullets shatter the windows, pepper the doors, but the car lurches forward into a sharp turn, peeling out of the yard.

My heart stops. I look over my shoulder, to the shadowy mass whirling around the form of a man, hugging close and sinking deep, until it lies somewhere beneath the surface of his skin. Our eyes lock, and that gaze is so calm, so secure in himself and in his goal.

No matter how long it takes, he'll never stop looking for them. Matty won't be safe anywhere.

I feel everything in those final seconds—the way Chad's claws puncture my skin, the weight of the humidity in the air, the thinness of the space between me and a bullet. Ford smiles right before my eyes squeeze shut, a joyous full-face smile that will be the last thing I ever see.

But it never comes, that tiny explosion of a bullet ripping through me. It's something else crashing into me, an impact to my whole left side. The breath is wrenched from my lungs as I'm swept off my feet. Clinging by nails alone, Chad cries in terror in my ear, a sound I've never heard her make. We never hit the ground. I sense bullets whizzing by, though the sounds grow fainter.

A thick band tightens around my waist. Arms in a relentless hug, keeping me from touching down. My nails rake at his arms, but he won't let me go. A scream tears from my throat, but we leave it behind.

*We.* I strain to open my eyes against the force of the wind. Chad's long fur is in my mouth and I clench my arms around her. There's nothing beneath me. Just air. And below the air, a world growing rapidly smaller. A neighborhood where forest and houses are one entity. It doesn't look real—it's a model of a town. But a flurry of distant gunshots ring out in the woods, sparks of light flickering among the trees. We're out of range. The men on the ground are specks, crawling ants. But one stands still, looking up at us.

*Up.* That's what Shandy said.

And there are no seat belts, no railings to grasp, nothing but human arms clasped painfully around my ribs. My stomach bottoms out and I hold on to Chad's trembling form for dear life.

"Please, for the love of Christ, stop screaming," Morrissey bellows into my ear.

# CHAPTER 8

*F*rozen, eyes squeezed shut, I think about how later, in my memoir, I'll describe the flight differently. The air up here will be crisp, not icy. I'll say flying is exhilarating, makes you feel truly alive for the first time.

I won't mention the turbulence as we fly against the air's current, or that I can't breathe. My cat has drawn blood down the side of my neck and the only thought I have in this moment is how fragile arms are when there is literally nothing else keeping you from plummeting to your death.

I won't mention shrieking, "How much do you bench?"

Or him gasping, "Do I look like someone who knows the answer to that question?"

I'm pretty sure it's stopped raining, which means he's sweating on my head.

Chad doesn't make a sound, her entire body tensed and shaking. This is a strike she'll hold against me. It's the second one. The leash was the first. If we die, it'll be the third and she'll hunt me through the afterlife.

"Brace yourself," he says, as he dips suddenly and my stomach suspends in air for a moment before slamming into my ribs. I make the mistake of opening my eyes just in time to see pavement rushing toward us. The scream building in my lungs is snatched away when we make impact.

His feet hit before mine do, but his legs buckle instantly, and we're tumbling forward in a mass of limbs. Chad yowls, leaping from my grasp, somehow landing lightly on her feet.

My hands meet hard road, the force of it shooting through my wrists. My body hits. And then my face.

The blow knocks everything out of me. My breath, my energy, my will to go on. Even the stillness hurts.

Something sharp digs into my cheek, a pebble, a fissure in the asphalt. The sound of the river, full to the brim after a rain, rushes in my ears.

Hands grip my shoulders, heaving me to my knees. If he's shouting something, I can't hear it. Slowly my gaze focuses on an object speeding toward me, eating the space between us.

Morrissey's probably yelling at me to get out of the road.

I stagger to my feet, staring blankly at the oncoming car, a car riddled with bullet holes. I notice for the first time it's a dark-green Jeep Cherokee. I remember that car because I was pissed its driver never once offered to take me to school. Dustin Miller was, after all, my neighbor. Is someone still your neighbor if they're dead?

Tires screech on the pavement and the car skids sidewise, coming to a shuddering halt two yards away.

The door swings open and Shandy leaps out, his mouth forming words. Blood streaks across one sculpted cheekbone. I turn slowly to face the fast-moving river, gray-blue ripples tinged with foam. We go tubing in the summertime. That won't be possible now, given the trees splitting through the water.

A giant fracture zigzags through the center of the bridge, but it still stands. On the other side lies thick forest again. We'll have to leave the car here.

"We drove straight through his perimeter," someone is shouting, but it's faint. Shandy. I hear him now. "They're following on foot. We've got to keep moving."

Numbly, I turn back around to see Shandy tossing my bag to the pavement. His and Brian's were lost back at . . . back at the crime scene. Shandy drags Brian to the edge of the seat by his leg. Brian stirs when he's yanked to a sitting position, but his eyes don't open. By the side of the road, Morrissey helps someone down from a tree. The delicate body drops the last few feet to the ground with a thud, already racing toward the car. A little girl.

"Brian!" Hyacinth's voice, thick with tears, finds me through the mind-numbing fog. "Brian get up! Please, please, get up!"

My cat mews by Brian's feet, winding around his ankles. Matty's cat. *Matty.*

And the world comes rushing back, a sledgehammer to the chest, everything painfully bright and loud. My pulse jump-starts. Pins and needles radiate up my arms and legs, reminding me I'm still alive, I'm here, and we have to go.

In seconds, I'm lifting my bag, hefting it onto my back.

Morrissey leans against the car, gingerly untying the saturated bandanna from his calf and rolling up his pants. There's a chunk of flesh missing, like someone took a bite out of him. The skin around it is red, swollen. A shadow falls over his face as his gaze shifts from his wound to the road, searching for pursuers. He turns to us, keeping all his weight on his uninjured leg.

"I can't fly with him; he's too heavy," he says, nodding at Brian.

"What the hell happened back there? You were taking so long, I decided to—" At Hyacinth's sharp glance, he hastily says, "Hyacinth decided I should go back."

"You didn't want to be stuck alone with a kid anyway," Hyacinth says, still clinging to Brian.

"Ford took Parker's magic," I say, unable to say she . . . what? Passed. She didn't pass. Died? She didn't simply stop breathing. If I close my eyes, the sound of a gunshot bursts through my mind. I see her drop. "He murdered her."

Morrissey isn't looking at me, but I see the way his throat contorts as he swallows. "He's going to murder us all," he says, almost inaudibly. "We're fish and Wellsie's the barrel." Finding my gaze on him, he rearranges his expression, but he can't clear that bleak terror from his eyes. "But she didn't have her Key on her. Ford only has Josh's."

"I tried to get it from him." Pressure builds behind my eyes, against a dam about to burst. "I tried."

"And nearly got yourself killed," Shandy says. "Priority one is staying alive."

As if that's so easy. I laugh, and everyone looks at me.

"Sorry, inappropriate reaction," I whisper.

"Ford probably has another power now that he has Parker's magic," Shandy says, raking his hair off his forehead. Blood sinks into the lines of exhaustion on his face.

It occurs to me that Matty does, too—his own, and one he got after Josh died. For him, that's a good thing. For us against Ford, it'll be a nightmare.

Morrissey still glances nervously between us and the road as Hyacinth struggles to wake her brother. She wipes at the mud on his cheek, smearing it further.

Shandy joins Morrissey's search of the road. "Once they get here, they'll see the forest. They'll know we're on foot. We don't have much of a head start. Campus is a half mile away."

Through a jungle.

"Morrissey, you can't walk," Shandy says, and they exchange a glance. "You need to go to Parker's grandmother's house and get her Key now that Ford has the ability to use it. Once you have it, you've got to get somewhere safe and stay there."

"You want me to go looking for Parker's Key alone? I've been shot." Morrissey digs his hands into his hair, the chestnut strands sweat soaked and limp.

Shandy's hands find his shoulders. "You can fly," he says gently, but firmly. "You can do this. We don't have a choice."

With a shaky nod, Morrissey says, "My family has an old hunting cabin on Blackbird Pond. It doesn't have an address. No one knows it exists."

"We'll meet you there once we've found the others," Shandy says. "Do we have the radios—" He stops short as he realizes everyone except for me abandoned their bags in the chaos. Only I have a radio, which does us no good. He closes his eyes briefly. "We'll find you. You can take Hya—"

"I will bite him if he tries," Hyacinth says. "I will kick him right in the bullet hole." Her gaze doesn't leave her brother's face, but the matter-of-fact way she informs them of this causes Morrissey to limp hastily away.

"Go," Shandy says. "We'll get him up. We'll be okay." But that perfect face, tight with worry, betrays the conviction in his voice.

Morrissey says nothing in farewell. *Be well. Stay safe. Take care.* He can't say that when two Guardians are already dead and any one of us could be next. We know without looking he's gone. Empty space can be felt.

The goal of all of this is to be together, stronger, but right now we aren't, and Ford knows it. He knows who isn't with us. He already has teams searching—they've been searching for days already. They could be on campus already, or at Matty's apartment, and we'll be walking into traps every place we go. But there's no other plan.

"Please get up. Please . . ." Hyacinth repeats over and over. She forced Morrissey to leave her and come back for us. She waited in a tree alone, with the possibility no one would return. Precocious, but only eleven.

Brian twitches as she pats his face, not gently. "The forest smells good," he mumbles. "Wet and green. Like moss. Like how gorgonzola tastes. Moldy, but you're kind of into it."

Hyacinth peers at me with a silent plea, lips trembling. She's been crying. I glimpse a reflection moving in the dark liquidy depths of her eyes, a person who looks like me, but isn't. I'm not the same anymore.

I bend down in front of Brian's slumped form. His jagged bangs are plastered to his forehead with sweat. When my hands touch his face, the skin is ice cold, clammy beneath my fingers. For a moment, I'm hit with a wave of dizziness. Darkness spots my vision. I swallow against the sudden nausea and focus on his face.

Even passed out, a deep fissure creases the space between his brows. His eyelashes are so long. My thumb brushes the curling ends. The queasy rolling in my belly passes as quickly as it comes.

"Brian." My voice comes out oddly steady. "Wake up."

Those eyelashes flutter, and I'm peering into bleary, bloodshot eyes—unfocused, but open. I breathe with him a moment, until his eyes zero in on my face and he inhales. Suddenly he's alert, glancing around wildly, pressing a hand to his chest. "Where are we? What's happening?"

"We have to go," I say in that same slow voice, practicing my yoga breath until my own heart no longer slams against my breastbone. "Hold my hand."

When his hand grips mine, it tightens in degrees until it's firm but not painful, damp, like his cheek, but warmer. As his breathing evens out, the strain on his face eases. A few spots of color emerge on his cheekbones. At my light tug, he stands, still weak but better, and he doesn't let go.

Four of us plus one cat cross the bridge, tiptoeing cautiously over the cracked middle that's losing bits and pieces of concrete to the water below. One of us travels alone. The other three could be anywhere in a town that has never felt so big before.

Somewhere behind us, our pursuers are closing the distance every second.

We enter the forest.


Traveling can no longer be defined as the process of moving from point A to point B. Instead, we clamber over intricate root systems and through bushes hiding sidewalk curbs and fire hydrants. I can't be sure if the ground beneath us is made of dirt or pavement anymore, whether it's stable or will collapse into a giant sinkhole. Better not to think about it.

I've unsheathed my machete, holding it out in front of me. While it's not particularly heavy, my arm shakes. I have the time to look at it now, the blade about the length of my arm, slightly curved and rounded at the tip, and smeared with dried rust-colored blood.

If I get out of this, I promise to hike more. My backpack feels loaded with bricks. I'm not sure if I stand behind the pillow decision. Chad has settled herself on the top of my backpack, indifferent to my struggle.

A thorny branch whips across my cheek. I cut it away, but the sting remains.

My fingers skim something damp but velvety soft. The moss Brian could smell. I step between tree trunks covered in flaking white curls or rough red-brown bark. There are more shades of green than I've ever seen in one place, from almost yellow to almost blue. Under the canopy, thin rays of sunlight burst through the gaps here and there. I can't walk soundlessly in this forest. The ground is both crisp and slippery, a carpet of twigs and pine needles and maple leaves, still wet.

"Did the forest come from the fault line?" I ask Shandy.

"Maybe. But there was a delay. So maybe somebody made it."

With their magic. The thought of that kind of power fills me with fear now.

Brian leads the way, each step stronger as the fatigue fades. Hyacinth walks on Brian's other side, but she won't look at him. She hasn't looked at him once since we set off. Brian's initial attempts to ask her if she was all right were met with stony silence.

Shandy walks closely behind them, his trekking pole resting across his shoulders, his arms draped along its length, like a scarecrow. His gaze never leaves Brian's back, as though worried he could drop at any second.

None of the Guardians mentioned a power could drain someone to that extent. They didn't mention it because it's not normal. Morrissey was tired from carrying me, not from the flight itself. He leapt into the air like it was nothing.

It's not nothing for Brian.

Shandy catches me watching him, meeting my gaze steadily, and gives a slight shake of the head. Not the time to ask.

A street sign juts from the ground at an angle. Beech Street.

Paolo's Pizza is still there. It's . . . not the same.

Pale creatures, emaciated and filthy, prowl around outside the huge front window. They move in fits and starts, like the signals from their brains come in surges. A shell—Wilhelmina, I name her—stands on the corner, neck bent to ninety degrees. She doesn't notice this. She doesn't notice anything.

Still, we freeze.

After a moment, Brian whispers, "South."

How close do we have to be for shells to smell the souls on us? I don't want to find out.

We veer right, passing through a bowed wrought-iron gate. We're in the park. It doesn't look like the park.

Something creeps over my shoulder, twitching.

With a shriek I claw at it, grip it hard in my fist and—

Chad screeches in my ear, nails sinking into my hand.

I release her tail with fresh punctures dotting my skin, eyes burning with tears, breath fast and heavy. I forgot she was there. Shaking, I grip the machete with both hands, and the blade quivers with me. I didn't mean to shriek. It takes so much effort to be quiet.

Both Brian and Hyacinth have spun around, weapons raised. He tilts his chin, looking down at me. In the green forest light, his eyes are bluer, though still bloodshot. He looks better, but those dark circles remain.

"You seem tense, Spencer," he says softly.

I move past him and Hyacinth. *I'm scared, okay? It's too quiet. I'm traumatized.* Brian moves up beside me but doesn't pass. I rub at my chest, reminded of the time my father was driving us home from a trip late at night and he was afraid of falling asleep at the wheel. I'd forced myself to stay awake so I could keep him awake, both of us talking nonstop to avoid dying.

"Could you talk to me?" I say. "Quietly. Just for a little while."

"Okay," he says slowly.

But he doesn't. When I peek at him again, his brows have knitted together into one thick, dark slash. So I guess he's not going to start.

"What's your favorite food?" I ask him.

"Chocolate."

A one-word conversationalist is tricky. The thing about that endless car ride with my father is I had to think of topics to interest him. My father likes sports and cars.

"Music is cool," I say inanely.

He glances askance at me. "Yeah."

"What's something people don't know about you?" I try. He rubs the back of his neck, grimacing. Nell always hated broad questions, ones without definitive answers—*everything*, she would answer nervously. I think he's like her in that way.

Next to him, Hyacinth bends to pluck a caterpillar off a root. As she watches it inch along her palm, she speaks for the first time. "When Brian was little, he had a pet caterpillar. One day, on the playground, a group of boys scooped it out of his hand, put it down the back of his shirt, and smashed it. Then they said, 'Now we've killed your only friend.'"

My mouth gapes open. Hyacinth looks calmly back at me like there are worse stories in the world, BUT ARE THERE?

Brian halts in his steps, his frown deepening as he regards her. "I'm not sure that story needed to be told."

"They killed your only friend?" I whisper.

"Okay, it wasn't my only friend," he mutters. "I have friends."

I glance back at Shandy, who grimaces. *NOPE*, his expression indicates.

"Also, his teacher used to ask the class if anyone played with him at recess," Hyacinth informs us.

"Whatever, that happens to everyone," Brian says, scowling.

I peek at Shandy again, who quickly shakes his head. *Say nothing*, his eyes communicate.

"I hang out with my boyfriend, Stuart, at recess," Hyacinth says.

Brian blinks. "Wait, what? Who's Stuart?"

She blinks back. "He's in my grade at Mountain Ridge—he rides the shuttle in from Plainville. At lunch, we read our separate books and don't talk. He's perfect." But as she stares solemnly into the middle distance, perhaps wondering if she'll ever see him again, her anger crumbles. "You and Daisy are the only family I have left. At the house, you made me go without you." Each breath is shaky, as though she's holding back a sob. "Don't ever do that again, Brian. You can't die. You can't leave us alone."

Her words, unsteady but firm, mirror his, the ones he speaks in his sleep. She lowers her head, pressing his lips together, and transfers the caterpillar to him before marching forward through the trees.

The fuzzy green creature slinks toward the two black marks at the base of his wrist, the violin f-holes. It's weird to see this extremely tall person gently holding a caterpillar. I don't know what my face looks like, but pink tinges his cheekbones as he hastily deposits the caterpillar on a branch. "It wasn't my only friend," he says emphatically, then rushes to catch up to her.

When he takes her small hand, she stiffens but doesn't let go.

"I'm sorry," Brian says quietly. "I need to keep you safe."

"I need to protect you too," she says in a small voice. Finally, she lifts her head and she's so little next to him, so fragile. "Those people who come to the apartment to monitor us. The site visits." Brian's shoulders go rigid at her words. "CPS is going to take us away from you, aren't they?"

Brian hesitates. "I'm eighteen. If I can show I'm responsible, they might—"

"Not if you're not here," she says, barely audible now. "They'll take us. They'll split up Daisy and me. You can't ever die."

As he immediately hugs her, she shakes like a leaf, and for a moment I imagine a bubble enveloping them, translucent and shimmering in the light. A separate haven where nothing bad can ever touch them.

"Okay, we'll both do our best to protect each other," Brian says, his tender gaze settling on the top of her head. He pulls a leaf from her braids.

"I'll be part of your family too," I say quickly, when they've broken apart. "So will Shandy. Found family."

Though she doesn't respond, her shoulders relax a little.

"I used to play alone all the time," I assure Brian. "I'd pretend I was a chipmunk, burrowing around in leaves and making little nests."

"I can't even pretend to be surprised by that," Brian says.

"Didn't you ever pretend anything?"

Brian is quiet for a moment. "I pretended I was a symphony conductor and my stuffed animals and action figures were my orchestra," he finally says.

Well. That is so adorable, I can't stand it.

"I pretended I was an assassin and my stuffed animals and action figures were my marks," Hyacinth says.

"I played street hockey with the neighborhood kids like a social person," Shandy mutters from behind us.

We're getting close to campus. The buildings in this neighborhood, most of which are old three-story homes with porches on each floor, rent to a lot of college students. They all lean, about to fall asleep on the shoulder of the house next door. One gust of wind might take them all down. But so many windows are covered in plywood. That means there must be people inside. Hope flutters in my chest.

*Don't come out. Stay alive.*

"Didn't your ex live around here?" Shandy says in a loud whisper, gesturing with his trekking pole.

Brian looks away from him. "She's not my ex."

"What ex?" Hyacinth asks. "You had a girlfriend?"

"No," Brian says, and speeds up.

"Maybe he was secretly in love with someone and she lived here," I say, matching his pace, though something tightens in my chest, a bit too painfully. "Were you secretly in love with someone?"

"No."

"Oh." Under my breath, so Hyacinth can't hear, I ask, "Were you sex buddies?"

"No. I briefly hung out with someone last year when she visited Wellsie for the summer. Why are we talking about this?"

"I get it. You were sex buddies. Do you have a lot of sex buddies?"

"*No.*"

"There's nothing shameful about having a sex buddy, Brian."

"I'm not ashamed. Stop giving me that look."

"What look?"

"That look like you're being understanding but you privately think I'm going around spreading syphilis."

"It's just my *face*, Brian, I can't make it any different. I don't judge people for having sex buddies. I wrote a love letter. Who am I to tell people what to do with their lives?"

He stops in the middle of the street. "You wrote a love letter?"

I stop with him. "You have syphilis?"

He sighs.

"If you had to choose, would you rather have a purple cloud come out of you every time you passed gas OR have your eyebrows wander around your face from time to time?" I ask him.

"Aaaand I'm done talking," Brian says.

"Purple cloud," Shandy says, as he and Hyacinth hurry to catch up. He touches his eyebrows lovingly. "Anyone who chooses the eyebrows is a straight-up serial killer."

"Oh, thank God," Brian says. "Behind you, Spencer."

*Behind me.*

I whirl around.

A shell roams the broken street, one leg dragging. Behind her, there are a dozen more.

*Isidora*, I name her. It's the first name that comes to me. Because even though an eyeball hangs from a veiny thread, her dark hair falls in ringlets like mine.

"It's easier with this."

It takes a second for Shandy's words to reach me, to cut through the shock that always comes first. Shandy hands me his trekking pole. More bodies approach from behind him, in the other direction. They're following the street and we're in the middle of it. I never see Shandy pull the knife from his boot or turn and let it fly. Just a blur, and a shell falls, a blade lodged in its forehead. As Shandy slips an ax from his belt loop, swinging it, testing its weight,

I clumsily sheathe my machete to hold the pole with both hands.

Brian's attention isn't on the shells coming at us from both sides. It's on the ground, on what they're tripping over.

Bodies. Bodies lying facedown.

I've seen that before. I've seen the way the back of the skull looks when it's been shot.

I absorb the clothing—bright instead of faded, intact instead of battered by time. Their flesh isn't thin, isn't covered in bruises and sores with dirt ground into every crevice.

These people haven't died from shell attacks.

Their blood is bright red and wet. Fresh.

My gaze drifts up the street along the lopsided houses, all with open doors, but falters as it lands on the house we're standing in front of. Closed, closed like the ones after it. They're not done with this street. It means—

"They're still here," Brian says under his breath, gripping Hyacinth's hand, nodding at the blue house one stop away.

I spin left, breath coming fast—oncoming shells. Right—oncoming shells. Their hands clench and unclench, reaching . . . if we kill a noticeable amount, they'll know someone passed this way.

"Into the trees," Brian breathes. "Go now."

But the swarm tilts their heads as we back to the edge of the road, swivel toward us, sniffing the air.

"Save your strength until we need you," Shandy says to Brian. "Run."

Brian leaps into the ditch beside the street, dragging Hyacinth with him. Chad jumps from the top of my pack as soon as I start to follow, scampering ahead of me into the trees. I hear Shandy's footsteps crashing through the brush after me, and then I don't. I hear shots.

Behind us, on the street, glass breaks.

Men are whooping. Another *pop pop pop* splits the air.

I duck behind a tree, covering my mouth with one hand. With each sharp explosion of sound, my muscles jump. Chad darts, soundless, away from danger, and I can't follow her. If I move, they'll hear me.

Brian stands next to me, completely still, clasping Hyacinth tight to his side. She looks up at me, eyes huge in her tiny face.

On my other side, Shandy carefully tugs a leafy branch to the side for a better view of the road.

I edge my face out from behind the tree. Through the branches and vines, I glimpse feet, legs, hands. The thick black barrel of a gun.

I count four in total, trotting down the front steps of the blue house one by one, leaving the door wide open.

They shoot into the air. Shells totter in confusion at their approach, attention diverted from the woods. As they shuffle toward them, hands outstretched, mouths gaping, the men riddle them with bullets. The shells sag to the ground in a wave. I cower back behind the tree. I haven't seen the men's faces, but I can hear their glee. They have rifles, and other weapons strapped to their backs and legs. These people armed themselves for a war. And they are not afraid. Unlike us.

But they aren't leading any people out of that house. Either it was empty, or they killed everyone inside.

Nell and Matty could run from shells, but not bullets.

Several yards from my tree, two men stand together on the street, monitoring the situation. The first one, in his early twenties, has a pink face and a blond buzzcut. The second one is dressed in full-on camo like he's living for this.

Brian edges himself in front of Hyacinth. His knuckles whiten as he tightens his hold on the tree in front of him, bits of bark crumbling in his hands. Shandy takes my hand and I grip Hyacinth's, guiding her behind the wall we form with our bodies.

". . . how many houses left?" Buzzcut guy is saying.

"The whole street," says Camo Guy.

"Are you supposed to be killing them?" Buzzcut asks hesitantly. "I thought this was a capture mission."

"We've run out of men to escort them back to base," Camo says indifferently. "We'll hold anyone with a useful power. Everyone else is expendable."

Buzzcut stares at him in silence for a moment. "Well . . . ," he hedges, fidgeting. "I don't know about that. I'm not a killer. I wanted . . . Mr. Ford said he would release the magic. That's all I wanted."

But Camo shrugs. "And these people are obstacles to that. Someone has to win and someone has to lose. So let's focus on making sure we're the ones standing at the end."

Buzzcut still averts his gaze. As though his silence absolves him.

Shandy's hand tightens around mine for a moment before he lets go.

I look over my shoulder, down at Hyacinth's small form, huddled against Brian. She stares at the stun gun in her hand.

"What do we do when the zombies aren't the monsters?" she whispers to me.

"We run," I whisper back. The moment they can no longer hear us, we run.

A man wearing flannel and a backward baseball cap surveys the row of houses, not appearing to notice the mass of shells heading his way. Or not caring.

"Keep checking every building on this block, especially the ones with boarded windows," he orders them in a flat voice. "You have physical descriptions and a list of their powers. The boss wants them alive. Anyone who doesn't match the profile or doesn't have a useful power . . . shoot them."

*They're looking for Guardians.* The boss ordered it—Paul Ford, the man who led them here, knowing there are countless tourists every month and we wouldn't blink at an unfamiliar face.

The men salute and continue on to the next residence, kicking in the front door.

But the man in flannel remains where he is, letting the shells close in. At the last minute, he leaps forward, unsheathing a machete like mine, like Brian's. He takes a shell down, and another, and another, doesn't stop when they no longer move. He hacks at them over and over, the blade hitting flesh and bone with crunching sounds that churn my stomach. I don't want to look at the mess on the street, but I can't not look.

Heat flares when he lights one on fire, when he sends an inferno at the mass of shells he hasn't killed yet.

*His hands. His hands are made of flames.*

He blows on his fingertips lightly and burning tendrils surge higher, completely engulfing his arms.

They keep moving, the charred shells. Their scent fills my nostrils, inescapable.

Ford's eyes had been the same shade of gray as the billowing smoke. *I know what it's like to feel lesser.*

Is that what all his men have in common, why they're loyal to him? Why they have powers like this . . .

*The magic shows you who you are,* Matty's voice whispers to me again.

And yet, Nell's tearful voice surfaces in my mind, that buried moment when I yelled at her, the only time I ever have.

*I'm sick of being the best friend.*

*I don't understand,* she'd whispered. *We're both best friends.*

Of course she didn't understand. The main character never understands how "best friend" isn't just a relationship, but a category of person.

I force my gaze away, shoving my thoughts back behind the wall I made months ago. *I'm not like them.* But the words in my head sound like a plea. And when I blink, the world looks sharper, no softness around the edges anywhere.

Hyacinth hides her face in Brian's side, refusing to look, but Brian wears a frozen expression. Flames flicker in his unblinking stare. This is what he imagines all the time. Though it's his parents, not shells, lying in ashes.

But Flannel has left the street, following the men into the next house. I grab Brian's hand to snap him out of it. "We have to run," I say, lips barely moving.

He glances at me, and slowly, he comes back to life from stone.

"Let's move," Brian says, and launches into a jog, leading the way, deeper into a forest of moving shadows.

Brian cuts down a shell right in front of him. I leap over it, and when I hit the ground, my bag slams against my lower back. Lungs aching, I push forward. A white blur darts in by my feet—Chad—and I'd sob in relief if I could breathe. Beside me, Hyacinth trips, and I grab her hand, pulling her up, running, running straight into a grove of evergreens. And more shells.

Brian flings out his arms, and the shells fly apart.

In the distance, I glimpse a wall of gray stone, the wall bordering

Hampton's campus. But the closer we get, the more of them there are.

Spindly fingers tear at my bun, dragging me down. Struggling to get up under the weight of my bag, I aim the pole up, impaling him straight through the middle. And into a tree.

*Crap. Crap. Craaaaap.* Tugging at the pole, I lean my face as far away as possible as the pinned shell reaches for me, broken nails slashing the air by my cheek. *Crap.* Shandy races up and wrenches my pole out. I manage to spring back as the shell surges forward and Shandy takes three of them down with one savage swing of his ax.

We run again, barely staying upright, but shells sail out of our way. Brian is making a path for us.

When I reach him, heart close to exploding, his hands grip my upper arms. "Climb," he orders. A tree limb swoops low, almost to the ground. I crawl onto it, my legs weak and screaming, and edge on hands and knees toward the trunk where I can grip the next branch. The trekking pole keeps getting caught, and Shandy has to climb around me. Hyacinth moves steadily above us. I follow at a snail's pace. When I am at least one story off the ground, I stop, clinging to a branch with both arms, and wheezing.

I can't run like this forever. I can't run like this for more than five minutes.

But we've reached the edge of the forest. On the other side of the tree is College Avenue, a stretch of dive bars and convenience stores and diners and delis. The stone wall of Hampton College is completely intact. The forest ends at this road so perfectly, it looks manufactured. If we can get across the road to Hampton, we'll leave this jungle behind.

The problem is crossing the road that's swarming with shells.

Down at the base of the tree, they paw the air.

They aren't particularly loud, but the sheer amount of them creates a kind of white noise. Not groaning or snarling, just gurgling in the backs of their throats. Choking on nothing, on words they don't remember how to speak.

I lean back, clammy, still panting. Someone touches my elbow. Hyacinth stands on the next branch over, pointing down.

Only Hyacinth, Shandy, and I are in the tree.

Brian remains below, with Chad winding around his ankles, a circle of shells held at bay around them. He bends to scoop Chad up, putting her on his shoulder as he wades through the shells, all the way across the street.

He doesn't so much climb the wall as he floats up it, balancing at the top in a crouch, both hands anchoring him there.

"Showoff," I mutter.

"Right?" Shandy says.

Brian wipes an arm against his forehead, signs of fatigue already apparent on his face. He meets our eyes and raises one hand, fingers spread, calling out something we can't hear over the gurgling.

"What's he saying?" I murmur to Shandy. "To wait?"

Shandy squints at Brian. "Long-distance high five."

"Oh."

We grudgingly make a high-fiving motion at Brian.

Hyacinth stares at us.

Brian blinks once, heaving a sigh. He waggles his hand at us—five fingers, four fingers, three fingers . . .

"Ohhh," I say.

"I mean, I can't read people's minds," Shandy says irritably.

*Two . . . one . . .*

Brian's hand does a quick *come hither* gesture.

And I'm yanked from the branch I cling to, screaming.

He jerks us forward out of the tree, all three of us. In seconds, we've soared across the street, high above the mass of shells, to the wall on the other side.

Brian catches Hyacinth.

The edge of the wall hits me in the belly. Shandy goes right over it, tumbling to the manicured lawn below, nothing like the untamed nature we've just come through. And there are no shells here at the edge of campus.

*Thank God.*

Brian hands Hyacinth down to Shandy, then sits to help me heave my legs over the top and slide down the other side. He hops off like it's nothing, but lines of strain etch his forehead. His skin is tinged gray, slightly damp.

"Are you okay?" I ask him, tense.

He nods, but his lips press together. Then he sneezes.

Chad leaps off Brian's shoulder and scampers off without a care in the world, no doubt to frolic among her flesh-eating brethren. I remind myself she can climb trees and scale roofs if need be. At the end of everything, she'll survive. She has to.

Shandy eyes Brian closely. "We need to find someplace where you can rest."

Brian ignores him. He reaches for Hyacinth's hand, scanning the campus in front of us. In one direction, there's Hampton's library, surrounded by gray-stone academic buildings. In the other lies the quad and the brick student dormitories. "I was hoping the campus would have no shells, since it's enclosed," he says. "But I'm guessing the front gate is open. I don't know how we're supposed to find Eleni."

There are no shells out here by the wall, but in that ocean of grass ahead of us, dozens wander aimlessly. The quad is a death trap.

"If we can get through them to a dorm, maybe people are holed up inside," I suggest.

Shandy's shoulders sag, his exhale ragged. "Sid. There are bodies on the ground."

There are bodies on the ground.

Meaning some, or a lot, of students are dead. Scared students racing out into the night to find help. Students who met the same fate as Dustin Miller. And there's no time for that to sink in. We have to keep going.

Shandy lifts the ax higher in his hands. "The library closes at midnight. It would have been locked, so no shells could have gotten inside. We'll go there and devise a plan."

I take Hyacinth's hand, the trekking pole in my other.

"Let's go," Brian says.

# CHAPTER 9

In those minutes of crossing the campus, minutes of watching my entire life pass before my eyes, Hyacinth and I devise a system. Once a shell gets past Brian and Shandy, she takes out a leg with her hatchet, then I stab it in the eye the moment it goes down. We don't communicate about it. Maybe it's a telepathy born from our mutual powerlessness.

The stench of death is lodged in my sinuses and no amount of exhaling expels it.

My arms ache. Blisters form as the pole rubs against my palms. But my mind stills. It's oddly methodical. There's a deep focus—

Then two come at us at the same time.

Hyacinth swipes the leg of the shell nearest to her, but I stab the ground next to the shell nearest to me who is, of course, still standing.

*Crap.*

Hyacinth adapts, pouncing on her shell and whacking it in the face with her hatchet.

I am rescued by Shandy, but whatever.

Hyacinth keeps her eyes on her brother the whole time.

Brian sends waves of shells careening backward across the grass, a human hurricane . . .

A guy running on empty.

Shandy moves like he's on ice, almost too quick for me to see—lunging, spinning, and wielding his ax with a combination of force and ease, like he's been doing this his whole life. He falters only once, when he tries to stop midsprint by turning both feet abruptly to the side.

Three-quarters of the way to the library, Brian drops to his knees.

Hyacinth and I dash to catch up to him. I stumble, fall, and for a second I lie there, cheek in the grass, staring into the foggy blue-white eyes of a student who used to be alive, who died when he was only a little older than I am. He has no arms. If I inhale, I'll smell him.

Hyacinth's urgent touch on my shoulder spurs me to my knees, and I crawl the rest of the way.

Gasping, drenched in sweat, I try to budge Brian. His eyes are closed.

"Brian, get up!"

His lids flutter open, gaze bleary as he struggles to focus on my face.

He has one hand on my shoulder, clenching down with his fingers, and a sound of raw pain escapes from his chest. Startled, I glance over my shoulder to see he's flung a shell that was almost upon me.

I throw Brian's arm over my shoulders and we lurch to our feet. The great wooden doors loom ahead like a cathedral in the midst of hell. A swarm of shells mill in front of the stairs, blocking our path.

I wrap my arm around Brian's rib cage, my muscles screaming as I fight to keep him upright. My eyes flick to Hyacinth, clinging to Brian's hand, to the blurry mass beyond her and then to Shandy's sweat-soaked face as he cuts in front of us, attempting to clear a path.

Shandy plows straight forward into a mass with a crunching *thwack*, a blur of blade.

*We're not going to make it.*

But a flash of motion catches my eye—something is racing toward us from the left side of the library, through a stretch of lawn free of shells. My heart hammers harder. It's a boy, moving straight toward us.

"Hey!" he shouts, raising a hand, and something thin and sharp glints in the light.

He's a person, not a shell. But people can be monsters.

"Drop your weapon!" Brian cries hoarsely, his whole body tensing.

The boy does not drop the weapon, instead motioning to us urgently. "This way," he yells across the distance, and his pace does not slow.

"I said drop your weapon!" Brian swipes Hyacinth behind his back, panic lighting his eyes. "Don't come any closer!"

But Shandy has his hand on Brian's arm, stopping him from using his power, and squints as the running figure skids to a stop in the grass. For the first time, I focus on the boy, glimpsing light brown skin and black hair pulled into a bun on top of his head. *Matty.*

Except it isn't. My vision clears, though the sharp pain in my chest lingers. His hair is shaved in an undercut, long on top, and not multi-colored. He looks about Matty's age and wears all black—track pants and a hoodie. The thin instrument he holds isn't a weapon, but a long paintbrush.

"Do you want to live?" he calls out, calm somehow. "Then come with me." With that, he spins around and sprints back the way he came.

I've never been asked that question, never asked it of myself. *Do I want to breathe?* The answer isn't a word, but a visceral response, and one all four of us have. Shandy shoves between Brian and me, throwing Brian's arm over his shoulders to take his weight. "Go," he says.

And we run. Toward the boy's retreating form.

With a horde at our backs, we close the gap between us in a frantic dash. Though we don't know this stranger, we have no other choice. Hyacinth and I follow him, veering left, with Shandy and Brian stumbling behind us, straight into the thick row of bushes bordering the library.

I crouch, ducking beneath the tangle of thorned branches, barely squeezing my backpack through. And my hands flatten against cold, gray stone.

There's no way through that.

I press my cheek to the library wall.

A hand snakes toward me, grabbing my wrist and hauling me toward a doorway I didn't know was there. I pitch forward into darkness with a shriek. My legs buckle, knees hitting marble floor, and then I'm curling up on my side, desperate for breath. Next to me, Brian and Hyacinth sag to the ground in a heap. Our gasps fill the great cavernous space.

Brian's watery gaze finds my face. "You're okay?" he mumbles, before his lids flutter closed and he passes out flat on his belly.

I roll to my back, still wheezing. Light streams in through the stained-glass dome in the ceiling, projecting colorful geometric patterns on the floor around us. I've been here before. We're in the library lobby. But we were nowhere near it. By my calculations, we should be in the reference section.

Behind us, through the open doorway, arms strain through the bushes, branches cracking as shells surge forward, and I tense, fingers still clenched around my trekking pole.

A shadowy figure slams the door shut and steps back into a shard of light. The boy.

The door he brought us through is made of thin, splintery wood, too flimsy to keep out a horde. Yet he remains composed, bending to lift one of the paint cans lined against the wall. A splash of royal blue hits the door, then another, then another, streaming down in sheets as he empties the entire thing.

His eyes close for a second.

In the space of that blink, fabric peels away from the wall, folds of blue fleece sliding down to pool on the floor at his feet. The door has vanished, nothing but smooth stone where it once stood.

He lifts a corner of the blanket, large enough for a king-sized bed, and turns to survey the four of us lying exhausted on the lobby floor. His eyes are golden-brown—like whiskey—and kind, though they narrow on the ax beside Shandy.

Shandy rakes his damp bangs off his forehead, summoning a weary but brilliant grin. "Hi, I'm Shandy."

The boy tilts his head curiously at him. "Angel Reyes." He turns to the rest of us and says, "I accidentally made a tarantula that is loose somewhere in the building. Just FYI."

I've always fantasized about living in a library like this, all gothic and old. Three large archways open into separate wings, with rows of shelves and tables, all ending in a stained-glass window. The building is shaped like a cross.

Brian is out. No amount of nudging, patting, or yelling stirs him. He sleeps like a star, arms stretched, legs splayed. Hyacinth sits by his side. She hasn't spoken since we arrived.

I unpack my pillow and wedge it underneath his head.

The longer we linger, the greater the chances we'll be found. But if we go out there now, we'll die. I'm not sorry about resting here, to be honest. My body feels like it's been chewed up and spit out by a lion.

I venture farther into the lobby, stepping over brushes and tubes of paint spread across the floor. Beneath the stained-glass ceiling, surrounded by a rainbow of light, is something more beautiful.

Wellsie. A mural of it, anyway.

Angel has painted our town, his style not quite abstract and not quite representational, some mixture of fantasy and real, both familiar and foreign. I see the mountain, follow the path from my house to the library, through Town Center to East Wellsie, then over the bridge into South Wellsie, all the way to my sister's house.

And there, halfway between my house and my brother's apartment, sits Hampton with its stone wall. I mentally place an arrow sticker.

*You are here.*

Angel's vision of our town is how it used to be.

There's a fissure running through the center now, one I have yet to see, where soulless creatures are crawling out. There's a forest in the north. And among it, men with guns.

About six thousand people reside within Wellsie's borders, if you count Hampton with its two thousand students, but it doesn't account for the tourists. We have no idea how many are alive, how many are dead, and how many are captured. Or how many followers Ford brought in from the outside.

By the library doors, I pick up what looks like a fried egg that won't bend from a heap of things stacked against the wall. Angel squats a few yards away, washing brushes in a bucket, but pauses when he notices me pick up a leather-bound book. *The Count of Monte Cristo* is embossed in gold on the spine but contains one line: *A dude breaks out of prison, I guess.*

"Experiments," Angel says. He wears a ribbed tank splattered with pigment; another paintbrush pokes from his bun now. His arms are slim but sinewy, hinting at a subtle strength, though hand-to-hand combat probably hasn't been necessary with a power like his. "It took some time to get things right—I have to visualize something in great detail. And some things, I can't make, no matter how well I visualize them." I glance over my shoulder at a door behind the reception desk. Yellow caution tape marks an X across it. "Don't go through that," he warns. "I tried to make a portal back to Oakland, and what lies behind that door is definitely not it."

Shandy avoids my gaze, but we both know not even Angel's power can get us through the barrier around Wellsie. Shandy crouches in the middle of the mural, a town frozen in time. A far-off tenderness flits over his face as he brushes a patch of dried paint, then traces the route to the old skating pond.

"What do you think?" Angel murmurs.

Shandy swipes at his eyes. "It's beautiful," he says hoarsely.

My feet shuffle to a stop over South Wellsie, over the spot Matty's apartment should be. "What you paint, what you imagine . . . it becomes real?"

Angel rattles his brushes against the edge of the bucket, flicking excess water from the bristles. "Only if I will it." His head bows as he surveys his masterpiece, sadness tilting the corners of his mouth down, and he answers my question before I can ask. "But I can't make this real, because this isn't Wellsie anymore."

"It would be an alternate reality," I say numbly, and he nods.

Shandy clears his throat. "You know, I've modeled for artists before," he says, changing the subject to something less heavy. As Shandy tilts his head at him, Angel's eyebrows inch progressively higher, but his gaze lingers on Shandy's cheekbones, then his lips.

At the thought of a Shandy clone, I say an emphatic, "*No*."

Angel's lips twitch. "Yeah, I don't think the world needs two people who look like you," he says. "It goes against the laws of nature." He tugs the paintbrush from his hair as he walks away, though he glances over his shoulder once, still with that hint of a smile.

Shandy coughs. "Anyway," he starts, but doesn't actually continue.

On the other side of the lobby, Hyacinth still hovers over Brian like a mother bird. "Can I talk to you a second?" I don't wait for an answer before pulling Shandy into a secluded alcove. "It's not normal what happens to Brian," I say. A statement, not a question.

He rubs his eyes. "It's normal for *him*. It's been like this for as long as he's been a Guardian. At first, we were hoping it would stop, but it hasn't."

"Has anyone tried to help him?"

Shandy shoots me the closest thing to a glare he can likely produce. "Of course we have. He doesn't want to hone his power. He wants to forget it's there. Unfortunately, we need it, and this issue is not something I can fix for him."

"Sometimes powers are instant," I say, thinking of Ford, of the men on the road. "Was his?"

"Yes. Sometimes they're triggered by something and sometimes it takes time to know what you have."

"Brian's got triggered by something?"

Shandy looks away. "His parents died."

I think of Brian's face, white, strained, the way his power took everything out of him, and a lump forms in my throat.

Still not meeting my eyes, Shandy opens his mouth, hesitates, and then: "Grief is an acute injury that becomes chronic," he begins softly. "The pain never fully goes away. You figure out how to live with it.

Sometimes you seek treatment, learn how to manage the scar tissue, how to strengthen the surrounding structures to compensate for it. But in the beginning, when it's fresh, everything seems to exacerbate it. And when that happens, you relive a trauma that's still ongoing. He's doing everything possible to avoid that."

For the first time, I think about Shandy's Wellsie origin story, and that he didn't grow up here. He moved in with his grandmother a couple years ago, I think. And he's never mentioned his parents. Yet he talks about Brian's pain like he knows.

*He talks about Brian's pain like he knows because he does.*

Shandy doesn't confirm my suspicion, only says, "It'll get easier for him eventually." He attempts a smile, but it doesn't look like his. "Powers change when people change. For now, we'll need to minimize the use of it as much as we can. We cannot carry him if he faints out there."

The lump in my throat remains no matter how much I swallow. If Matty dies, nothing will heal me, not even time. If Nell dies, I'll know the last thing I said to her was, *I don't ever want to speak to you again.* It takes a moment for me to continue. "Are you going to tell Angel who you are?"

Shandy bites his lip, and I know he's thinking of the men on the road when he shakes his head. "It's not safe."

I'm not sure I agree, but I'm not a Guardian. It's not my secret.

Back in the sunlit lobby, Brian and Hyacinth are gone.

"They went to the bathrooms," Angel says as we approach, nodding toward a shadowed hallway. "He didn't look good. He's possibly vomiting."

Angel must've been alone here for days. "Why are you not in the dorms?" I ask him.

"I had to flee," Angel says. "On night one, when the earthquake woke me, I didn't get any emergency texts, so I thought it was just a particularly hard-core tremor. There was some commotion in the hall, but people still get *really* excited whenever the fault line rumbles happen, so I didn't think anything of it."

As evidenced by the tourists who flock to our town in droves, that tracks. But Angel just shrugs. "I'm over it, to be honest, so I put on my noise-canceling headphones and went back to sleep. When I woke up, everyone was gone. The RAs must've evacuated people, but somehow zombies had gotten inside the building, so I was trapped inside my room at first. It quickly became clear that magic had been released from the fault line when I accidentally made a unicorn."

I blink. It takes a second. "Wait, what? Where is it?"

"Oh, it's still in there, but it was vicious as fuck," Angel says, grimacing. "I didn't know where I'd be safe, so I made a door to the first place I could visualize clearly. You're the first people I've seen since then."

But sadness lingers on Angel's face, and I remember the students lying in the grass on the quad—he must've seen them; he might've *known* them. What Angel means is we're the first people he's seen *alive*.

"There might be others hiding on campus," Shandy says softly. "In fact, we're looking for our friend Eleni."

Angel takes an unsteady breath. "Phone service and internet have been down for days. I couldn't contact my family. I need to know they're okay."

Shandy hesitates, and I'm worried he won't tell Angel *anything* specific about what happened.

"Some of the magic has been released, but part of it formed a barrier around the whole town," I blurt out, not giving him a choice.

"Nobody can get in or out. Everyone outside of Wellsie is okay. Your family and friends are safe." He needs to know that, at least.

Relief washes over Angel's face, but it's brief. "The Guardians," he says flatly. "They did this?"

Shandy falters, managing only a shrug in reply. But as he turns away to hide his expression, I see the realization dawning over his features that everyone will blame the Guardians. Everyone will blame them.

It feels wrong not to tell Angel the whole truth. People are alone in this chaos when there are men out there shooting people. He's vulnerable just being around us. But if the Guardians trust the wrong stranger, if he tells someone who they are, the more dangerous it could be for all of us.

I glance off in the direction of the first-floor restrooms. "I'm going to see if Brian and Hyacinth are okay," I say, starting off through the arch.

I don't have to go far.

Though he doesn't call out to me, a giant Brian-shaped lump is hunkered down in an alcove with his back against a bookshelf, sitting in broody silence. Shandy's distant laugh echoes against the stone.

Brian blinks up at me when I stop. God, he looks terrible. Red-rimmed eyes in an ashen face.

"Waiting for Hyacinth to come out," he says, nodding at the narrow hallway nearby.

I sink down against the opposite bookshelf, facing him. "Are you okay?"

"I'll live." He hesitates for a moment, not meeting my gaze. "Hyacinth is upset about . . . about the men we saw. She's scared she won't get a power to protect me."

The men with the guns, at least one of whom takes "kill it with fire" literally.

He leans his head back wearily, worried about his sister, who is worried about him.

"That night, outside the café," I say, and clear my throat. "I'm sorry I implied you could be a rapist or a white supremacist." Suddenly it's imperative he know that I've seen monsters now and he's not one of them.

He shakes his head slightly. "I'm a dude and you were alone. Also, isn't Southington the KKK capital of the state? That's, like, two towns away." He doesn't look away from me, and for the first time, that sharp gaze doesn't make me feel exposed, just . . . seen.

Something unfurls in my chest. I crawl across the space and sit next to him against the shelf.

Brian's gaze travels over my face, lingering on my nose—small, wide, with barely a bridge—"cute as a button," my mother always says. I wonder what he thinks of it. Not that it matters. What matters is he's stopped sweating and the color has returned to his lips. But I can't help thinking his sharp nose is perfect for him—he's meant to be a dagger, not a spoon.

"Do people assume your family isn't together when you go places?" he says then. "That always happens to us when we go out to dinner, on vacation, anywhere."

This is the first time anyone outside my family has understood this. Nell never did, not really. "All the time. They think my parents and sister are together, and my brother and I are these randos standing near them. And when they find out we're family, they say, 'Oh, good for you!'"

He smiles a little. He only ever smiles a little, never a lot.

But it's enough. "Sometimes it's . . . it's hard to live here," I say hesitantly. "To grow up in a place where most people don't look like you. You're totally separate—the something in this picture that doesn't belong. But because you aren't like everyone else, people decide not to register you at all. They don't even see you."

I stop as a voice comes back to me, clear, as though Ford is standing right next to us.

*You know what it's like when people don't see you.*

His eyes had been emotionless, but his voice was so firm, so completely certain. He thinks I'm like him, that I get it. And maybe I do. I keep my head bowed, deciding not to tell Brian this.

Nell looked at us like we were the same. Like race and beauty didn't matter. Theoretically, as people, it didn't. But in reality, when the model of beauty is white, she was always going to be the main character. All I'd ever be was her invisible sidekick. I never asked if she saw how differently we were treated. Because if she didn't, I wouldn't have been able to love her the same way.

"Matty—" My voice cracks on his name. "Matty's the one I talked to about this stuff. About everything."

Brian's hand rests on the ground next to mine. I study it—long, narrow fingers, a little knobby, to be honest, with veins popping out above his knuckles. I move my hand closer.

He takes a deep breath. "Daisy will find him. They'll take care of each other until they can get back to us."

He's as terrified as I am, more so, because he might lose more than he already has. Everything, this time.

"I bet Hyacinth will have a power stronger than yours," I predict, and the way his smile gets a bit bigger sends a quiet thrill through my body.

"You're right," he murmurs. "I'm the average one in my family."

"Okay, I don't think you understand the definition of 'average.' I bet you were in Gifted and Talented, weren't you?"

He decides not to respond to that. Instead, he says softly, "You know, the Guardianship is meant to be passed around. It's why we can transfer at will and why we'll gradually forget being Guardians at all. It's why there are different Guardians on every fault line. So, in some small way, power shifts and remains distributed in the hands of ordinary people." His gaze sears into the top of my head. "Every person makes an impact in some way, average or not. We change one another."

I look up at him, not sure I believe that, watching as he lifts a small bag from the floor on his other side.

"I need you to do something for me, Spencer. I need you to do it *because* you're not a Guardian."

I don't understand until he holds it out to me, and something clacks inside. Bone against bone. Their Keys.

"These can't stay with us," he says. "We could be captured at any moment. You'll have to hide them, and not tell us where. Hyacinth can't—she's just a kid."

*And I'm not anymore.* He lets me absorb his request for a long moment, and then, in almost a whisper, "I will never tell anyone. I will never give you up. No matter what happens."

Fear bubbles in a slow rolling boil in my stomach. I remember something Parker said in the darkness beneath the porch. *No one knows who they are until the moment presents itself.* But as I study his face, I know beyond a shadow of a doubt he's not a person who says things he doesn't mean.

I glance down at his pinky again. "Okay."

"Thank you," he murmurs.

When I take the bag from him, feel the outlines of the Keys through the fabric, they seem so fragile, so breakable, these tiny things that could end the world. Their fate is in my hands. No pressure.

"Maybe I'll have an awesome power to bolster my credibility as Keeper of the Keys," I say, pretending that I'm not terrified of being a potential target. "But Ford would never be able to, like, rip out my soul, right?"

"Only a Key lets you control magic to that degree now," he says gently. "To do anything you want with it."

Which is what Ford wants. Still, I relax because he can't do any of that without Matty. "That's good. Because if I get something like fast hair management—like turning it from curly to straight, then back to curly, with the snap of my fingers—I wouldn't want to lose that."

A frown dimples his brow. "Why would you want to straighten your hair?"

A kaleidoscope of colors from the window hits his face, softening the hard edges, and in that moment it makes total sense to me why Matty sent him to meet me that night outside the coffee shop. Hyacinth had been right. Brian is a champion among men.

We sit there in the silence, pinkies almost touching. Almost.

I quickly stuff the bag under the hem of my hoodie when Hyacinth walks out of the darkened hallway housing the bathrooms.

"Brian?" She peers at us, pausing by the end of the shelf. Her voice sounds thick, like she's been crying.

"Hey," Brian says, his voice tender. "Come here."

She comes toward him, and he pulls her down for a hug. "We're gonna be okay," he murmurs. "And you're my favorite person with or without a power."

She clings to her brother for a moment, and I ignore the lancing pain in my chest that I can't hug mine. "Okay," she says seriously. "It's fine if I'm your favorite as long as you love me and Daisy equally." She tugs Brian to his feet, leaning back with all her weight.

A smile touches his lips. "Do I have to?" She swats his arm.

He looks a bit better, no shakes, less pale. When he reaches out a hand to me, it's steady.

I give him a resounding low-five, the smack echoing.

He sighs, looking at his open hand, then leans down to take hold of mine and pull me up.

"Oh," I say. "Right."

And then we're standing there, holding hands. His engulfs mine in a way that might feel overwhelming if it wasn't so gentle. I feel the calluses on his fingertips, like the last time I held his hand, in his sleep.

I hastily disengage when Shandy runs down the wing, sees us in the alcove, and halts.

"So, the bad news is the shells aren't dispersing," he says. "But the good news is we have a door to almost anywhere on campus."

Dishes upon dishes of food have been set along the reception desk.

Shandy eats a steaming bowl of red soup, chewing on something white with a honeycomb texture. "Tripe," he says to me, mouth full.

Brian and Hyacinth hang back while I inspect the options.

The food offerings are eclectic, to say the least. The normal side of the desk includes a plate of steamed tamales in corn husks, stacks of corn tortillas, grilled meat, several varieties of salsa, and a pot of the red tripe soup. The abnormal side contains a casserole of fish sticks and canned pineapple; a loaf of egg salad, chopped ham, and tuna covered in cream cheese; and a lime Jell-O salad with cheese cubes and olives.

"My grandmother found a box full of seventies casserole recipes in the back of a closet in our apartment," Angel says, when I jiggle the molded Jell-O salad. "We experimented with the recipes to figure out what white people ate."

This food reminds him of home, the way my mom's prize-winning lasagna as well as her terribly dry pot roast remind me of mine—I'd take sawdust meat right now just to have something of her with me. I'd take the two-hour drive to get Korean barbecue with Matty, where, for a short time, we wouldn't be the only Asians in a room.

"Menudo," Angel says to us, nodding at Shandy, who slurps the last dregs from his bowl.

Noticing Brian and Hyacinth aren't eating, Shandy says, "You both need to keep your strength up."

For me specifically, eating is not the correct course of action before we leap into undead territory. But Brian looks like he just rose from a weeklong coma, so I'll make him eat his weight in Jell-O salad if it comes to it.

Hyacinth's fingers trace the edge of a plate loaded with frosted Pop-Tarts.

Brian eyes Angel suspiciously. "You're not from Wellsie. How long have you been a student here?"

Shandy grimaces. "Sorry about him. There's a bunch of armed vigilantes gallivanting around town killing people, and we think they probably posed as tourists. But my sense is that's not really your thing."

It takes Angel a few moments to process this new information, fisting his hands to keep them from trembling, but when he answers Brian, his voice is even. "I've been in Wellsie almost a year. I was here the day the sheep escaped from Windswept Farm and jammed traffic for six hours. I may not be a local, but I care about this town, and I would never hurt anyone here." He pauses. "Except maybe my ex-boyfriend."

Shandy looks like he wants to expand on that topic, but decides against it, shooting Brian an *I told you so* glance instead.

The sheep disaster was last September, months and months before Ford would have arrived here. Angel couldn't possibly be one of them.

"Also, I saved your lives," Angel adds. "So there's that."

Frowning at Brian, I point out, "You're forgetting *we're* strangers. He has no reason to trust *us*. Maybe we should all go around and reveal something no one else knows, so our shared embarrassment will bond us for life."

"No," Brian says.

"Brian only recently gained friends so he doesn't know how this friendship thing works," I say to Angel, wondering if I should tell him the caterpillar story.

Angel rubs a fist over his bun, brows drawing inward. "Uh . . . sometimes I spray-paint dicks on cop cars."

"I would tell everyone that," Shandy says, a faint smile playing about his lips.

"Seriously," I say. "To be clear, it should be something humiliating." I turn to Brian. "Your turn."

Brian ignores me and crosses his arms. "Why did you help us?" he asks Angel instead.

Angel tilts his head at him as he considers the question, and then one shoulder lifts in a shrug. "Because I could."

It's such a simple thing to say. And yet, I've never heard it before.

Brian stands rigid for another moment before the sharp line of his shoulders releases. I'm not sure if it was this statement or the dick revelation, but he takes a Pop-Tart and starts eating it like he's never seen food before.

"How do your doors work?" Brian asks. A crumb wedges at the corner of his mouth. I do not tell him this.

"Since we want to go to a real place, I have to have been there before. Say we're trying to go to the Elm Restaurant. I've never gone there, so I'd be imagining what it looks like, and we'd end up in some alternate version of that restaurant. I haven't been inside every dorm, so that'll be an issue too."

Hyacinth glances up from her plate of hot-dog mac and cheese. "We need a central location. If you can get us close to the fountain in the center of the quad, Shandy could hang a message. That way, Eleni will see it from any building." When I turn to look at her, she shrugs, like this plan should have been obvious.

"Shells are concentrated near the main gate and the student residences," Brian says, rubbing his jaw. "They might sense us once we get close."

"Shandy's an athlete," Hyacinth says. "He can lead and climb the fountain. The rest of us will follow and fend off shells."

Shandy shakes his head adamantly. "Angel can make the door, but I should go alone."

Angel scowls at him. "Something you realize when you're alone in the dark is how much you need other people to survive. The only way through this is together."

I remember waking up alone in the dark, and the days that followed. Had I left my house alone as I'd planned, I would have died. "We'll all go," I say slowly. "Except for Brian. I think we all agree he should stay here."

Brian's eyes narrow on my finger pointing squarely at his chest. "Brian will not be doing that, thanks. Spencer and Hyacinth can stay here."

"Spencer will not be doing that, thanks," I say testily.

Hyacinth matches my tone. "Neither will Hyacinth." She meets his sharp stare with zero discomfort. "You are not at your best."

"She's right," Shandy says quickly. "And your logical mind knows that." Brian looks like he's raring up for an argument, but Shandy's expression is firm. "If you come with us and pass out, it's game over. It would jeopardize us all."

Frustration rolls off Brian in waves, but he can't deny the truth. In some ways, he's the strongest. In other ways, he's the weakest. But I'm not about to broach the subject of his power with him, not after what Shandy told me.

"It'll only be a minute," I say with a confidence I definitely don't feel.

Brian doesn't respond to that, just stalks off to stress-eat the rest of his Pop-Tart in a corner.

As Shandy jogs off with a paintbrush to yank down one of the maroon school banners hanging from a balcony, Hyacinth approaches Brian's broody corner, hand out, palm up.

"There have to be enough of us to circle the fountain," she says evenly.

Angel and I on opposite sides isn't going to cut it, and he knows that. She still has to wait several beats until he reluctantly hands her his machete.

"Stay as close to Spencer as you can, okay?" he says thickly.

Hyacinth nods in her solemn way. "I will protect her."

A faint smile touches his lips.

When Shandy returns with a newly painted banner wound around his neck like a massive scarf, he pins Brian with a serious gaze. "Stay ready, but only use your power if we are all about to die."

I rest a hand on the hilt of my machete.

Angel is already standing at a blank patch of wall where he dips a brush into an open paint can and draws a thick black outline that drips a little.

It's just a rectangle.

Then it's a door.

We step out from a large oak tree, maybe fifty yards away from the fountain, far enough away that we wouldn't be walking straight into a pack of shells.

It only takes the one step for terror to seize my entire body, familiar in the way that it's all-consuming every time, but different because I'm not who I was an hour ago, or five seconds ago. I unsheath my machete, holding it firmly but keeping my limbs relaxed. I know that now, not to be too tense.

I look back at Brian once—he's watching us through the doorway—and it helps.

We start to run.

Shandy is our only athlete and it shows.

We sprint behind him, but the distance grows, and *his* protection detail morphs into us just protecting ourselves.

We underestimated how many shells were out here, for one thing.

*Oh God*—swing. *Oh God*—swing.

My machete slices across a shell's chest. Blood splatters across my face. *Keep your mouth closed.* It's almost not real, almost not me. I know what I'm doing—sticking a blade into a human head, a face, a throat—but it doesn't feel the same as before. They are wax figures come to life. They are shells.

Yet each of my breaths sounds like a sob.

Angel has the trekking pole. He hesitates with the first few, the way I once did.

Hyacinth doesn't hold back. She cuts their lower limbs, and Angel catches on to the system, spearing them when they go down.

Digging a blade into bone means jerking it out again. Slash and jerk . . . Slower and more difficult each time.

My blade slices a throat open. The head drops back, hanging there. The image will be with me forever.

I go for the rotten ones. The ones who have been living with growing infections for years and years.

*Smush.* Easier.

Four close in, all around me—bodies, hands, faces contorted with silent screams. I breathe, and the sour scents of sweat and rotten meat fill my lungs. I can taste them.

When we were young, Matty and I got lost in a crowd at Disney World, caged in by bodies. *But we got out.* Through the panic, I remember that. I remember: we were small.

Tucking my limbs in, becoming compact, a boulder, I crouch below their outstretched arms, as small as I can, and dart between them.

It's at least five seconds before they realize I'm through.

Shandy's stride barely breaks each time he swings his ax. He nears the fountain, hurtling over the short stone wall of the well and landing in a crouch in the knee-deep water.

He unravels the long swath of silk. It's the first time I've seen it fully. Once a school banner, it now displays a series of painted images running vertically down the fabric—a stick figure, followed by a hockey stick, followed by a book, all a bit smeared. It's not the most covert code to let Eleni know he's here, but it might have been sufficiently vague if not for the embroidered gold words at the bottom that we all stare at now.

HAMPTON COLLEGE LIBRARY

"Shit," Shandy says slowly. "I definitely did not notice that."

We're risking our lives to hang a banner that's broadcasting our location.

But Angel dashes around to our side of the fountain. "What's the holdup?" he says urgently. "Hang your sign."

We don't have a choice.

More of them have seen us. Or felt us. Around the quad, they stop, they turn. Whatever it is swirling around inside us, our souls, it calls to them. In pulses, they move toward us, quick and slow and quick again, as one writhing unit.

Shandy begins winding the fabric around the wide center column, which is no longer spouting water.

Angel, Hyacinth, and I edge backward, the backs of our legs against the edge of the fountain. I hold my machete up.

"Shandy," I say, looking left, right, and inching closer to Hyacinth.

Angel looks anxiously over his shoulder at Shandy as he climbs the column and struggles to tie the end of the banner to the golden ornament at the top.

I swing, hit a cheek, cleaving it open. When the shell falls, I bring the machete down into its skull with all my weight.

Shandy leaps down onto the ledge of the fountain and launches three knives in a perfect W, landing dead center in three foreheads. But it's not enough.

Both Angel and Shandy lunge forward, hacking and stabbing, trying to make a path for us, but any gaps between bodies have disappeared.

I cut down two that reach for me, but not before one of them latches his teeth into my bun.

I hear the clunk when my temple crashes into the edge of the fountain, and the world disappears in a burst of pain.

Nails scrape at my neck. Through the haze, I realize I'm on the ground, and it's hard not to panic, to not curl into a protective ball. Hyacinth sinks to her knees next to me, clutching her head—*is she hurt?* I brush the side where she cups it, searching for an injury, but there's nothing. Slowly her eyes focus on my face and she stares at me in confusion.

A face materializes above us, mouth gaping.

I yank Hyacinth against me as they crowd in, but their reaching arms never find us. They've halted in a near perfect circle they don't breach, hands up as though they're pounding on windows. It doesn't matter why—I launch to my feet despite the dizziness, dragging Hyacinth fully into the fountain. The moment we move, the shells break from their holding pattern, lurching forward.

I trip in the stagnant water. Coins dig into my knees, each one a wish that probably never came true.

Hyacinth and I splash to the other side of the fountain, where Shandy and Angel face a line of the undead all bunched together, arms extended, mouths stretched open like masks cast in the throes of agony. Every route is blocked by a sea of bodies. Through the crowd, our door in the tree is wide open. Brian stands, one arm up and shaking with effort as he sweeps about twenty away from the fountain.

Brian goes down hard on one knee, and one large patch of the horde moves forward, freed from his hold.

I drag Shandy and Angel back into the fountain. More shells surround it, knocking their knees against the short stone ledge. They stare down at it, unsure. Shandy shoves a couple away from the edge, but they'll eventually make their way over it. Any moment.

Hyacinth grabs my hand, then, pointing. "Something's coming."

*Brian?*

No, not Brian. But *something. Someone.*

A girl. Running through the crowd from the direction of the chapel near the main gate. Hordes rush in from all sides to take her down in one ginormous football tackle.

Except that isn't what happens.

She barely slows as she physically tosses the shells aside. Flying bodies collide with others, bringing down large sections at once. Whoever she is, she barrels through the pack, punching, kicking, with enough force to send them fanning out.

"Oh, thank God!" Shandy breathes, his entire body slumping in relief.

Bursting through the mass surrounding the fountain, the girl leaps into the water.

"Seriously?" she says, standing from her crouch. The person glowering at us now is of average height with an athletic build, wearing baggy gray sweatpants and a black off-the-shoulder T-shirt—sleepwear—though her sneakers are bright red. "You thought it'd be a good idea to run into a sea of zombies?"

"Well, you spotted us, so it worked," Shandy retorts.

"I spotted a giant zombie exodus toward the fountain," she shoots back.

Heavily fringed green eyes turn to me, cold, hard—emeralds that don't sparkle. Her nail polish—red to match her sneakers—isn't chipped at all. "Don't just stand there," she snaps. "Get behind me.

The kid, too." She glances at Angel next. "This is the posse you chose, Shandy? How in God's name have you survived this long?"

Shandy gives her a long-suffering look. "Get us to the tree," he says, pointing.

She turns, stepping onto the fountain ledge to look out over the swarm of bodies. "Come at me, bitches."

They press in on her, clawing at her legs. One wide backhand, and four of them sail back. In a bound, she leaps into the throng. With each hand, she lifts a shell by the neck and tosses them backward.

They go down in a wave.

We follow this goddess of destruction, jumping over the trail of bodies she leaves behind. She has no weapons on her, but she doesn't need any. Though not as graceful as Shandy, she is undoubtedly stronger. No hard breathing. Not a drop of sweat.

Her hair streams in a silky dark curtain down her back. A spindly hand grabs it, and she plucks it off and flings the creature down, stomping one red shoe into its skull.

As we near the tree, a white blob leaps protectively in front of Brian, and the girl shrieks, drawing back one foot to kick it.

"No!" I cry, rushing forward to grab her arm. "Don't hurt her!"

Chad stands frozen, green eyes huge in a wad of dirty fur. She cowers there for a second, and I have never seen her cower.

The girl whirls on me, her arm slipping from my grasp so fast it's like I never held it. Her fingers clench the front of my shirt, jerking me forward. Her eyes flare with recognition, though we've definitely never met, before a shadow falls over her face. "Don't ever touch me again," she says, dead soft, and lets go.

Shaken, I bend to scoop up Chad, who, for once, hangs there, docile as a lamb.

The girl doesn't break stride as she grabs Brian by the arm, hauling him to his feet and dragging him through the door.

As we all rush in behind her, Brian is already bending down for Hyacinth to dive into his arms. He hugs her tightly, his eyes moving to me, to Shandy, to Angel, scanning us all for injuries.

The girl, around Angel's age, maybe a little older, stares up at the stained-glass ceiling, absorbing the fact that we stepped into a tree and ended up in the library without any outward reaction, before finally dropping her gaze to Brian's.

"Eleni," he says.

"Brian," she says, with a twist of her lips that isn't a smile. "You're welcome for saving their asses."

# CHAPTER 10

Ten minutes ago, we were a team of five—four genuinely good people plus me—and now, the universe has decided we need more balance.

"These extra people will slow us down," Eleni says.

"They can help us," Shandy argues.

"With what, screaming and running away?"

Eleni doesn't think much of me and Angel, and she *really* doesn't care if I know it. Angel decided about eight minutes ago to search for the elusive tarantula so none of us would wake up to find it crawling on our faces, but I'm pretty sure he left to avoid asking loudly why we risked everything to find her.

She's removed her bloody shirt to reveal a black tank. Her skin is close to my color—a pale tan—but that's the only commonality we have. She sits on the library floor, feet bare, totally relaxed, hair all glossy and skin all glow-y. The rest of us slump on the floor in a sweaty, dirty, bruised, and exhausted heap.

When girls look good like right after gym class, I wonder if they've made some sacrifice to pagan gods. I know it shouldn't matter. I know I'm not supposed to hate them a little. I wonder if Nell knows I did.

Eleni's staring at me, fully aware it's making me uncomfortable.

I have never met her before—I would have remembered. But I can't shake the prickling at the back of my neck every time my eyes cross paths with hers. The sense that *she* knows *me*, the way predators know the weakest member of a group.

"That thing is disgusting," Eleni says. I can tell she's talking to me because her voice changes when she does—everything sounds like a taunt.

"That thing" is Chad, and none of her licking cleans the knotted fur. I might have to shave her. Still, I'm allowed to dislike my bitch cat, but no one else can. Those are the rules.

"So you're one of *those* people," Eleni says. "You cry when dogs die in movies, and, in the event of a zombie apocalypse, you're worried about your pet when you should be thinking about yourself. Do you think *he* can save you?" She doesn't specify who she means by "he."

"Well, no one can save anyone."

I glower at her over my cold tamale. "And you're one of those people who kicks animals. That's how serial killers start out."

Her eyes narrow. "Your point?"

They have similar eyes, she and Chad. The same green. Similar temperaments, too.

Brian takes that moment to step between us, staring down at her with arms crossed. "Did Matt or Daisy come here?" he asks curtly, moving straight to business.

Those narrowed eyes shift up, in no way intimidated. "No, but someone did. You must know that, because they came for you, too. I was in a dude's room during the quake. When I got back to mine, the door had been busted in and the whole place ransacked. By then, all chaos had broken out. I went to a place no one would think to look for me."

"How do you know someone came for us?"

"So many questions." Eleni leans back. "It's like you don't trust me, Brian."

"Why should I?" he says coldly. "I barely know you."

"I don't know this girl you've brought along with you, but apparently you've decided to trust her with my secret too." She raises one perfectly shaped brow. "Zombies were everywhere. Obviously, that meant Josh probably bit it. That surprised me, honestly, that they got Josh. I would have put money on Parker or Matt."

The cavalier way Eleni talks about Matty dying hurts, though it's not the first time I've considered it. I avoid making any expression with my face.

"You, Morrissey, Shandy, and I are the only ones who stand a fighting chance against attack," Eleni continues indifferently. "Daisy is smart, but she's physically weak."

Hyacinth stares at the floor, her eyes dimming. I give her hand a quick squeeze she doesn't return.

"Josh and Parker are dead," Shandy says, voice hollow. "Morrissey was alive as of this morning. We don't know about Daisy and Matt."

As Shandy relays everything that happened, I don't contribute. It's replaying a horror movie before it's ended. I see a blond man dressed all in gray, men in riot gear with guns, and Brian holding them off alone. Rain comes in sideways. Wind rushes through me, catching in my bones. A woman dies in front of me.

When he finishes, Eleni says, "Well, that explains everything." Matter-of-factly. Like she's not even sad.

"Given what's happened, I recommend giving your Key to me to hide," Brian says. "For your own protection. And ours."

I lower my eyes. He doesn't say to give the Key to *me*—she'll think he has them. They all will. *It's like you don't trust me, Brian.* And I can't blame him, to be honest.

"Are you recommending or telling?" Eleni shoves herself to her feet. "We're supposed to be equals. Or we were. If everyone has power, my Key is my last advantage. It's mine, after all."

"What do you mean by 'advantage,'" Brian says sharply. "The only advantage the Key has is to open your segment of the fault line."

She smiles sweetly. "I'm keeping it. Stay mad."

The tension in the lobby is palpable when Angel passes through, still searching for the tarantula he's apparently named Rodrigo.

"And who the fuck is *this* guy?" she says, pointing at him.

Angel just flashes her the finger, not even slowing down.

"That's Angel," Shandy says coldly. "And that's Sid, by the way."

"Why are they with us, again?"

"They're friends of ours, and there's safety in numbers," Brian says.

Eleni grinds her jaw. "He's got a power, but those two"—she gestures at me, then Hyacinth—"they don't know what they can do. We're carrying dead weight." She sweeps up her shoes. "Are we leaving?" She looks up at the stained-glass dome. "The sun will be down in a couple hours."

Brian shakes his head. "We're exhausted. We should rest and go early in the morning."

Eleni rolls her eyes. "Already slowing me down." She takes one of the flashlights we brought and pads off, her bare feet soundless on the marble floor.

"She'll stay," Shandy murmurs, as though I was worried. "She needs us. She can only use her power when she's protecting someone. It's how it works for her."

· · ·

The library darkens in degrees, feeling huger, emptier. We could each claim a wing and not see one another until morning.

I follow the traces of candlelight to one of the bathrooms, looking for the bubble bath Angel made for me. The door is open, and Shandy and Brian are bent over the double sinks. Shandy's hair is twisted into a sudsy pompadour and a toothbrush hangs out of his mouth, dripping foam down his chin. Brian's face is half-covered in shaving cream, and he holds a hunk of dark bangs between two scissor blades. He snips the wad without hesitation, leaving them at a severe diagonal. Chunks of hair already litter the sink and floor.

A of all, boys are gross.

B of all, neither one is wearing a shirt. Their shoulders and chests and forearms are all out and everything.

Shandy looks like one of those naked statues in a museum, while Brian looks lean and ropey, more like a picture in an anatomy textbook with each muscle labeled in Latin. How do their pants stay up? They hang on their hips like straight-up magic.

Brian jerks, his spine rippling, his shoulder blades pulling together, as though someone poured ice water down his back.

"What's with you?" Shandy says, giving him a strange look.

Brian rubs the back of his neck, his upper arms. "It's cold in here, I guess."

"You could try putting a shirt on," I say loudly, as gooseflesh travels up my arms.

As they turn to face me, I book it down the hall.

Even after I take a long soak in vanilla orchids and change my clothes, the smell of death still clings. The new bruise on my temple has swelled to an alarming degree, both red and purple. My headache concentrates in that area, pulsing with each heartbeat.

I pass the darkened wing Eleni claimed. Her still figure stands at the end, studying a stained-glass window—two women facing each other, one with a sword and the other with a harp.

I choose the wing as far away from hers as possible and sit at the end in front of my own stained-glass window—a million tiny pieces forming a flower. Maybe a person's soul looks like that. Different shapes, different colors fitting together to make one picture. The fading light shining through it projects a reflection. The way the magic does with us.

Hyacinth wanders in, sitting in a corner with a stack of books, one of which is just titled *Poison*. "Go for the knees," she mutters to herself, scribbling on a notepad. "Kidneys, jaw hinge, trachea, armpit, ankles, eyes." She glances up when Chad trots past, a fuzzy arachnid clamped in her jaws, then shrugs and dives into a book on witchcraft, protective spells, and wards. For someone so logical, this is an act of desperation. I remember her expression when she told Brian she had to protect him, too, large and anguished eyes in a small face. Terrified. Just a kid. If she gives Brian a little pouch filled with herbs, he better never take it off.

I turn on the two-way radio for the first time. "Matty," I whisper. "Matty are you there?"

Silence.

I imagine him lifting the radio from our kitchen counter, scrambling to answer me.

"Matty."

But he doesn't.

I place it on the ground next to me and continue to stare at the window as it dims.

Muddy shoes shuffle up next to me as I hug my pillow to my chest.

Brian watches me fluff my pillow on my lap, then dive into it face first, rubbing my ear against it. "Spencer, what are you doing?"

It's a thing I do when I'm anxious. "I'm making a comfortable hollow."

"Burrowing," he says. "As I suspected. Making yourself a tiny nest and storing nuts for winter."

I lift my head. "I don't want to be dead weight," I blurt out, thinking of Eleni's comments about carrying us. "Are you worried you'll have to save me all the time?"

He frowns. "Remember that time you tasered me? Because it was yesterday."

"Right." I dive back into my pillow.

"But if you were in trouble, Spencer . . . I would try to save you."

My words are muffled by the pillow. "I would try to save you, too."

"Thought you didn't like me," comes his soft reply.

I implied that, didn't I? After tasering him. I glower into my pillow. "Shut up."

When I lift my head from my lap, he hunkers down across from me, folding his legs in. In his hands, he holds a bottle of rubbing alcohol and some paper towels. Leaning in, he examines the fresh wound on the side of my head. I watch him slosh a bit of the alcohol onto the paper towels.

He touches the bruise. I wince, and so does he.

"Sorry," he murmurs. "This is gonna sting." He presses the paper towel to the cut on my head.

"Ow." I suck in air through my teeth. My eyes water. Profusely.

He blinks rapidly and looks away.

"What?" I ask him.

"Nothing. Allergies." He swipes at the corner of his eye. "Your cat is a menace."

When I look up at him, I can't help but notice how short his bangs are. Maybe I should rethink what I'm about to ask him. But he's here. "Do you think you could help me with something?"

His eyes move briefly to mine, all deep blue and direct. "What can I do for you, Spencer?"

"The shells grab my hair." I touch the mass of wet curls hanging down my back. "Can you help me cut it? The current circumstances require me to be a sensible person. Like Elinor Dashwood."

"I don't know who that is." Brian looks at the pair of scissors beside me, and again at the cut on my head. He touches the curl by my ear, rubbing it between his fingers. "If it makes it harder for shells to hurt you, I'll do anything you want."

He doesn't have any of his own wounds to tend to. I wonder that he would think of mine. One large hand cups my cheek. I steel myself for the next deep sting, trying not to stare into his eyes, but the thing is, his face is so close.

"So, who'd you write a love letter to?" he asks casually, concentrating on cleaning my cut with gentle dabs.

Unexpected. My face heats, but I can't move with him holding it. Did I tell him that? Yes. But why? "No one. A friend. It's just . . . it's just a ridiculous thing I did." I focus on his nose. "Those things don't matter anymore."

He frowns at the side of my head. "Of course they matter."

"Well, no one should ever write a love letter. Ever. But I'm shy."

He raises a brow, not looking away from my wound. "Um. Are you?"

I glower at him. "Why do you want to hear about this?"

"Maybe I need a distraction. Maybe you do too."

Maybe we need something other than fear and death. "Fair enough."

"So . . . I take it this letter didn't yield the results you'd hoped?"

"Sometimes you think someone's secretly in love with you, but it turns out they are secretly in love with your best friend, Nell."

"Nell," he says slowly. "She sings, right?"

Something in my stomach twists, but I nod. I haven't heard her sing in six months. "Yes. She's very good."

"I've seen her around." He shrugs out of his hoodie and tucks it around my neck and shoulders. It smells like a forest. Like him. He sets my pillow out of the way and lifts the scissors. "Are you ready for this?"

I toss the cloud of curls and frizz over my shoulders. I try not to look at the side of his head where I can see a hole in the hair.

He holds a lock between the blades and snips it. No hesitation, all confidence. Musicians have steady hands. A long coil drifts into my lap. I hold it in my hands, pulling it straight, then letting it spring back.

Curls float down around me, light as snow.

My eyes grow wet, but when he pauses, I motion for him to keep going.

Brian hesitates when he touches the little baby corkscrew by my ear again. "We'll leave that one," he mutters to himself. "So this guy liked Nell?"

"Everyone loves Nell." I try to say this matter-of-factly, like it's definitely not something I resented even if I loved her too. "It's always been that way. Also, she looks like a model." Another curl hits the floor. "And she's got straight hair."

"Hmm," is all he says, snipping another curl. My head already feels lighter. I find the sound of blades shearing through hair soothing. Or it's his hands, sinking in close to my scalp.

"I didn't think she was into him. They barely spoke. But then he played the guitar for her and it was all over."

He leans back and raises his brows. "Only tools play instruments to get girls, Spencer." He lifts a large hank of hair on the top of my head.

I'm pretty sure that applies to a whole lot of musicians. "He showed my letter to his friends on the basketball team. They called me creepy AF."

The cutting stills. He looks like he's going to say something, but he only releases a gust of air to ruffle his bangs. He tosses my hair— more pieces fall—and turns my chin one way, then the other way. When he shifts positions to sit behind me, he says, close to my ear, "What an asshole." And that's all.

It's enough.

One long leg extends on either side of me and I wonder for a moment what it would be like to be hugged by him. He probably engulfs you like a phagocyte. But there's a comfort in the silence, like I don't have to rush to fill it the way I normally do. I struggle to remember what Finn and I used to talk about. All I remember is writing my texts out first, making lists of things to say to keep the conversation going.

"Anyway, they're dating now," I say stiffly. "And we . . . we don't hang out anymore."

His voice lowers. "Because you liked him so much?"

*No. I didn't.*

The response is immediate, but it dies in my throat. I don't want to talk about this part. That a straw snapped inside me and I couldn't handle it one more time. That I broke up with both of them, but I didn't miss Finn the way I missed her.

If I don't answer, though, he'll think I did; he'll think I still do. And somehow that's worse.

The next part comes out a whisper. "I don't know. He would tell me I was sweet and funny and I . . . liked that."

*Liked being loved more than I wanted to love.*

He doesn't say anything, not even a "hmm."

I breathe in the soothing smell of evergreen as tears pool beneath my lids. "When Nell started dating him, it felt like she chose him. She chose him over a decade of friendship, like . . . like I was no one. Like I was right all along."

He pauses again, absorbing that. "Right about what?"

I shake my head, swiping my eyes quickly. "I . . . nothing. In conclusion, that's why no one should write a love letter. The end."

Brian's hand rests against my head. "You know," he muses. "Most people would not be able to do what you did."

"You mean humiliate themselves?"

"No, be brave like that."

"Pisces aren't brave," I mutter. "We're doughy blobs of feelings oozing around, crying, and eating everything in sight. It's limiting."

"I see. What about Scorpios?"

My head whips around so fast I almost pull a neck muscle. "You're a *Scorpio?*"

He jerks the scissors back, studying my expression. "I take it Pisces are cute and likable and Scorpios aren't?"

"That's not it," I hedge, eyeing him suspiciously. "I can't decide if everything about you makes perfect sense or if everything I know is a lie."

With a gentle nudge, he guides my head to face forward. "Maybe you can advise me. How would a Scorpio make himself more likable?"

In that moment, I wonder what his secret sex buddy tourist girlfriend was like. "Oh. I wouldn't know." I scowl. "People think I'm creepy."

"People like you, Spencer," he says. "You're focusing on the *one* person who didn't. I bet most people like you immediately, and I bet this has happened all your life. Teachers. People at the store. Random children on the street. I bet people talk to you in class. I bet you've always had friends."

Maybe. Maybe the majority of people find me easy to talk to. I've never counted a caterpillar as my best friend. I've never been alone at recess.

I don't tell him the worst person in the world looked at me like he knew me, and thought I was like him. That in the quiet moments, I've wondered if what made Ford isn't so different from what made me.

"What are you saying to yourself down there?" he murmurs.

"Nothing," I say. "Do old people ask you to teach them how to use the self-checkout register at the grocery store? Because that happens to me all the time."

I feel him shake his head. It's never occurred to me that those things don't happen to everyone, or that people might actually want them to. "You don't need to do anything to make yourself likable," I say softly. "You . . . you think people don't like you? That's not true. People think you're cool."

"Is being cool good or bad?"

Do cool people seriously not know? "It's good," I say.

He maneuvers himself so he's facing me again and takes hold of two tufts of hair, measuring their lengths by eye. I watch his eyes dart back and forth as he bites his lower lip.

"It doesn't matter if it's even," I say, sifting through the pile on the floor. I've never cut this much.

"Of course it matters," he says, tugging the hoodie away from my shoulders.

Despite that protection, I'm covered in hair, and when I shake my head, tiny bits fly everywhere. It's short and springy, longer over my ears, and curling at the back where cool air touches the base of my neck. "Do I look okay?"

He tucks a tuft gently behind one of my ears, taking his time as his gaze travels over my face, not my hair. Then he nods.

My cheeks warm. "I'm going to be itchy forever," I mumble.

"Lean forward."

I do, resting my forehead on my knees.

He blows on the back of my neck, a burst of warmth turning immediately cool. "Ack . . . ," he mutters.

I glance up and he's flexing his shoulder blades, shooting me a thoughtful look. "Are you cold, Spencer?" he says.

I smooth the bumps on my upper arms. "Maybe."

He blows on my neck again, and the ripple travels all the way down my spine.

He shivers, a quick jolt, and murmurs, "Hmm."

A tension settles in the space between us and I lunge to my feet. "Anyway, thanks," I say, too breathlessly. "Should I cash in my IOU coupon?"

He tilts his face up to look at me. "Save your coupon for something you really want."

After an awkward pause, I blurt out, "I like you fine." Because yesterday I told him maybe I didn't. And it wasn't true.

He smiles a little, but it's only ever a little. "Good."

"Did your head get caught in a lawn mower or something?"

These words greet me when I walk into the lobby in the morning to find everyone already eating. Brian's gaze is sheer ice as he looks at Eleni—he doesn't need to say a word.

"I cut it," I say. "I didn't want it to be easy to grab." From what I saw in the mirror with a flashlight, it doesn't look that bad. It's shaggy, to be sure, but my hair was non-uniform to begin with—part curl, part wave. It flips up in the back, and two longish tufts sit in front of my ears, framing my face. The rest has increased in volume without the weight to drag it down.

Eleni's brows arch upward. She leans forward to fork up a mouthful of huevos rancheros straight from the shared platter. The gold chain around her neck swings forward—a tiny gold heart and an arrow dangle from the end. "Changing yourself will make no difference if someone wants to hurt you," she says flatly.

I don't reply.

She's found the small bag of dry cat food I brought, which she pelts at Chad piece by piece while Chad sits there, *purring*.

Angel sits with Brian and Shandy, studying a map of Wellsie. "I don't know the south of town well at all, so I'll take you as close as I can," he says to Brian. He has decided to travel with us out of Hampton, with the vague notion we're headed south to find more friends. I don't feel great about letting him stay with us without all the facts, but we need him. Yesterday proved we're no match for a horde without Eleni and I'm not sure anyone trusts her.

After we eat, we sort through weapons, taking our usual. Except for Eleni, who goes without. She doesn't offer to carry my bag and I most definitely do not ask.

I take one last look around that beautiful library as we cross the lobby to a blank stone wall.

But my cat stops in the middle of the floor mural, ears twitching, hair rippling down her back.

I nudge her with a toe, but she doesn't move. "Chad, come on," I mutter.

Eleni glances back, jaw ticking in annoyance. "Do we have a problem?"

Arching her back, Chad hisses at the library doors once, then bolts, racing down one of the wings. A memory surfaces of Chad hissing at our front door. Of her bounding into the bushes before bullets started firing.

*Someone's here.*

Slowly, I turn toward Angel. "*Get us out now*," I whisper to him, as his eyes widen.

He doesn't have time to reach for his paintbrush.

The fireball bursts through the locked library doors, hurtling toward us.

Eleni dives out of the way. Angel and Shandy sprint left toward one of the wings, right before Brian barrels into me and Hyacinth, knocking us both down.

My shoulder and hip hit the floor, fast and hard with the added weight of my backpack. Marble has no cushion. Pain registers, but dully, the way it does when the body is half-frozen. I will feel this once I thaw.

The firebomb crashes into the stone wall, toppling Angel's buckets, spilling rivers of paint over the floor, over the mural of Wellsie.

We've seen him before, the man stepping past the library doors now hanging askew, singed and smoking. He still wears the flannel shirt and backward baseball cap. I didn't see his eyes the first time, though. Dark, and hard, and blank—I once described Brian's eyes as hard, but I didn't know the difference then. Brian's eyes have never looked like this.

The man's hands are ablaze as he tosses a burning length of fabric onto the lobby floor. Shandy's banner.

"Morning," the man says, and launches another ball of fire directly at us.

## CHAPTER 11

*T*he table in the wing behind us goes up in flames. A lamp explodes.

Shandy is shouting in my ear, hauling all three of us up. My body has the sense to follow him as he pushes us around the corner of the nearest stone archway and I see Eleni and Angel on the other side, pressed up against the wall.

Eleni's furious gaze settles on Shandy. "If we die, thanks for giving the murderer a literal map to us," she says under her breath.

"Okay, *my bad*," Shandy whispers back. "Does something about me scream strategic mastermind to you?"

"Listen," Brian cuts in, directing his words at Eleni. "They want us alive. We'll try talking first so these three çan escape."

He means me, and Hyacinth, and Angel. Not them.

Eleni rolls her eyes. "Yes, try diplomacy, Brian. See how it goes. I stand by the old adage: if someone tries to fucking kill you, fucking kill them right back."

"They have our descriptions, but they can't be totally sure it's us," Shandy mutters. "Once we use our powers, they'll know. We don't know what they can do, so proceed with caution."

"Wild guess: one of them makes *fire*," Eleni snaps.

In the old world, no one had any idea what another person was capable of doing. In this world, the possibilities include magic.

The stare Angel levels on Shandy is accusatory. "Who are these people?" Harsh breaths punctuate each word. "What do you mean they want you alive? How do they have your descriptions?"

Remorse deepens the lines puckering Shandy's forehead. "I'm so sorry we put you in this situation," he says. Angel's jaw tightens, but before he can demand answers, the flannel-clad man calls out, words echoing against stone.

"If you don't reveal yourselves, things will get messy."

I name him Fireball.

But Fireball is not alone.

Three more men enter the library behind him. One has a long, scraggly, black beard. The other two I recognize. Buzzcut and Camo both position themselves behind Fireball.

Hyacinth's hand tightens painfully around mine. I squeeze back, focusing on that contact. Brian is counting on me to keep her safe.

Eleni points at Brian. "Fire guy." She points at Shandy. "Buzzcut. We all split Beard. I'll take Camo Guy." She glances at me, Angel, and Hyacinth. "You three . . . try not to die. Go when you can."

Shandy looks once more at Angel, who stares instead at the advancing strangers cutting through the puddles of spilled paint that were to be our salvation.

Before the men can cross through the lobby, the Guardians move out from opposites sides of the arch, fanning out across it.

Angel, Hyacinth, and I remain hidden. Hyacinth peers over her shoulder. Flames glimmer in her dark eyes. An image of her face with trembling lips comes back to me, when she told Brian he couldn't leave them alone. Her and Daisy.

One of the nearby chairs is on fire. We don't have anything with which to extinguish it, and everything in here is flammable.

From across the archway, Angel's hard gaze comes to rest on me.

"They're the killers we saw," I whisper.

Angel's lips tighten as he's likely already surmised that these are the "vigilantes" Shandy mentioned, conveniently omitting that they were after us specifically. "I don't know who any of you are, not really," he says flatly, and the statement hurts. "But I do know who I am, and I don't leave people to die."

He jerks his chin in the direction of a single remaining paint can out in the lobby. Scanning the area, he lifts a hand with a quick shake of his head. *Wait until the right moment.*

As heat dampens my skin, I peek around the corner.

Fireball and the other three men stand in a line, blocking the door so we can't get out.

Fireball's calculating gaze scans each Guardian, sizing them up.

"What can we do for you today?" Brian asks, voice clear of fear, of warmth, of any emotion at all.

"We're looking for survivors," Fireball says, matching his tone.

"Do you throw fireballs at all the survivors you come across?" Shandy says.

"You could be dangerous," Fireball says. "We wanted to be clear right off the bat we'll have zero tolerance for violence. There are people out there who can do horrific things. Our orders are to collect everyone we find—for your own safety. If you cooperate, no one needs to get hurt." Both hands are glowing—a threat.

"We mean you no harm," Buzzcut says quickly.

"But if you attack," Fireball interrupts smoothly, "we can't be held responsible for self-defense. You understand." And he smiles in a way that confirms he is definitely a serial killer.

Eleni has her eyes on the three men behind him, all of them pointing guns. She glances over her shoulder, not at us, but at the fire eating the rug, well on its way to the next chair. "Well, thank God," she breathes, turning back to them. Her voice notches up in pitch. "We're all Hampton students, and frankly these guys don't know what they're doing." She throws Brian and Shandy an apologetic smile. "We need someone who can get us somewhere safe. You'll get no trouble from me." Eleni takes a small step forward, hands in the air.

The bearded man has a somewhat dazed expression as she approaches, pulling her long dark hair over one shoulder.

This can't possibly work.

"Where are we going?" she says brightly, smiling at Beard, and his ears redden.

Fireball watches her closely. "Cuff her," he barks.

Eleni offers no resistance as Beard proceeds to cuff her hands behind her back.

"Just a precaution," Camo says to her. "It's not personal."

"Oh, I don't mind handcuffs," Eleni says.

His cheeks flush and he averts his gaze.

Fireball's attention is fixed on Brian. "The library is surrounded. Every exit is covered. Make your choice."

Eleni stares hard at Brian. *Guns*, she mouths.

Brian makes a sharp jerking motion with his hand, ripping the guns forward out of their grasps. With a wild swing of his arm, the library door flies open.

In the next instant, Fireball is hurled backward through the doorway, but not before he sends another blazing mass hurtling in.

Ducking, I shield Hyacinth. "I hate fire," she whimpers from within my arms.

Camo is dashing forward, headed for Brian, when Eleni breaks the cuffs apart. Catching him by the neck, she spins him, smashing him headfirst into the wall. "Just a precaution," she says in that supersweet voice. "It's not personal." She whacks him again and his body goes slack. The third time is probably for fun.

Brian attempts to lock the doors, but they're loose on their hinges, unable to fit back into the frame. Something, a blur that used to be a person, tackles him to the ground.

I glance desperately to Shandy, occupied with Buzzcut—no, five Buzzcuts, all slowly circling him.

"Now," Angel says to us, tucking the trekking pole beneath his arm. Without hesitation, Hyacinth lifts her stun gun. I tighten both hands around the hilt of my machete.

As one, we race out into the lobby. Glass crunches beneath our feet. I slide, fall, and sharp diamonds dig into the palms of my hands, my knees.

Angel grabs the container of paint, dodges one of the Buzzcuts, and sprints toward the unstable doors. A shower of white hits the burned wood, streaming down its surface. By the time it reaches the floor, it's no longer liquid.

A wall of ice stands where the doors once were. Fireball can't get in, not without slowly, painstakingly melting it from the outside.

But the building is sealed now. With us inside.

The first window shatters, then another, and another—too high off the ground to climb through, low enough for Fireball to lob his flaming orbs.

Shards rain down as fireballs crash inside. Little fires rage everywhere, morphing together fast—too fast. All the shelves will go up. *All those beautiful books.* If we can't get out, we'll burn alive.

Eleni and Brian stand with debris glittering in their hair, facing off against . . .nothing. A blur. Their eyes dart around, heads swiveling left, right, left again. One second, Beard's by the wall, and the next second, he's charging Eleni, moving faster than they can see. Brian tries to sweep him away, but the man keeps changing direction. A stack of papers flies off the reception desk, a stapler, a lamp, even balls of flame, but Beard evades him.

"I don't want to have to hurt you," the Buzzcuts say to Shandy, looking remorseful. "I'm not like them."

Shandy's lips press together. "You don't get to divorce yourself from the people you've chosen to join. You can't say you're not like them when the damage is the same."

But Shandy's gotten too close to one of the Buzzcuts, who panics, letting a fist fly.

I don't see Shandy move, but the fist never connects. He spins, graceful as a dancer. All the Buzzcuts charge him.

"I'm going to shock them repeatedly," Hyacinth says, and takes off toward them.

I unsheath my machete, my focus shifting back to Brian and Eleni, who stand blinking, at a loss, as they search the empty space.

"Brian, behind you!" I scream, as the blur zooms up behind him and whacks him in the head with a paperweight. Brian pitches forward onto his knees and I lunge toward him.

Beard stops moving, materializing in front of Brian, his watery blue gaze settling on me.

*I should run.* I only have time to think it before he's there, fingers squeezing my throat, the other hand twisting my wrist until the machete drops.

"You think you can fight me, little girl?" he sneers into my face, breath stinking of tobacco and beer. His grip tightens.

I claw at his wrist in desperation, but his fingers are a vise, strangling me where I still have bruises from Thaddeus. Eleni will be here. Any second.

Except she doesn't come.

I cry, *Help,* but it's soundless.

Beard's jaw drops open, but no words pass through his lips.

He jerks back, tugging me forward, and gasps again. As he clenches harder, my vision fogs. It's just glimpses now, of his skin growing redder, his mouth working as he struggles to draw breath. One of my hands finds his face, pushing. *I need to breathe. I . . .* A lightness fills my brain, and I no longer feel my body.

Beard sags to his knees, bringing me with him. He chokes, his free hand clawing at his own neck, but there isn't anything there.

Suddenly his fingers release. I suck in a breath but gag on smoke. It's too hot, too thick.

For a second, Beard stares at me, touching his throat, attempting deep gulps of air, but retching instead. Eleni is on her hands and knees two yards away, trying to reach me. Grasping at her bare throat, she looks up, red-faced, gasping. "Stop," she croaks. To *me.*

Images flicker through my mind one by one: Hyacinth clutching her head by the fountain. Brian's eyes watering as he cleans my cut, shivering when he blows against my skin.

And the machete is back in my hands, and I'm bringing it down hard, straight through Beard's foot.

The force of his scream vibrates in my teeth, but in the corner of my eye, I see one of the Buzzcuts running toward us. A fist sweeps toward me.

Pain explodes across half my face, like someone ripped out my eye. Another jolt as the side of my head whacks the floor. For a second, the light blinks in and out. I clutch at my cheek, already bracing for another strike.

But something soft nuzzles my cheek, a tickle of whiskers. Through the stinging tears, I see Chad, anxiously padding back and forth by my head, terrified of the spreading fire. Buzzcut lies on his side next to me.

He cups his cheek.

I force myself to roll to my belly, my backpack a giant sandbag weighing me down, and brace my palms on the floor—the marble grows hotter. Shandy stands, his fists raised, glancing around. "What the hell happened?"

The Buzzcut copies are scattered around him, clutching their faces.

Eleni yanks Brian to his feet, pointing at us. "Get out of the circle!"

*Circle?*

I struggle to my knees, gaze on the floor. There's nothing but shattered glass, spilled paint, footprints—

*Lots of footprints. Angel.*

Angel edges along the wall, slowly so as not to draw attention, leaving wet paint tracks and scuffmarks behind. A border around the entire room.

I snatch Chad, clasping her hard to my chest, and she clings, nails digging into the fabric of my hoodie.

Shandy pulls Hyacinth onto his back and rushes toward me, hand out, and I seize it.

Angel reaches the edge of the lobby at the same moment we do, crouching to douse his hands in a pool of paint on the floor. Out of the corner of my eye, there's movement, the Buzzcuts huddling together in the middle of the circular path.

Angel closes his eyes. "Sinkhole," he murmurs.

The floor collapses.

We're already running as the library lobby implodes, marble breaking into great slabs beneath the Buzzcuts, a gaping mouth opening wider and wider, swallowing them whole.

Angel sprints out ahead with Shandy, who carries Hyacinth. We need to get out of the building, but everything is ablaze. Flames engulf furniture, entire rows of shelves. We can't make it through without Brian. Still, we keep running, doubling over, hacking against the smoke, and Brian and Eleni close the gap, coming up behind me.

Brian splits the fire ahead of us and it bends away as we run through the narrow path. The blistering heat singes Chad's fur, stray sparks scorching holes in my pants.

I glance back once and see an orange haze.

And a dark blur. The man, Beard, moving quicker than a floor can crumble.

"Hurry," I cry to Brian, a warning. But Beard is on our heels now, coming too fast even with a wounded foot, skirting through the parted flames, and jumping.

I don't see it happen, but I'm staring at Brian's face when it does. And for a split second, I feel a snap inside me. A pain part physical, part horror.

Brian lets out an agonized cry, and his leg gives way.

*No.*

I leap forward to catch him, but sag under his weight.

The blur darts past Eleni, who swings out a fist and misses.

Shandy stands at the end of the hall in front of Hyacinth, both of them somehow free of soot and singed clothes. Hyacinth struggles to look for Brian through the waves of smoke billowing between us. She doesn't know what happened. She's screaming his name.

But Shandy remains still as a statue, focused on the blur coming at him.

When he lets his ax fly, the butt slams into Beard's temple.

"Goal," Shandy murmurs to the blur who is a man again, sprawled unconscious on the ground.

We have no time left.

"My leg," Brian says, white-faced, breathing in light, quick gasps. "It's . . ."

*Broken.*

Eleni appears at my side and simply throws Brian over her shoulder like a sack of potatoes. She turns as the flames grow hotter, nearer. "Move!" she bellows.

Beyond Shandy and Hyacinth, Angel stands at a wall, smearing his paint-covered hands in an arch over its surface.

Then we're gone. The library full of books and colored glass burns behind us.


We're in an art store. Angel gathers more paint. We keep moving.

A burger joint. Sal's. Not the best burgers in town, but the cheapest.

In the convenience store down the road, the smell of rotting food in the no-longer-refrigerated section is so pungent that catching my breath is not a relief.

Each stop is only a few blocks away from the last, and Angel's rapidly running out of places he knows farther south.

We end in a playground.

Angel says he used to draw here on the weekends, giant chalk pieces the rain would eventually wash away. Now he stamps his feet over the surface of the door, covering it in smears of black paint. It becomes asphalt, a slightly darker shade, like a patched pothole.

I know this place, this blacktop surrounded by a chain-link fence with a brick building on the far side. I went to school here as a child, but Stony Peak Elementary looks different to me now—smaller, but also like I'd dreamed going here, like I'd dreamed my whole life. On a normal day, we might have heard voices, seen kids running around on the pavement. Today, nothing moves, not even the swings. Nothing can be as still as that empty playground. Nothing feels as horrible as the thought of those kids never coming back.

There's no forest out here, just normal stretches of road and sidewalk and parked cars. If silent streets can ever be normal. The stoplight at the corner swings listlessly from its cable, all dark. We're southwest of Hampton, farther from the fissure cutting through Town Center, and thus, farther from shells. Until they migrate.

I'm seconds from collapsing. My cheeks hurt—a raw soreness— from the heat. The stench of smoke and that rotten egg odor of burned hair permeates the air around us. I let my backpack fall with a thud.

I hear birds, but mostly the sound of my own gasps. Gently, I pry Chad's claws from my hoodie, letting her free, though she doesn't scamper away. Instead, she crouches at my feet, eyes alert, ears twitching.

Eleni deposits Brian onto the ground, carefully, though Brian still makes a sound, his face white with pain. "Don't come near me; I need my strength," she snaps at me, and paces off into the yard, rolling her shoulder and putting distance between us.

She means my power. She means she can't afford to start wheezing and probably crying and throwing up. I mean, I agree. *Way to make your power about your feelings, Sid Spencer. Way to get the one no one will respect.*

Hyacinth kneels beside her brother, silent tears streaming down her face, dripping off her jaw. She touches his arm. His lips are dry, cracked, but his head lolls to the side to look at her.

"I could really use some pie," he whispers. "Do you have any?"

She doesn't have any, and her face crumples.

I hover over his leg, not wanting to touch it. If Brian can't walk, we can't get south, for one thing. But that problem is secondary to another. If Brian's leg goes untreated, it's possible it won't heal right. He could be bleeding internally right now.

A hand wraps around mine, large and icy cold.

"It's okay, Spencer."

I make the mistake of looking at his pale face, though his eyes are as steady as they always are. A tear slips down my cheek. His lids drift closed.

Eleni stalks back, looking down at Brian, her hands on her hips. "We're not going to make it. Not for long."

A few yards away, Shandy and Angel are having an agitated conversation.

Shandy touches Angel's arm, but Angel shrugs it off. He turns to us, eyes darkening. "I've had several observations over the last day, things that were a little strange that I let go. One: No one seemed at all shocked that Eleni had super strength, almost as though you already knew she had that power. Two: You said you're friends, but she clearly hates you all."

Eleni can't argue that, and lifts her shoulders in a shrug.

Angel's face hardens to stone. "But I thought to myself, you know what, these four seem like good people; one of them is a kid, for God's sake . . . and why would they lie to someone who saved them?"

My eyes lower. He's saved us twice now, proving that we were right about him even if he was wrong about us.

"What are you not telling me?" Angel demands, voice rising in frustration.

When no one answers, Angel shakes his head and turns on his heel, taking a few angry steps away from us. Bending down, he scoops up a stone and lobs it at the fence.

Where it vanishes.

The air shimmers for several long moments before settling like a puddle.

Chad's tail goes taut. Immediately, I sling my backpack onto one shoulder. When I lift Chad, she allows it, mewing plaintively.

Slowly, Angel backs toward us as we instinctively bunch together.

"Get him up," Shandy says to Eleni, low, but she's already heaving Brian over her shoulder again. His hand falls limply away from Hyacinth's.

I stand in front of Hyacinth, clinging to my shaking cat, eyes darting around the playground. There's nothing but empty jungle gyms, a slide, a swing set . . . a swing set that doesn't move despite the breeze ruffling our hair.

Shandy and Eleni spin around at the sound of boots.

They materialize out of nowhere, stepping away from the fence through an invisible curtain. The two men wear all black, like Ford's posse at the house.

I turn to the school—we all do—desperate for a direction to run.

The air wavers in front of the staircase to the doors. Four more people step through, and as they do, I see past the barrier for a moment. A makeshift gate of corrugated metal stretches across the six entrances into the school. Yet the windows overhead are open. On the playground ahead of us, swinging, running around the pavement, and climbing to the top of the slide, there are about a dozen kids. Then the air hardens again, and they're gone, and the building and the swings are as silent as before.

The six men surrounding us all wear ski masks.

Eleni radiates aggression, one arm tightening over Brian's hanging legs, but the other remains free. She could take them in a physical fight, but who knows what magic they could unleash.

"Come with us," one of the strangers says. It's not a suggestion.

Eleni looks at Shandy, a question in her eyes. *Fight?* He glances at Brian, then shakes his head. Angel looks toward the playground where the kids were, then back at the school, and then at us, the people who have been less than truthful with him. He decides, breaking away from us, walking across the playground and ascending the stairs. He doesn't glance back.

Eleni looks down at Hyacinth, who holds Brian's hand again. Sighing, she moves forward toward the steps, following Angel's lead, but not without getting all up in one guy's face as she passes.

As Shandy and I follow, we pass through the glamour. Faint sounds grow louder all at once, and we hear the children again and the screeching sound of the metal gate opening. A tall, broad man, a little older than my father, emerges to stand at the top of the stairs. He has a red beard shot through with threads of white, and he looks familiar, like I've seen him before, like I've served him coffee. A Wellsian. The knowledge soothes the tension running under my skin.

And though he doesn't smile at us as we join Angel at the top, the lines in the weathered skin indicate he often does. He wears worn cargo pants and a name badge—IAN MCNAMARA. Also, a fanny pack. No one wearing a fanny pack can be all that bad.

Light cinnamon eyes scan each one of us as we stand there, not saying a word. His gaze settles on Brian, passed out over Eleni's shoulder, and Chad enduring my embrace. Eleni and Chad stare at him without blinking, and I know personally how intimidating both of them are. Soot clings to our skin, the odor of smoke and blood. Still, he looks at the weapons we carry, and his face stiffens.

"No one enters with weapons," Ian McNamara says. "You'll leave them with the gate guard before we bring you to the doctor."

They have a doctor? Relief is so strong in that moment, I almost burst into tears.

"And we should listen to you because why?" Eleni says.

Ian looks at her. "Because you need help."

When no one argues further, he says, "Follow me." But he pauses as he slides the gate open wider. "And please keep any magical powers in check."

CHAPTER 12

They have electricity.

Ian follows my gaze to the rows of fluorescent lighting along the hallway ceiling.

"Mike charged the generator," he says. A rosy-cheeked blond man, who removed his ski mask upon entering the building, raises his hand to display sparking fingertips connected by a flickering current. I take a couple obvious steps away.

While a guard remains by the door—a slender woman in her twenties who wears dog tags around her neck—Ian beckons us to follow him down the hall. Mike walks beside him. A precaution.

Children's drawings decorate the walls. Paper mobiles hang from the ceiling, spinning slowly above our heads. Most of the classrooms are empty, but a few are filled with backpacks and clothes, sleeping bags and blankets. And people. A number of people, young and old, sit in circles on the floor, or in the hallway against cubbies and lockers. Some smile as we pass. Yet terror haunts every face.

In the back of one of the rooms we pass, all the furniture—beanbags, bookcases, easels, and tiny desks—has been pushed against the wall, but a pile of winter coats, gloves, and hats sits in the center.

Ian answers before I can ask. "It's snowing in the south of town where we lived. We wouldn't have been able to survive there without heat."

I glance back at Shandy, absorbing our newest obstacle. Matty's apartment is in the south of town—would he be there?

"Andrew triggered the forest currently overtaking the entire north side," Ian continues. "Lillian can't turn off the snow. People panicked. They didn't know they had powers to control. A lot of people still don't."

Hyacinth focuses her gaze on the ground.

But Ian shrugs, indicating the powers are the least of his worries. "We've mostly been concerned with finding survivors and keeping them alive. There were a few creatures—zombies—who made their way south, but the cold saved us. It froze them."

"How did you come to be here?" Shandy asks.

"The first day, we sent a small group farther south to the border, but they couldn't get out." Ian pauses, watching our faces, lingering too long on mine, as though I'm the weak link. "We couldn't stay in the south without heat, so we went door-to-door, gathering any survivors who wanted to leave and as many supplies as we could. We would have searched more neighborhoods, but a truck came through carrying men with guns. They questioned us, asked us where we were going, suggested we wait for their leader. I have no doubt if we hadn't outnumbered them, it might not have been a suggestion."

None of us say a word, staring at Ian, not daring to look at one another, even as I feel Angel's tension, his eyes boring holes into each of us in turn. Ford's men let Ian and the other survivors go, but they know where they are. More than that, the men were headed south. We'll be walking into a trap.

There's no mistaking our ominous silence, but Ian continues. "It took a day and half to get here, and people have been trickling in from other areas." He rubs his forehead. "We want to run search-and-rescue missions, but it's a lot to organize and we have no idea what we're dealing with here."

We walk silently behind him, pretending we know nothing.

"If we stay here for the long haul, we'll set up the gym and library as the common areas," Ian muses. "Cafeteria is where we put all the food. There are bathrooms on every floor, but our water situation is precarious. Water is a number one priority. We have someone who may be able to clean it, but we'll need a long-term solution." He says all these things while jotting notes on a small pad.

Ian leads us to the nurse's office. Brian is clearly injured, but all of us have visible cuts and bruises too. Well, not Eleni, who appears slightly sweaty in that cover-of-a-fitness-magazine way, but otherwise uninjured. Not Hyacinth either, for that matter.

Two women sit at a table, drinking coffee. One, birdlike, with red-brown hair and kind dark eyes, wears a name tag reading, DR. KLEIN. The second is tall and bony, with dark curly hair and an unsmiling face.

"This is Dr. Katherine Klein and Shea O'Neill," Ian says, and pauses, waiting expectantly.

There's an awkward silence as we exchange uncertain glances, and then Hyacinth, stone-faced, says, "Jane."

Ian looks to me next.

So it appears we're giving fake names. "Mingo Salamanca," I say.

Ian heaves a sigh. "My name is Ian McNamara. My wife and I have lived uneventfully in South Wellsie until five days ago when the power went out, it started snowing, and a little while later, we saw a boy being chased by half-frozen creatures. He was running on top of the snow. On top of powder, without making a mark."

I stare at my hands, already flashing back to that night with Dustin Miller. And Thaddeus.

"And the next morning, I could see clouds around people, swirls of color following them wherever they went. My wife calls them auras. The boy walking on snow, the aura thing, was just the beginning, as I'm sure you know."

Yes. There are people who can glamour whole buildings, apparently, and people who are made of electricity. And there are people who throw fire, and people who multiply, and people who can't be harmed.

Ian doesn't blink as he peers at us closely. "According to the refugees from Town Center, the fault line is partially open. Obviously, magic is back. All this to say, we have no reason to trust one another, but the alternative is to trust no one, and where does that leave us?"

He lets the question hang there, rhetorical, but not really.

It's Angel who decides to answer it. "I'm Angel Reyes," he says.

"We're glad to have you," Ian says, his face relaxing.

And though we can't be sure about anyone, I whisper, "My name is Sid Spencer. Is there anyone else named Spencer here? Matt Spencer? Or Finn Warren? Or . . . or Nell Ambrose?" I clasp my hands tightly, heart inching into my throat.

Whatever Ian sees in my face softens his tone. "I haven't had a chance to do a full registry," he says. "And it's only been a few days. They could be here—don't lose hope."

If these people are alive, some of them children, the people I love could be too.

Though the others don't volunteer names, Ian lets it go. "We can talk more later, after you receive medical attention," he says quietly. "I imagine you may want to get cleaned. I'll be back in a bit." With no explanation of what "get cleaned" entails, he leaves us, though Mike stays at the door.

Dr. Klein's gentle face sets me at ease, but she quickly morphs into all-business when she sees Brian. She motions for Eleni to set him on a vinyl bed by the window.

Shea regards us, expressionless. "While the doctor scans the boy, I can take care of any minor things. But if any of you have some private issue you want addressed, please know I'm not a doctor and it would gross me out to hear about weird warts. I can help you heal quicker, but there are limits."

She picks up a two-way radio by the door. "John, please report to the nurse's office."

Neither Hyacinth nor I take our eyes off Brian. Dr. Klein sits on the edge of the bench. Her palms hover a couple inches over his body.

"It's his leg," I say quickly.

"I know," she says, moving slowly from the top of his head down. "But I want to make sure I have a complete picture. How did this happen?"

"High-speed blow." I couldn't exactly see it, but I have to assume Beard jumped on his leg at a run.

Hyacinth sits in a chair by the bench, gripping his limp fingers. Dr. Klein murmurs something to her I can't hear.

"I'm not injured," Hyacinth says, and guilt lies heavy in her voice. "He always protects me. I don't get injured because he gets injured for me." She rests the side of her head on the pillow next to his.

"No one should get injured at all," Dr. Klein says firmly, with a gentle touch on her shoulder.

A tall man with glasses and a thick tuft of brown hair appears in the doorway. His bored expression changes immediately to one of distaste as he takes in our less than pristine appearances.

Dr. Klein stops what she is doing and stands, holding out her hands. Shea sighs and leaves the room.

Instead of a giant cat licking us, which is what I pictured, John literally waves his arms in our direction, then leaves without a word. The sensation of being instantly dry-cleaned feels like the gust of wind at the doors of a butterfly house. But afterward, the scent of Lysol hovers in the air. My skin is squeaky to the touch, my clothing tight and stiff. My hair . . . well, that's the one drawback. There are rules to blow-drying my kind of hair and John clearly doesn't know them.

Instead of curls, or sleek straightness, Angel and I have giant clouds of frizz, the strands brittle, like straw. Interestingly enough, Eleni's hair lost its sleekness and resembles a triangle—flat on top, poufy at the ends. Shandy looks like an anime character with bangs sweeping off his forehead in a perfect wave. UNFAIR. Chad, now a giant dandelion-seed head, reveals it could've been worse.

Hyacinth at least had the presence of mind to distrust any suspicious cleaning process on her hair and yanked up her sweatshirt hood beforehand. The fabric took the brunt of it. Her clothes look brandnew, though the rest of us remain dotted with blackened holes. Hyacinth fingers her braids now. "I wonder if there's anyone left in this town who can do my hair. Daisy could, but she . . ." Her small voice trails off.

"Daisy's alive," Brian whispers, eyes closed, halfway between sleeping and waking. "She's coming for us. I know it."

Hyacinth's eyes brighten with a hope that was the barest flicker before.

Shea makes each one of us sit on the other nurse's bench. She suggests Shandy first, as he has an oozing cut on his cheek. He tenses at first, bracing himself. Her face a mask of concentration, she stares at him like she's seeing through his skin, watching his heart pulsing inside his chest. After about thirty seconds, she relaxes.

I watch, astonished, as Shandy's wound closes, as the bruises on his knuckles fade from blue to purple to yellow before disappearing entirely. His split lip scabs over, ending up plump and pink as ever. It's watching a video of time passing—whole days in the space of a minute or two—except it isn't a video, and hardly any time passes at all.

"What's happening?" Shandy says anxiously, watching our faces. "This feels weird."

"Does it hurt?" I ask, awed.

"Not really." His gaze has moved past us to Angel, who stands with his back to us, staring out the window, disinterested in whether Shandy heals or not.

"How are you doing this?" Eleni asks Shea, and it must have been a struggle to sound so unimpressed.

"I accelerate things," Shea says. "In this case, the natural healing process, things your body would do on its own without intervention."

"Can you speed up anything?" I ask. "Like hair growth? Or time?"

"Who would want to speed up time?" Shea says, scowling. "Time is abstract, not easy to see the same way bodies are. If I tried, I might make a mistake, and we'd suddenly be old and gray with no way to reverse it. Or possibly dead."

She has a point.

"If something's going to get infected, would you speed that up?"

"Anything is possible," she says, which is in no way reassuring.

It does feel weird. Not painful, but not great, either. Parts of my body are sore and tight, full of pressure one instant, perfectly fine the next. There's a definite heat element, too. The one time I needed to get a CT scan with contrast, they told me I would feel a flush of warmth down my lower body like I was peeing, and it felt exactly like that. So did this, kind of.

But after, I feel better than I have in days. My cheek no longer throbs. All my head wounds are closed. Now that I know what it's like to have my neck wrung, feeling nothing is heaven.

"Inflammation is a part of healing," Shea says, watching me poke my own face in wonder. "Luckily, it's so fast you don't feel it much. But your body is working overtime, so it could make you sleepy."

Shea eyes Eleni's sullen form. "There's nothing wrong with you. I feel your youth and vitality from here. Please leave." Obviously, Shea can't know for sure, but Eleni is happy to oblige, retreating out to the waiting area, away from the rest of us.

Brian's hand is as squeaky clean as mine when I pick up the one Hyacinth isn't holding.

He takes that moment to lift his head, fully awake, his static-filled hair sticking straight up. He blinks at his surroundings. "Where are we?" He squints at Hyacinth, then at me again. "Did you do something to your hair?"

But he utters a terrible sound as Dr. Klein gently touches his lower leg. Quicksilver emotions flicker over his face, ones I can discern now—fear, dread, resignation. Dr. Klein slowly rolls the cuff to reveal the swollen, bruised shin, all red, white, and purple. I tighten my grip on his hand.

Dr. Klein smiles at Brian, warm, confident. "You're going to be okay. You've broken your tibia, and there's a fracture to your fibula, but you're lucky the bones haven't displaced much and I don't see any fragments. I'm going to reduce it to make sure the bones are completely aligned, which will hurt." She glances up at all of us. "Please give me space."

Shandy, who hovers over her shoulder, backs up a few steps. Hyacinth and I edge away but don't let go of Brian.

As she gently but firmly presses on his leg, he clenches his jaw and again looks at me. He's trying not to make a sound, breathing rapidly through his nose. Dr. Klein makes a quick motion and his grip becomes painful. But Beard flashes through my mind, gasping for breath. And I remember Brian thrashing in his sleep until I held his hand.

"It's okay, don't be scared." I seek out my own shin, concentrate on how it feels, every sensation or lack of sensation. "This doesn't hurt at all." His face slackens in degrees. "See? No pain."

"Your bruises are gone," he whispers.

"Yours will be too."

He hesitates, looking around. "Spencer, is it safe here? Can we trust these people?"

I don't know for sure, but I think so. "Don't worry about it."

Shea moves forward, peering down at him. "I've never tried to heal a broken bone. It'll be a bit of an experiment."

Brian's entire body tenses.

"But I feel great, totally healed," I rush to say. "It's going to feel like you're peeing, but you're not."

He does not appear to find that comforting.

Shandy pats his shoulder. "I feel great too. You'll be fine."

Dr. Klein nods at Shea. "I'm going to splint the leg loosely, so he doesn't jar it."

As she eases his shoes off, using a cardboard splint and an ace bandage to brace his leg, Brian looks at me in alarm. "If I pass out . . . what if you need to run? What if something happens?"

I don't point out he can't run anyway. "We've got this," I say with zero confidence. "It can't always be you, Brian."

Hyacinth nods emphatically. "You can't keep flinging yourself into harm's way," she says, scowling. To which he makes a weak sound of defensiveness.

Shea steps forward and stands at the foot of his bed. For a moment, Brian stares at his leg in trepidation, but I watch his eyelids grow heavy. "My leg feels fat," he informs me.

"That's the inflammation," I say gently.

"I can't move my arms," he says, voice slurred, and he laughs, turning his head on the pillow to look at his sister and ask, "Hy, is there pie here?" as he drifts off.


Shandy tells Angel everything. They've retreated to a corner, speaking in murmurs so their voices won't travel to the waiting area where Dr. Klein and Shea are playing cards, but I can see the horror slowly darkening Angel's face during their conversation. I think some part of him must have suspected they were wrapped up in what happened, but nothing truly prepares you for the moment all your fears become real.

They're Guardians. They were found out. The man who did this is now a Guardian too. And we don't know how to beat him.

Whatever Angel says to him after that makes Shandy cry, a single-tear, beautiful cry that I, and ugly criers everywhere, can't relate to. Angel cries too.

I make a note to tell Shandy he should expect this reaction from everyone once they realize we truly are trapped and there is no plan.

Mike has deemed us non-threats and says he'll return for us when lunch is served. He charges all our phones before leaving, not that we can call anyone.

I loop a name tag on which I've written MARIANNE DASHWOOD around Brian's neck. Each name card they give us has the words THE LIGHTHOUSE scrawled across the top. "The Lighthouse must be the name they gave this place," I say to Brian. "They're either a shelter or a cult. Don't freak out."

Brian doesn't stir, breathing deeply, peacefully.

"Once I stole a book from the library," I whisper. "It was a smutty book and I was worried the librarian would judge me. I still feel bad about it. I don't know why I'm telling you this."

His lips curve in his sleep, and for a second, I think he hears me.

*God, I hope not.*

"You have calluses on your fingertips, but just on the one hand." I rub Ella's rosemary lavender lotion into his dry skin.

He kicks out his good leg in his sleep and I reach out to make sure he doesn't move the broken one.

"We could be Gandalf and Frodo for Halloween," I suggest.

The lines in Brian's forehead relax a bit, though not all the way. His bruises disappear, even the circles under his eyes. He never told me if my stun gun left a bruise, but I can't stop wondering if I hurt him.

Shandy falls asleep on the nurse's bench, finally betraying some exhaustion, and possibly to avoid Angel's anger.

Hyacinth is the one who gets Angel to talk to us again, telling him not the Guardians' story, but her own, the one about a girl who lost her parents, her town, and possibly her sister, who is out there alone in this chaos.

I envision two people sitting under Lulu's portico—one of them doesn't understand the other, not yet, but she will soon. Maybe I only understand people by filtering their experiences through my own, and that doesn't feel right to me. Maybe I began with the ability to look outside myself, but I lost it over time. The way Ford did.

"We need to tell each other so many stories there's no experience outside the realm of understanding," I say to Brian, using a ruler to measure his eyelashes. They're like a half-inch long.

I give Hyacinth my seat by Brian's bedside so she can whisper her random thoughts, or more likely, sit in silence while communicating telepathically like two people who are exactly the same. I sit tentatively next to Angel. The terror ignited by Shandy's earlier revelations remains behind his eyes. Though he knows everyone outside of Ford's magical barrier is safe for now, that's only a partial comfort when *we're* still trapped here.

I broach the subject of Shandy. "What did you say to him to make him cry?"

Angel chews his lip. "I told him I wasn't going to forgive him. We talked all night at the library. I told him things I've never told anyone. I told him my Avatar The Last Airbender fan-fiction username."

"Oh wow, so you really went there."

"He told me on his parents' first date, his dad drank a beer and his mom drank a lemonade—mixed together, those two drinks make a shandy. He told me about the car crash he survived and they didn't. Not once did he mention he was a *Guardian*. That's a pretty huge omission from his life history."

"Do you feel differently now that you know why they were so scared?"

Angel lets out a whoosh of breath. "You all put me in danger. You didn't give me a choice, not trusting that if I had one, I'd still help you. I understand why, but I also don't."

At my quizzical expression, he turns to face me fully. "I was born here, but my parents and my grandmother immigrated from Mexico. They didn't have family here, they didn't have friends, and they didn't know the language. And yeah, that was profoundly isolating in many aspects of their lives. But in their neighborhood in Oakland, where people spoke their language and knew their story because they, or their family, or their friends had lived it too, they had a whole community." He watches my face intently and his eyes soften, as though whatever he sees there confirms a suspicion—that I never had that.

He stares wistfully at the phone Mike charged for him. No service, it says. "Not everyone is good and I get that, but where I'm from, people do for each other, even people who are not blood, because no one is looking out for us but us. Every brown person you meet is family. Community is a Mexican thing. It's a queer thing. So no, I don't really understand any other way."

"Not blood," I whisper to myself, because *that* I understand. For a moment, I think about the time my mom signed Matty and me up for an Asian Students Alliance retreat a couple years ago—basically a giant pan-Asian sleepover party with kids from across the state. We were not all the same, obviously, but when Matty stepped out of the car and dramatically shouted, "My people!" it felt true. It felt like belonging. And the food was on point.

I look down, nodding slowly. "I'm sorry for my part in it," I say. "I would understand if you don't want to be involved with us anymore."

He doesn't answer right away. Finally, he flicks his eyes to Shandy, who is curled up on his side like a puppy. "I'll probably forgive him," he says grudgingly. "He's very pretty and I'm not above being totally shallow."

"You saved us at the library," I tell him. "You and Shandy are alike that way. Like Brian. Like my brother. Not like Eleni. Not like me, either. I'm not the sort to willingly put myself in danger."

Angel's forehead puckers, and he shakes his head slightly. "If that were true, you wouldn't be here. You didn't have to join them."

When I don't answer, he continues. "You're doing this for loved ones, right? When I came to Wellsie, it was the first time I was the only Mexican dude everywhere I went, the first time I didn't have a support system. Like I said, I have family back home, both blood and found. If helping you means getting back to them, then I'll do it."

When I meet his gaze, he smiles a little as though he knows I feel the same way. My experience is not the same as his, but the sense of recognition is there.

"If you can make people feel what you're feeling, you crave connection," he says gently. "If it had been you, you would have saved me too."

He doesn't know me, not really, but I hope he's right.

# CHAPTER 13

Maybe a hundred survivors sit throughout the cafeteria, all with trays of spaghetti and marinara sauce. Two individuals plop mounds of pasta and sauce onto paper plates as a line of people trickles past. Behind them on the gleaming metal tables, bulk boxes and cans of food are stacked all the way to the ceiling. The food they brought won't last forever. Angel can help, but they'll likely have to make another run and hope the grocery store hasn't been emptied out by Ford's men. I forgot all about these things until Brian broke his leg. Reality. Needing water so we don't all get cholera. Needing antibiotics so an infection won't kill us.

I can't help looking for a rainbow bun bobbing among the crowd, even if I know deep down Matty wouldn't be here.

After collecting my spaghetti and garlic bread, I choose an empty table in the corner. Eleni stands near the wall, hands on hips as she surveys the cafeteria for any potential threats, then eyes my tray of mushy pasta with a wrinkled nose.

As he throws one leg over the bench, Shandy chugs from a glass of viscous fluid the color of pond scum that he made himself.

"What the hell is that?" Eleni asks flatly.

"I blend smoothies every day after hockey practice," Shandy says, gesturing to his body so we can both agree it's worth it. "It usually has bee pollen in it."

Eleni raises a brow. "Do I look like someone who knows what that is?"

"You look like someone in a sci-fi thriller who sleeps with weapons," he says.

She tosses her hair over her shoulder. "You look like a——"

"Brutally hot man-Asian?" he finishes, smiling widely. "Thanks, I know."

Rolling her eyes, she stalks off to get her own spaghetti.

Hyacinth settles in next to me and, after a moment of hesitation, Angel places his tray next to Shandy. Though the coldness has dissipated, Angel doesn't quite return Shandy's hopeful smile.

I'm opening a can of tuna for Chad when a guy with a long, scraggly ponytail approaches us. His knee-length sweater looks like he knit it himself.

"What's up, newbies! I'm Casey." Grinning, he straddles the lunch table bench, smelling strongly of body odor and weed. He produces a plastic bottle of neon-green-yellow liquid and a stack of paper cups. "Anyone want Mountain Dew? I made it myself. In fact, I peed it. But don't worry, it's legit."

Everyone in the cafeteria looks toward us, then quickly away. Direct eye contact might encourage him to approach them next.

Angel, Hyacinth, and I shake our heads. Immediately.

Casey's smile fades. He stands, holding his bottle high. "ONE DAY I WILL FEED THE WORLD."

"Can you make anything else?" I wonder, because if not, one day he will malnourish the world.

"Working on whoopee pies. I want to produce food with my body.

Like a chicken makes eggs." But his face falls. "It's not going well." I don't even want to know what his experimentation process entails.

When no one says anything, Shandy shrugs and reaches for a cup. Casey looks so delighted that clearly no one has ever taken him up on his offer.

"*No*," Angel says emphatically to him, but Shandy raises the "Mountain Dew" in a mock glass clink.

None of us can watch Shandy as he tests the sample. But I *hear* him swishing it around his mouth before he swallows. "That *is* legit," he says to Casey. "Just needs to be chilled."

I don't want to experience a pee-temperature beverage ever.

"Never kissing him again," Angel says to me.

Beaming, Casey moves on, peddling his wares to the next group. Shandy places his empty cup on the table, and we all shift away.

A little girl clinging to a woman's hand pauses a few yards away, staring in awe at the Disney prince at our table.

Shandy bends down to one knee as she hides her face. "I'm Shandy, what's your name?"

"Penny," she whispers shyly.

"It's nice to meet you. What's that in your hand? Is that for me?"

She holds a wilted crocus in her fist. As she holds it out to him and opens her hand, the flower petals unfold, fluttering.

Shandy laughs, gazing at the purple butterfly perched on his wrist. The butterfly takes flight, bobbing through the air toward us.

Chad dives off the table, clamping her jaws around the butterfly midair. She hits the ground and sits there, the picture of innocence, except for the delicate wings half hanging from her mouth.

"*Prrrrrrow*," Chad trills, which no doubt translates to, "MURDER!"

Penny bursts into tears.

I dash forward and seize Chad, lifting her struggling body. "I am . . . so sorry. So, so sorry."

The woman shoots me a stern look as she hefts the sobbing girl into her arms and coos to her.

"Bad cat," I mutter. "Bad, bad cat." Preoccupied with containing Chad, I vaguely notice Shandy straightening, his eyes finding someone behind me.

"Oh hey," he says. "It's good to see you alive, man."

I glance distractedly over my shoulder, glimpsing a red-and-white letterman jacket.

And then, "Sid." Just my name. Low and flat.

My arms tighten around Chad. So hard she yowls and leaves a long scratch down my arm. I know that voice. I let Chad go and she bounds away.

As I turn, my stomach sinks, suddenly filled with lead. "It's you," I say, staring blankly at him.

Finn Warren stands in front of me, holding a lunch tray. "Yeah, I'm alive," he says without any emotion at all. "Sorry."

How many times has he stood in front of me holding a lunch tray? I don't remember the last time, but it was a different school and a different life. I can't remember the last normal conversation with him. He looks the same. Of course he does. I saw him a few days ago. Still handsome, same sandy hair and green eyes, but the smile is absent. He stares at me distantly, the whites of his eyes a faint pink. My gaze shifts automatically to the space beside him. The empty space.

Finn looks to the space, too, then back at me, with emptier eyes. "Oh. Nell's dead."

. . .

When Nell and I were kids at this school, we were in the same class every year. Our parents said it was luck, but sometimes I think the school did it on purpose, because they didn't have the heart to separate us. "You must be the giggle twins," the teachers always said at the beginning of the year.

The first time we had a close friend other than each other, we were in the third grade. The girl's name was Katie. She had pale blond hair and a toothy smile, and for a time, it was the three of us. Until the day I said, "Let's not be friends with Katie anymore. Let's just be friends with each other," and Nell agreed. In the fifth grade, we became good friends with Riley. Riley was small and good at gymnastics, and for a time, it was the three of us. Until the day I said, "Let's not be friends with Riley anymore," and Nell agreed.

I was always going to be her favorite. She was always going to choose me.

In junior year of high school, we became friends with Finn. For a time, it was the three of us.

And now Nell's dead.

"Did you hear me?"

I sit at the table, staring at the dollop of plain tomato sauce on my spaghetti. My mother makes spaghetti with Bolognese sauce. I wonder if this new world will have Bolognese in it.

"Do you care?"

The table is warm under my hands. My fingers leave prints when I pry them up. "She was supposed to be okay. Nell wouldn't have known what to do. But you were supposed to be with her."

He's somewhere in front of me, but I don't see him, just the table with my sweat drying on the surface. "I was supposed to save her? Where were you? Where were you for the last six months?"

"She was supposed to be okay. She had you."

"And you think I was enough? I was with her when it happened. She just . . . there were too many. I lost her in the horde. There were too many." His words come in hard bursts, like he can't breathe. "But you know what? Even if she hadn't died, even if this world was the same as it had been before, I wouldn't have been enough. She needed you. And she died thinking you hated her."

My hands find my ears, covering them. The scream I hear is a shattering explosion. And it's mine.

Cold fingers seize my upper arms, tight and painful. A face appears within the haze of too-bright light, the eyes cold and green.

Eleni shakes me, hard. "Stop it. I mean it." She slaps my cheek with enough force for it to smart, enough to bring me back. She looms over me, her red lips set in a thin line. "I *will* slap you again."

Hyacinth is on the ground next to me, curled in a ball. "Sid," she gasps.

*I'm hurting them.*

All the tables are empty.

Finn still stands next to the table as Shandy, Angel, everyone in the cafeteria writhes on the floor. He presses his palm to his chest. "Do you think I don't know how this feels? I already know."

I tear myself from Eleni's grasp. And I'm running.

Out through the swinging doors, down a hall. People sag as I pass.

I have to get out of here, but there's nowhere to go.

My legs take me somewhere, though. They find a dark, small place for me to tuck myself into a ball.

The gym is empty. And under the bleachers, at the end against the wall, no one will see me. There's no one to hurt.

She knew me most of my life. She knew, right? She had to know.

"I was jealous of you," I say to her.

It must have been hard for her to be friends with someone who was jealous of her. She never mentioned it. Not once in eleven years.

"I'm not like you," I say.

*I'm not like you.* She used to say that to me, too. I don't know what she meant. Now I never will.

*I know what it's like to feel lesser.* When Ford said those words, he was saying *you are like me.* And I do know what that means.

They turn the lights on in the gym sometime in the evening. Though people walk in through the doors beside the bleachers, no one looks into the darkness underneath. At least no one falls or cries. The thud of a basketball echoes against the walls for a time. Someone tromps up the bleachers overhead, then down a little while later.

"Matty," I whisper into my two-way radio. "Matty, I need you."

Silence.

At some point, they turn the lights off again. That's when I creep out, when everyone is asleep, finding my way to the locker where I stowed my backpack.

I bring the plastic bag stuffed with her notes back under the bleachers with me, but it takes maybe an hour to unfold the first scrap of paper, to read the tiny, slanted handwriting by flashlight. I open them one by one. Until I'm afraid I'll run out.

*I'm thinking of dyeing my hair rose gold, but my mother would HATE it. So . . . do it, right?*

*I finally got the courage to take driver's ed. I passed. I have a license now.*

*Finn hates Cheetos. Can you believe that? I honestly think you can do better.*

*Your hair is so long. You look like a beautiful mermaid.*

*Les Mis is coming to the Asheville Theater in the spring and I'm so mad at you today.*

*WHAT IS YOUR FAVE SONG ON THE NEW TAYLOR SWIFT ALBUM I MUST KNOW.*

*On my birthday, I once again asked the universe to bring back fried apple pie at the diner, and I'm sure you already know it did not come to pass.*

*I need you to know I thought he liked you too. It's why I didn't talk to him much. It was self-preservation. It wasn't supposed to happen this way.*

*If we were BTS members, I know you think we'd be VMIN. The truth is I'm the person who stands near you with a tiny fan when you're overheated.*

At some point, I start crying.

At some point, I sleep, because it's morning when I blink my eyes open. It has to be morning since Brian is pushing through the gym doors. The side of my face is pressed against the cold wall. Still balled up, my legs are numb. I don't want to move anyway. I want to stay here until my body fossilizes and becomes part of the wall.

He's not limping, so the accelerated healing obviously worked. After a quick scan of the premises, he walks out again, and, honestly, that's for the best.

Until he backtracks, pausing by the bleachers and squatting to shine a flashlight in the dark space underneath.

I flinch as the light comes to rest on me, deep in the corner.

"Sid?" My name is being called somewhere in the hallway. I know that voice. I curl tighter inward.

Brian switches off his light and straightens, backing up his body so it blocks me from view.

The double doors push open.

"She's not here," Brian says immediately.

Over his shoulder, I see Finn jump, having not seen Brian lounging against the side of the bleachers. He lets out a breath, a weary laugh. "You scared me. I didn't see you there."

Brian pushes away from the bleachers. "Yeah, well, I'm *creepy as fuck*," he says, and walks out.

Finn stands there, watching him leave. "Okay, that was weird," he mutters to himself. But after a moment, he leaves as well.

*I'm safe.*

A wild laugh bubbles in my chest. What a ridiculous thing to think in a world like this. *I'm alone.* That's more accurate.

Until maybe ten minutes later, when a shadow blocks the passage into the bleachers once again.

"Had to be a dark and tiny place," Brian says. He ducks, completely bent at the waist, and climbs in through the horizontal bars beneath the highest bleacher level. He carries a tray, making slow and clumsy progress.

"Ow," he says, his head hitting a diagonal support.

I hear him shuffling along, but don't look up when he stops beside me. The scent of food wafts downward, though, and my stomach lets out an involuntary growl.

With several grunts, he slides, back against the wall, until he's scrunched next to me.

"This is the most uncomfortable place I've ever been," he says, easing his legs forward and threading them beneath a metal rung.

"Is your leg okay?" I mumble.

"It's like nothing happened."

Good. That's good. I turn my head on my knees and glimpse the tray of food resting on his lap. "Is that a chicken?"

"Apparently all the food in the south remained cold because of the snow and lack of heat. This is a mostly defrosted rotisserie chicken from the warehouse store. I also have pancakes. And half-frozen fruit salad." He lifts a Tupperware container. "And green beans."

"I don't need a whole chicken."

"I don't think you've eaten since yesterday morning. Have some water. You're probably dehydrated."

"Is that a pie?"

"An apple pie I made last night." He lifts the dish edged with a delicate, fluted golden crust and unceremoniously forks into the middle. "Unless you eat enough food to qualify for dessert, it's all for me."

"You can't eat a whole pie."

"I can and I will, Spencer."

"Are you high?"

He takes a bite of pie. "My biological mother struggled with addiction. I don't do drugs."

Light filters in through each stair overhead, dust suspended in the beams. One shard falls over his face. "When did she leave?"

"I was eight. I don't know where she is now."

"Do you miss her?"

"To be honest, not really."

"Are you mad at her?"

He pauses, thinking about it, and I study his sharp profile. "She was rarely at home, just a person who would show up sometimes, not know what to say to me, then fight with my dad. After she left, she sent postcards for a little while, then nothing. But I had my dad then. I had Rosie." His head lowers.

His sisters are all he has left. He's hanging on to them with both hands, the way you do when you've always known family is not guaranteed.

He gives me a bite of pie though I haven't qualified for dessert yet. It's probably the best thing I've ever had—buttery flakes of crust, hints of cinnamon, slices of apple firm enough not to disintegrate but soft enough to absorb all the syrup.

"Do you ever think about your biological parents?" he asks me.

"Sometimes," I say softly. "I don't really have the drive to know more. But it's not just two people I didn't have, it's a whole culture. I think about that more than I think about what they were like or what their reason might have been. I do wonder where I got my hair or if I have a history of heart disease. I think I'd wonder more if I didn't have—" *Matty*.

"Have some chicken," he says gently, handing me a drumstick.

"Your mother was a musician like you?" I ask him, nibbling on the leg.

"Yeah. She played the guitar."

He has a music measure tattooed on the outside edge of his forearm. His dad had one too. "Your tattoo. What song is that?"

"It's my dad's favorite song." He pulls out his phone, newly charged, and scrolls through.

"What's it called?" I ask, when he plays the song, a gentle voice accompanied by a guitar.

"'The Wind.' 'I let my music take me where my heart wants to go.' That's the line. My dad used to sing it to me before I went to sleep."

"You miss him."

He doesn't say anything, but I know. I see his face in the light of the phone—peaceful. The lines of his forehead have loosened. As the base of my own spine relaxes against the wall, I realize now, when it's gone, that his tension permeates the air around him. You can feel its presence or its absence the closer he is. *The music calms him.* He lowers the volume so only we can hear it, and sets the phone down.

"I didn't know what to say before, but I'm so sorry about your parents."

"I know you are," he says.

"You liked your stepmother?"

He swallows. "Rosie married my dad when I was ten." I see the flash of teeth in the dark. "She was an architect. My father would sing her 'La Vie en Rose' terribly while they danced in the dark in the living room. She was that person in the movie theater to let out one really loud laugh during an inappropriate moment." His chuckle fades. "She understood me, sometimes better than my dad did. I loved her."

"Do you and Daisy get along?"

"Um . . . we have our differences. She's . . . strong-willed."

I decide not to say, *so you're the same.* "Do you fight a lot?"

"It's more like she shaves off one of my eyebrows while I'm sleeping."

"But how do you frown without two eyebrows?" I feel him frowning at me after that comment. "Did you retaliate?"

"I didn't have to. I said nothing. My parents saw my tragic face in the morning and signed her up for two weeks of Extraordinary Leader Camp somewhere in the woods. I may have mentioned six months prior that Daisy's least favorite thing is team-building exercises. Nature being a close second."

"You were plotting this for six months?"

"I play the long game, Spencer."

"I heard Daisy is super smart."

His voice turns wry. "She's the kind of person who decides to do something one day, learns it, and excels at it."

"Daisy is a year below me, right? She goes to your fancy school? Nell could have gone there, but she decided not to. She never told me why, but I used to wonder if . . . if she didn't want to make me feel bad." She knew me too well. The chicken turns to ash in my mouth, and I whisper, "You should know I'm secretly a bad person."

"It's true," he says softly. "You steal erotic literature from the library. What kind of person does that?"

"You *did* hear me."

"I hope that vampire book was worth it."

"That was my sister's!"

"A likely story."

"That was not the book I stole. I was young, and I did eventually return it. Haven't you ever stolen anything?"

"I stole that chicken for you at great personal risk. This is a community where people are encouraged to *share*, not surreptitiously sneak off with things to eat under the bleachers."

"You and Shandy are obsessed with feeding people."

"He grew up in a restaurant. I grew up in a bakery. We find it physically painful if people don't eat."

"Okay." I eat some of the pancakes, saturated with maple syrup. "Brian?"

"Yeah?"

A tear runs down my face, and I had thought there were none left. "I miss my mom. I miss my dad. I miss Matty and Ella and Zora."

"I know you do," he says.

"I'm afraid Matty is dead."

"I know you are."

"I won't—I won't be able to . . ." I shake my head. *Survive.*

He reaches down and grips my shaking hand. It's sticky with syrup, but he doesn't seem to notice.

"I can make people feel what I'm feeling," I say through the tears. "Can you feel"—I rub my chest for lack of a way to explain it—"this?"

He shrugs a little. "I'm not sure. It could be you. It could be me."

Because he still hurts. I don't want to add to it. "If powers enhance who you are, does this mean I want to inflict pain on people?"

"It's not always pain," he says with a hint of a smile. "Have some cold, disgusting green beans."

I eat some cold, disgusting green beans.

"You're not a bad person," he says softly.

I don't know if I believe that.

"Do you feel like coming out?" he asks. "It's so small in here. I don't know how you've been here all this time, sitting like that without dying."

It's only to save him from numb legs that I agree. "Okay."

I stand shakily. He has to hold on to the supports and climb his way to his feet. I wait for him, my hand resting on top of his head to keep him from hitting anything when he bends down for the tray.

When we're out from under the bleachers, I rub at my face, not wanting to look at him. My eyes are so puffy, I can barely open them.

He looks down at my face, his eyebrows drawing together, and I can't imagine him with just one. "I'm sorry about Nell," he says.

My chest hitches. "When we die, what happens to the magic inside us?" I whisper, because I wonder if she got a power. "Does it transfer, like yours does? Or does it . . . stay?"

He touches the curl by my ear. "Death is a clean break between body and soul. Ours was built to transfer through touch. Yours will just leave when the soul does and drift back to where it came from." His voice lowers as he says, "She's not a shell. I promise."

*He always knows the words I need.*

I want to ask where her soul is now. But there are some things nobody knows.

He never got to meet her. He would have liked her. Not because she was pretty, but because she was a good person. And all those many months ago, she didn't choose Finn over me. She chose herself. Once in her whole life.

# CHAPTER 14

*T*here was a large-scale fainting accident the day before you arrived, so you shouldn't feel like you're the only one to ever
incapacitate people," Ian says from behind me.

He's found me peering into the library while everyone else is at
breakfast.

I don't look at him, so as not to directly see the pity on his face.
It's already in his voice, and all around him, like a wet mist that doesn't
clear. He's obviously grasped enough from the cafeteria situation to
know I received bad news, but perhaps my aura is painted black.

"I brought the survivor registry in case you wanted to look at it.
We're also going to send search-and-rescue missions today."

From the corner of my eye, I see a spiral-bound notebook in his
hands. I shake my head. It's too late. Not for everyone else, but it is
for me.

Brian told me Finn was part of a small group of survivors from
Town Center. It was Saturday night when it happened; there were
enough people in the bars and restaurants to band together and get
out alive. They waited out the forest growth before heading south to
avoid the shells.

I only hear about half of what Ian is telling me, the reassurances that more people may be alive. All I can think about is how few people we saw on the way here. Empty streets and dark houses. If they were hiding inside, there were men going door-to-door. If Ian goes out searching for people, he'll encounter more of the wrong sort of people. I have to believe there's safety in numbers, but Ford likely has more.

"The men in the truck you saw, they know where you went," I say softly, cutting him off. When I meet his cinnamon eyes now, they're troubled as they search my face for answers. They're not mine to give, but I can't let more people die because they didn't know what to expect. "The shells can sense you. The more they migrate through town, the more they'll congregate nearby. But they're not your biggest threat."

Ian's brows knit together as he absorbs that. "I've seen many auras in the past few days, but you and your friends are the only ones with a matching color element—same size, same shape, same location. You share a common secret."

I neither confirm nor deny that, but I hold his gaze.

"You're Guardians, aren't you?" he asks flatly.

"No one in my group caused this to happen, if that's what you're asking," I say. "I swear to you. But there's a man named Paul Ford who did, and he wants to open the fault line completely. He's killed people; his men have killed people. He's the reason none of us can get out of Wellsie. Are you able to protect yourselves?"

Though deep lines of exhaustion have settled on his forehead, Ian's expression is set. "I will do whatever it takes to keep these people alive," he says.

The thought of pink-cheeked Mike with the sparking fingertips is very reassuring now. "What did you do before this?" I ask then.

Ian shrugs. "I was an accountant." He starts down the hallway but pauses, glancing at me over his shoulder, hesitant. "The boy, the one with the injured leg. He's a protector. But his aura doesn't flow. It's a solid thing, completely closing him in. I thought you should know that."

"He's not dangerous," I insist, instantly defensive.

Ian, utterly calm, says, "I never said he was. But there's always more to a person than we can see. Our powers are proof of that."

"What does my aura look like?"

Ian's eyes dart around the space surrounding me, much like he's seeing a cloud of gnats. "It's expanding."

The library is much smaller than I remember. The powder-blue carpeting remains the same, but the beanbag chairs and the art projects displayed along the walls are different.

In the nook in the back corner, the one Nell and I always claimed, I pull a tattered copy of *Anne of Green Gables* from a shelf and clutch it to my chest. I was Anne. She was Diana. We would sit here to whisper our secrets or read books together. We didn't have to talk. Someone's presence can fill the air the same as words.

It's not the same in the nook, but I sit for a while anyway.

Someone arranged the items on the librarian's desk by color, from the pens to the Post-its to the stacks of papers. It flows in slight gradations through the whole spectrum of the rainbow, from left to right. For the first time I study the furniture, realizing it's arranged like that too.

"I did that," says a clipped voice to my right. A short, bespectacled man with gray hair sits at one of the wooden tables. I hadn't noticed him, probably because his cardigan and trousers match the wood. His eyes fall to the book in my hand. "Are you going to put that back?"

I need to hold on to something, a good memory, for a little while. "I'll put it back."

"Fiction is alphabetical. Nonfiction, please use the Dewey decimal system. There were so many things shelved improperly when I arrived, I had to redo it."

"So you put things in order," I conclude.

"The world is complete chaos," he says. "You can allow me this one library, can't you?"

I can. We all deserve to feel okay about something.

"I'm Marcus Severin," he says.

"Sid Spencer."

Marcus walks over to one of the huge windows. "In the world before this, it was stress management, you know. When the world got to be too much, I organized things. At night, before I went to sleep, I would put my thoughts into boxes."

"You can order your own mind?"

Small papier-mâché animals line the windowsill, ordered from largest to smallest. "Yes, though it's different now that it actually works." He almost smiles. "It's like a file drawer. The other day, I compartmentalized my fear, filed it under 'Only access this when it is in my best interest.' Fear has its uses. If I encounter an undead person, I want to have the presence of mind to run. But right now . . . I don't remember what fear feels like. I can survive these moments in between."

It's on the tip of my tongue to ask him if he can order my mind. If he can put my fear in a box—all the emotions, really. If he can keep them all separate so I won't feel every single one of them at once. If he can put Nell in a box . . .

All the air leaves the room. I can't put Nell in a box. I did that before, and now the box is a coffin.

I must have been silent for a while, because when I look up from the windowsill, Marcus Severin has drifted to the other side of the library, leaving me with my disorganized mind.

More people trickle into the library as the day goes on.

A photographer made the glamour that cloaks the school. "When people look at a photo, what they're seeing is one moment in time, with life happening before it, after it, all around it," she explains to me. What we saw when we arrived was the school the first day *she* saw it—empty, still, and quiet.

I ask a man with detachable body parts if it means he can remove his eyeballs and leave them places in order to spy on people. He seems offended by the question. But, like, there's no way someone gets a power like that without being a little creepy. Is there a non-creepy reason to detach one's hand and let it wander off somewhere?

"Say you are in the shower," he says coolly. "And you realize the shampoo you've bought is in a bag on the kitchen counter. You can send your hand off to fetch it for you."

I can't pretend that wouldn't be useful.

It's about 50 percent. Half the people I meet know their powers, and half don't.

"That's cool," a girl named Amaya says, as she practices increasing and decreasing the size of my aquamarine ring. "You'll never need to explain yourself again."

It doesn't feel like that; it feels like the naked dream only real.

My ring feels smaller when I slide it back on my finger. Or she made my hands larger. But I say nothing. We're all doing our best.

I wander over to the giant library windows, gazing out at the playground—empty but for the lone figure on the swings wearing that red-and-white jacket.

Again, I wonder what power Nell would have had. To everyone else, she was quiet, reserved, reluctant to speak in a group. She always wedged herself a little bit behind me.

But that shyness disappeared when she stood on a stage to sing. When she sang, she was loud and expressive and confident. Maybe with magic, there wouldn't have been a dichotomy. If she'd survived, she would have woken up that first day and everything would have been different. Every day, every moment, she would have been her full self.

Finn uses his feet to rock slowly back and forth. The breeze tries to catch his hair, but the strands flop limp over his forehead, refusing to play.

He always carried himself with a kind of swagger, shoulders squared, sauntering instead of walking. But now he slumps in the swing, chin to chest. He's lost weight already, like he's losing pieces of himself.

Though he doesn't look up, I know he sees my shoes.

I lower myself onto the swing next to his.

"Shandy said you're leaving," he says tonelessly. "Why?"

"I have to find Matty. And they have to find . . . they have to find people."

He laughs. His laugh was once everything, full and unselfconscious. He laughs now like he's never done it before. "Nell always said you were the strong one."

I don't know what I expected but it wasn't that, and it's difficult to breathe when you've been struck in the chest with a brick. "I know why she said that," I say unsteadily. "It's because she always made me lead whenever we reenacted *Dirty Dancing* moves."

Finn finally looks at me, his green eyes still bloodshot, but at least they aren't angry anymore. "We called and called you. For weeks. She knew you'd blocked her, but she called anyway. You stopped talking to us, Sid. You wouldn't look at us. You ran from us in the hallway. You wouldn't come downstairs if either of us stopped by. We did one thing you didn't like, and you were done."

I want to look away. I want to walk away. "I didn't think it mattered if I was there or not," I whisper.

"Of course it mattered! You think because I loved her in a certain way that I didn't also love you? As though some love is real and some isn't? There are a million different ways to care about someone."

"I know that." It barely comes out. "But sometimes you can know something and feel something else. I felt embarrassed." *For thinking anyone would want me when they could have her.* But I don't say that because . . . because it would make Nell sad. "I felt *creepy*," I say instead, leaving it hanging in the air.

Finn drags a hand across his face. "I didn't call you creepy," he says. "I didn't know what to do. I asked the team because I thought they were my friends. I told them to stop making fun of you, but Adam wouldn't let it go." He takes a deep breath. "It was a mistake. I made a mistake and I'm so sorry."

He's telling the truth. It's all over his face, and maybe some part of me knew he wasn't that cruel, that I'd judged him right a year ago. "I don't always react well when I have an emotion," I say, hugging myself.

"For what it's worth, your letter was the nicest thing anyone's ever done for me."

The world blurs. "She died before I could . . . she died thinking I—"

"I shouldn't have said that," Finn says, and his voice is thick with tears now. "She was waiting for you. She said you needed to talk to yourself about it for a little while, and then you'd come back. She kept a list of things she kept wanting to tell you. I don't know where she kept it."

I cry, hearing that. I have her notes, but one day I'll run out of them and there won't be any new ones to read. I cry because coming back had never been my intention. But maybe she knew me better than I knew myself. Maybe I would have. Maybe she was stronger than I treated her.

"I . . . wasn't . . . my best self when she knew me."

Finn shakes his head slowly. "I don't think it works that way, otherwise she never would have loved me." He wipes the corner of his eye with his thumb. "It's not just the best parts that you love."

*Maybe I'm not the best, but I'm enough.*

At that moment, I feel someone's gaze upon me.

Brian stands at the window of the library, looking down at the playground. Our eyes meet and one corner of his mouth lifts.

He raises a hand, beckoning, and my swing sways forward—light, teasing—and back again. A laugh forms despite the tears on my cheeks as I swing without any effort at all. Not fast, not slow, but safe, as solid as if he were holding my swing with his hands.

Finn follows my gaze. Brian's brows flatten to a harsh line before he turns away from the window, and my swing slows to a gentle stop.

A ghost of a smile touches Finn's lips. "Nell would have liked that guy."

"You think?" I say doubtfully. "I don't think she would have known what to say to him."

"She was a musician. Not like me. I played a lot of pop songs to get people to like me." He gives me a rueful look. "She and I went to the winter concert at Mountain Ridge. You should hear him play. I know nothing about classical music, but I know I've never heard anything like it."

Finn's songs were enough for Nell and me. "Do you have a power?" I ask, standing.

Finn shrugs. "I don't know yet. Maybe I won't have one." He grips the swing's chains tight in his fists. "And if I got one now, one that might have saved her, I—" He swallows hard and shakes his head.

*Wind whistles next to my ear, carrying a scream that sounds like hers. White and gold blur against a writhing mass. And then she's gone. But the scream remains because it's mine.*

I shake my head against the image, holding my breath until it passes. Finn rises next to me, shoulders tense as he waits for me to ask about her, but I don't. I don't want to know if it was as bad as I imagine. I can't.

His forehead creases with worry.

"When are you leaving?" he asks. "She would want me to look out for you."

"Tomorrow, I think." It's not safe to linger any longer than we already have. Not safe for us or for the people here.

Uncertainly, he holds his arms out. I walk into them, but it's not a hug I remember. My hands hover a few inches away from his back, above a layer of tension. It's not the same. I'm not sure it ever will be.

Finn rests a chin on top of my head the way he used to, but it's hesitant. We don't know how to be us anymore.

Still, I close my eyes.

It's almost dinnertime and I can't find Chad. I even check under the bleachers on the off-chance she has hidden Spencer qualities deep down inside, but any possibility of that disappears the instant I walk into the girls' bathroom and find her sitting in the sink in front of Eleni.

Eleni's long hair falls in a mane of damp, spiral curls, far different from the straight curtain she sported when I first met her.

She plucks her brows in the mirror, having procured tweezers and eyeliner from someone. The dark kohl wings out dramatically at the edges of both eyes in a way I'd never be able to replicate if I tried for fifty years. "You look like Einstein," she says.

I catch a glimpse in the mirror of my round face surrounded by a cloud of frizz and make to leave, but she turns to face me before I can haul the door open.

"God, you are so sensitive," she says.

I pause at the door and subject myself to her supercritical once-over. "Get over here," she says, and shoos Chad out of the sink. Chad complies immediately, tiptoeing along the edge of the counter. Her fluffy tail caresses the underside of Eleni's chin before Eleni bats it away. Eleni rummages in a small bag for a bottle of water and small pump container.

"Is that mine?" I say, recognizing the curl cream that had been in my assigned locker.

"I went through your stuff," she says, as though that explains everything.

Reluctantly, I stand in front of her, wanting to take Chad and leave. My last memory of Eleni is of her smacking my face. She doesn't appear to remember this.

Eleni motions to the sink. "Put your hair in there."

Because my hair is reminiscent of those fluorescent-haired troll dolls, I do so. Not because she scares me. Yes, because she scares me. Eleni shakes the bottled water over my head, which is not a practical use for it in these times. When my hair is well soaked, she motions for me to flip my head up. She combs it while it's sopping wet, surprisingly gentle, before rubbing a dollop of cream into her hands.

"I know how to do my own hair," I say to her.

One brow arches. "Do you, though?"

Maybe she has a point. "Well, once I had bangs. Curly, frizzy bangs. None of my friends said anything to stop me."

"And that's why friends are overrated." She massages the cream through my wet curls. "Bend over and scrunch it."

I sigh, but I follow her instructions. When I straighten, wet coils spring up around my face. "Are you done treating me like a child?"

"Not really. Let it air-dry. Once it's dry, scrunch it again to break the cast if it's stiff." She stares at me for a long moment, her eyes traveling over my face. My eyes are puffy. She can see that. But all she does is murmur, "Your skin is my color," and I'm not sure at first if she's talking to me.

"My skin likes the sun," I say. "And I freckle."

She nods and presses her lips together tightly, her fingers closing around the charms on her necklace. "When you show emotion, you're showing someone exactly where you're weakest."

I've thought of that before. "I didn't mean for that to happen yesterday. I couldn't help it."

"I mean, of course that's your power. *Of course* it is," she says, rolling her eyes. "But it's not just your power. Everything you feel is all over your face. People will take advantage of that." She lets the arrow and heart fall through her fingers.

"Why do you care?"

She rips a piece of paper towel from the dispenser. "I don't." Wiping the residue of hair product from her hands with rough, angry movements, she brushes past me.

But at the door, she pauses. "Despite what everyone thinks, I do care about my responsibility." When she faces me, it's with narrowed eyes. "I saw the Keys in your bag. You're not a Guardian, and after what Josh did, Brian trusts none of us to do the right thing when our lives are on the line. And to be honest, neither do I." She digs into the pocket of her jeans, then reaches for my hand, slapping a glowing Key into the center of my palm. The light fades the second she removes her hand. "I am giving you my Key to hide. It's what he wants, right? For all the Keys to be out of Guardian hands."

I stare at the Key, as delicate as the bones under my skin. So tiny. Such a little thing can unleash so much power.

"Do you know when people transfer their Guardianship to a new person, they're supposed to choose people who've suffered loss or hardship?" Eleni says softly. "Like they'll take this seriously because they understand on a personal level what's at stake."

I did not know that. I've lost someone now too. But it strikes me as faulty logic. "I don't think you need to suffer to be strong."

"No," she says, even softer. "But it changes you irrevocably."

Whether that's good or bad is left unsaid. "But Matty didn't lose anyone."

*Or did he?* Maybe we both did when we were too young to remember it. Maybe a hollow spot remains, and that's what drives me to find him now.

"He's my brother, you know," I say, though she never asked. "We'd do anything for each other, no matter what. It's a sibling thing."

Eleni flinches.

I rub at the sudden sharp pain in my chest.

And the lights go out.

*In the darkness, I hear sniffling. She's crying again, trying to stifle it.*

"Stop crying," I whisper. "He'll hear you."

The floor squeaks under a pair of wet boots outside the door. A wisp of fear flutters into my belly, but I punch it down until it no longer moves. "Get behind me," I say through gritted teeth. "Get. Behind. Me."

As the door slams open, I turn, calm somehow, facing the light.

Snap. I blink, shielding my eyes for a moment until the glare dims to pale but harsh fluorescent lighting. A pair of fingers with red-polished nails hovers in front of my face. Eleni snaps her fingers again, and I take a step back. The gray tile of the school bathroom comes into sharp focus and then Eleni, standing with hands on her hips now. "What's wrong with you?" she says. "You just completely spaced out."

It takes a second to register her words. "I don't know," I say hesitantly. Lowering my hand, I shake my head to clear the confusion. "Were you just . . . crying?" It sounds ridiculous even as I say it.

She glares. "Do I look like I cry?"

"Never mind," I say, rubbing at my eyes. "Have you ever been so tired you have lucid dreams?" I only slept a few fitful hours last night under the bleachers and now I'm hallucinating.

"Suck it up," Eleni says. She pushes the door open and leaves without another word.

Chad doesn't bolt after her fast enough to get out through the swinging door. She paces, mewing, until I push it open for her, and she bounds down the hall after Eleni.

Eleni halts, looking over her shoulder.

Chad freezes, gazing up at her.

Eleni walks; Chad darts forward, getting caught between her feet.

"Stop following me," Eleni mutters.

Chad rubs against her ankle.

Eleni points a finger at her. "If you choose to walk beside me, you will answer to 'McRib.' Don't expect me to carry you or pet you or use little baby voices." She looks down the hallway at me. "Your cat has chosen her allegiance. She knows the fittest survive."

I shrug because when has Chad ever been wrong.

Eleni turns on her heel and strides off, Chad following, and when Eleni reaches the door at the end of the hall, she holds it open for her.

Hard ridges of bone dig into my palm as I close my fingers around her Key. I have four in my possession now. Brian, Shandy, Morrissey, and Eleni are depending on me.

We can only hope Morrissey got Parker's and that we can retrieve Matty's if he hasn't already. But the one that truly matters, the one Josh transferred to Matty, is in Ford's hands.

In the morning, we'll go south, into the snow, where Ian says his group couldn't have survived without heat. Because we have no other plan.

I can't keep them on me.

*I will never give you up*, Brian said.

The question is, will I?

A memory drifts through my mind. I take a step down the hall. And another, my pace quickening.

*No. I won't.*


Near the street corner, I stop, blinking. Shandy's trekking pole slips in my sweaty grasp.

Uncertainly, I glance up at the yellow DEAD END sign. Though the sun has set in shades of pink and purple, the streaks will fade to navy and black, and I'm outside, standing alone on a silent road.

It takes a second before it comes back to me. *A walk*, I'd said to the gate guard who had extreme reservations, but zero authority to stop anyone from leaving.

I'd insisted. For some reason.

And I'm not quite sure what possessed me or how long I've been outside, zoning out. My newly charged phone reads 7:29 p.m. The others are probably finishing up dinner.

I'm reminded of a night I couldn't sleep and I strolled the neighborhood in the dark. I pretended it was the end of the world, that I was the only one left alive, and at the time, I thought it was peaceful.

It is most definitely a different time now, and I need to get inside immediately.

I glimpse the school down the street, shadowy and dark from the outside. Beyond the veil of the glamour, it'll be lit and bustling with life.

The moment I turn the corner, a shell totters out of the shadows and into my path. At first glance, she's lost, a confused woman waiting for someone with a kind face she can ask for directions. When she jerks her head in my direction, the blank eyes gleam silver from a distance. Her skin is thin, papery, ancient the way skin would look if it aged but never died. Then she lurches forward, mouth gaping to reveal a black hole with no teeth at all.

I keep walking.

She doesn't trudge, more of a glide. No limbs hang or drag. It's almost like she's not broken. Almost.

A spidery web of blue veins lies visible through her pale skin. Blond hair, thinning in great patches, blows like cornsilk in the breeze. The same color as Nell's.

She reaches out a skeletal hand, uttering a choking sound instead of words, but it feels like she's speaking, like she's saying *help me*.

My pole swipes the back of her knees and she sags to the ground, limbs twitching, fingers still clenching and unclenching. She stares at me, not blinking, mouth moving. A plea.

I drive the point of the pole through her eye. My body absorbs the shock.

And she's gone, dying at last on a dead-end street.

I hurry toward the school at a jog, clinging tightly to my weapon.

The scrape of metal against metal has me instantly freezing in my tracks. Without moving a muscle, my eyes scan left, right, but the neighborhood is still.

I take a tentative step and the sound comes again, this time with a clank.

Slowly, I lower my head, eyes fixed on the ground, at the manhole cover several yards away as it lifts an inch, then two.

I edge toward it, silently, lifting the pole like a spear.

With a loud clatter, the heavy metal lid is tossed aside. There's a gleam of bright white as something bobs through the open hole in the street. A delicate figure climbs out with a grunt and crouches there for a moment, back to me, tense as she surveys the area. *Not a shell.*

The girl rises, fingers spread, arm outstretched and moving slowly back and forth like an antenna until it points at the school. "Nailed it," she murmurs.

When she spins to face me, the point of my spear brushes the underside of her chin.

At first, I see thick-rimmed glasses. Then, deep brown eyes, curious, brimming with intelligence. A slim Black girl in a white shearling coat stands in the fading light. A grin spreads over her face, though her gaze flicks down to the spear.

My mouth falls open and when I forget to step back, she casually forces the tip of the pole aside.

I've seen her around town with Mountain Ridge people. More recently, I've seen those eyes and that mouth on someone else.

"Well," Daisy Radcliffe-Aster says brightly, pulling off the white scarf around her neck and shaking out four thick cornrows long enough to reach her waist. "That was easy."

## CHAPTER 15

"Easy?" I say numbly, because that is not a word I would use to describe the last week, or, like, anything in my life ever.

Daisy's face is round instead of Hyacinth's triangle; she has a wholesome, apple-cheeked prettiness, like her mom. Her eyes dart around, taking in every detail of our surroundings. But as they zero back in on me, I realize she has something in common with her siblings. At least I'm used to people looking directly at me now. Like, if I have something on my face, I know three individuals in the same family who would definitely tell me.

"You're Matt's sister," Daisy says, tilting her head. "The fact that you're with the Guardians made finding you a lot easier than it could have been."

"You're a glass-is-half-full kind of person, aren't you?" I say.

She tilts her head the other way, contemplating that. "It's not one or the other, just two halves of the same coin, isn't it? Like, inside me, there are two squirrels."

I blink. "You mean two wolves?"

"They feel more like squirrels," she muses. "There's the one who—" Her light, musical voice slams to a halt. She swallows several times before continuing. "The one who wanted to die the day my parents did, because what kind of world shatters your life but expects you to keep doing laundry, and eating, and going to school, and averting the apocalypse?" There's a sheen of moisture in her eyes, but she manages a small smile. "And then there's the one who remembers there are things it used to want to be, to do—one who has never been to a BTS concert and is determined to live at any cost."

I point at her, my mouth falling open.

She shoots me a finger heart. "Neither squirrel really wins; they just fight each other until the end of time." She drops her hand, and there's a relief in the sigh she exhales. "We are in the worst possible timeline, but I've found my siblings and I've found you, and I'm taking that win." She sheds her backpack and coat, one meant for winter, and stands there looking so impeccable in a white turtleneck sweater and leggings that I'm not sure she knows this is the zombie apocalypse. I'm the sort of person who will randomly drool coffee all over my shirt for no reason, so white is never an option no matter the circumstances.

*Don't compare yourself.* Nell's voice drifts through my mind the way it has for months when I least expect it, except this time she's not gone from my life, she's just gone.

The trekking pole drops to my side as Nell fades, leaving an emptiness behind. "How did you find us?" I ask, and it hurts to speak. If Daisy's wearing a winter coat, she's coming from the south. There's one reason she'd be coming from the south. And if she's alone, it means she never found him.

"I track people," Daisy says, and swivels toward the elementary school, arm out again, fingers spread. "They're in that building, yes?" When I nod, she nods, like she didn't need me to confirm. "Traveling by sewer when I could was the smartest option, obviously. I saw a map of the whole system once. If I've seen something, I remember it." She shrugs, as if that's completely normal. "But it's harder to sense people when I'm underground. Distance makes it harder, lots of obstacles, certain materials like metal. Plus, they were on the move. I'd come up once in a while and have to backtrack." She talks fast, with these quicksilver expressions, moving with a barely contained energy. But when she spins back, scowling now, she looks just like her siblings. "It was really annoying. Brian couldn't just stay put somewhere and wait for me."

Hyacinth and Brian said Daisy would find them. Now I know how. Still, I'm compelled to say, "You know how he is. He wasn't going to leave you alone out here to fend for yourself. Also, he was determined to save the world. He's, like . . . selfless."

Her eyebrows have inched progressively higher during all this. "I mean, you're talking about a guy who once shoved me into a gourmet cheese display in his haste to get to the lady with the sample chocolates."

Well. Chocolate is his favorite. I don't say this. Instead, I press a hand to my heart. "Matty," I say. "You were looking for him, weren't you?"

Wincing, she rubs at her chest. "Maybe we should get out of the street."

But there are no shells, only the dead one on the corner. I realize I didn't name her. It's easier that way. She won't be like Nell, who left behind a name and a family and a whole life. "Tell me," I whisper.

Eyes on mine, she pulls a hand out of her pocket. For a second, I stare at her open palm, at the white Key, like ivory. It doesn't light up. A tie-dyed rabbit's foot hangs off the intricate loop on the end. This is his rightful Key, the one that made him a Guardian.

I'm choking then, on nothing, just pain. If she has this . . . if she has this, it means . . .

"No," she gasps, doubling over. "Look."

A rolled-up scrap of paper lies next to it.

With a trembling hand, I take it, unroll it . . . The nearly illegible handwriting, worse because it was rushed, is his.

*Daisy—*

*You know by now Josh's part of the fault line has opened. Josh is dead and his Guardianship lies with me. But his Key is in the hands of a man named Paul Ford. Ford is after all the Keys— all of us. I'm on the run as he'll be after me first. I'm the only thing standing in the way of him being able to use the magic loose in Wellsie. It's not safe for me to stay at my apartment. It's not safe for me to go home.*

*You need to get Josh's Key from Ford and get it to me so I can relock the fault line. But in case this letter falls into the wrong hands, I can't tell you where I am. Find my sister. She'll know. She'll know where I'm going. Please protect her.*

*In the meantime, I can't have my own Key on me in case they get me. Keep it safe. Stay alive.*

*—Matt*

The tightness in my throat eases little by little as I clutch the piece of paper in my fist. I may still be gasping because Daisy keeps rubbing her chest. She reaches out her other hand to grasp my upper arm. "Breathe, Sid. He's alive."

"How did you get this?" I say when I'm able to speak.

"Matt and I had a system worked out for emergency situations."

She straightens up, beginning to pace. "I went to our drop-off spot first—his Key was there with this letter. I went to Matt's apartment, but the place was surrounded. He's not there. I can't sense him and I don't know why."

"The other Guardians didn't have plans with their buddies."

"Not everyone is me," she says, breezy AF, but the brightness in her eyes fades a little. "I have been preparing for anything since the day they died. It helps me cope, to have plans."

Her parents. She thought it wasn't an accident, same as Brian. "I don't know where Matty is," I say hoarsely. "If I knew, we wouldn't be here." Where could he hide that Daisy couldn't find him? Where could he hide where Ford or a shell couldn't get to him? Again, I can't help but wonder if I don't know my own brother the way I thought I did.

Daisy chews on her cheek. "Hmm. Well let's put a pin in that because it's not the biggest challenge."

I blink at her. "What is?"

Those eyes swivel back to me. "Getting that Key back from Ford. That is and always has been the most important thing."

And we failed from the beginning.

"I need to find us a safe place," Daisy says, glancing around the neighborhood. I gesture toward the school, but she shakes her head. "No, there are over a hundred people in there; I can sense them. They can't know I'm here."

Confused, I say, "It's a shelter full of survivors."

"Do you know that for certain?" she says gently. "Even if they're all innocent people, if Paul Ford comes here, these people can't know anything. They can't know anything that would give Ford an advantage."

Her eyes roam the street again with a sharp intensity. "You all

have to leave tonight, right now, without anyone seeing you or knowing where you're going. Get them out and . . ." She pauses, squinting
at a darkened building a ways down the street. "There's no one in
there. Take them to that church. That's where I'll be."

I squint at the church. "How are you going to get inside?"

But Daisy, already rummaging around in her backpack, pulls out
a small black pouch and unzips it, tilting it for me to see a line of thin
metal tools. A lock-picking kit. "Should be easy," she says.

Okay.

"Bring them to me and we'll go through the plan I've devised,"
she says.

She has a plan. That makes one of us. I turn toward the school, but
she stops me, with a hand on my arm. "Don't tell Brian I'm here yet.
Wait until you're out."

"Why?"

"I don't want him to react in a way that will draw attention,"
Daisy says.

I'm not sure what she means by that. "He's very stoic."

She snorts. "He's the most emo person of all time."

"Okay, I don't think you've met him."

"Just because something's under the surface, doesn't mean it's not
there." She surveys me thoughtfully, her fingers drifting to her chest
again, like she wants to say something.

"Sometimes people feel what I'm feeling," I mumble.

"It's pretty apparent."

"I'll try to rein it in, but I don't always know when I'm doing it." I
think of Eleni smacking me in the face in the cafeteria. "Are you going
to tell me to stop being emotional?"

A faint smile touches Daisy's lips. "The only family I have left are two people who are probably stewing over something they experienced years ago, and one day they'll accidentally drop their cake in the mud, and everything will explode. They'll simply sprint into the ocean. No, I'm not worried that you feel things. I'm worried that Brian is refusing to."

But I think of the entire cafeteria collapsing in pain because of me. He chooses to suppress things because sometimes it's unbearable to feel them.

Daisy takes a step forward. "It won't always be this way," she says softly, in a way that makes me think loss recognizes loss. "My mom used to say that. Even if the circumstances stay the same, you won't."

I don't know if that's good or bad. Both. Neither. It just is. Time will pass. But as Shea said, time is abstract.

"You seem to see your power, the way you are, as a burden," she continues, slowly shaking her head. "But you're sharing yourself with someone. It is your gift to give. And it is their choice to accept it or not." She studies my face. "The shells are not affected by you, are they?"

"No. They are most definitely *not* terrified, which is how I feel whenever I'm near them."

"I find that fascinating." Daisy is one of those people who gets visibly excited by problem-solving. As she looks at me, her gaze takes on a strange, single-minded focus, the same look I get when presented with dumplings. "Some powers affect the individual," she says. "Yours affects other people. On some level, you have to connect with the world, with people who have souls, for it to work."

I hadn't thought of that. That means Daisy has to connect with the world too. Brian told me she's the kind of smart where she could excel at anything she chose. Her power could have been like that as well. And yet it's this, it's finding people. It's keeping her family together.

On impulse, I grab her hand and it's as small as mine, but warmer. "We should be friends after this," I say, wishing I had been before. "If we don't end up getting murdered."

Her smile grows wider and she looks so much like her mom. "I bet he likes you," she says. She does not feel it necessary to reveal whether she does or not. She hauls her bag over her shoulder and walks off down the street.

We're staying in a classroom marked VISITORS LOUNGE. I find the others there, lounging on sleeping bags and discussing tomorrow's journey in hushed voices.

"A wild Sid appears," Shandy muses, looking up, and I have no doubt I look as nervous as I feel. "Where've you been?"

That part is not entirely clear to me, but I don't have time to freak out about it. "I went for a walk, apparently. But I need you all to listen to me and do what I say."

It's possible I've managed to sound authoritative for the first time in my life because they all go quiet, even Eleni.

"Where's Brian?" I say, noticing for the first time the absence of his gigantic presence.

"Music room," Hyacinth says, her solemn gaze never leaving my face. "Should I get him?"

I shake my head. "I'll do it." My gaze settles on Angel. "Make a door out to the street so no one will see you leave. Head to the church two blocks down. Wait for us there."

Angel shoots me a bewildered glance, but Eleni shoos Chad off her lap and rises slowly. "Why?" she demands.

I keep my voice steady. "Leave the cat."

At this, Eleni's brows settle, and she regards me thoughtfully.

That's what it took for her to decide I might have a legit reason, I guess.

*Chad will be safe here,* I tell myself. *They'll take care of her.* I couldn't abandon her back at my house—she was an orphan once the same way I was—but I have no idea where we're going next. I have to leave her—and I'm definitely about to cry. Without another word, I leave the lounge, and they can follow my instructions or not.

I remember the way—it's where I took violin for a single year, a requirement for all Asians. But halfway there, it doesn't matter if I'm treading a familiar pathway. I would've found him anyway.

In the distance, I hear a chord.

It sounds like it's right next to me. Or somewhere inside me.

The sound catches in the space between my stomach and my chest, the same ache I get when I'm so full of emotion, I can't breathe. Haunting and beautiful, and so very sad.

It's not even music. It's *him*—all the layers and textures of a person. I understand now why Daisy said he's emo. The music is as solid as his hand squeezing around mine. As real as the shivering I sometimes experience when I look at him, the same chills I have now that have nothing to do with the cold.

Months ago, I heard someone at the café mention they heard him play at his parents' funeral. I'd always heard he was good, though never knew personally.

He's not *good*; he's amazing. I have never heard—*felt*—anything like it. The music hurts, the way hope hurts sometimes.

*Finn was right.*

As I approach the open door, there are crowds of people gathered silently in the hallway, listening. The air around them shimmers.

When I lift my hand, I see it against my skin—glitter. Years and years of elementary school glitter that couldn't be removed from the carpet until now floats on the air, still and peaceful.

The way he feels when he plays.

I used to think growing up in Wellsie, in a place where magic rested, that I'd lost my sense of wonder. But I haven't, because some kinds of magic *are* still here. They're in us.

Slowly I peek my head around the doorframe. Though he's turned slightly toward us, his eyes are closed, his forehead smooth, mouth relaxed. His lips turn down naturally at the corners.

Nell would have loved this—she closed her eyes when she sang, too. She said when she sang, she felt real, instead of fake. I never knew what that meant until now. She was releasing a wall each time.

As the last strains of Brian's music fade into the night, I remember the first time I spoke to him, in the rain, and how direct his eyes were and how strange it was. Strange, because it felt like the first time any-one had looked at me.

He lowers the violin, eyes still closed, and the glitter showers down.

I sneeze. Blinking his eyes, like he's waking up, he turns to see me standing in the doorway and the curious faces peeking in behind me.

A flush rises up his neck as he realizes he's had an audience this entire time.

I shuffle into the room as he hastily lays the violin and bow on a chair and lifts a mug of water.

"You've got glitter all over you," he murmurs. "Like a vampire."

Because I don't know how to tell him it was him, I shake my head, coughing a bit as I inhale a few specks. "Do I? Super weird."

A line of people are making their way into the room, smiling hopefully. "You play so beautifully," a woman says. "Would you play some more? We'll sit quietly. It'll be like we're not even here."

"Um, well," Brian says, staring at the ground, the redness deepening. "I suppose I can."

And then I remember. "No," I say quickly. "He can't."

His brows pinch together at that, as the others let out sounds of disappointment. "One or two more songs," they cajole.

Everyone is looking at me then, wondering why I'm blocking their impromptu concert. We need to get to the church. I need a reason for him to leave. Something not suspicious and totally believable. I turn to look at him, at a loss, as he shrugs and takes a sip of his water, one hand already reaching for the violin.

"Brian and I are going to go make out," I say loudly.

Brian chokes on his water, spitting a mouthful back into the mug.

A lot of awkward throat clearing and eye aversions are going on in the crowd by the door.

Brian swallows, coughs again, and stares at me with a genuinely bewildered expression. "Um, are we?"

I reach for his hand and squeeze, hard. *Please. Also, I'm hurt.*

"Okay," he says, searching my face. I yank him toward the door and he trips on a chair. "Okay, off we go." Dazed, he follows where I lead.

The crowd parts to allow us through. No one says a word to stop us.

Well, that worked, though I pretty much want to die as we walk down the hall. Still, he doesn't let go of my hand. "I just said that to get you out," I mutter as soon as we've gained some distance.

There's a pause, and I find his gaze darting away from my lips. He clears his throat. "I gathered that. What's wrong? You feel antsy."

This slows my steps and I remember to breathe. "Everything's fine, but we have to leave."

We've reached the Visitors Lounge where my cat sits in a square made of masking tape probably created by Eleni. After I've closed the door, I pull up the tape to free Chad. "If I don't come back, know that Matty is alive, and eventually you'll find each other," I tell her. I lay her bag of food on the ground, with the top open, blinking back tears the whole time. I feel Brian watching me as I stroke her head, and she allows it. "Is there anything you need?" I ask him, sniffing. After my experience running with a backpack, I've made the decision to leave it behind, stuffing only the two-way radio into my pocket.

Brian shakes his head, scooping up his hoodie. Something falls from the pocket, drifting lazily to the floor. He hastily bends down to pluck it off the ground. It's a long dark coil. "Still finding bits of your hair everywhere," he says, with a weird laugh, shrugging one shoulder. He stuffs it back into his pocket, then clears his throat. "What about our weapons? They're with the gate guard."

I move to his side, taking his hand but afraid of the fluttery feeling in my stomach that caused so much hurt the last time, when it was crushed. "We'll leave them." I tug him over to the door I've spied in the corner. This one is subtle, a thin line in the plaster that you wouldn't notice at first.

As we face it, I look down at our joined hands, and then up into his face.

He had one of my curls in his pocket.

A grain of glitter sits in his eyelashes.

"What?" he asks.

This is the moment, the one I'll remember if anyone asks me when I knew.

"Your music was beautiful," I tell him, my gaze dropping to his lips. "It sounded like you. I didn't know it would sound like you."

He shifts uncomfortably. "I don't usually like playing for people," he confesses. "It's like everyone can see me. Everything I feel."

"Yeah, it's not great."

"But I feel . . ." He searches for the word. "Lighter?" He rubs some glitter from my cheek, peering at the sparkle on his thumb in a contemplative way. When he blows it away, he flexes his fingers, bending them, playing a melody in the air.

*This is what his power could be. The magic doesn't have to hurt.*

But concern flickers in his eyes as he meets mine. "Spencer, where are we going?"

"Do you trust me?"

"Yes." He doesn't hesitate.

I lead him through the door, shutting it before Chad can get through.

I hear her mewing as I look around at the small parking lot. I know where we are.

Quickly, because we have no weapons, I lead him down an alley and onto the sidewalk. There, we jog, and he shortens his steps to match mine.

But he tenses a bit as we ascend the steps to the church, and his hand tightens around mine. He enters first, standing slightly in front of me, as though he's expecting an attack.

Shandy, Angel, and Eleni turn at the sound of the door creaking open, the light of two dozen candles flickering over their faces.

Past the rows of wooden pews, at the front near the altar that she's lit, two small figures are locked in a tight hug. The straight, rigid lines of their bodies, the way I realize they both held themselves— stalwart in a hurricane—have released. They breathe like they've never breathed before, deep and gasping.

I touch a drop on my cheek, watching them. The person I want to hug is so far away from me, but everything I've done in the past few days, everything, is to get to him, to the moment the storm passes.

Daisy pulls away from her sister, gazing down the aisle at us as she wipes her cheeks. "Brian," she says unsteadily.

Brian stands frozen, his face curtained in shadow, throat working as he swallows. "Daisy?" A harsh sound escapes him, a sob.

The rush of sudden wind extinguishes the candles in a rippling wave seconds before the windows cascade inward in a shower of shattered glass. Not an explosion, an exhale.

In the pitch-dark, wood creaks as the church bends inward and shudders, before going quiet once more.

Nobody moves.

Daisy's voice breaks the silence. "Really, Brian?"

They're shouting. Well, they're whispering, but the tone is one of shouting, as Hyacinth stands to the side, looking from one to the other with a silent plea in her eyes.

I busy myself with relighting the candles and pretend not to be listening.

Brian towers over Daisy's slender frame. "Where the hell have you been?" he grinds out.

She juts her chin out, her finger poking him in the chest. "Where the hell have I been? Where the hell have *you* been?"

"I, unlike you, do not have the ability to find people," he says. "Was I supposed to use my ouija board, Daisy? You weren't at home. You didn't tell anyone where you were going; you never do. I had no idea where you were."

"When I leave the house, I don't consider whether you're going to throw yourself into some life-and-death battle before I make my decision. I don't know *everything*. Why does everyone think I know everything?"

"I was alone with Hyacinth and I needed you there."

"I thought you could handle yourself, Brian. Was I wrong?"

"I had no idea if you were alive or dead," he explodes. "I'm responsible for you and Hyacinth. And if I can't do that well, they will take you away from me, okay? I was—I am—worried *every single second*."

The delicate flames of the candles flicker as the altar trembles. Daisy ignores the groan of the pews straining against some unseen force, and says softly, "They're not going to take us. The paperwork keeps being deleted from their system and they keep having to start the process over. Weird how that keeps happening. Firewalls, am I right? So easy to get past." She tries a smile. "And if that fails, I will find another way."

For several beats, they stare at each other. Then Brian takes two steps forward and hugs her. His shoulders slacken as he breathes deeply, lips pressed together.

"I didn't mean to . . ." Brian's breath hitches and he gestures at the damage.

"I know," Daisy says. She's on the verge of tears, her arms hovering in the air before she pats him on the back.

*The scent of fresh dirt and mown grass fills my nostrils. A hand, my hand, brown and slender, but dry today because I haven't moisturized, haven't done anything normal or human or alive, slips over a fist so tightly balled it trembles. In front of us are two newly dug graves, gray stones engraved with names we know. He won't leave the cemetery, though everyone else has. He stays with me while I cry, hot tears stinging my face, already tight from all the other tears that have dried on my cheeks. He doesn't cry. He doesn't cry because someone needs to hold us together. Or they'll say he's unfit. I wonder if he'll cry later when he's alone. I know he won't.*

Shoes crunch through debris. Blinking, I stand, gripping the back of the bench in front of me, and the image fades. Of our hands held fast. *No. Their* hands. And I know this isn't the first time I've seen, felt, something that seemed like mine, but wasn't. I see Eleni's figure stalking around the church, back turned, like she can't watch them. Her feet scuff though broken windows as she peers out at the night. *Something is happening to me. I wish Matty were here.*

I watch Brian rest his chin on Daisy's head briefly. Like how Matty does with me.

"There are bad people out there," Brian mumbles.

"Okay," she says, sniffling. "Thanks for that newsflash, Brian."

He pulls back, rubbing his jaw. "Why did you take so long to find us?"

Daisy's hands are on her hips, annoyance creeping back into her face. "Let's see, the first thing I did was secure the Keys. I knew Parker and Matty don't carry theirs with them, so I went to her place first to make sure it wouldn't fall into the wrong hands."

"We sent Morrissey there two days ago," Brian says, arms crossed.

"I got Parker's Key maybe an hour after the fault line opened so he wouldn't have found anything," Daisy says. "Then I went looking for Matt. What have you been doing?"

"Trying to find Guardians, trying to stay alive," he says wearily.

Daisy bites her lip. "The Keys matter more."

Brian spins away, raking a hand through his hair. "You weren't there when he shot Parker," he says to Daisy. She flinches, though she must have gathered what happened, given that Parker isn't here. "He'd already killed Josh, and you and Matt were missing." Panic brightens his eyes as he looks out over the darkened church, then back at her. "That man murdered our parents."

Daisy inhales. Moisture pools along the bottom rims of her eyes. She closes them, and as she does, a weight bears down on her shoulders, a crushing pressure. I feel it. But Hyacinth slips her hand into her sister's, and as Daisy breathes, the weight dissipates a bit, until she meets his eyes again. "Tell me what happened."

As Brian and Daisy talk, I walk toward the back of the room, approaching Angel and Shandy, who sit in the center of the aisle, surrounded by votives and solemn vibes. "I really am sorry I didn't tell you everything," Shandy murmurs to him. "In my defense, I got distracted."

An image pops into my head instantly, of the library before it burned. They've sat like this before.

*Candlelight flickers in the depths of Angel's golden-brown eyes as his face inches closer and I—*

Heart hammering, I hurry past, steering clear of Eleni, who paces slowly in front of the windows. I sink down in a corner free of broken glass and lean my head against the wall, eyes closed.

I pull out the radio in my pocket. "Matty," I say into it, a whisper. "Please answer."

But of course there's nothing. There's nothing, and I don't know where to find him.

I let the radio drop into my lap, staring listlessly at it, remembering how my father would make us use these on ski trips when our phones didn't have service. "Where are you now?" he'd boom into it every three minutes. Always channel two, our family channel. I lift it, squint at the dial. I'm on channel one. I didn't check. And though I know it's useless, I switch it to two.

"Matty . . . Matty, are you there?"

Silence. I thump my head softly against the wall.

Nothing but silence. And static.

A voice. "Random girl."

My heart comes to a thudding halt, my fingers digging painfully into the plastic. And then I'm on my feet, breathing hard. "Who is this?" I say, loud enough that Brian whips around at the front of the church.

"I've been trying to reach you for days," the voice, a man's voice, says smoothly, not answering my panicked question. But he doesn't need to. I already know, my mind flashing back to that moment of putting the other two-way radio on my counter.

He was at my house. He went inside after we escaped.

"Matty, radio me on channel two if you come home," Ford says, reading my words back to me. He pauses before finishing. "Love, Siddy."

Eleni is the first to reach my side. "Turn it off," she says fiercely. "He doesn't know where we are. He can't hurt us—he's just a voice."

"Before you rush off," Ford says casually, like he knows. "There's something you need to hear."

"He's going to try to manipulate us," Eleni says in the brief silence, glancing up as the others crowd in around us. Eleni makes a grab for the radio just as someone speaks, and she freezes.

"I'm . . . I'm so sorry," Morrissey says, his voice breaking.

William James Morrissey III, who saved me once, who was injured but was supposed to be okay because he flew away to a safe house where no one would find him. We planned to meet him eventually. We're too late.

"They found me," Morrissey says, thick, through tears. "He's going to kill me if you don't . . . if you don't do what he says. Please. Please just do what he says. Please——"

Morrissey's voice cuts off.

My hand holding the radio shakes uncontrollably, and Brian takes it from me, his face a stony mask.

Ford has Morrissey. Morrissey is going to die. Another Guardian lost.

Daisy slowly raises her gaze to Brian's. "People have powers now," she says gravely. "We need to confirm."

I don't understand immediately until Brian lifts the radio to his lips. "What was my father's favorite dessert?"

When Morrissey speaks, his voice is a whisper. "Trick question. He was a baker who didn't like sweets. He was my buddy, you know. Before you. He was the father I always wished I had."

Daisy's breath hitches.

Brian looks away. "It's him."

And Ford's voice, pleasant now, drifts through the radio, "Tomorrow, noon. Town Center by the fault line. I've said from the beginning I'll let you live. Brian Aster, Shandy Ohno, and Eleni Christakos, bring your Keys and I'll keep that promise. Or don't show and I'll chain your friend to a lamppost and leave him to get eaten alive. If he dies, his blood will be on your hands."

He says nothing more. There's only static, and beyond that, the sound of my heartbeat in my ears.

Nobody speaks, staring at the radio like it's a live thing, a monster.

Eleni sets down her candle and paces, hands on her hips. "If we show up there, there's no way Ford lets any of us live," she says finally, her voice betraying no emotion. "It'll be a massacre."

Daisy takes a deep breath, holding tight to Hyacinth's hand. "We're not going to Town Center."

"Hold up, are you suggesting we leave Morrissey to be executed?" Shandy says in a low voice. "Is that what you're saying?"

Daisy meets his incredulous gaze. "We need to get that Key from Ford."

"How do you propose to do that, Daisy?" Brian interjects. "We faced him, we—"

But Daisy lifts her hand. "And we have to face him again," she says, though a quiver betrays her confident words. "We have to end this. We are the only ones who can."

"You want to launch an offensive," Eleni surmises, tilting her head.

"There's a problem," Shandy says, clearly not on board. "We don't know where he—oh."

Daisy raises a brow at him. "Souls have different energy than the shells do. I can see survivors scattered everywhere. I can see clusters, like the one at the elementary school." She pauses, her expression darkening. "There's a cluster on the mountain, too. He's at Mountain Ridge Academy."

Ford has a base. He and his followers need somewhere to sleep, somewhere to keep all the survivors they didn't kill. He chose Matty's alma mater, the school on the mountain for gifted kids, and of course he would. Of course he'd choose a place for the extraordinary.

"No one knows I'm with you," Daisy continues. "Not him, not his men. Ford has no idea we know where he is. That is our advantage. We won't be expected and we can control this situation. We'll go in tonight."

This has been her plan all along and the reason she wanted no one besides us to know she was here.

Though nothing on Brian's face reveals what he thinks, he says, "He can't be killed."

Daisy regards him thoughtfully. "Maybe we're approaching it wrong. Killing him may be impossible, but we don't have to. Between all of us and our powers, we can go in, find him when he's alone, and restrain him. While we're in there, we'll get Morrissey."

Shandy looks slightly mollified now that the plan doesn't include a human sacrifice, but Angel watches us with serious eyes, knowing it's not going to be that easy.

"You think Ford will just give us his Key?" I say slowly.

A small voice behind us says, "He can feel pain." When we all look back at Hyacinth, she merely lifts her shoulders.

Okay, so this plan involves torture. Eleni cracks her knuckles at this, so at least we have a volunteer.

Daisy crouches, pulling her backpack off and peering into it.

"Do I need to make bombs," she says to herself. "Probably, as a last resort."

We don't even ask.

She pulls a folded length of paper from her bag, spreads it over the ground, careful not to let Eleni's candle singe it—a student map of Mountain Ridge. I've only been there a couple times. She shakes a slew of jelly beans into her palm, placing seven, each a different color, at different locations on the map's surface. They look very cute, happy even. Not like they're about to get murdered. Maybe we'll be fine.

"Are the beans supposed to make the situation feel less dire?" Brian mutters. "Because they don't."

Ignoring him, Daisy says, "Given the number of Guardians present, we'll need the civilians to help. And given our limited timeframe, our plan hinges on him." Her gaze settles on someone over my shoulder.

Angel blinks at Daisy. "Wait, do you mean me?"

# CHAPTER 16

We go to a place in Wellsie everyone knows, but a place no one would go after a disaster when the last thing you're thinking of is the town's number one tourist attraction.

Angel brings us through a solid slab of mountain rock onto the thick ledge running behind the Llewellyn Falls, right where the water crashes into a pond so clear, it always looks like the sky is exploding.

Maybe it's the perfect place to be, though. A reminder that life is equal parts terrible and beautiful. And if we die tonight, some good things will remain, for years after us, maybe forever.

Daisy says most of the shells are concentrated in the valley below, in town, not up here. Our danger lies about a quarter mile up the mountain. Ford's base.

She wants to go after midnight, which gives us about three hours.

To chill, I guess. Literally. Behind the waterfall, the cold spray tickles our faces no matter how far back we edge. But Angel's pack is full of art supplies he pilfered from the elementary school. He makes sleeping bags to ward off the cold and a lantern that splays our shadows across the stone.

There's an issue. Not insurmountable. Angel has limited knowledge of Mountain Ridge. He can get us in, but once we're inside, we'll have to travel without shortcuts.

"You should make her stay," Eleni says to Daisy, loud enough for me to hear.

I don't have to look at her to know who she means.

Daisy shakes her head. "The person who stays has to have knowledge of Mountain Ridge, someone who can navigate your direction, and someone who can act fast if things go awry."

So definitely *not* me.

"I'll be staying here with Hyacinth," Daisy says.

"But I—" Hyacinth protests.

"No," Daisy and Brian say automatically, arms crossed.

"You can't keep doing this," Hyacinth bursts out, eyes flashing. "You can't protect me from everything bad in the world—"

"Sure we can," Daisy says.

"End of discussion," Brian snaps.

Hyacinth lifts her chin mutinously as her siblings stare at each other, share a single nod of solidarity, then walk off in opposite directions. Hyacinth can't win if they gang up, and she's got no argument. She's a child. She doesn't have a power. She retreats to the edge of the cave, sitting forehead to knees, and I suspect she's crying.

Eleni stalks up to me, Shandy, and Angel where we sit conversing in the lantern's glow. "You three," she barks. "My concerns about the plan exist on many levels, but the first and most major one is you having some kind of moral code."

Shandy glances at Angel. "If I found a briefcase full of money on the street, I'd return it," he admits.

But Angel shrugs one shoulder. "How much money are we talking about? And do I know how to launder money in this scenario? To be clear, if I found a snack someone left in a vending machine, there's a hundred percent chance I'd take it."

"Once, I stole a book from the library," I blurt out.

Eleni absorbs that. "We're gonna die," she mutters. "When you're in there, there are no gentlemanly rules of conduct. Go straight for the balls. Zero hesitation."

I tilt my head at Brian as he helps Hyacinth unroll her sleeping bag. "You're not concerned about him?"

Eleni's gaze flicks to Brian. "If it comes down to it, he'll kill," she says flatly, and she walks off, conversation over.

Before we left my house that day, I didn't think I had it in me to kill anyone. But I hadn't yet faced gunfire and flames and hordes of zombies. Nell wasn't dead, and I hadn't known the true consequences of magic. I'm not the same person anymore, and I don't know if that's good or bad. Morrissey might die unless we can save him. He might have died the moment after he provided proof of life.

We would probably all kill if it came down to it.

On my way to my sleeping bag, I pass Daisy standing by the waterfall, holding another lantern. When I look closely at the dim glow surrounding it, I see a rainbow shimmering among the droplets, like the remnants that used to remind us of what was possible.

Over the roar of the falls, I almost don't hear her. "I saw him," she says faintly to herself. "At a cabin in the woods on the east side of town. I didn't think to keep checking on him. I should have checked. I would have known when they took him."

I asked her earlier what it looks like, when she tracks people, and she said it's like she's a magnet looking for metal. Once she gets closer, the detection becomes more distinct. "When I get close to Brian, I hear music," she said. "When I locate Paul Ford, I sense a black hole."

"We can't know everything," I say to her now. "We're supposed to be kids."

Daisy jumps, not realizing I'd approached. She doesn't open her eyes. "Kids die," she says unsteadily. "People die all the time."

Her terror lies just under the surface, one squirrel rising up to attack the other.

*Mama's on the phone, talking to the mountain rangers about organizing a search party. Her voice is high, not like her normal one. Our neighbors are here, but they're not helping.*

*I'm supposed to sit quietly in the living room, but I slip out into the backyard, into the trees, and no one notices. Fat drops of rain fall from the leaves overhead. If anyone can find him, I can. We're alike. "Two peas in a pod," he always says.*

*I can do everything easily, but this is too easy. Because he's there, just beyond the forest's edge, just steps from home. It's Daddy, except it's not, not really. It's just his shell. And that's when I scream.*

"I've been through grief before," Daisy says, snapping me back. "There are things that got me through it, that continue to, but if those things are gone?" She turns to me with glasses speckled with moisture. From the falls, or maybe something else. "Tell me Brian will write a symphony. That Hyacinth will become an elite assassin. That I'll live in a tree house the way I've always wanted. And I'll fall in love. And I'll survive."

"You'll *live,*" I say, because living is different from surviving. Because I need to believe it too, that there will be an after, where I'll have the space to grieve Nell, and another, where I'll keep going.

Because if we don't win, if there is no after, it'll be my fault.

The reality is the plan doesn't hinge on Daisy or Angel. Guilt sinks deep into the spot between my shoulder blades. If we get that Key, only one person can use it to end this. And I don't know where he is.

I don't *have* to go on this mission. My power will only be useful if I need an attacker to sob uncontrollably. But I have to do something.

And when I'm huddled in my sleeping bag, facing the wall, barely touching the food I ordered from Angel, all I can think about is failing.

The rush of water gets softer the more I listen to it. I hear conversations fade one by one as the others fall asleep, but I stare at the wall.

Maybe an hour passes when a noise startles me. Close, like right next to me.

I sit up immediately, looking over my shoulder. It's a sound I've heard before.

Brian lies several feet away, close to me when everyone else has spread out. The lantern remains lit, outlining him in a bluish glow. He murmurs in his sleep, agitated, breathing rapidly. I hear a choked sob, and I scoot closer, reaching immediately for his hand.

I breathe, deep and slow, imagining snow again. Something light and fluffy. I imagine glitter hanging in the air.

Inching up beside him, I peer at his face as his brows unfurrow. I study the dark fringe edging his lids. So thick. Like fans, or brooms, or those rubber curtains in a car wash.

His eyelids open, revealing a foggy blue, and I struggle to fling myself back to my prone position.

Brian levers himself up on his elbows.

"Were you . . . watching me sleep?" he asks all scratchy voiced.

"No, because that would be creepy," I say. "I was looking at your eyelashes."

"Um. Okay." He looks at our clasped hands.

I snatch mine back. "You were freaking out in your sleep. I was . . .

trying to comfort you." I dive deep into my sleeping bag, but I still feel his eyes.

"I didn't realize I did that," he says finally. "Okay, well . . . I guess I'll go back to sleep."

I sneak a peek at him as he flops back down and stares at the cave ceiling.

"As you've obviously decided to let me fend for myself over here, what happens if I freak out again?" He turns his palm up, fingers open and slightly curled, and lets out a deep sigh. "It could get real bad."

I wind my arm outside its covering. After a moment, I slide my hand back into his. His fingers close around it.

I shiver. He shivers.

His head turns toward me. "Are you cold, Spencer?"

"Am I making you feel something? My anxiety? Grief? Everything?"

"I have anxiety, grief, everything—you can stop worrying about that," he says. The forehead lines are back. "Daisy is right. I should have done everything I could to get that Key from Ford."

"You did do everything you could. I was there."

"Rosie could sense danger. She knew something bad was coming. Do you think"—he swallows—"do you think they told Ford everything, and that's how they found Josh?"

I think of my parents, my mother who made me wear glowing stars when I jogged. My father who forced me to take a defensive driving course in case I ever hydroplaned. "If they had, it wouldn't have taken Ford three months to act. He probably found Josh because he used his powers, the way he found your dad. Your parents definitely didn't want you to die. They thought giving you magic was protecting you."

He hesitates. "I'm scared."

Daisy said my feelings are a gift. If that's true, Brian usually accepts. I want it to be *sharing*, though. I want to be the kind of person who gives comfort, too.

I roll closer against Brian's side and burrow in against him, rubbing my ear against his chest, because . . . because we're all going to die anyway. His arms wrap around me, engulfing me.

"Like a phagocyte," I mumble, and a soft rumble of laughter escapes him.

I hug him tighter. He's quiet for a long time, but I feel the moment it happens, his tension releasing, the rigid muscle and bone surrendering beneath my cheek. When the aura Ian said was a solid thing begins to melt. Someone's playing music somewhere. Faint, like it's traveling on a breeze. A bow draws long plaintive notes on a few strings, a melody echoing inside my chest, a little sweet and a little painful. It's not a song I recognize, though it feels familiar, familiar like the heartbeat against my ear.

"I know," he says, almost inaudibly. "I know that if I try to stop myself from feeling, it'll keep building up until it explodes. Until the magic explodes. I know that. It's just . . ."

*It hurts too much.* I want to tell him that I know, that I think I'm starting to feel him, feel everyone. "It's not always going to be this way," I whisper instead. Rose Aster's words.

A wave of sadness washes over me; it feels cold and smells like evergreen trees. It's his, and I accept the gift.

We remain like that, half-asleep, half-awake for a couple minutes, an hour.

A phone alarm goes off, and we're both sitting upright.

A slim shadow stands over us.

"It's time," Daisy whispers.

. . .

In the early aughts, a famous architect vacationed in Wellsie for a summer. On a hiking trip with his young children, he came across a crop of untouched forest on Mount Hemsworth's eastern side, where mountain springs poured melted snow into crystal pools. It was there, dreading the return to urban life, that he decided to buy this land and build a state-of-the-art school where gifted kids could learn in the peaceful embrace of nature.

A year later, he brought his vision to life. Made of mirrored glass, the school reflected the world in the same way that mountain spring had.

The admissions process was highly selective, bringing in kids from all over the state, some of whom would board in town during the week. They reserved some spots for local kids, but of course the architect's own children were automatically accepted.

I'm not sure what they do now. I think they're just rich, like, as a job.

As someone who'd need to support myself with labor, I'd never given much consideration to what I'd do when I was grown. I assumed I'd have time to figure it out. Years.

*I'm not ready to die, but the world won't take that into account.*

I climb up through Angel's door into a courtyard of stone paths, trees, and a whole pond full of lily pads, all of it surrounded by glass. There are six main hallways jutting out from this central courtyard, all connected by bridges in concentric circles. Like a spiderweb.

People who design oddly shaped buildings should think about what it might be like to perform a rescue mission inside them.

"Settle your nerves," someone utters next to me. Eleni.

That's not happening, and there's no space within me to feel bad about it.

"Okay, it's imperative you follow my instructions exactly," Daisy says through the in-ear pieces she gave us. From her Black-Ops kit, apparently. "Most of the men are guarding the outside perimeter of the school. The internal rotation will be back in approximately five minutes. Morrissey is at the end of the east hallway. The guards in that hallway will exit to the bridge in about thirty seconds. Once they do, you can go down that passage without being seen."

I picture her staring out into the trees, hand out in the direction of the school, fingers outstretched, sensing us through space. She can't hear us, but we can hear her, and she's watching over us.

There was a hiccup in Daisy's plan—Angel has been inside Mountain Ridge's walls exactly once, to an art show, in this very courtyard. The rest of his knowledge is limited to Daisy's map, which doesn't cut it in the real world. He could get us here, but movement inside is entirely up to us. Up to Brian, who's the only one here who knows the building well. Up to Daisy, who can see the enemy.

They have electricity due to Mountain Ridge's extensive solar panels, but at least here, on our bellies in the dark courtyard, we feel invisible. For the five seconds we stay.

"Go," Daisy says urgently.

And though I'm not ready, Brian leaps up, motioning for Eleni and Shandy to follow—the strongest physically. Angel and I move behind them. Brian opens the glass door soundlessly, then turns right into the walkway surrounding the courtyard. At the corner of the east hallway, he flattens himself against the wall, waiting. Heart hammering, I glance right, left, expecting men to march out at any moment.

"It's clear," Daisy says in my ear. "Go, but quietly."

My hiking boots squeak despite my efforts to run lightly, despite Eleni's murderous glance over her shoulder.

"Hold," Daisy says suddenly. "Guard near the courtyard, he might come down your hallway."

Brian stops us, and we stand, trembling, in the brightly lit hall, in plain view, breathing hard through our noses.

"He's going to pass the hallway entrance. Turn left onto the bridge for a second."

Brian darts through the door, holding it open for the rest of us to sprint onto one of the bridges circling the building and connecting all the hallways. We stand in the open air now, no roof, just a railing, and breathe in the scent of trees.

Angel takes hold of my hand, squeezing tightly.

"He's passed," Daisy says, relief in her voice. "Morrissey is in the room at the end, he—"

When Daisy stops short, Brian pauses, his hand on the door handle.

"Wait, he's on the move," Daisy says then. "Morrisey's on the move down the hall, coming straight toward you. He's alone. There are no guards with him."

"Now's our chance," Brian mutters, and he and Shandy push through the door into the hall with Eleni at their heels.

Angel and I skid into the hallway behind them to see Morrissey limping slowly in our direction, eyes on the tiled floor in front of him. His head jerks up at the sound of us.

The last time I saw him, his clothes, soaked in blood and rain, were plastered to his body. Now he wears a clean, button-down shirt and trousers, looking like a less attractive Timothée Chalamet. Still wounded, but alive.

Morrissey stops in his tracks, blinking rapidly, as though unable to comprehend us somehow materializing in front of him. "How did you—? W-what are you doing here?" he manages.

"We've come to get you out," Shandy whispers.

Brian glances over his shoulder, down the hallway toward the courtyard. "Follow us. We've got to go."

Morrissey stares at us with wide eyes, not moving to join us. Instead he takes a step back, breathing unsteadily.

And in my ear, Daisy mutters more to herself, "Flight would be ideal right now. I wonder how he escaped his room."

Eleni's gaze is locked with Morrissey's, and comprehension flickers in the cold green depths of her eyes. Her lips curl as she utters, "Oh shit," and advances toward him, hands balling into fists. "You little bitch."

Morrissey takes another step back, and another.

"You joined them," Brian says, voice hoarse.

Morrissey's lips tremble at the question, gaze pleading. "I don't want to die, Brian. We can't win this. You know we can't. They . . . they said they wouldn't kill me if I joined them, if I transferred my Guardianship, if I . . ."

"If you helped bring us in," Brian finishes.

"If you give up your Guardianships, they won't kill you," Morrissey hurries to say. "We can all live."

"Why are you standing there?" Daisy asks. "Ford is two hallways over in the north wing. Pick up the pace."

She doesn't know. She doesn't know Morrissey betrayed them.

Shandy hasn't said a word, but there's a new hollowness in his eyes.

Emptiness is something you feel. When the flutter of hope goes quiet, you feel its absence, you miss it like something vibrant and alive just died. My gut wrenches, searching the space for one glimmer, but there's nothing left.

I don't know Morrissey. This pain isn't mine.

Angel inches slowly toward the nearest wall, shoving his backpack straps off his shoulders.

But Brian throws Morrissey violently backward with a sweep of his arm.

Morrissey hits the ground with a cry, his body sliding several yards. But as Brian pins him in place, he's already screaming. "Here! They're here!"

"Guards," Daisy is gasping. "Guards on the move. Get out of there."

The doors to the bridges swing open and men file into the hallway, cutting Angel, Shandy, and me off from Brian, Eleni, and Morrissey.

I grip Angel's arm, but he's already moving, lifting a can of spray paint from his bag and shaking it hard.

But there's the sound of running footsteps, as a line of guards, guns drawn, crosses the hallway entrance by the courtyard, trapping us. One of them shouts a warning and I throw my hands up in surrender even as Angel faces the wall, paint can raised.

A gun fires.

Angel flinches and goes still.

But he doesn't fall.

Shandy stands in front of him, blinking at the guards, that bleak expression still on his face.

He can see bullets. He can move fast enough to dodge them.

Or block them.

I feel the impact, already sagging to the ground, unable to breathe, as my hands clasp at the searing pain ripping through my chest. But my hands are dry.

There is no wound. Not for me.

Above me, Shandy staggers once, his hand brushing his chest and coming away painted red. "Seriously?" he says, and crumbles to the ground.

In the echo of the shot, it's Morrissey I hear gasping. "No. You promised. You promised me."

*The world comes in flashes—a harsh overhead light, a ceiling, a face hovering over me, in and out of focus. Something's crushing my chest. Can't breathe. Can't breathe . . .*

As the pain in my chest morphs from a suffocating weight to a burning numbness to nothing, gloved hands grab me by both arms, dragging me to my feet, hauling me backward toward the rest of the guards. They rip out my in-ear, and Daisy's panicked voice is gone.

But I hear thuds, crunches, pained cries, as Eleni fights her way through the bridge guards to get to us. She twists a man's arm, breaking it, and he sinks to his knees with a bloodcurdling scream.

Suddenly all of them, including Eleni, come sailing at us, crashing into the men holding me. We all go down.

On my belly on the ground, a tangle of bodies weighing my limbs down, I twist my head toward Brian.

He alone remains standing, his arm stretched toward us, his face a mask of fury.

Morrissey crawls on the ground, hand reaching toward Shandy, his face twisted in horror. "You promised you wouldn't kill them . . ."

He speaks to the men, pleading, as if they care. But his voice breaks, as he's dragged back. By Brian.

Brian has Morrissey up in the air, throwing him hard against a wall and pinning him there. And as more guards sprint in from the bridge, Brian freezes them in their steps, guns ripping from their hands and skidding over the floor.

Shandy isn't looking at them. Instead, he looks up at Angel, who clutches him against his chest. Blood spreads over Shandy's chest, pooling around their bodies. There's too much of it. Shandy is gasping, face leached of all color.

*Pretty. He's so pretty. And I didn't have enough time.*

A man's knee has settled in the middle of my back, keeping me on the ground, bringing me back to the cold floor under my cheek.

Eleni reaches us and in seconds has him by the throat. But she goes still, staring down the barrels of a dozen guns pointed at her.

Angel looks up from Shandy, his golden-brown eyes glazed with panic, as Shandy's chest rises and falls in quick, short breaths. He wouldn't draw guns earlier, when Eleni asked, afraid a gunfight would lead to this very thing. His eyes dart to his bag of art supplies several feet away. He lifts one hand in surrender, dripping with Shandy's blood, but his gaze locks with mine.

There's no choice. He has to leave us. And I nod. *Get him out.*

Angel's other hand moves, just one finger, drawing a line in the blood.

*A*, he writes. *M. P. Letters.* He repeats them. *A. M. P. I don't know what that means?*

"Grab him," someone bellows behind me.

But both of Angel's hands are in the puddle of blood now, sweeping through it, making a circle around his and Shandy's bodies.

When the men start shooting, Angel and Shandy are gone, falling through the floor.

By the time the men stumble toward that round red door, it's disappeared, revealing tile and a few splatters of blood, the only evidence they were ever there.

Through the line of guards struggling against his hold, Brian sees me on the ground. Eleni sinks down with her hands up. There have to be twenty men here. *Too many.* As I struggle to my knees, they still grip my arms. Someone wrenches my hair, and I let out a cry.

Brian's eyes darken, rage burning black.

The air explodes around him, like a bomb detonating, sending a massive wave radiating outward, taking everything and everyone down with it.

Wind whistles in my ear and I'm digging my fingertips against tile, grappling for something to hold on to, to keep from flying away. Men peel off me like shingles in a storm, slamming into the walls, hairline fractures spider-webbing around them.

The ceiling is cracking. Bits of plaster spiral away into the hurricane the hallway has become. The floor moves beneath me as the building rattles. Glass shatters, blasting to pieces like those windows in the church.

*It's too much power. He can't control it.*

When I force my head up, eyes stinging, Brian stands in the center of a tornado of debris, his whole body shaking. He turns slowly to face Morrissey, who still hangs against the wall. Teeth gritted against the pain, Morrissey squeezes his eyes closed at Brian's approach.

"Look at me," Brian snarls. A thick slab of drywall falls at his feet, crumbling into pieces.

*He's going to bring the whole building down on top of us.*

I'm dragging myself forward on my stomach, against the wind's current, inch by inch. "Brian," I gasp. "Brian, stop."

A chunk of ceiling falls, and I cover my head as it lands mere feet away.

Brian doesn't hear me, not over the raw sound ripping from his throat. He braces one hand against the wall as the other wraps around Morrissey's throat. "Was it worth it?"

When Morrissey opens his eyes, filled with tears, he whispers, "Will it be worth it for you?"

To kill him, he means.

As the walls bend inward, Brian's hand falls away, his legs buckling beneath him. Morrissey sinks to the ground beside him.

But I've reached him, cupping my hands around his fist. "Brian."

His face turns in my direction, gaze liquid and filled with pain.

This is what Daisy feared, what he always feared: the whole world coming down when his walls did.

I don't try to suppress him. I just hold his hand as he feels all of it. "You told me every person makes an impact in some way. We change one another. But you get to choose the impact."

The floor still vibrates beneath me, but it slows, growing gentle.

"You decide who you want to be," I say, holding his hand to my cheek. "The magic will show that."

A shudder runs through his body once, before he slumps to the ground in a faint.

The school, his school, seems to let out a sigh before it stills, dust and fragments drifting down from overhead like snow.

Footsteps sound at the entrance of the corridor.

"Get up," a man says calmly, and I keep my eyes closed because I know that voice. It is in my head every day.

There's a bustle of motion as men stumble to their feet, muttering apologies.

"Call the powered individuals back from Town Center," Paul Ford continues. "Clearly, it's no longer necessary to camp them there."

Eleni's voice, quiet but menacing, comes then. "If anyone touches me, I'll break every bone in their hand."

"You can't break mine," Ford says. "Eleni Christakos, it's a pleasure."

There's a sound, like a puff of air, a wet splat, and I force myself to look at him. Pale blond hair lies combed back from his forehead, and his eyes are the same shade of gray as the fancy suit he wears. Too fancy, like no one told him the dress code.

"Charming," Ford says, casually producing a handkerchief to wipe her spit from his face.

Eleni stands, tall and uncowed even with her hands up and guns pointed at her heart.

"Keep your distance," Ford orders. "She can't fight bullets no matter how strong she is. Separate her from her people. Her power only works if she has someone to protect." As they jab her forward, down the hall and away from me, she looks back, but Ford blocks her view. He stares down the hall, his gaze lowering to me, to Brian.

I look him in the eye, a man I would have passed on the street with zero awareness, the same way he would have passed me. Someone standing in line at the bank. Someone whose coffee order would be for Paul F. because Paul isn't an unusual enough name to stand on its own. Someone I'd take notice of if his breakfast order was a bacon, egg, and cheese without the cheese, because who does that? And then the moment would pass and I'd forget him just like that.

Except I can't forget a killer.

His men are hauling me up. I cling to Brian's hand until we're ripped apart.

Ford saunters up to me, hands in his pockets.

He nods at Brian. "Sedate him and keep him that way."

Someone crouches down, producing a hypodermic needle, and I struggle, but the hands gripping my upper arms tighten like manacles.

Though fear churns my stomach, I don't look away as Ford smiles at me. "We meet again," he says.

# CHAPTER 17

*I* focus on his pores. Close up like this, it's the only part of him that won't scare me. Better than the mild smile. The blank eyes the color of pond ice deep below the surface.

"Take him away," Ford tells his men.

Next to me, Brian is a limp mass. They lift him roughly, carrying him out through the crowd, and I don't know where they're taking him, or where they took Eleni. Swallowing back my panic, I rack my brain for something, anything, to do. Daisy and Hyacinth are back at the falls, and Angel left to save Shandy. *He won't know where we are. He won't have been there. He can't come back for us.*

A man steps up to Ford, murmuring something in his ear.

"Daisy Radcliffe-Aster is no longer MIA and she's at Llewellyn Falls," Ford muses. "I suppose she's how you found me." Obeying some silent command, several of the men jog off, and I press my lips together, praying they've already run.

"The boy goes by the name of Angel?" Ford continues, listening to his man. "He can't get back in, not without knowing where he's going."

*How does he know this?* My heart thuds painfully in my chest as I glance at the man, small with thinning hair, only to find his dark beady eyes boring into mine.

"What is her power?" Ford asks him.

The man's eyes narrow for a moment, and when he speaks again, it's loud enough for me to hear. "It's useless. She makes people feel what she's feeling. And more recently, she feels what they're feeling as well."

Hearing him say this out loud, this thing I might've always known but never said aloud is such a small thing, but it matters more than they could ever know. *It goes both ways. It always has. If I let it.*

But it's a momentary relief as it sinks in that this man knows things, things he shouldn't, like he's plucking them straight from my head.

"We'll start with the Christakos girl," Ford says, and waves a hand at his men. "Take this one to the cell block. We'll talk later," he adds, as though I might feel slighted to be deemed less important.

I've been dismissed, and they're dragging me away. I don't look back, but I hear it when Ford says, "You did well," and I know whom he's speaking to. He's the man I let into my home, who wore my father's sweater. A man who saved me once. And maybe I saved him today, too, though he sentenced us all to death.

As I'm propelled forward, my feet slip on a slick patch—Shandy's blood—and I won't know if Angel got him to Dr. Klein or if Shea can even heal something of this magnitude. I trip through bits of wall and ceiling, over a crack in the floor where the tiles have tented, to the courtyard where I see two men open the door Angel made, the door to the falls.

*Daisy. Hyacinth.*

But we're past it, even as I crane my neck, straining to hear their voices, to know if they've caught them, too. My breath comes faster, rough against my dry throat. They shove me more forcefully.

*What hallway are we in?* I catch a glimpse of intact white walls, classroom doors.

We turn into a new corridor, this one sporting dark wood panels and doors with small windows revealing cluttered offices lined with bookshelves. I glimpse a gold name placard on a door. A faculty wing—it must be.

"Occupied," someone mutters—the man holding my upper arm tight enough to bruise. He pauses to peer into a darkened office. "This one looks vacant. I thought this whole row was full."

The men in front of me come to a halt and I just manage to stop myself from colliding with their backs.

These doors usually don't lock from the outside, but they've installed metal bolts. For survivors. For prisoners. For me.

One of them slides the bolt over and opens the door.

"No," I whisper. "Please." But he's already throwing me inside with enough force that I hit the desk in the middle of the room.

I spin, rushing to the door as it slams and the lock clinks. Pressing my palms to the smooth wood, I stare out into the black-masked face until he turns away.

The thunder of footsteps fade as they retreat back down the hall.

I'm alone. We all are. It's over.

Turning around, I lean my back against the door and take deep quivering breaths.

A sound breaks through my panic, a sharp gasp.

At first I see only a desk stacked with books, the shadow of a chair behind it. But in the darkness, one of the curtains framing the window seat moves.

A flash of white, a translucent shape, flickers in and out of focus.

She appears out of thin air, sitting with her knees hugged to her chest, wearing a white sundress that's not even wrinkled, not a single rusty smear of dried blood. Her hair lies over her shoulder in a shining gold river. Those eyes, ones I know as well as my own, widen. They're wet, glistening, as she stares at me like I'm a figment of her imagination.

Nell's lips tremble. "You cut your hair," she says.

*She's not here. She's dead. She's gone.*

My fingernails dig into my palms as I look at her, and something huge bubbles up in my chest, catching in my throat, choking me.

When the sob explodes out of me, I sink to the floor, weeping like I'll never stop.

The last time I cried like this, she was there.

When Matty was sixteen, he left home for a while, truly running away, and I couldn't go with him because he didn't want me to, because it was real. We don't talk about it; sometimes I forget it ever happened. I remember it now, though. How he left after a fight with our dad, and it was raining. It was the first time I saw my mother cry.

For an entire summer, he was gone. He did call our mom, telling her he was with friends in Vermont. I didn't know if he'd come back, but he did. He did, and the moment I saw him, I walked out of the house, all the way to Nell's. And on her porch, I cried. He promised he would never leave again, and I believed him, and I put it out of my mind. He didn't leave again, until now.

Nell's beside me on the floor, sitting on her heels, white skirt in a perfect circle around her. Ethereal, like an angel come to life. I thought that the first time I saw her in the first grade. She's turned on the desk lamp and I can see the smattering of freckles across her nose. Ghosts can't turn on lamps. Ghosts don't have freckles.

My breath comes in quick hitches that don't bring in enough air, right before more bouts of sobbing. The pattern repeats. "Can't. Breathe," I force out between gasps.

"You're hyperventilating," she says softly, putting a hand on my back and rubbing lightly. "Breathe through your nose."

It's been so long since I've heard her voice that it's strange, like I'm hearing her from across a great distance, but also like no time has passed at all, like we've always been here, sitting across from each other, our spirits waiting for our bodies to catch up. I suck air through my nose though it feels like I'm suffocating, but her eyes are so calm, blue, like the sky. She pushes in one of my nostrils, so I'm only breathing through one. And as I look at her through the blur of tears, I'm afraid she'll feel this too. One hand pressed to my thundering heart, I manage to say, "I . . . project. Can . . . you . . . feel it?"

She tilts her head, face softening. "A bit, but it's like a memory. I used to have panic attacks sometimes. You know that."

I didn't. She never told me.

So I whisper something I never told her. "I'm . . . afraid I'm not enough. I'm afraid everyone will see that, even the people I love. And when they do, they'll find someone better, someone extraordinary. And I'll be alone."

She lets out a long exhale. "I know." Gently, she releases my nostril and my next breath is unbroken. A smile curves her lips. "Why are you like this?"

At my own flicker of a smile, she hands me a bottle of water. "From the desk drawer. But we should probably ration it."

I nod grimly, taking a tiny sip to soothe my throat. "Eventually one of us is going to have to pee in a corner. When it happens, let's make a pact to never speak of it again."

Her smile falters slightly. "Maybe that's not always the best idea."

Maybe it isn't. I press my fingertips to my eyes where the skin is hot and puffy, to my cheeks stiff with salt trails. The explosion of built-up pressure, the grief, left a residue of guilt behind. "I thought you were dead. I think I glimpsed it. Finn said——"

Suddenly she's launched herself across the space, gripping my upper arms. "You saw Finn? Where? He's alive?"

I nod slowly. "He's alive. He's at Stony Peak Elementary, in a shelter for survivors."

Her hands slip from my arms and she's sinking back against the desk, covering her face with trembling hands. But the smile peeking out through her fingers is wide and beautiful.

*A gust of wind washes over us, bitingly cold, filled with tiny snow crystals. He holds me as I wobble on the ice. Wisps of my hair blow across my face, across his. "I love you," he says, hot breath against my ear. It's the first time he's said it. And there's no cold anymore, just a deep warmth filling my chest, wrapping my heart in a blanket. "I love you too," I say.*

The bright white of that afternoon fades to dim light, and the icy wind dissipates to the stagnant air of an office. It's spring, not winter. But I know what this is, now. It's not my memory, it's hers.

*There's a flash of limbs and gaping mouths, a panic engulfing every thought and emotion, a scream ripping from my throat.*

"You can get out of here," I say, realization dawning. "You can go to Finn. You disappeared that day. That's how you survived."

She lifts her head, sweeping aside that length of blond hair, to frown at me. "What do you mean? Those *things* were clawing at me and I just . . . ran. I ran through the horde and kept running until I couldn't run anymore."

I blink at her. "You can't run through a solid horde—believe me, I've tried. No, you had to have physically, like, poofed." As she shakes her head, I push myself to my feet, hands on hips. "You literally appeared out of thin air five minutes ago. You know that, right?"

Nell pushes herself to her feet and walks straight at the door. "Ow," she mutters as she hits it. Turning, she spreads her hands wide. "I would know if I could become both invisible and incorporeal. I've been here this entire time."

"Well, you're solid *now*," I say peevishly. "You weren't before. And you weren't that day. So you need to figure out how you did it. Maybe it's only when you're scared."

"You don't think I've been scared this entire time?" Nell cries. "All I know is I ran until I got lost in the woods, woods that appeared out of nowhere, I might add, and then I saw . . ." She clears her throat. "I saw Adam O'Brien."

"He survived?" I burst out. "Of course he did."

"Yeah, well, he told me he heard people were holed up at Mountain Ridge, that it was safe this high on the mountain. He led me here, and the next thing I knew, I was locked in a room for days. There are others on this floor—I've knocked on the wall and they knock back, but that's it." She shrugs helplessly. "Just so you know, I have *already* peed in here, Siddy, in that vase over there."

I tactfully do not look at the vase in the corner. In the silence that follows, I rise, leaning my back against the door. "Adam joined them," I say faintly. "He was out collecting survivors. He brought you here and locked you up." Rage builds somewhere deep inside me as it all clicks into place. "It was a punishment. For rejecting him."

She perches on the edge of the desk, but her face is turned away. "Yeah" is all she says.

I know what she's thinking, the words on the tip of her tongue. *It's not as great as you think to be me.*

"Are we going to talk about what happened?" Her voice is quiet, though there's an edge to it.

"Now?" I say, pacing the entirely too tight confines of the office. "Is this really the time?"

"Why, is there somewhere else you need to be?" she says coolly.

"Yeah, actually," I mutter. But I can't go find Brian or Eleni. I'm trapped in a room with no way out. When she doesn't say anything, I gather she's waiting for me to start.

I face the wall, not looking at her, shoulders by my ears. "Finn told me what happened with Adam and the other guys on the team, that he didn't mean for the whole school to know about the letter. But that doesn't change the fact that it was humiliating." It all comes rushing back. How it felt to walk through the school hallway and hear whispering, laughing. How the support I would usually have wasn't there because she was on the enemy side. And how, for the weeks afterward, I understood why Adam was such a jerk to me. After you're embarrassed in front of the world, time is endless, and you can't snap your fingers and be over it.

Pressing a palm to the back of my neck, damp at the memory, I say what I've always known. "I know it was wrong to be mad he didn't like me that way. No one is owed that. But"—I turn to point at her—"you don't know what it's like to be humiliated. To share a part of yourself you never have before, only to be mocked for it. It made me never want to try again. I felt like I was right all along."

Though she presses her lips together, they tremble. Her eyes lower. "Right about what?"

"That it was never going to be different for me," I say, voice cracking. "That I'd always be an insignificant sidekick. I'd never be a person who was special in my own right, who had something just for me."

At this, Nell shoves off the desk. "Sidekick? It has *never* been that way. You're the one who talks in a group. You're the one they listen to." It's her turn to pace. "And if this is about boys, oh my God. Millions of people in this world will think you're hot. It's math. It's a statistical certainty. They just aren't here, in this tiny homogenous bubble of humanity. Are you really so mad about that? It's one town. It's Wellsie."

It's the dismissal I'd always feared, and I explode. "Don't say that. Don't say it doesn't matter. Because I have to live here, Nell. I have to deal with existing in an extremely white town where no one really sees me, and it doesn't matter if it's not forever. It's been seventeen years. That's a long time to 'just not care' that I'm invisible here. To boys and everyone else."

For a long moment, minutes, I think, we sit in the echo of those words.

Nell keeps gulping. It's that thing she does when she's trying not to cry. And I feel bad. It's why I've never said this. I didn't want to make this difference between us a solid thing. But I should have anyway.

"When people here ask me where I'm from," I say thickly. "Or if I can read a Chinese menu. Or if my parents love me less because I'm Asian—like, they literally ask me this—I feel like I can't talk to you about it. Like, maybe you'd shrug and say, 'It's just the way Wellsie is,' as though that makes it less bad. As though what I feel doesn't matter. As if the whole world isn't like this, which it is."

Nell stares at her hands, still swallowing. "I-I'm sorry. I shouldn't have . . . I know it matters. I-I just w-wanted to make it better, less hurtful somehow. I didn't want you to think everyone here saw you that way. To think I saw you that way. I don't want you to think I'm like them."

"But you already know I don't. That's why you trivializing it is worse."

"I want to be the kind of person you can come to about anything," Nell says, so quietly I almost don't hear. "But right now, I don't even know what to say because . . ."

Because we're not exactly friends now.

I was worried I'd never get the chance to say so many things, when I thought our separation was final, but now I can. "Maybe we can be friends again," I say in a small voice, feeling her peek at me from behind her curtain of hair. "But I'm not rejecting boys for you any-more. Not just boys. When people in general are literally kissing your ass, I'm going to stare at them and slowly arch one brow."

"A of all, no one has ever literally kissed my ass," she says, sniffing. "B of all, you can't arch one brow. I've seen you try, and it's ridicu-lous."

I ignore that. "No, it's a fact. I don't know if it's because you're pretty or rich or aloof in a way that makes people want to earn your approval, but I want to stab something every time they wear something you wear, or like something you like—no one should put ketchup on apple slices, okay? And next time they take a random selfie with you and post it on Instagram with the caption *here with my best bitch!!!* I'm commenting with a series of skull emojis."

"No, that was so embarrassing!" she cries, wiping furiously at her eyes. "You can't actually want that to happen to you!"

"The point is, I have good qualities too. I'm better than you at Flip Cup."

"That one time you drank, you mean, and Matty had to pick

you up off a street corner," she says, glaring at me. "Is it my turn? Because—"

"No, no it's not," I snap. "I'm not done. I don't like your mother. Now I'm done."

She crosses her arms. "Okay, let's roll right past the fact that I don't like my mother, and talk about your self-absorption and wild insecurity." And when I shrink back, she levels a finger at me. "There are lots of things you're good at and I'm not. I *like* that about you. I liked you the moment I met you. I was alone at recess and suddenly there was this weird girl who was like, 'Oh hello, you don't talk much, let me fill the silence with endless chatter about myself to ease the tension.'"

I scowl at my hands. "I feel like that's not necessarily a good trait."

"It was a good trait to me," she says quietly. "You made it easy to talk to you when it's never easy for me. You became my friend when I was a lonely child who didn't have anyone. It's not about being better, Sid."

She knows. She always has. That I've wondered why some people were chosen to be extraordinary while others would never be. Ford was right when he asked me that question. It would come to me in odd moments throughout the day. I would be looking at someone in a magazine. I would be looking at my family. Or my friends. I would think it wasn't fair.

When I don't respond, she says, "No one has everything. You said you want something just for you, but no one can *be* that for anyone. If I just had you, I'd have no one to go to hockey games with or go fishing with." I make a face, and that finger is back in my face. "I love violent sports and I love fishing, okay? And if I just had Finn, I'd have no one to watch k-dramas with or eat straight trash with. I wouldn't have my best friend."

And the tears are spilling down her cheeks now, punctuated with quick little sniffs. There's an ache behind my own eyes, a tightness in my throat. I remember this feeling. When you're missing something you used to have, a limb, gone, except you feel it in the space it used to be.

"People give you different things and you need all of them," she says then. "I like that you aren't like me. You think I'm perfect, but I'm not. You make up for the things I lack and vice versa." She looks at me for a long moment, studying my haircut, and decides not to say anything about it. "Do you know what I did when Finn asked me out?"

"Did you make a pro/con list?" I ask, thinking of her anxiety every time she had to make an important life decision.

She shakes her head. "I asked myself, 'What would Sid do?'"

Anything else I was going to say disintegrates in that moment.

"I was going to say no at first," she says, voice lowering to a whisper. "But I've always wanted to be more like you."

*I mean, what?*

"He didn't handle it right, the letter," she says with a sigh. "But I thought about what you would do if you were me. Once the truth came out, that he never laughed at you, that Adam and those guys on his team betrayed his trust, I thought you'd be angry at me for saying no."

If it had been me, if the roles were reversed, I would have said yes immediately, and that's the truth. I'm more selfish than she is. "If my letter had worked and Finn and I lived happily ever after, you were going to secretly like him forever and never say anything." She pauses for a moment and nods. Something leaves me then, a pent-up tension I didn't know I was carrying until it's gone. "Why are *you* like this? You're so shy. If I looked like you, I'd walk around in slutty clothes all the time. You're not like this when you sing."

A flush spreads over her cheeks. "You can walk around in slutty clothes whenever you want. And singing is different. When I'm onstage, I'm not me. I'm who they think I am. I'm who I want to be." When I grimace at that, she says, "I relied on you for a lot. I saw that when you were gone. I let you do the things I didn't want to do."

She moves to stand beside me, back against the door, and we both slide down it. Tentatively, I let my head tilt against hers, the way I used to. "We're both insecure," I say. "We should probably work on that."

She nods.

It's not as hard as I thought it would be, now that the moment is here, but my voice wavers. "I'm sorry I hurt you. I'm sorry I did it over a dude I had no claim over."

"Over a *jock*," she points out.

"I wasn't a person who could handle it then." I'm not sure if she'll understand what I mean. "Maybe that's not okay. But maybe we all suck sometimes and can be forgiven anyway."

"I forgave you a long time ago," she whispers.

"I forgave you like a couple days ago."

She lets out a sound, part snort, part sob.

I don't know if we're okay now. But I think she's a better friend than I am. Maybe, in this moment, she's making up for what I lack.

We don't say anything for a time, breathing together. There's nowhere to go and nothing to do for a couple blessed minutes. Exhaustion clings to every muscle, tugs at my eyelids, but I feel lighter than I have in a long time.

Eventually, footsteps sound at the end of the corridor, growing louder as they grow closer. I'm glad I got to have this moment, that she and I aren't broken at the end.

"What now?" she whispers fearfully, as the boots come to a halt outside the door and the bolt clicks.

Eyes still closed, struggling to keep my voice even, I say, "Well, I've gotten myself into something very bad." Despite my best efforts, my voice cracks. "Just know that Finn is alive. You can figure a way out of here. Survive, okay? For me."

Her eyes widen at that last part, as the closed door pushes at our backs, and a voice barks, "On your feet."

We leap up as the door shoves open, and a man in black lifts his gun in warning in case we try to run.

"Who were you talking to?" he growls.

I blink at him for a second, barely stopping myself from looking to my right, where Nell should be, where I'm guessing she's not anymore.

There's an almost imperceptible gasp next to me.

Images flash quicksilver through my mind—Nell disappearing in a horde, Nell seeing Adam O'Brien, someone she knew, Nell disappearing when the men were here, reappearing when it was me.

"No one," I say shakily. "Myself."

He steps back into the hall, gesturing with his gun to walk ahead of him.

"People you don't know," I say under my breath, not moving my lips. "Strangers. Crowds."

"What was that?" he says impatiently.

"Nothing." I walk out of the office without looking back.

He leaves the door unlocked.


They always tell hikers to tell someone where they're going in case they get lost on the mountain. Because someone died up here once.

This man is going to open a door leading to the outside. Any second, he'll take me through the dark. I won't be able to see where I'm going, but eventually we'll stop in some secluded place, surrounded by trees. No one will know what happened to me. If my parents and Ella get back into town eventually, they won't know where I am to say goodbye.

Yet we don't head outside, remaining instead in the labyrinth of this building, and I'm not sure that's good or bad. I should be counting my steps, memorizing the turns. A sign on the wall directs us to the west hall. There are no breadcrumbs in my pockets. Brian and Eleni won't know where I am any more than I know where they are.

*They could be dead.*

The gun pokes into my back, bringing my entire body into focus. Clothes have weight, they're too tight, they cling in patches of sweat. Hairs I don't usually feel stand up straight, and every breeze travels down their lengths straight to the skin.

His eyes bore into the back of my head. And despite the stiffness in my neck, the way I'm too afraid to move a muscle, I keep wanting to look over my shoulder, to study his face and see if he would actually shoot me if I made a sudden movement, if I run. He tenses when I'm unable to stop myself from looking back at him. He's jumpy, eyes darting nervously away. One arm wipes his brow as he prods me forward. I don't recognize his face, not that I'd know what to do if I did. But I forget it the moment I turn back, as though my mind is unable to hang on to anything except for the moisture on my upper lip and the tightness of this thin passage we turn down now—an alley, narrow enough that I could touch the walls if I extended my arms. The door at the end drifts closer.

*Radio Lab.*

Matty had a show that aired during prime time where he played nothing but nineties grunge and occasionally took calls where he gave dubious advice. Last year, I called in with a question about asking a boy out and he instructed me to try slipping him a note, then never speaking to him again. That didn't work out great in retrospect. But I cling to this memory when the door opens and I'm flung inside, even though I can't feel him in this room lined with CD cases. There's no one I love here.

Despite what must be newly installed bars on the outside, the windows have been opened all the way. The night air dries my sweat in an instant. My escort shoves me into a chair in the center of the room. I perch on the hard seat, brutally awake and shivering.

Ford stands on the other side of a long table. Beside him, a man sits, hands folded in front of him. It's the beady-eyed man, the one who plucked thoughts from my mind like scraps of paper from a bowl. But my gaze drifts beyond him to the rectangular pane of glass in the wall and the girl sitting alone in the recording booth.

*Eleni.*

There's a momentary relief—that she's not bruised or dripping blood—until I realize she's blindfolded, hands cuffed to the arms of her chair. Periodically, she twitches, jerking her chin left, right, as though she's listening to something, but she doesn't react as the door closes behind me in this outer room.

Gripping the edges of the chair to stop my hands from shaking, I stare into the gray eyes across the table. There's a spark of recognition in my mind, like I've seen these eyes before, but not on him. Eyes that are hungry, yet dead.

*I have.*

I've seen them many times. In the soulless faces with gnashing teeth, in the people who aren't people, who are alive but not.

"What do you want from me?" I say, and it comes out too high-pitched, too obviously scared. "I'm not a Guardian."

Ford lifts his brows. "No, you're not. You're just like me."

"I'm n-not. This . . . this is what cult leaders do. They a-act like they understand you, like they'll give your life meaning. You find people who seem lost in this world. But I'm not like that." All the while, my teeth are chattering.

"No?" he murmurs. "Consider your power. It tells me you desperately want someone to notice you. It's a cry for help."

When I shake my head harder, a pitying sound leaves his lips. "Try to relax. I just want to chat."

I'm not bound, but there's a man standing at the closed door with a gun. There will be no chatting involved, only interrogation. A glance at Eleni reveals she slouches in her chair, looking incredibly bored. *Okay.*

I direct my attention to Beady Eyes, who swipes a hand awkwardly across his comb-over at my pleading gaze. "I don't know what's happened to you in your life to—" *To make you like this?* I try again. "If you've had a hard life—"

But Ford rounds the table, strolling so close, I scoot my chair back. "So we're doing this, are we?" he muses, resting one hip on the edge of the table in front of me, blocking Beady Eyes from view. "Why ask him and not me? Let me see if I can satisfy your curiosity."

Breathing through my nose, trying to stave off the panic, I watch him cross his arms, head tilted slightly. "Who hurt me?" he says. "That's what you're wondering. What's my damage?" A smile touches his lips. "I grew up normal. I wasn't beaten as a child. I never went hungry. I had a mother and a father who were reasonably content together. We lived in a house in a neighborhood in a town. I was educated. I was employed. I had a cubicle. I was average."

His eyes are intent on my face as it twitches, an involuntary reaction at that word.

"And the truth is, I could have lived that life," he says slowly. "But at the end of it, what would I have had to show for it? It would've been like I never existed, a footprint in the sand—there one instant, gone the next. And if no one is there to see it before the water washes it away, was it there at all? I could have lived an entire life the way so many of us do." He leans forward slightly, and I lean back, my neck aching with it. "Without magic, that's your future, Sid Spencer. The real truth is, your heart is sinking at the thought of it."

I try for the first time to summon it, the power that goes both ways. To search for something, anything I can grab on to. I dig my nails into my palms. *Can you feel this?* But as I leave raw crescent moons behind, heart hammering violently enough to explode out of my chest, I already know. He can't.

I come up against nothing. Emptiness, a pit you throw things into, straining to hear when they hit bottom. *A black hole*, Daisy said.

No matter how much power he gets, it won't be enough. Because he has nothing else that matters to him. "I didn't ask you," I whisper, "because I knew you couldn't be reached. You are someone who gives off the average-white-male-aged-twenty-five-to-thirty-five vibe."

Lips twisting, he finally leans back. "That's a little harsh. Serial killers are compelled to murder. I do it if it's necessary."

The quaking fear isn't strong enough to conceal the hate. "That's a lie. You'll want the world to know you did this. To know you."

"They will know me," he agrees with quiet fervor. "They'll know I'm allowing people to be more than what they were told they had to be. I know some people will think I'm a monster. But more will be grateful."

Maybe he doesn't think he's the bad guy; maybe he truly believes he's right. And yet . . . "What happens if you bestow this gift on all of us, and one of us has a power stronger than yours?"

He hesitates for a second. Just a second. "I can't be harmed, which means I can't *die*. Eternal life is absolute power." But I hear the catch in his voice. Uncertainty.

"Is it, though?" I manage a stiff shrug. "Not to me. To me, it would be a real-life easy button from Staples. It's a matter of perspective. There could be a whole lot of people who look at what you are and say, 'I've seen better.'"

"Not when I open the entire fault line—I'll be limitless," he says curtly, then clears his throat. "So will everyone."

That hasty add-on doesn't matter. He's already shown himself. There's nothing noble in his actions, no freeing of the people. He wants, needs, to be better than others.

*It's not about being better, Sid.*

Ford looks over his shoulder, nodding at Beady Eyes. "I always give people the choice, hoping they'll see what's best for both themselves and everyone else," he says. "The way your friend Morrissey did."

When Beady Eyes approaches, I turn my face away. "But there are other ways," Ford continues. "I know Daisy Radcliffe-Aster has three of the Keys. The same way I know you hid the other four. You and only you. Because Eleni told me."

"She's lying," I say, voice rising. "She said that to stall you."

"A mouth can lie, but a brain can't," comes Ford's light reply. "In theory, maybe it's possible to withstand a mind reader, to not think of the exact thing you're trying not to think. For instance, where did your two friends escape to? Shandy Ohno and Angel . . ."

"Reyes," Beady Eyes mutters. "Stony Peak Elementary, most likely."

Tears sting at the corner of my eyes as I cover my head, uselessly.

"You clearly don't have that skill. What a pity. I've known about that school for some time. Do you think I don't already have men closing in?"

There's no way to warn them. It'll be an ambush. "You don't have to hurt them. We're trapped here. I don't know anything. Why would I know anything?"

"Where are the Keys?" Ford says coldly now, losing patience.

"I never had the Keys," I say, as something scrapes against my skull. Whimpering, I clutch the base of my head. "Please."

And, mercifully, the digging pauses.

"We have a problem," Beady Eyes says, voice low.

"What do you mean?" Ford says, controlled, but with an edge.

"I can grab thoughts that float to the surface," Beady Eyes says hurriedly, fear hovering in his voice. "The knowledge is there; I can sense it. But I can't get to it."

"She's actively suppressing it?"

"Something else."

I glance up to see them both regarding me—Ford, jaw clenched, and Beady Eyes, staring at me in confusion. He makes a swift, pulling motion, wincing.

For a moment, everything goes black at the pain, a radiating pressure.

*"Can you make a filing cabinet in my mind like the one you have?" a voice says. Mine.*

*Marcus Severin stares at me a long moment, blinking slowly. "I have never tried to make a box in someone else's mind."*

*"You said you'd filed your fear, but you allowed it out sometimes. How does that work?"*

*"For people who are able do this to a degree in the normal world, they're the ones who control when they access the box and when they don't. The same rules apply to the boxes I've made." He hesitates. "This isn't a decision to make lightly. Be careful what limitations you make on your thoughts and feelings. There are things that need to be thought. And felt. Even if they're unpleasant."*

*"I need this one. One I can only access when I decide to, and not because I am being forced, threatened, tricked, blackmailed, coerced, or tortured in any way."*

*The word "torture" makes his whole body stiffen. But he doesn't say, "Who would do such a thing?" Not when we both live in this new nightmare world.*

*I hand him a note to give to Brian, telling him I won't remember it, but I took care of the thing he asked me to do.*

Beyond the pain, beyond that conversation forced into the light, I can feel it, briefly, like it's a solid thing. A metal box like the one my mother uses for recipes. Except this one doesn't hold handwritten cards for lemon squares. And there is no lid.

I did this. Because I realized it might come to this. And that I would break. Unless I couldn't.

The pounding slows, fading to an ache, and then numbness. My vision clears in degrees, and from a distance, I hear Beady Eyes's nervous voice. Nervous because he's scared. Of Ford.

"It's impenetrable. I can't get in by force. Whoever made this box followed her instructions. *She* can't get into it. Not this way, anyway."

"I'll need to keep the people at the school alive for now," Ford mutters to himself. "I'll need Marcus Severin." As I focus on the two of them again, Ford regards Beady Eyes with contempt. "You're useless to me here. Go get ready to wake the boy. We'll see if he knows anything."

Beady Eyes moves to the door like he's being chased, and I can't feel bad for him that he, that all the people who fail Ford, might die.

"It seems I made an error in judgment," Ford says in a tone no longer civil. "I never expected you to do something clever."

When the wave of pain hits me, whatever words I meant to say fly away with my scream.

# CHAPTER 18

*T*here are moments in between, when I know I'm on the floor, that it's hard beneath my hip and head, that I'm curled into a protective ball, and the air in the room is so very cold, but that's all I know of myself.

Pain doesn't rip or tear or punch. It engulfs. It becomes. Until there's nothing else left.

And while my body contorts, pain is also a whisper in my ear. *You're nothing. You're alone here. You'll die here. And when you've gone, the world won't have been made better by your presence. When you're gone, it'll be like you never existed at all.* It's my voice, the one in my head that feeds on pain, finding me now, telling me to give up.

And then nothingness, blessed nothingness, like I've passed out. But no, because the hoarse sounds of my sobs are filling the space around me.

"I have other powers," he says, standing over me, voice emotion-less. "In fact, I have three. The magic from William James Morrissey and Parker van der Kamp. Did you forget?"

I don't have a chance to lift my arms, to try to fight the hand at my throat that feels like a steel manacle. I'm lifted, but not to my feet. Choking, I claw at his wrist, toes scraping the floor, and then air, as he holds me with one arm like it's nothing.

*Can't breathe.*

Spots dot my vision. But through the recording booth window, I glimpse Eleni slumping in her chair, mouth open like she's fighting to breathe. Because she can feel this when Ford can't. The guard at the door doubles over, face going red, then white, then pale blue.

"Tell me," Ford coaxes. "Open the box."

But I can't, even though I beg it to open.

I hit the ground, my legs crumbling, knees then palms thudding hard against wood. My cheek presses into the floor and I gasp in air that burns my throat. Coughing, I suck in another breath and another.

Ford sighs heavily. "I have to admit, I struggle with all this self-sacrifice when there is ultimately no benefit to you. You didn't have to help them, but you'll die because of that choice. Have you no survival instinct at all? Are they worth the suffering they brought down upon you?"

When I squeeze my eyes closed, Brian holds a candle, brushing hair away from the bruise on my forehead. Curls fall into my lap. The smell of rotisserie chicken reminds me I have to keep going. Arms fold around me, protecting me from the cold. His gaze is filled with such certainty that I'm braver than I think.

There's a plate of bruschetta in front of me that Shandy made because he can't bear it when people are hungry. Hyacinth stares at the picture of my family over the mantel like she understands when no one ever understands. Even Morrissey, his arms shaking as he carries me over the forest, holds on.

Angel rushes out into a quad crowded with soulless creatures to save us. Because he could. Daisy smiles as she tells me my feelings are a gift. I'm the strong one, Finn says.

Nell . . . Nell forgives me.

And somewhere, Matty is alive, and that's enough.

*It's worth it.*

Ford stands over me, experiencing no bittersweet pang. He doesn't know every beautiful thing given was more beautiful because they didn't have to.

Stiffly, every limb pulsing with the memory of pain, I lift my head. This man is eternal, he causes physical suffering at will, he's strong enough to snap my neck with one hand, and still, the fear fades. I hold his gaze without shuddering. "You talked about having an existence that didn't matter, being a footprint in the sand no one would remember once it washed away. But if you kill me, I will be remembered. My brother, who you'll never find, will remember me. Matty and I had no one once. It's why we'll do anything for each other. It's why——" My words die in my throat, palms pressing hard against the floor. It's why he told Daisy I would know where he is.

*I can't really sense people when I'm underground or when there are certain obstacles, lots of metal*, Daisy says in my mind.

One rainy night, the night I met Brian, Matty was late meeting me. He was with a customer. Chester Graves. An image of Matty slicking back his rainbow hair flashes in my mind. *He basically admitted he has a bunker in his backyard.* The one we'd always imagined was there, the one we were going to run away to once. A bunker, probably made of reinforced steel, buried under the earth.

A smile spreads across my face as confusion spreads across his. "We're not the same, you and I," I whisper.

Ford absorbs this without reaction. "If you care about people so much, then I wonder if you can refrain from telling me what I wish to know if it's someone else's life you're risking." He crouches, covering my mouth with his hand. He nods at the guard, who straightens, rubbing his neck, visibly shaken.

The guard hurries to open the door to the recording booth. I hear a noise. The snap of teeth, a gurgle. I lift myself to my knees and Ford lets me. He wants me to see the emaciated figure of a shell whose wrist is bound to the door handle, as the guard skittishly moves to cut the thin rope with scissors.

As I scream against Ford's hand, I hear Eleni drawl from inside the room, "Did you miss me?"

"Eleni Christakos," Ford calls pleasantly. "Hypothetically, if I were to tell Sid Spencer we're letting a zombie eat you alive, would she be amenable to our requests?"

There's a brief silence before Eleni's voice comes again, resigned. "If you think I've never fought someone off without superstrength, you'd be wrong. Go ahead and tell her. But joke's on you, bitch, she doesn't even like me."

The guard severs the rope. I scream again as the door closes.

"Let's get you up so you can see," Ford suggests, but as he forces me to my feet, the floor begins to shake gently, a rumble.

Somewhere in a distant hallway, I feel his eyes snap open.

*Blurry, everything a fog. "Spencer."*

Ford lets go of my arms, thrusting me away. His eyes flick toward the ceiling, where a hanging light sways. "He's waking up," he says grimly, and lifts a radio from his pocket. "Sedate him again, I'm on my—"

Explosions, one after another, send us crashing to the ground, emptying my lungs of air.

The floor tilts, and for one second I think the building will cave in around us.

The scent of smoke wafts into the room.

I push myself to my knees, ears ringing.

"Boss, someone is blowing holes in the wall——" a tinny voice bellows from the radio.

*Daisy.* My heart lifts, filling with hope.

"All guards to the south hall," Ford barks into the radio. "Are the powered people back? The ones that matter," he adds.

There's a brief pause before the voice comes again, quieter. "The most powerful people are split between here and the elementary school, like you ordered, waiting on your command."

"Good. Instruct them to secure Brian Aster." Ford lowers the radio, pointing at the guard. "Stay here. Do not take the gun off her for a second."

He storms toward the door, flinging it open and slamming it behind him. I hear his footsteps sprinting down the hall.

There's a soft gasp, instantly stifled.

For half a second, a heartbeat, I see her, standing in front of the door, hands clasped under her rib cage with a confused expression on her face. But when I blink, she's gone again.

"Don't even think about moving," the guard warns, advancing toward me as he fumbles with the gun on its strap.

"You know you don't matter to him, right?" I say quietly, and he hesitates. "What's your power? Do you see colors no one else can see? Summon bunnies? Turn objects to chocolate? If you can't blow people up at will, you're of no consequence to him. A faceless minion who can hold a gun."

The floor creaks behind him.

The guard blinks, bewildered, then spins around.

The wooden chair I'd been sitting in slams into his forehead with a sickening crack.

He topples backward, hitting the table first, then the ground.

Nell stands there, holding the chair raised, shaking a little but face stone-cold as she steps toward him, peering down at his unconscious face.

Her eyes flick to me, wet with tears. She tosses the chair away and rushes to my side. "Siddy, are you okay?"

"You followed us?" I croak. "You should have gone, walked through the wall."

"Not without you," Nell says firmly.

She stands, holding a hand out to me, and when I place mine in hers, she hauls me to my feet. I stand there, clinging to it. The aching in my bones, the weight of exhaustion, fade to the background as she squeezes my fingers.

But I whip around to face the wide window of the recording room. "Oh. Crap. I guess we should save her."

Eleni, still blindfolded and cuffed to the chair, is on her feet, hunched forward to carry the weight of it on her back. She's somehow managed to pin the shell to the wall with the four wooden legs as spindly arms reach over the back of it, clawing at her long hair.

We race to the booth door, flinging it open before realizing we have no weapons on us.

Eleni's face swivels toward the door. "Who's there?" she yells. "Did you think I couldn't take one undead creature? Really?"

"Eleni, it's me," I say, scanning the room for something to stab it with. I grab a microphone attached to a metal arm bolted into the table.

"Oh. What are you doing here?"

"I wasn't going to leave you to die," I snap. "I thought about it, not gonna lie. And thanks for telling Ford I was the one who had the other Keys."

"Whatever," she growls. "Brian told me you couldn't remember anything when I had severe reservations about you coming on this mission. Anyway, I'm gonna move away from the wall now. Make a commotion so this bastard goes for you."

"What? No," I cry as Nell pauses in trying to help me yank the mic from the wall to give me an *is she for real?* glance. "Stay like that until we get a weapon."

"Oh for fuck's sake," Eleni mutters, trotting away from the wall.

"OH MY GOD, ARE YOU SERIOUS?" I shriek. Loose from the chair prison, the shell jerks its head toward us, teeth snapping. It limps closer, arms already reaching.

"Help," Nell squeaks, backing up, and then she disappears.

Eleni rips her cuffs free from the chair arms, straight through the wood. They hang from her wrists as she yanks the blindfold off, blinking, swiveling until she sees me.

Raising a brow, Eleni stretches, cracking her neck, moving at a glacial pace. Casually, she lifts the chair in one hand and tosses it at the wall.

I have my hands at the shell's throat, trying to hold it away from me, as Nell reappears behind it, slapping at it timidly. "ELENI."

She picks up a broken chair leg, flips it lightly in her hand, and saunters toward us. "I can't believe you've survived this long," she says. With that, she drags the thing back by the neck and stakes it in the head.

I stand pressed to the wall, watching her drop the body like a sack of potatoes. "Oh. Right." She needed someone to save.

"It sucks to be me sometimes," Eleni says, dusting her hands off. She pins Nell with a hard stare as Nell flickers without meaning to. "You brought a holographic princess as backup?"

After a brief struggle, Nell remains solid and stares back at her, eyebrows slightly raised, her trademark "cold" look when she's secretly terrified. "I'm not a princess."

Eleni gives her a once-over, from her perfectly straight blond hair down to her feet in ballet flats. Eleni's mouth, lipstick totally unmarred, releases from its sneer. "I like your dress," she says grudgingly. "Does it come in black?"

Nell brightens. "Oh, thank you. It's my favorite—"

"Yeah, hi, can we do this later maybe?" I say abruptly. "We need to get out of here and find Brian. I figured out where Matty is."

Eleni looks at me, chewing her lip. "We don't have the Key."

Right. *Right.* "And Daisy's plan to come upon Ford by surprise and force him to reveal the location is a no-go."

"I've known men like him before," Eleni says suddenly, eyes darkening. "He won't keep it anywhere but on his person. He'd never risk hiding it where someone could find it. He has it, but he's narcissistic enough to think no one can get it from him. We'll see about that."

"You can't get it from him," I say, hands drifting to my neck, tender and bruised. "He's as strong as you, with no limitations. Subduing him will be extremely difficult. Especially if he's mentally torturing us." When I was on the floor, racked with pain, with every muscle contracting, I had no ability to do anything. Eleni wouldn't be immune to that.

Nell's hand is on my arm, squeezing. There's no time to explain everything, but I'm guessing she heard enough of the interrogation to know what's at stake.

But there's a peculiar expression on her face as one hand hovers at her midsection. "Are you talking about a Guardian Key?" she asks tentatively.

Eleni gives a curt nod.

"When he left, he walked through me. I shouldn't have felt any-thing—I never did before—but this time, it hurt? There's something *in* him, something powerful that's not like the rest of him."

In him? My mouth drops open. *Inside* him. "He swallowed it," I mutter. "That's why he thinks no one can get it." Eleni and I exchange a glance. She can't punch through impenetrable skin. "We need—"

"Brian," she finishes grimly.

"The south hallway," Nell says. "That's where they said he was. That's where Ford and all his men went."

I take a deep steadying breath and take her hand. "Let's go."

We have no mirrors to peer around corners with.

But we have Nell. At every intersection, every turn in the hallway, she steps out first like a guardian angel, holding her breath, looking both ways before waving us forward.

*They're all in the south hall. We may be able to get there unimpeded, but once we're there . . .* I try not to think about it, even as my body remains taut, nerves on edge.

We keep low, but only Nell moves soundlessly in her ballet slip-pers. None of us have a clear idea where we are within this building until, up ahead, I see the darkened courtyard. We're headed to the middle.

A lone man enters the hallway from the bridge, crossing directly in front of us. He's looking up at the sound of our footsteps when Eleni's fist connects with his jaw, knocking him out with one blow.

She catches him before he can fly backward, waving us past as she lowers him lightly to the ground instead. When I glance back over my shoulder, she's checking him for weapons, but he has none. It's Beady

Eyes, and he's alone, far from the action. A coward at heart. None of these men are truly brave. Not even guns can give them that.

Nell moves out into the corridor, staying close to the wall, away from the windows. The scent of smoke is getting stronger, and somewhere across the garden, we hear distant shouting.

We creep along, stopping to peer down every hallway we pass, reading the signs. NORTHWEST HALL. WEST HALL. SOUTHWEST HALL.

Eleni squints through a set of double doors to a room—the cafeteria. Except it's not a cafeteria anymore. Instead of rows of lunch tables, there are rows of shelves, shelves lined with weapons. An armory.

If we go in, we could grab some, though none of us know how to load or use a gun. Eleni's thinking about it, though, chewing her lip again, glancing at us, at me, a helpless person, when voices sound in Southwest Hall, running boots growing closer.

"Out of ammo—we have to load up," someone shouts.

Nell grabs my hand and we're running toward South Hall, skidding to a halt at the corner, as she peeks out to check. *It's clear,* she mouths to me.

But then I realize no one is shoving me forward from behind. I know Eleni isn't with us even before I spin around to see her still down the hall at the cafeteria doors, pushing one of the bookshelves along the wall to barricade the doors, to delay them getting inside and filling up their empty guns. She presses a shoulder against an armoire filled with trophies. She's fast, but not fast enough.

Men spill out of the hallway as she slides the heavy wood cabinet into place.

A dozen, maybe, crowd into the narrow circular passage surrounding the courtyard, slowing as they see her blocking their way.

They wear all black, like all the others.

Something flickers over her face as she glances over her shoulder, pinning me with that emerald hard stare. "Go," she says, and turns back around without another word.

"She's buying us time," Nell says in my ear. "She can catch up to us."

I let her pull me around the corner. The sounds of blows, glass breaking, men grunting in pain, grows distant. We're halfway down the north hall when I hear her scream. I've never heard her scream.

"No. Wait, she can't do it," I whisper, staring at Nell with a rising dread. I turn slowly, facing the way we came. We're too far away. Eleni faces them alone. Her strength will fade.

*White lights. The ground rises up fast, too fast, to meet me. A cry escapes my lips when I promised myself I wouldn't make a sound. Never again. But they're too strong. And I'm not.*

In the next instant, I'm sprinting. I feel Nell at my side as we turn into the passageway, because she knows without me saying a word—I can't leave Eleni. Even if there's nothing I can do, even if I die, I need to be the kind of person who rushes into a quad of zombies to save strangers, to step in front of a bullet I could dodge. I can't leave her. And Nell can't leave me.

But by the time we reach the blockaded cafeteria doors, Nell has disappeared.

Three men lie on the ground, not moving. Sitting with her back against the wall, legs curled to her chest, Eleni presses a palm to her cheek, staring blankly into space.

I step in front of her as the rest approach, hesitantly, as though wondering what I can do. "You should know," I say, voice barely above a whisper, tensing for a blow. "Whatever you do to me, you will feel."

I don't know this for certain, I don't know if they're too lost, but it's all I have.

One of them barrels toward me, sneering—and runs face-first into a trophy thrown by an invisible hand. Nell flings objects from the armoire beside us. There's something stronger than fear inside her now, the same thing that allowed her to lift the chair in that room, allowing her to control it, to be both incorporeal and not. Love. For me.

There's another man coming, and I crouch as he dodges a glass sculpture hurtling at his head. I grip Eleni's shoulders with both hands. "Eleni," I beg, shaking her gently. "We're here. Eleni, get up. You have to get up."

Her green eyes, liquid with tears, don't register my presence, fixed instead on some spot in the distance. One of her cheekbones is bruised, bright red with the promise of purple, but as I pat her upper arms, her knees, searching for a reaction, I don't detect other injuries. Unless she doesn't feel them. Unless she retreated somewhere far away from here.

They're coming. There's nothing I can do to stop them. In five seconds, I'll be on the ground too. Still, I touch the edge of her bruise with a fingertip and something shifts inside me, terror beginning to burn, igniting into something else entirely. Rage bursting to life, contained by skin and bone. My hands cup her face, gently, and I block everything else out. "I know you protect people, that you always have. But you never should have been in that position in the first place. Either of you." Slowly her eyes shift, meeting mine, flickering with something, a memory, of a sister. "You're a person too," I whisper fiercely. "You have to protect someone, so protect *yourself.*"

She's reaching for my hand desperately, and I take it, and though her fingers squeeze tightly around mine, I barely feel it. Her grasp is weak; it's little more than air against my skin.

*I hear sniffling. She's crying again, trying to stifle it.*

*"Get behind me," I say through gritted teeth.*

I let go of Eleni, rising slowly at the rush of footsteps behind me, close, any second now.

*As the door slams open, I turn, calm, somehow, facing the light.*

My eyes focus on the man, ducking out of the way of a hurled plaque.

*There's a shadow there, a monster. Weakness disgusts him even if fighting back makes it worse. If I fight, though, I can take the brunt of it. I can save her. I look him in the eye . . .*

"Come at me," I murmur. "Bitch."

His eyes widen for an instant before I hear the smack his fist makes, connecting with my palm. He stands there, slack-jawed, his arm trembling with effort as I hold it mid-swing. I stare at our hands, stunned. Tentatively, my fingers curl around his. I squeeze.

He screams as his bones break, dissolving like powder.

And as he's sagging, clutching his crushed hand, I'm bending, lifting his body, and it's nothing, like a pillow, and I send him hurtling through the glass into the courtyard.

Slowly, I turn, reaching down for her. Blinking, like she's waking up, Eleni lets me grasp her wrist. She's weightless as I pull her to her feet.

When the rest of them come at us, simultaneously this time, I close the distance, meeting them in the middle. *Impact.* I feel nothing, just free. One wide swipe of my arm sends three fanning back. Easy.

I send one man headfirst into the wall, but as I let him crumble to the ground, one man skirts past me. At first I think he's getting away, until I hear Eleni roar.

When she barrels into him, he topples backward, head thunking hard on the tiles. She crouches over him for one beat, lips curving into a smile. As he groans, attempting to lever himself up, Nell passes her a trophy in the shape of a crystal vase.

The sound of shattering glass follows me as I spin to face the last man.

He's hanging back, a hulking figure in black, making no move to advance.

Red hair. Red face. He stares at me, sweating, trying to inch back with every slow, casual step I take in his direction.

When he decides to run, I've already seized him by the shoulders, slamming him back against the wall.

The first thing I do is bitch-slap him, hard enough that his face whips to the side. My knee jerks up hard, straight into his balls, zero hesitation.

I honestly think Adam O'Brien has blacked out from the pain, though I stoop over him, lift his head by the hair, and punch him any-way. "That's for me and Nell," I say.

Nell stares at me with her mouth hanging open as I jog back to them. "Who *are* you?"

I shake my head, because I REALLY DON'T KNOW? I don't think the voice that comes out of me is fully mine when I nudge Eleni with a toe and snap, "Get up, we've gotta go." She's straddling her foe, the base of the broken vase clenched in her fingers. But when I pull her to her feet, I stumble slightly, strength gone.

"Everything you just did was all me," Eleni says, pale but composed. "You're welcome."

We make our way through the fallen bodies, picking up the pace as soon as we're clear of them. When we reach North Hall, it's empty, but clouds of gray smoke billow toward us, ash floating on the air, trapped by blackened ceilings and walls. At a fork in the hallway, the air is thick with heat, dampening my skin with sweat. Eyes stinging, I peer left, then right, then left again. Beside me, Nell doubles over, coughing. Eleni tries to duck lower so as not to breathe straight smoke, but I can hear her wheezing. My own lungs burn. Men are shouting—*how many, how close?* Somewhere, the all too familiar sound of gunfire echoes outside the building. I flatten the three of us against the wall, covering my mouth to stifle the coughs.

Eleni, hands braced on her thighs, gasps, "We don't know which direction—"

"Not that way," I say, staring toward the left.

Both Eleni and Nell squint, but the hallway curves and smoke obscures the view. "How do you know?" Nell asks faintly.

Facing right, I hear—*I feel*—music. The same music I heard in the cave, in the dark, next to him. *Brian.* "This way. We need to go this way."

They follow me, all of us hacking as we try to outrun the smoke.

In the distance, a wall comes into focus through the haze. No, a way out. EXIT in red letters over the thick metal door.

But a familiar shape, fanning away the smoke, stands in front of it.

I thrust my arms out, stopping Eleni and Nell, several yards away.

Morrissey's eyes, reddened with smoke, find us through the haze, and he freezes.

Nell flickers beside me and it's just as well. He's carrying a gun.

Eleni brushes past my arm, strolling closer, daring him, and though his fingers clench around the gun, he doesn't raise it.

His gaze shifts past her, toward the sound of voices somewhere in the hallway behind us.

He opens his mouth and I think—*I know*—what he wants to say. Regret is an ocean without borders and there's no part of him not drowning in it. *I'm sorry. I made the wrong choice. I was so afraid.* But the words are not enough and he knows it. Instead, he says, "If Shandy lives, tell him he can have all my cars."

The gun falls from limp fingers, clattering on the floor. Without looking at us, he steps to the side. "Hurry. They'll be here soon."

Eleni passes him without a backward glance.

Nell and I step out behind her, and we're outside, inhaling cold, wet air into our raw lungs. The pillars of smoke spiraling into the black sky glow red-purple. But beyond the fog, there are stars and the faint light of the moon to show us the way.

We're running again, sticking to the shadows, over wet grass, gaining distance.

Behind us, on the other side of that closed door, there's a shout, and a single shot splits the night.

# CHAPTER 19

*I* wonder if I tried to reach out to Morrissey, if I'd feel him. A gun can obliterate life, but not the soul.

He saved me twice. I tell him that's not nothing. I hope some part of him knew that.

*Bang.*

The grass kicks up ahead of me. Next to me, Nell blinks in and out, a white beacon in the dark. She touches her belly—there's no hole, no blood—and she disappears again.

*Shooters on the roof.*

Eleni and I are solid.

"Run," I gasp to her.

But the echoes of the gunfire surround us. I wait for a million tiny bombs to pepper my body, explode through my skin.

Nothing hits.

In the darkness, someone staggers toward us, one hand lifted, and the music in my mind crescendos.

A sob escapes me, and I'm moving across the open grass toward that ridiculously tall figure, knowing I'm safe.

He exhales when he sees me, nearly tripping in his relief.

Bullets glitter in the dark, like falling stars that have halted mere feet from our heads.

With a roar, Brian sweeps his arm. The bullets hurtle back toward their shooters and—

He crashes into me as his legs nearly give out. I'm vaguely aware of screams—something falls behind us, a body, thudding in the grass.

Wrapping my arms around him, we both sink to the ground.

I stare up into a pale, strained face I know, the eyes that pierce straight to the heart of me. "Hi."

"Hi," Brian says hoarsely.

"You're here," I say, clinging to his arm, weakly at first.

"We were coming to you," Brian says. "Daisy was tracking you, but you kept moving around. It was annoying."

"We were trying to find *you*," I say.

He's studying my face, a soft smile at the edges of his mouth. "How did you make it out?"

"Um," I hedge. "Something happened that hasn't quite sunk in yet. Ask me again in three to six months."

Then hands are gripping Brian's arms from behind, lifting him like he's not gigantic. "Up, now," Eleni is saying, already pointing.

A flash of white glimmers over her shoulder. I see Nell across the expanse of grass, waving for us to follow her. Behind her, a maintenance shed sits close to the trees, and someone peeks her head out. Daisy lets out a visible exhale.

We follow Eleni at a jog.

Daisy waits, back against the building, one arm stretched across Hyacinth's chest as though she wants to keep her from running out to meet us. Daisy's covered in leaves, dirt staining her white coat, finally embracing the apocalypse.

As she surveys us, plus one vaguely see-through Nell shyly hanging back, she closes her eyes in relief and rests her head against the wall. A gray smudge of soot curves over one brown cheek. "Come on," she says in a low voice, opening the door. "We don't have a lot of time before they search every building on campus. The woods are already crawling with men."

She gently guides Hyacinth in first, with Eleni following.

Brian finds me scanning him anxiously and straightens up. "I'm okay," he says, in a voice raked over gravel, tucking a sweaty curl behind my ear.

I reach over, tugging Nell forward. "This is Nell."

Brian, noticing her for the first time, blinks several times in quick succession. "Oh. Okay."

Nell's gaze lingers on Brian's hand, hovering by my cheek, before darting to me.

"I'm friends with Brian Aster now," I say awkwardly, as he enters ahead of us. I find myself facing a human version of the eyeballs emoji. "He's my . . . traveling companion. Like Gandalf. If Gandalf had . . . like . . ."

Nell lifts a brow. "Hot vibes? That's Aragorn, Siddy. Get inside."

It's pitch-black within the shed, and we're crowded together among rakes and lawnmowers, sharp and unyielding.

Wincing, I make my way somewhere toward the center, hearing nothing but heavy breathing.

"We are in an unideal situation," Daisy's voice says from the corner. "We have to abort the mission. No one knows where Ford is and even then——"

"Nell found the Key," I say, feeling for her hand next to mine. "It's inside him."

Daisy absorbs that. "Oh God, is it up his ass?"

"He swallowed it," Nell says in her quiet voice, the one she uses when she's around a lot of people she doesn't know. I squeeze her hand and it grows more solid in mine.

No one says anything for a moment, weighing the options. Try to find Ford when we have countless men standing between us and him? Get through them and face off against him? My body tenses involuntarily at the memory of the agony ripping through it.

"None of us are at our best," Daisy admits. "You did everything you could. I need time to devise a new plan. We should go, but we're on a mountain and getting down in the dark will be hell."

"*She* could get us out," Eleni says suddenly. "She could use Angel's power. Back inside, she used mine."

It strikes me at this moment when there is more than one "she" present that Eleni has never actually addressed me by name. In the confused silence, while everyone is looking around in the dark, I shrink back. "She means me," I say in a small voice. "But I . . . I don't even know how I did it. Or if it even works with everyone."

"You could *try*," Eleni says impatiently.

"Well," Daisy says slowly. "The larger problem is . . . does anyone have paint?"

Their silence is answer enough.

"Angel had all the paint in his bag," Brian says.

Nobody has to say it's unlikely all of us will make it several miles to the bottom of the mountain alive. Angel would have known that when he left, but there was no other choice. He had to—

*A-M-P.* An image of Angel's fingers forming letters in the blood flashes through my mind.

"A-M-P," I blurt out. "What is A-M-P? Angel wrote that to me before he left."

"A. Murder. Palace," Eleni mutters. "We're already in one."

"No . . ." It's Hyacinth's voice that speaks from the corner. "Angel knew we needed him. He doesn't leave people to die." It occurs to me that she's been by Daisy's side this whole time, without a power, probably terrified, helpless while people battled around her. She sniffs, soft but audible. "He was telling you he'd come back. It has to be a place he's been before, somewhere he thought we could get to. Amp."

"The amphitheater," Daisy says then, and I sense movement as she stretches her arm toward the back of the shed. There's a brief pause, then relief fills her voice. "He's there."

In the woods behind the gardens, carved into the mountain, a series of stone levels lead down to an open space. Steps for giants, my mother used to say, bordering the stage in a crescent moon. It's where Mountain Ridge would put on their spring musical performances, and in the summer we'd go and watch the community center perform Shakespeare.

But it lies on the other side of the school, and in between there's an army.

As my eyes adjust, I glimpse a hint of white as Daisy faces away from us, as though staring through the wall. "Ford's men are everywhere," she says faintly. "And they have powers. He had the strongest outside trying to find me, to make sure none of us could leave. I was able to avoid them, but there are more of us now. If we have to cross the yard, or enter the woods, we will not be able to remain undetected."

We'll have to go straight through them.

We don't have a choice.

"We stay together," Brian says, resolute. "All of us are getting through this. Protect each other. Protect Hyacinth."

Though Hyacinth makes a soft sound of distress in the dark, we all agree.

We will lose no one else.

Right before Daisy hurls her smoke grenades, I catch a glimpse of Mountain Ridge, like a nightmare version of the school it once was. A shadowy outline of a building, the warped reflection of a dark forest covered in smog within the cracked mirrored glass. Whole wings are crumbling, burning.

Clouds of red smoke billow from both hands as Daisy runs forward, pitching the canisters directly into our path. To cloak us.

All I see is a scarlet wasteland, no concept of where I am, what might be in front of me. Wrapping my arm across my face and breathing into the fabric, I sense her moving ahead of us straight into it, and I follow the glimmer of white. There's no way out but through.

Beside me, Brian has Hyacinth's hand, keeping her at his pace. I can't see Eleni or Nell, but I feel them on my other side—shadows in the smoke.

Through the haze, a massive black shape crawls toward us. A dog. No . . . a wolf. Teeth bared, growling, it crouches as though to spring.

Eleni swats it away like a gnat the moment it leaps at us. A yelp pierces the air, but a man hits the ground, and we're jumping over him without breaking stride.

"Go right," Brian shouts, strides lengthening.

Ahead of us, Daisy banks left.

"Really, Daisy?" Brian has no choice but to follow.

Daisy shouts something over her shoulder. *What did she say?*

But then I glimpse men creeping in from the right, groping wildly as they search for us.

They're lost in the fog, but they won't be for long.

The red wafts around us in wisps as we veer off, toward the spindly black outlines of trees. Booted feet clomp through the brush. There are men in the woods, moving in. But there will be men no matter what direction we go.

We creep along the forest border. A rich earthy scent cuts through the smoke. My fingertips brush splintery bark as thorned branches snag the fabric of my pants, digging into the skin beneath.

Nell's ethereal form flickers up ahead. She turns back, shouting a warning, disappearing a millisecond before a thin, glowing red line slices through her middle.

"Daisy, down!" I cry, ducking behind a bush.

But she's already on her belly when the ray of light sweeps toward us, sawing straight through a copse of trees as the air sizzles and pops.

As they topple, Brian is next to me, halting the laser that bends against his power. With a gasp, he forces the beam up, then back the way it came, through even more trees. Beyond the wave of cracking, I hear a distant bellow. The red fades, though the air tastes of burned sap.

My hands fly up to cover my head, an automatic reflex, when a massive trunk tips toward us from overhead. But Eleni is next to me, catching it before it crushes us.

"Under," I gasp to Hyacinth, who dives beneath the trunk with Brian.

Eleni lowers it with a grunt, and together we climb over broken branches, twisted limbs that claw at our hair. I crash through to the other side, spitting out a leaf.

"Keep going," Brian says, grabbing my arm, and we're moving again.

But I hear something, something toward our left, a soft pitter-patter against leaves. Like rain, but ending in a hiss.

I look up at the same time Brian does. A barrage of glistening droplets shower down like arrows. He swerves them left, falling to one knee at the effort. One gets through, hitting Eleni's arm.

Staring at the hole in her sleeve, she curses. "It's acid," she cries, shimmying out of her jacket. "Run."

We sprint right, out of the woods, onto a stretch of grass on the left side of the school.

Someone jumps into our path—from where, I have no idea. And then he's gone, blinking out of existence.

Brian lashes out, eyes darting around in panic. He can't move what he can't see.

The man appears for an instant before disappearing again.

I crouch low, my eyes on the ground. *There.* The grass flattens. Indentations made by booted feet appear faster, running. Invisible—invisible like Nell—but not incorporeal. My hand fists in the soil beneath the grass, and I throw, sending an arc of mud.

A glistening outline of a man materializes out of thin air, splattered with sludge, half there, half not. He's recoiling, arms shielding his face.

With a flick of his hand, Brian crashes him into the building.

Nell pauses to look back at us, making sure we're okay, and then keeps running. Her white dress is a beacon, spurring us forward.

When she disappears without warning, we know what that means, even as Daisy says, "A man," a moment before he steps out of the trees.

My body goes limp. The ground rushes up to meet me. My chin hits first, and then the rest of me, in a contorted heap. But I can't move. My arms and legs are dead weights. No strength, no sensation.

Eleni falls on top of me, facedown. I make a sound through frozen lips as her weight presses my ribs into the earth. But she doesn't roll off me. She can't move, either.

Footsteps, squeaking against the grass, move closer. Boots halt by my face. "I've got them," a man murmurs into a radio. "Incapacitated. Left side of school."

"Good work," a voice responds.

*Ford.* A black hole somewhere behind us.

I'm unable to blink, even as the man squats, tilting his head to look into my face.

"Five," he says, his eyes moving over the pile of our bodies.

Panic rising, I meet his gaze, trying to reach him, to find something in him that'll connect with me. "Uhleez," I say, unable to move my mouth. *Please.* It's elusive, but there. Humanity. For a moment, he falters, like his legs are giving out—like he can feel this, the effect of his own power. But he steadies himself, steeling himself against me, turning at the soft *pat pat pat.*

*Feet in the grass. Nell.*

There's a crack, a branch against skull, and he does go down this time, with a low exhalation of shock.

Though he stirs weakly, my limbs jerk as feeling returns, pins and needles running up and down my arms. Eleni rolls off me in an instant, punching the man until he stills completely. Beside us, Brian is helping Hyacinth to her knees.

Nell holds a hand out to me, to Daisy, but her blue eyes are wide and terrified, fixed on something in the distance. "Hurry. They're coming."

There are people behind us, catching up. We're almost around the school, almost at the other side.

Clamping down on my fear, I lurch to my feet.

And we run.

Ahead, where the border of trees curves, we'll find a staircase made of stone slabs leading us down into the woods, to the amphitheater.

Something hits the ground in front of us. Brian manages to sail us all over a massive ball of fire just in time.

*Oh goddammit.*

I turn my head, glimpsing a shadowy figure gaining ground. In his hands, he conjures another flaming ball. Daisy, Nell, and Eleni race faster, widening the gap between us.

Hyacinth's tiny sob reaches me, and with it, memories of fire. She's chased by fire wherever she goes. In dreams. In life. She can't escape it, and the terror slows her body, making her stumble. I grab her hand and run with her, pulling her along.

It's only when we're nearing the staircase at the tree line's edge that I notice Brian isn't with us.

Whirling, I search behind me and see him stopped halfway back.

A flaming wall spans the stretch of lawn, inching toward Brian, eating the space between. Brian holds it back, but barely.

I don't think, just run, sprinting back to him, faster than I ever have in my life. The wall sears my skin, but it doesn't matter.

Sweat pours down Brian's face, bright red in the heat. His blood-shot eyes turn to me, wet, glistening, but clear. "Get out of here, Spencer," he says through clenched teeth.

I shake my head, trying to take his arm, but he shakes me off.

"Please," he says, straining to hold the fire back. "*Please*. We can't outrun it. I have to do this. You have to go. I can hold it until you're gone."

"You can't hold it forever." I'm crying now, screaming over my shoulder for Daisy, for Eleni, who don't have the power to help, even as I see their shadows dashing back toward us anyway.

When the first wave of pain hits, Brian sinks to his knees, mouth open in a silent scream.

My back arches and I'm falling, breath knocked from my lungs.

Behind us, the others go down like dominoes before they can reach us.

I remember this; I've felt it before. Like my bones are tearing from muscle. Like sandpaper underneath my skin. Like swallowing glass.

*Ford's here.* Behind the wall, he waits for us to let go. For the fire to burn us alive.

Tendrils lick at my skin.

Brian's on his knees, containing the flames, teeth clenched. He bears the pain like it's not the worst kind he's faced. "Go."

"No." I struggle to get up.

But Brian just looks at me as no one has ever looked at me. Like he sees me. Like he always has, from that moment in the rain outside the café. Beyond the low roar of the burning wall, there's music, music I heard when we were lying on the floor behind a waterfall, music I heard when I was searching for him through smoky hallways. A tender, sweet melody more like an emotion than a song.

Music that plays in his head when he's with me.

"Isidora," he whispers. "Please."

When I asked him if he believed I could be brave, he said he did. He said my name.

Slowly, I lift my palms, though the heat threatens to melt the skin from my bones. I push with everything I have. It inches back slowly, painstakingly. And not enough.

A wave of exhaustion washes over me. My arms shake with exertion. Numbness spreads up to my shoulders. And as spots dot my vision, my hold breaks.

*This is how his power feels.*

Brian's hand grasps mine. In that moment, I feel the bone-to-bone contact through our skin, and I know what he's going to do before it happens. Because I know him.

It's not like Ford taking the magic from Parker's dead body, when the magic glowed black. When Brian transfers his magic to me, it's bright white, hotter than the sun, but not painful at all.

Golden threads snake up my wrist, sinking into my skin.

"No!" I scream. "No!"

I struggle to pull away, but he won't let me. Our locked hands glow.

The golden web beneath his skin slowly fades, his power leaching out of him, and the wall moves as he loses his power to keep it back.

A faint smile crosses his face, and he uses the remnants of his magic one final time.

A force more solid than wind sweeps me away, toward the others, pushing all five of us back to the tree line and the path that will take us to safety. Just as the fire reaches him.

Before the flames swallow his body, Hyacinth screams. I feel it everywhere, exploding around us, exploding inside me. A burst of anguish so strong, it's a solid thing.

In his last moments, Brian knew what this would feel like for us, and he did it anyway.

This pain, losing someone you love, is the worst kind.

I kneel on the ground, arms wrapped around my middle.

Nells's hands touch my shoulders, trying to get me up, to get me to run. Her hands are gentle, though, not tight or urgent. I don't remember how to stand. If I don't move, the inferno will eat us like it ate him. I can't be sure it matters to me even as I wonder what it would be like to burn.

Brian knows what it's like. That thought destroys me.

Hyacinth still screams, so much louder and so much higher pitched than her normal voice. So much pain.

"Siddy." Nell's voice comes in my ear. She's gasping, on her knees with me. Because of me.

She wants me to run and I can't.

She grabs me by the face, though, tilting it up.

I don't want to see it, but she makes me, makes me face the blaze raging toward us.

Except it isn't.

It's stopped, lashing at some barrier, something I can't see unless I look for it—something shimmering and iridescent.

Something solid that began as a burst of energy exploding around me, through me. Past me.

When Hyacinth screamed.

A tall, lean shadow walks out of the fire, dark against the bright, and the force field follows him.

I laugh. Inappropriate.

Brian stands, dazed. Somewhere on the other side of the flickering mass, Fireball strains to keep it moving, to engulf us all, but Hyacinth's shield doesn't flinch. Tipping my head back, I see it, the dome, with faint swirls of shining pink, and purple, and blue, like the surface of a bubble.

My mind travels back to a moment by the Hampton fountain, shells standing frozen in a circle around us.

She and Shandy had no scorch marks on their clothes after they ran through a fiery corridor, no singed hair. Hyacinth never had a single cut nor bruise—she's remained untouched all this time.

We didn't know. None of us did. Not even Hyacinth.

Until the grief.

"I knew she'd have the strongest power," I murmur, then I retch into the grass.

Hyacinth stands behind us with her hands up, tears streaking her sooty face as she screams his name. Daisy sits in the grass next to her, fist pressed to her chest, staring up at the sky as she takes deep, gasping breaths.

Brian moves at a slow jog, then breaks into a run. When he reaches her, he folds his arms around her as she sobs against his chest.

He stretches an arm toward Daisy, and slowly she stands, letting him pull her in against his side. "You asshole," she says, voice breaking. "What is *wrong* with you?"

A harsh laugh escapes him as his arm tightens around her. "Hyacinth, you saved me," he says hoarsely.

She's inconsolable. "I told you not to do it again," she cries. "I told you not to leave us. You didn't listen."

Brian pulls back, eyes wet with tears. "I'm so sorry," he says, wiping hers away with a blackened thumb. "I just . . . I have to make sure you both survive. It's what they would have wanted me to do."

"Oh, Brian," Daisy says, sadness seeping into her voice. "Mom, Jack, they knew something was coming. They didn't tell the other Guardians. They didn't try to save themselves. But it was because they thought the three of us would have one another afterward. Not two. Three. What's survival if you lose everything that matters to you?" Her gaze hardens as she says, "If you *ever* do anything like this again, I will shave off *both* your eyebrows." And when he nods wordlessly, Daisy smacks a hand across the top of his head. "Always gotta be the goddamn hero," she bellows.

Hyacinth takes that moment to punch him in the stomach.

As he hunches, with a soft *oof*, he tries to reach for my hand. "Spencer."

Shaking my head, I don't look at him. I refuse. The tears don't stop, though. Nell gently helps me to my feet, wisely saying nothing.

Only Eleni is completely dry-eyed, standing a few feet away, staring back toward the fire. Or what remains of it. "The Key," is all she says.

The flames have lowered, revealing Fireball standing outside the barrier, his hands glowing.

Beside him, Ford throws a fist at it, rage twisting his usually controlled face. He directs his men to fire bullets that ricochet, sending them scattering back. An acid spray slides down the surface like water. Someone throws a grenade, and when the smoke clears, one of them is dead. If these men have names, identities, I will never know.

The wall doesn't waver.

Brian disentangles himself from his sisters, straightening to his full height.

I stare at my hands for a moment, the skin that absorbed that brilliant white light.

"Spencer." Brian's trying to get me to look at him, and I lift my murderous gaze, finding him watching me warily, his face pale. I plow both fists against his chest.

Brian stumbles back, but he's silent when I place a palm on his cheek, which is all scratchy with stubble. Afraid I'll start sobbing, I don't look at him when I pass that white-gold light back into him, a connection searing through the skin, bone-to-bone.

I thought I might have to ask the magic to transfer, but it understands what I want without words. Glowing tendrils wind down his neck and sink below the surface.

"What you did tonight?" I say in my lowest, most dangerous voice, which is to say slightly below a shriek. "Don't you *ever* do that again."

Brian's lips twitch, but he forces them still. "Noted."

I push him again, but this time a sob bursts out.

Though he flinches at the sound, I point over his shoulder, at Ford beyond the veil.

Ford refuses to back up as Brian crosses the grass, the rest of us a few steps behind him.

Brian stops, face-to-face with Ford, close enough that he could grasp him by the throat if a barrier didn't lie between them. The dome has closed in around us, and his men quickly surround it.

"You can't kill me, Brian," Ford says softly. "I'll survive anything."

Hyacinth steps up next to Brian, her face screwed up in concentration. Brian's gaze settles on the top of her head, tender. Tentatively, she pushes the energy out a bit with two hands, and the force field expands. By the time his men reach to pull him back, she's sealed Ford inside with us.

I brace myself for the pain Ford will unleash, but she's pinched off a second bubble to encase him, shrinking it close to his body until it's like plastic wrap clinging to his skin. Only his lips remain uncovered.

With one savage swing of his arm, Brian throws Ford onto his back, pinning him to the ground with his power, one booted foot planted in the center of his chest.

He rests his arms on his bent knee, leaning over Ford, whose face has gone red with rage as he struggles at Hyacinth's barrier, at Brian's power.

"What's survival if you lose everything that matters to you?" Brian murmurs, not breaking eye contact. He flexes his hand with a *come hither* motion.

Ford chokes, coughing, gurgling on bile and saliva, struggling against the inexorable pull as Brian summons the Key from inside him.

When Ford retches and it sails out of his mouth moments later, his eyes grow wide, horrified—the first time I've seen him afraid.

"No," Ford rasps, as Brian floats it farther and farther away. "That's mine."

Except it never was. The Key drops into my open palm and I close my fingers around the bone, all slimy and warm. It was Josh's Key. It's Matty's now. *Matty.*

Ford's head whips to the side, his wild eyes finding me. "How did you know?" he croaks. "What magic do you have?"

I let him watch me slip it into my hoodie pocket and zipper it closed. My gaze comes to a rest on Nell in her white dress, hair barely tangled, and I smile. "A random girl," I tell him.

Something feral crosses his face as he lifts himself up on his elbows. "I will find you," he spits out. "I will never rest. I will kill you and everything you love. You will never be safe from me."

But we're already walking away.

It's dark in the woods, but the staircase down to the amphitheater is made from gleaming stone slabs. We don't see anything at first, but as Hyacinth's shimmering dome expands, illuminating the space in a faint glow, we see the figure sitting in shadow, huddled on the ground, arms wrapped around his knees.

When the gleam hits the stone around him, Angel looks up. He lunges to his feet.

"Thank God," he chokes out, gesturing to the door he's been sitting on. "We have to go. Shandy's at the elementary school, but it's under attack."

*The most powerful people are split between here and the elementary school, like you ordered, waiting on your command.*

"Wait," I say suddenly. "I can't go. Everyone else should go to the school, but I know where Matty is." I scoop up the can of spray paint Angel brought and hold it out to him. "Make me a door," I say. Maybe I could do what he does, but I might not picture the location well enough, and I don't have time to experiment.

No one says anything. They know the stakes; they know I have to do this.

"Town Center," I say, somehow keeping my voice from shaking. "Near the fault line."

Angel kneels next to me, taking the can of spray paint. Though worry creases his brow, he begins spraying a large square. "You can't go alone," he murmurs.

I stand, my hands finding Nell's shoulders as she starts to volunteer. "Finn's at the school," I say. "He doesn't have a power. Ford will go there thinking that's where we've gone. He won't find me, but he'll find them. You all have to go, especially Hyacinth. There are children there."

Whatever Daisy sees in my expression causes her to exchange a glance with Hyacinth, who bites her lip. Angel hauls open the door to the elementary school. Through it, we hear explosions.

Brian is waiting for Hyacinth to look at him, and I'm not sure why until she tips her face up to his. "You have my permission to go with her," she says solemnly.

Daisy glares. "To be clear, you do not have permission to sacrifice yourself. You are not allowed to die." Hyacinth clings to Brian tightly for several seconds before letting Daisy lead her through the door. Her force field fades.

"We'll send whoever we can to Town Center as soon as possible," Angel promises with a quick squeeze of my shoulder, and follows them.

Nell doesn't hug me, doesn't say anything that'll sound like good-bye. She looks back once, eyes glistening, and disappears through the door in a glimmer of white.

Eleni catches it before it falls closed, but hesitates for a moment. As she tilts her head at me, emotions war across her face. When the expression settles, it's one of uncertainty. "No one has ever saved me before," she says in an oddly quiet voice. "Why did you?"

I don't know what to say to that. It hadn't felt like a decision. I lift one shoulder in a half shrug. "Because I could."

She blinks rapidly before turning away. "Try not to die," she says. But not in the flippant way she said it once before. Like she might mean it this time. In the next moment, she's jumping down.

The door closes with a thud, leaving us alone. I stare at it for a moment, then let my gaze shift to the one next to it.

"Spencer." Brian's voice is soft as he says, "Back there, you used my power. I saw you do it."

I did, briefly, but it didn't make a difference.

"You're very brave," he says. "You're saving us, you know that?"

"Go screw yourself, Brian," I snarl, but I reach out my hand for him to take. Because all those days ago, when we were preparing to travel into the unknown, he said he'd help me and that I wasn't alone. He meant it.

Together, we jump down.

## CHAPTER 20

*T*he world tilts.

One moment we're falling through a doorway, and the next minute we're flying up through one on the other side, landing hard on a white wood-plank floor.

I stare at a vaulted ceiling, trying to place it.

I know where we are.

And to be honest, I forgot about *them*.

"We've got to go," I gasp, already scrambling to my feet.

Saturday night is midnight movie night. People come with blankets and beer hidden in paper bags. When it rains, they sit on camping chairs underneath umbrellas.

It isn't Saturday night, but it was when the world changed. And on this stretch of grass, those people would have been the first meal when the ground opened.

Angel's door led us to the gazebo on the town green, less of a green and more of a sea—of bodies lurching forward, stumbling, tripping over the humans lying broken and rotting.

But I can't think of that now.

"Chester Graves's house," I manage to say before one of them crawls up the two stairs into the gazebo. "It's off Main Street. Matty is there. We have to get the Key to him."

Brian doesn't ask how I know this, just jumps over the railing of the gazebo and reaches for me.

*Oh God. The smell.* A gaping mouth, purple with blackened teeth, snaps the air by my ear as I leap down. *Bad.* But I can rank the bads now, and I've experienced worse.

We have no weapons.

Nails rake down my arm, piercing the fabric, and I scream through gritted teeth.

Brian hurls bodies out of my path. I see the wall of fire again and my stomach clenches. With the memory of his music in my ears, I sweep out an arm, sending a couple sailing back. As his power bursts out of me, exhaustion ripples down my body, turning my feet to lead. I stumble, nearly going down in the grass. "Brian," I manage, "Your power is . . ." *a pain in the ass.*

Every time he uses it, he grows weaker.

And I will too.

He struggles to clear a path through the forest we'd forgotten about, driving us closer to Town Center, closer to the fissure, but he's weak, quivering. It's a crowd of hundreds.

*Too many. Surrounded.*

The shells move in, fingertips swiping at my curls. With a raw cry, I send them fanning out, but a wave of dizziness brings me to my knees.

"Don't use my power," Brian gasps, hauling me up and behind a bush. Sweat beads on his forehead.

And yet, if he keeps using it, he'll pass out and we'll both die. In retrospect, he wasn't the best choice to come with me. I don't say this, though, as I see the same realization on his face.

I look right, then left, searching for a pathway. But we are beacons. In every direction, they morph into one unbroken unit. Sunken faces, limbs moving in fits and starts.

A shell launches itself at me, teeth gnashing. I fling out a punch, willing Eleni's strength to find me. Pain explodes in my fist, but the shell barely budges. *It doesn't work . . . Why won't it work when Brian's does?*

I leap back against an unyielding trunk of an oak tree as it comes at me again.

"Spencer, up!" Brian shouts.

*Up?* I glance up blearily at the tree limbs overhead. And then I'm shooting upward, with barely enough time to keep my head from crashing into its branches.

The tree leans slightly, but its limbs are sturdy, protective, like outstretched arms, and I reach a hand down.

He doesn't need it, but he takes it anyway, his feet brushing the trunk as he leaves the shells below. They reach for us, fingers skimming the underside of our branch. Brian helps me stand, and I grasp his arms for a moment, breathing in trees and sweat and blood.

I yank off my hoodie, using a clean patch to wipe blood from my face, from his. I transfer the Key to the pockets of my pants and let the hoodie fall.

The shells don't notice. They aren't even aware of each other. Just us.

"Keep going," Brian says.

I climb higher. My nails dig into bark. He follows beneath me, struggling to maneuver his long body in and around limbs.

We stop in a crook high enough that the shells can't reach us, low enough that the tree can handle our weight. I slump back while Brian rises to his full height next to me.

I watch him edge carefully out as far as he can go, holding a branch to keep himself steady, scanning the forest for a path out.

They keep coming, milling on the ground beneath us. The longer we stay, the more impassable the area will become.

I whisper, "Angel said they'll send help when they can. We just have to wait."

That's assuming things at the school are going well. Brian's head lowers, shoulders hunched. He's thinking they may not get here anytime soon. He's wondering how to use his power without passing out. I stare down at my hands, dirt and blood ground into the lines of my palms. If I can use Brian's power, I should be able to use Eleni's again, and the others' as well. I try to summon a force field, as Hyacinth did, an unbreakable barrier to protect us.

Nothing happens. I try again and again, my heart sinking further with each failure. I could do it when I was with Eleni in the school. Maybe it's proximity? But all of them are miles away.

I wonder how much pressure it would take, how many bodies, to fell a tree, and I stare up at the canopy edged in faint light, blinking back tears.

Streaks of pale pink are creeping in to melt the night's shadows. Perhaps it's not so bad if this is the last sky I see.

A cooling breeze flows over us again. The leaves rustle amid the scuffling and scratching, the soft gurgling sounds as the shells beg us for what they lost. Life, *real* life, only possible with a soul. I should have made mine count. A heavy sorrow settles in my chest, not just for them, but for all of us, for me. Because even now, beyond the fear and exhaustion, there's so much that I want.

"I'm sorry I tasered you," I say, committing his profile to memory, watching the slight rise and fall of his shoulders.

And he turns toward me. "Where is this coming from?" he says gently. "I thought we'd established I was in the wrong."

But I see the fire again, feel the heat burning the skin of my face. I see his eyes, the reflection of orange-red flames. "You almost died tonight," I say.

Half his face remains in shadow. "But I didn't."

"You would have if Hyacinth hadn't become one of the Incredibles. It felt like you died." It was a shocking breathlessness, my body hollowing out in an instant. When I thought Nell had died, it felt the same way. Like there were so many things I'd never gotten to say. Not everyone comes back the way she did. Some people die and stay that way. And now there's the rising panic that I'll lose him when I've just had the chance to know him.

"I'm still here," he says. "And so are you."

"Not forever." I clutch at my chest, remembering Shandy, bleeding out, thinking, *I didn't have enough time*. "I'm wondering if I can ask you for something. My IOU."

"I'm not going to die, Spencer, and neither are you. We'll figure a way out of this. You'll have a long time to cash in your coupon."

Another fear seeps in. He'll think this is a silly thing to want now of all times, when we're both straining to remain awake and fighting for our lives. "You're right. I changed my mind. And I'm mad at you anyway."

"What were you going to ask me for?"

Should I say it? What's the worst thing that could happen? He could say no when I'm stuck in a tree and can't flee. I could jump out of the tree. It's not that far. The zombies would break my fall. Once, I wrote a love letter to a boy, and he texted, *I think really highly of you as a person*. This would be even worse.

"What are you saying to yourself over there?" he asks softly.

"I have no requests and I never will," I say quickly. "If you die today, it's fine. I don't need anything."

He's quiet for a moment. "Maybe you could tell me what you would have asked so I won't have to haunt you forever."

It's possible he'll think there's something wrong with me. And yet . . . he had my hair in his pocket. "Remember that time I said we were going to make out?"

He goes still for a second, and I think about preemptively jumping. But then he clears his throat. "I remember."

"I have never . . . I have never made out with anyone before, not even one kiss," I say in a small voice. I have also never admitted that to anyone except for Nell. "Maybe it's not so surprising to you that no one ever wanted to."

"I don't think no one's ever wanted to," he says, even softer. "In fact, I know that's not true."

"You almost *died* tonight," I say again.

"But I didn't." He takes slow steps toward me along the length of the branch.

I still don't look at his face. "Anyway, I was wondering . . . if you don't have any plans right now, if you might want to? Just a peck."

Pause. "Did you ask for a peck?"

"Only a small one." I shrink back against the tree trunk. "You don't have to. Never mind, it doesn't matter."

"Of course it matters."

In desperation, I look for a way to climb to the other side of the tree. "You think I'm weird, don't you?"

"I think you're weird for many reasons, but not because of that." He catches my hand. "Where are you running off to?"

"I'm gonna go over there."

His fingers play lightly over my palm, then close firmly around my hand. "But the thing is, if we're going to do this, we're going to have to get a little closer."

He is a gigantic person. Obviously, I've always known that, but I didn't *know* that. He stands so close I could rest my face against his chest. His arms brace on the tree limbs on either side of me.

"Um. Okay," I manage.

But I look up, finally, to see his head tilted down and that blue gaze waiting for me. A smile, a tiny tug at one corner of his lips, draws my eyes to that spot. A shiver runs through me before it runs through him. He rubs the back of his neck and laughs, husky, and both corners of his mouth curve.

He isn't the sort to shiver. I am.

He lifts me until I sit wedged inside the crook of a branch. My heart beats against the inside of my chest, and I breathe far too quickly. His cheek is an inch away from mine, and still he doesn't move. My God, it cannot be worth it if it means being this nervous.

"I don't have my coupon," I say anxiously.

He tucks a curl away from my face and sighs, the air tickling my forehead. "This situation is so problematic. You're so short. I haven't shaved. We're trapped in a tree. You don't even have your coupon."

Still, he tips my chin up with his thumb and forefinger. "Okay?"

"Yes," I whisper.

I do not know what to do beyond silently scream, *Do what he does and act natural!*

Yet I look into his eyes, and the scream fades.

"Spencer," he murmurs. Before I can respond, his lips smack mine, all quick. "*That* was a peck."

Oh.

Leaning forward, he says against my ear, "Is that what you wanted?" His lips brush back across my cheek to the corner of my mouth. "Or did you want a *kiss*? He grazes his lips, feather light, against mine.

"I . . . I mean, you're already here."

I feel him smile. "Save your coupon for another time."

He holds my face in both hands the way I always imagined but never thought people actually did, resting his fingers along my jaw and the sides of my neck. He tilts my head and the sides of our noses brush. His mouth fits over mine.

His lips part, just a fraction, catching my lower lip gently between his.

Then he does it again. Soft, so soft. He tastes of woodsmoke.

His chin scratches mine and sends a thrill through my limbs. Somewhere on the edges of the blood, the death, I catch hints of the forest, of his soap or his detergent or whatever, and the smell of his skin, all sweaty and boyish.

His mouth opens against mine.

I put my hand on his chest where his heart touches my palm in quick little taps, and he inhales. His hands fall away from my jaw, arms wrapping around me hard and hauling me against him.

I used to think everything would stop, that the world would disappear if someone was kissing me. That's only partly true. I'm awake, hearing everything, feeling everything. He breathes, and his breath is mine. The rhythm of our heartbeats is the same. From somewhere deep inside him, the music comes again, and with it, a rustling of leaves showering down, dancing in the breeze. *We* are the entire world.

My fingers trace his jaw.

He shivers. I shiver.

It goes both ways.

The last kiss is slow, and lasting, though not nearly long enough.

When he pulls back, his nose and forehead rest against mine, our lips an inch apart.

I open my eyes, but I don't move away.

Brian smiles, then, a full smile, and he looks . . . he looks . . .

"This might be a weird thing to say right now, but you look like your dad when you smile," I say. "I know you think you don't."

His eyes open, an inch from mine. Moisture gathers in the corners, but they're bright, lit from within. "Really?" he whispers, and his exhale is part sob, a breath he'd been holding all this time. Something leaves him, some tightly bound energy unravels, passing through him and away.

I burrow my face against his chest, though the anxiety has returned and I know this moment has to end. But I have this thing I can remember forever. That one spark of joy gives me the strength to peek at the ground below.

The *ground* below. Grass and roots and earth. Not an ocean of reaching hands and open mouths.

We are alone in these branches. Like they were never there, a nightmare all along. We are alone, like two normal people in a normal world who wanted to kiss in a tree.

I clutch the front of his shirt. *"Brian."*

At the urgency in my voice, he follows my gaze downward and freezes.

Maybe we're both hallucinating. Maybe we fell out of the tree when we kissed and we're both dead.

Then I see shells have become blurs in the distance, like mere shadows the mind molds into dangerous things. They've been pushed deep into the woods, to the edges of Town Center, pushed with magic that was an extension of his soul.

I cup his cheeks. "Brian, look what you did."

He shakes his head slowly. He isn't pale. He isn't tired. "I didn't . . . I didn't feel it."

He's not supposed to. My palm hovers over his heart—his power will flow when this does.

*There are things that need to be thought. And felt.* Marcus Severin said that to me. The memory surfaces of a gray metal recipe box filled with knowledge, a box that doesn't exist until I need it to. Brian also has a box, one of his own making. Someday that box's lock will break completely. Someday the frozen aura Ian warned me about will melt.

He has time. Neither of us are dying today.

I should probably kiss him more often.

"Go," I say, pressing lightly on his shoulders, and we weave ourselves through the branches, our bodies lighter, free of fatigue.

On the last limb, he reaches up to me from the ground. I jump, and he catches me against his chest, in the circle of his arms. He stands tense, glancing around at tree trunks and branches, black in the pale light.

He grabs my hand, and my chest fills with certainty for the first time. *We're going to win.* It's a brief moment before I hear the echo of voices, distant shouts.

A chill seeps down my back.

I picture a man, a black hole crawling out of the gazebo floor.

*Angel always destroys his doors from the other side. We couldn't.*

"Ford's in Town Center," I whisper.

. . .

In the cemetery by Stony Peak Elementary School, the centuries-old tombstones are nearly black, covered in moss and dirt, and they lean crooked, rather than in the neat rows they once did. In Town Center, trees have knocked buildings askew. Moss and vines and fungus creep up the walls and leafy canopies replace rooftops. Town Center is a graveyard too.

A redwood, the kind I've only seen in pictures, splits through Llewellyn Hotel. Evergreens block our way to Main Street. There is no way out but through.

Brian runs behind me as I fling branches out of my path, light footsteps on a bed of leaves. It's easier now, using his power. Still taxing, like lifting a heavy box, but at least my body isn't on the verge of collapse. Dew drops hit the forest floor as we pass, and a silvery fog rises as though the ground is still hot with magic. The smell of the shells clings to my hair, my skin, but that pine-fir-spruce scent, as sharp as their gray-green needles, pierces through the blood and rot.

The night the ground opened and sent rays of light into the sky, I thought I'd never see anything like it again. And that was true. But everything's astonishing now. Everything is a memory I'll never forget. If I leave this place and time, fire and smoke will take me back. Trees will take me back. Some part of me will never leave.

I don't dare look behind us.

Brian's hand finds mine, gripping hard. "Main Street," is all he says, pointing to a break in the trees. Together we leap through, and there's broken pavement, and then mud squelching beneath my feet, and—

I dig my heels in, skidding; my arm goes taut as I reach the edge and only Brian's grip keeps me from sliding straight into the fissure.

He yanks me several steps back.

Gaping and jagged, the fault line is a wound with serrated flesh. Hundreds of shells latch on to the crumbling sides with hands and teeth. Pale, bruised fingers claw at the edge, struggling to climb their way out.

The slash cutting through the middle of Wellsie continues to hemorrhage without clotting, a dark splotch creeping slowly outward, stopped only by a magical wall. Unless we staunch it, it'll bleed until there isn't a single bit of unsaturated fabric left in this town. Brian sends a wave of power along the length of the crevasse, shoving shells away from the cliff. They fall soundlessly, not screaming, not hitting bottom.

The fault line lies in the middle of our path to Chester Graves's house. To Matty. It's only a segment and has to end somewhere, but there's no time to go around it.

"We'll float over it," I say, as I take a tentative step toward the edge.

But his hand slackens in mine as he inhales, quick and sharp.

"Spencer." There's something peculiar in his voice—shock, not pain. His fear hits me then, a wave so intense my stomach drops at the force of it. Fear for me.

I turn, searching his face for signs of fatigue. They're there, but faint, and his skin hasn't lost its color—

A feathery yellow tuft flutters in the breeze, adorning the dart sticking out from the side of his neck.

Brian stumbles once, then slumps into me. Desperately, my arms lock around his rib cage. "No, Brian, no, no, no, stay awake," I plead, even as we both sag to the ground.

Brian's eyes struggle to focus on my face. "I'm sorry . . . ," he says, carried on a soft breath, before those thick lashes come to rest on his cheeks.

My panicked mind races through the options. I could sail us both over the fault line, but then what? There are shells on the other side of it. Can I fend them off while floating him all the way to Chester Graves's house?

I could go without him. I can't. I can't leave him here defenseless. And Ford knows that.

"Matty!" I scream. "Matty! Please, Matty, please. Please." He won't hear me in the bunker. I know he won't.

Every muscle jumps as something rustles in the forest, maybe ten yards away. My vision blurs as I whip my head around, but I already know.

Ford emerges from the trees, flanked by guards, a dozen of them.

Despite the quivering in my arms and legs, I lay Brian on the ground as gently as I can and rise, backing up closer to the drop into nothingness. All it would take is a light push and I'd be gone.

We've been here before—a girl, a man, and his army. We're running through all the same scenarios over and over again like a version of hell. But this time, I truly am alone.

The mild facade Ford wore when I first met him is wiped away, replaced with the darkness he no longer hides. His gray eyes, burning with hatred, seem paler in this early morning light, like the gleam on a dagger. But he looks rumpled now, hair tousled, suit stained with smoke and dirt. Just a man.

"I was wrong about us being alike," he utters in a low, dangerous voice. "You are exponentially more irritating."

"Have you met yourself?" I say in that warbly voice that comes no matter how hard I try to be brave. There's an echo in this place where the world falls away. Magnifying my fear.

As the line of guns lift, I sweep their barrels up to the sky, but my legs wobble even harder. The exhaustion that comes with Brian's power is less debilitating and more of a constant pressure, like moving against a current.

The men struggle to inch forward as I freeze them in place. I know that it can't last, that I'm pressing against a door while a flood of people try to batter it down.

But Ford wasn't expecting this.

His eyes dart to the guns tilted away as his men strain to move them, to his own feet glued to the ground. "How are you doing this?" he utters. "The boy has telekinesis, not you." Something else flickers over his face, an emotion I recognize. Jealousy.

It should be satisfying. Except I don't know how I'm doing it. And as my outstretched palms waver, he sees that answer in my face.

"No matter," Ford says with a shrug.

The pain hits me in the middle of my chest, a rib-shattering punch, except it isn't physical. I crumble to the ground, racked with convulsions, unable to breathe or even to scream.

*You're nothing,* voices whisper, tearing into my skull, writhing around. *You're weak. You're going to die and it won't matter. Just give in to the pain. Death doesn't hurt.*

I can't feel fear anymore. Nothing is stronger than pain.

Yet I remember music. His hands cradling my face like I'm precious. I made him smile, a full one, when he only ever smiles a little.

I cling to his power. *Keep holding them. Hold them.* A plea against the fog of agony filling up every corner of my mind. *I can bear this. There is worse pain. I've felt it.*

"Call them," Ford barks.

I don't know who he's talking to, what he means, but somewhere outside my body, in another world that hasn't contracted in on itself, there's a rush of wind. A chorus of screeching caws. My eyes squeeze shut, arms wrapping about my head, shielding my face.

They swoop down in a flurry of flapping wings.

Claws dig into the back of my neck.

His man doesn't have to move to use powers.

*A group of crows is called a murder.*

A sharp stab pierces through fabric. A beak. Another, and another, as birds peck at my body, searching . . . *They'll find it.*

Scrunching tighter, I let one hand fall away from my head, shielding my pocket. They attack my fingers, peppering them with tiny wounds.

My hold on the men is breaking apart. I feel it disintegrate, as they push harder against it, inching forward. Including Ford.

*I can't. I can't. I can't do it anymore.*

"Matty," I whisper, my throat raw like I've been screaming. Maybe I have. "Matty, I need you."

But he's not here. And neither am I.

*Matty and I sit at the end of our driveway as the sun sets and he asks me if he's unlovable. He asks me if that's why his parents gave him away.*

*"If you think that, then it means you think I'm unlovable," I say. "Am I?"*

His soft brown eyes disappear and his answer never comes, though I already know what he said. *Never.* In my mind, Wellsie appears. Not the way it used to be, but the way it is now. Filled with nature that would be so beautiful if not for the shells lurking within. Buildings wedge between trees and ruined roads, yet birds are singing. My mind travels faster than I can walk, flying to the end of Main Street, searching for a house, a one-story cottage at the end of a narrow dirt road, and past it, to an overgrown yard full of tall grass. Hidden among it is a hatch, the one we'd always believed was there.

"Matty," I say.

A boy with a rainbow bun sitting hunched on a cot lifts his head in the dim glow of a camping lantern. All his worry, all his fear, lie etched in his forehead and the tense corners of his mouth. I stand before him, reaching out a hand.

"I guess Chester Graves wasn't as unhinged as we all thought him to be."

His eyes widen, lips forming my name but no sound comes out.

"Matty, come to the fault line. I need you to come now."

And then he's gone, the image of the bunker disappearing, leaving only darkness. A dream dissolving. A last vision my mind makes because I'm never going to see him in the flesh again.

"Knock her out, but keep her alive," Ford's voice barks at the corner of my mind. "Her head contains the location of four of the Keys. Radio the school—ask them if they have Daisy Radcliffe-Aster yet. I want all eight Keys within the hour. Kill the boy."

*No.* My eyes snap open. A feather sticks to my lips, bruises swell under my clothes, but the birds are a distant black swirl in the sky. Ford's deep, hollowing pain has faded, but the memory of it, the aftershocks ripple through me. Someone has Brian by the leg, dragging his limp body away.

And a blurry gray figure is almost upon me. My hand fists inside my pocket.

"Where do you think you're going?" he muses, as I crawl stiffly on my belly, through wet mud.

But I don't stop, not until I brush that torn cliff's edge and I thrust my arm out, hovering it over the fault line. "Do not come any closer," I manage, barely above a whisper.

His footsteps halt immediately.

"Stand down," Ford barks, and the men obey at once. "Don't move; don't use your powers."

A few lower their weapons, but not all.

I struggle to my knees, then my feet, standing hunched, arm straight out over the side.

"I'll drop it, I swear I will," I say, feeling every rough contour of the bone Key in my sweaty hand. "If you shoot me, hurt me, it's gone forever. Stay where you are. You will not touch me or Brian."

Ford says nothing for a moment, eyes on the Key in my hand. At his nod, all the men let their guns hang by their straps. "If you drop that Key, the fault line remains open forever," he says in his reasonable voice. "The wall around Wellsie will never come down. Your life and the lives of everyone here will be constant war, forever."

"Tell me how it would be different if the Key is in your hands." My eyes flit to a man on my left, who has inched half a step forward. Behind me, there's open air, where brown-red dust hovers. It's impossible not to imagine falling backward, arms pinwheeling. My foot is so close to the edge; a pebble skitters into the fault line, knocking lightly against sheets of rock on the way down.

*Don't think about it. Don't look down.*

I face Ford again. In my mind, I trace the lines and corners of the metal box that I know is there but shows no signs of opening. It won't; it knows the rules. "If I jump, the location of the four Keys I hid will die with me. Even if you get the last three Keys from Daisy and kill the Guardians they belong to, without *this* Key, *you're* still trapped here with nothing but your posse. That'll get old fast."

Emotions war across Ford's face. Anger, impatience, yearning. I can identify the emotions, but I can't feel them.

"If you are the most powerful man in the world," I continue, "but there's no one around to witness it, does it even matter at all? Do you?"

Something happens then. He flinches. I struck a nerve. But he doesn't respond to the question. "It appears we are at an impasse," he says instead. "But for how long? Do you intend for us to stand here forever?"

It's not the greatest plan, especially as the scraping behind me grows louder, of shells once again nearing the top of the ravine. Shells don't stop moving; they can't. And they've been inching back up this whole time.

I don't have an answer.

I don't need one.

"Siddy? SIDDY."

My name. Bellowed. From across the gorge.

It wasn't a pain hallucination. He heard me.

"Matty," I breathe.

I didn't pay much attention to the other side of the fault line. I didn't think about the shells climbing out on the other side, milling around aimlessly until now, when they've caught the scent of a live soul.

He only has a hammer as a weapon. When Chester Graves imagined the apocalypse, he went with nuclear war, something real, something human.

Matty swings wildly with the hammer, eyes never leaving my face. He's young and he's strong, but there are too many and he's alone. He must've known that, but he came for me.

"Shoot him," Ford says.

Matty dives to the ground.

Above him shells jerk, stumble, as a barrage of bullets tear through their bodies. Their mouths gape, always choking out a plea, but they feel nothing.

As more gunshots sound, I swing wildly to swerve bullets away from him. My muscles burn and throb, but I turn toward Ford and his men, pulling desperately, trying to yank their guns from their hands.

"She won't drop it," Ford snarls, calling my bluff. "Get her."

There's nowhere to go, I can't back up any farther. I shove the Key back in my pocket and sprint along the edge of the fault line, leading them away from Brian. My lungs seize.

Pain rips all the air away. I'm falling—no matter how fast I go, Ford's power can reach me anywhere.

Gasping, on hands and knees, I crawl. They'll be on me in less than ten seconds, five seconds . . .

A man's hand clenches around my ankle, dragging me back. My hands fist in the mud, but there's nothing to hold on to.

He looms over me, but his hands have morphed into blades that glint in the light, razor sharp against the skin of my neck. I freeze, panic fills my chest, igniting a scream, and then—

*Thump.*

The ground shakes beneath me, a faint vibration.

The blade lifts as the man leaps to his feet, tense.

*Thump.* The pebbles on the ground skip. *Thump.* A tree trunk cracks in the forest. *Thump.*

Behind me, Ford and his squadron have paused, seeking the source of the impact, steady like a drum. "What is that?" he mutters, his whole body rigid.

Behind them, the forest canopy is moving, rustling, branches breaking. The thumps come faster, and more trees come down.

*Footsteps.* Something's coming. But whatever it is, it's massive.

And when the giant white monster springs from the forest, leaping over us and the fault line like it's nothing, we all duck.

Matty flattens himself to the ground as a fluffy beast the size of an eighteen-wheeler lands lightly somehow and proceeds to crouch protectively over him, before letting out an ear-splitting, "*Rowrrrrrr.*"

Ford stares, uncomprehending.

*Oh. My. God.*

They sent backup. With the help of a girl who can change the sizes of things.

Matty always was her favorite.

Chad bats at the shells surrounding Matty, crushing five as she pounces on them. White furred jaws clamp over bodies, razor-sharp teeth puncturing skin and bone. She tears off a leg.

The familiar cracks of multiple guns firing draws my attention back to Ford. He and his men have recovered from the shock, sending a torrent of bullets in her direction. She barely notices—they're burrs to her—and clears the fault line again, hissing in a gust of foul-smelling wind while swatting down eight of Ford's men.

The man with knife hands is lifted full off the ground.

Still, I cower as one giant fluffy paw settles a foot away from me. The claws dig into the ground, each one about the length of my arm. I should have clipped those. Shaking, I lift my head when a whisker tickles my face. Yet Chad doesn't eat me the way I was sure she would; she rubs one side of her face hard against my torso and bounds off to the other side of the fault line.

Staggering to my feet, I move sluggishly, barely aware of the scurrying bodies of men attempting to flee. Gunshots, screams, fill my ears, but I keep going. My hand, covering the pocket where the Key lies, has gone numb, dripping blood from a dozen tiny punctures.

Brian lies unconscious, but unguarded where they dragged him, close to the forest's edge.

*I have to get to Matty——*

A man with a running start springs past me. Before I realize it, he's leapt to the other side of the fault line. An impossible jump—or it used to be. He vaults himself straight at Matty, bowling him over.

*No. Matty will survive. He has to.*

But a wall of gray steps in front of me, blocking my path.

"I changed my mind," Ford says. "If I have to tear through every inch of this town, if it takes me until the end of time, I will find those Keys myself." The words are quiet, but somehow filled with more rage than I've ever heard from him. "Without you."

He points a pistol straight between my eyes, and fires.

The clap of sound is thunderous at this range, exploding in my ears, a sound so familiar now. So familiar . . .

They say that right before you die, your life flashes before your eyes.

Time slows, a suspended moment.

But before you die, eyes squeezed closed, waiting for a darkness more total than that—for nothingness—*everyone's* lives flash before your eyes. Entwined with yours.

Not just images. Everything. You *feel* everything.

Joy swells in my stomach. There's a rising pressure in my temples, the one I get before I cry, followed by the radiating warmth of a hug. I'm holding Zora for the first time, handing her to Matty as my sister smiles through tears. My parents are telling the story of when I arrived as we sit around a table at Chuck's Steakhouse for my Adoption Day dinner. There's always a sense of relief every time I see them. When I wake up, when I come home. When I'm in pain. When I'm happy. Every time. No matter what. Not blood, but love.

And Nell . . . Nell is with me too. A tiny slip of a girl, six or seven, sits alone on a swing, staring up at me with huge eyes as I approach.

"Do you want to be my best friend?" I ask. It's the first thing I ever said to her.

"Okay," she says timidly, but without any hesitation.

She gets up off the swing, and suddenly she's older, standing in a smoky hallway, wearing a white dress. She grips a baseball bat, bloodied at the end. "Siddy," she cries as she sees me, voice trembling with fear.

"I love you," I say.

There's no pain. I'm dead before I feel it. My soul is floating away on the breeze.

And yet the earth is solid beneath my feet.

I open my eyes, blurred with tears, and squint at the man still pointing his gun. A thin tendril of smoke wafts from the barrel.

"Where the hell did she go?" he says incredulously.

My fingers fly to my forehead, smoothing over clammy but intact skin. Looking down, I see my body, alive and definitely solid. Except I'm not. Not to him.

The bullet went through me.

*Nell.*

Ford blinks, focusing on my face, and his expression twists with fury.

*He can see me again. Crap.*

One of his hands closes around my hair, the other my throat. Always the neck. But this time, he squeezes without stopping. He'll crush my throat, as I fumble at his fingers.

Except I know now what to do, how it works. How *I* work.

I have to . . . *You have to connect with the world, with people*, Daisy says in my mind.

So much distance between us. They're miles away.

My eyes flutter closed.

She stands in an elementary school hallway, glasses fogged, her hand stretched out, searching for me.

I reach, fingers spread the same way, sensing . . . energy. Shadows dot a map of a school. Bodies like inkblots bleeding over paper.

I see them the way Daisy sees them.

Eleni turns toward me, eyes narrowed, flushed but barely sweaty. "Don't just stand there, put some muscle into it."

I lock eyes with Ford, bending his fingers back with mine, slowly, painstakingly, strength against strength.

His eyes widen in shock, and behind it, envy. "How?"

He's not prepared for my backhand, one that sends him sailing backward, crashing into the ground with a force that cracks rock.

I expect the gunshot, don't even jump at the sound. The bullet leaves a white tail in its wake, like plane tracks in the sky, inching through the air as though moving through molasses. Time has slowed, or I move faster, ducking, easily. *Powers change when you change*, Shandy says in my mind. He lies on a nurse's bench, unconscious. But alive.

I stalk forward as Ford scrambles to his feet, stuffing the gun in the waistband of his pants.

The pain he sends next is momentary. *We're stronger together.*

Hyacinth lifts a shield, expanding it outward, sheltering the school and everyone in it. A force field materializes between Ford and me, shimmering, thin as a bubble, but as impervious as he is. And the pain ceases. Instantly.

Hyacinth's solemn eyes meet mine. "You—"

"Can't beat us," I say.

Ford and I stand, unmoving, staring at each other through the invisible wall.

His gang of armed followers have scattered, running from the monster that used to be my cat. It's just us now.

Slowly, we circle each other.

I inflate the barrier, shoving at him with its impenetrable force. Hands pressed to its surface, he pushes back, though his feet skid all the way to the ragged border of the fault line.

He sinks to a crouch, driving his fists into rock, holding on.

Gritting my teeth, I try to bowl him over, but he won't let go. Sweat runs down the side of my face. I ease the pressure, panting, just for a second.

He punches at my dome, not managing to puncture it, but hard enough that I stagger back.

Slowly, he stands, not looking over his shoulder, not afraid, the way I was, of falling backward. He's too strong for me to budge.

I pace back and forth, wiping the moisture on my brow. I meet Matty's eyes across the ravine. His face is bruised, lip split. His hammer hangs at his side, dripping blood. The man who leapt over the fault line lies on the ground, unmoving. Matty paces as well, pale, unable to cross a canyon.

*Ford can still hurt him.* Determined to distract him, I raise my brows. "Does it bother you that I have more powers than you do?"

His nostrils flare at my words.

"I don't own them," I add. "I borrow them. I couldn't do that with you, though. You'd have to be open to people, to letting them affect you and giving something of yourself back, and we both know that's never gonna happen. I can't make you feel anything at all."

Triumph lights his eyes now. "All you're doing is listing reasons why I'm stronger."

"But you're not. You're broken," I say quietly. "Did you know powers evolve? Even if you live forever, yours never will. Because it's the people in your life who change you and you don't have anyone. I pity you."

With those words, a flash of anguish, a memory, maybe, washes over his face. But I'll never know the details of his life. I'll never know what made him, or if he ever had a normal dream like being a fireman or traveling the world or falling in love. His face is already hardening, and with another burst of effort, he rams against the force field with both hands.

I brace myself against it, though my feet slide back a few inches.

Face-to-face through the shield, he smiles. "All that *borrowed* power, and for what? I'm still here. You're not better."

If I can't beat him, he'll be a constant thorn piercing everyone I love. We're deadlocked, and I stare desperately at the ground where he stands mere feet from the fault line's edge, feet firmly planted.

His once-polished dress shoes, now caked with mud, draw my attention.

The same mud coats mine.

My messy footprints smear the ground surrounding Ford, a splotchy semicircle completed by the sharp precipice of the cliff behind him.

Slowly, I lift my head. "I don't have to be better to matter. All I have to be is this."

My force field disintegrates as I lower my hands, and with it, the last of my fear. It stuns him that I've done it, those gray eyes in that nondescript face filling with sudden trepidation.

I step back.

Across the miles, Angel turns, paint smeared over his hands, up his forearms. His warm eyes meet mine.

"Sinkhole," I murmur.

Ford's lips form a word—*No.* But no voice escapes them.

I only see his face in the moment before he's gone.

Lost. Hollow.

Slabs of rock and earth crumble into nothing as the crescent of ground beneath him breaks off and collapses, and the fault line swallows him whole.

He doesn't scream as he falls, even when the cascade of rubble becomes distant and fades completely. Paul Ford never makes a sound. Maybe the drive for this Key—for all the Keys—was the only thing making him *him*, and without it, there was nothing. When he hits the bottom, if there is one, maybe he'll just be a body. A shell.

In the silence, I stumble the last few yards to the forest's edge, to Brian, collapsing next to him.

Across the fault line, Matty watches me. I've never seen him tired before, but he looks exhausted now, moving with his back hunched.

*It's not him, it's me.*

Wearily I hold out my hand to him. Josh's Key. His Key. I'll have to float him over here.

He shakes his head. One hand brushes his heart as he looks at me, tears in his eyes.

My outstretched arm stops shaking. My breathing slows. Energy, shared from his endless pool, courses through me, chasing away the fatigue. I straighten up as the weight lifts from my shoulders—awake, and it feels like the first time.

"Siddy, the Key," he says over the distance, hoarse, but clear. Like he's next to me. A part of me. "Look at it."

The moment I do, everything else is blotted out by light. My fist, radiating a bright white glow. The Key burns like it knows me, like it belongs to me.

We always thought it was a blood sacrifice bonding Guardians to their Keys. That the magic passed on to every successor matched that which was within the bone—a physical connection. Like calls to like.

But the Guardians told me magic merges with the soul—it doesn't work otherwise.

A soul, a formless thing, fills every part of you.

As Matty's Key activates in my hand, I feel something in my chest hum in response.

It doesn't see a difference between Matty and me. Because in those moments, when I feel a person or they feel me, we're the same. And maybe he and I always have been. Because it was never blood that connected us anyway. Because we made each other who we are.

As I lift the glowing Key to my lips, it vibrates against my skin, listening.

"Let the wall fall," I say to it. "Bring the magic back to me."

I don't have to explain; it understands what I mean.

Whispers—faint, like leaves rustling—travel on the wind as the Key calls to the magic.

And the magic answers.

I was never close enough to see what the wall around Wellsie looked like, but I feel it explode into mist, sense the golden tendrils snaking toward me, through air, over ground, between trees, catching shells in a web. There is movement all around me as the squirming bodies are swept past me to the edge, and over.

The magic travels, searching for the rest of the magic. It finds only people. Wispy golden fingers reach inside them, seeking something shapeless and incorporeal, and tugs . . . gently at first, then harder.

My eyes snap open as I feel the tug in my own chest. There's no give.

*Magic is meant to be ephemeral, Shandy once told me. But if it's used too often for too long, it'll fuse to the soul. If someone tried to take that magic from someone it had merged to . . .*

The tugs turn painful, burning, forcing a stretch.

The magic has been trapped here too long with nowhere to go, no new people to drift to. It's tied to us now, for better or worse. The only way to take it back would rip our souls out along with it. Leaving shells.

"Enough," I murmur, and the magic stops yanking. "Go home."

It skims past me, slipping over the edge. With a sigh, like it's about to go to sleep, the magic drapes itself within the chasm, like folds of shimmering ribbon.

The earthquake isn't jarring this time. A rolling wave ripples beneath me as the two edges of the fault line drift back together, puzzle pieces locking into place. The seam, a lightning bolt zigzagging over the land, smolders only for a moment. But the scent of scorched earth lingers after the shifting ceases, when the magic rests once more.

Everything is quiet. Tears pool beneath my lids. When I open my eyes, I know they're there, but I can't see the rainbow ghosts tethered to the fault line, the evidence that magic was here. You can only see them when it rains.

I let the Key slip through my fingers and clatter on the ground. Huddling in next to Brian's sleeping form, all spread out like a star, I brush the badly cut hair from his eyes, and press my nose against his cheek.

Through a blur of tears, Matty's face appears as he falls to his knees beside us.

In the distance, a giant white beast is prancing about, searching in vain for more shells.

"Do you have *any* idea what I went through this past week?" I say through dry cracked lips. "While you were sitting in a bunker doing literally nothing?"

Matty wisely doesn't answer, just bends over me, arms coming around me and hugging tight.

We stay that way, listening to the sounds of the forest and the rhythmic spinning of helicopter blades somewhere overhead.

## CHAPTER 21

### One Week Later

$S$ometimes I think about some of the mean things I said to people in elementary school and I want to die."

Dr. Banerjee sits in a weathered leather armchair, watching me with zero judgment from across the coffee table. I'm not sure the moose head on the wall is her style. The bright silk tunic she wears is the one pop of color in a very monochrome brown room.

We sit in a suite in one of the hunting lodges on Mount Hemsworth.

Most of the displaced people have been temporarily relocated to one of the hotels or vacation houses up here. Though the fault line opened partway up the mountain, the majority of structural damage is concentrated in Town Center. At least they managed to restore power to the south. The snow has yet to melt and no one, least of all the person who did it, knows if it ever will. The area of town to the east, the rich side, remains the same as before—it's surreal to walk through the quiet neighborhoods of mansions that don't have a scratch on them. Figures.

But even if they didn't lose anything, no one in Wellsie came out unscathed. I suppose that's why the town is mandating these therapy sessions.

"What did everyone else talk about?" I ask, drumming my knees.

"You know I'm not going to tell you that," she says gently. "This session is for you, not them, and not me. You can talk about elementary school if you want. You can talk about anything. You can talk about nothing. Or you can come back when you're ready."

"Well, the thing is, I saw people die," I say hesitantly. "So, on top of all my, like, regular-person issues, how many sessions do you think this will take?"

Dr. Banerjee takes a sip of what looks like black coffee. "Well, the good thing about therapy is it doesn't have an expiration date. Like Cheetos." I sense a bone-deep weariness matching my own, but you wouldn't know it from her face or the fact that she sits in her chair without slouching, which is impossible for me no matter the circumstances. "What happened here will never be okay. We are all grieving and trying to heal. But I promise you a day will come when you feel normal again, you won't think about zombies for long stretches, and you'll be a person who laughs and makes plans for the future. And even then, regular-person life can be a lot. You can always come back."

"You're nicer than the military guy who debriefed me. I think he was military . . . I don't know who he was, to be honest."

"Well, I'm not a part of that," she says. "I live in Wellsie. I was here during the crisis, which I guess is what people are calling it. I was at Stony Peak. I'm not sure if you know this, but Ian McNamara is my husband."

I didn't know. But I do know that under his leadership, everyone at that school survived.

"Anything you tell me regarding your experiences in the last two weeks, I understand on some level," she continues. "If that makes it easier."

Because she experienced it too. "Sometimes I wonder about empathy," I say then. "Do we always have to feel something ourselves in order to understand someone else?"

She contemplates that. "I think it depends on the person. There's no right way or wrong way. If one assumes all empathy to look the same way, they are therefore expecting everyone to behave the way they do ... which is not empathetic, is it?" She leans forward, elbows on her knees. "There are always going to be people we can't relate to, people we'll never love, people we'll never meet. In those situations, you have the opportunity to see how far your empathy can be stretched."

"Some people suck, though," I mutter.

"Whether someone is worthy of empathy isn't something you need to decide. You do get to decide if it's something *you* wish to extend to someone. If it'll harm you or not. Caring for yourself and caring for others is a balance."

"So, what you're saying is, maybe it's fine that I don't care that Paul Ford fell into the fault line where he will be imprisoned for eternity because he can't die."

She doesn't respond, because it's my emotional well and therefore my choice. Okay.

"I hurt friends once," I tell her. "I decided what was best for me was not being friends with them, but I was wrong. So, what then?"

"What then?" Dr. Banerjee lifts one shoulder. "You changed your mind. And she decided to forgive you. That was her choice, too."

My mouth hangs open. "How did you know that?"

"On the one hand, I seem to be able to sense what people might need from me in terms of healing. On the other hand, I can quite literally feel what you're feeling, so there's that."

"Right."

Her dark eyes are very soft. "People make mistakes, but you know now that you get to choose the person you want to be. It's not a straight path, there are obstacles, and the journey never ends. But you're not alone on the road."

The lobby is packed with people when I make my way downstairs.

People might be looking at me. They might be looking at me wherever I go.

Eleni says they aren't looking at us; they have their own shit to worry about.

She's probably right, but I weave through as quickly as possible until I reach the door to the massive deck with its unparalleled view. That's what our travel brochures say about Wellsie. Unparalleled views. Majestic peaks. Lush foliage. Paired with small-town charm.

The air stays cool on the mountain, turning icy the higher you get, no matter the season. Up here, the world smells fresh and clean, the way snow smells. Up here, the town looks beautiful, half-covered in forest, half-covered in ice. The smell down there will dissipate slowly the more bodies they find and bury. Some won't be found, though, and will become one with the moss and the roots of the forest floor.

They have two different lists. They've been careful to focus mainly on one of them: Missing Persons. But as that list diminishes, the focus will weigh more heavily on the other: The Death Toll. It shifts by the day. It was over a hundred the last time I checked, on Day One. I haven't checked since.

Most of Dr. Banerjee's sessions will be grief or trauma counseling.

You either lost someone or witnessed it, and the knowledge of how people died, the violence of it, will make peace harder to come by. She knows that, yet she's here every day, with all the other therapists in town.

When I come up beside him at the railing, he doesn't speak at first. He stands, looking down, past the thick evergreen forest—Wellsie's real forest—to the magic one below. At night, you used to be able to stand anywhere on the mountain and see nothing but sky and stars above, and below, a scattering of twinkling lights spread through the valley, representing lives. It'll take forever to rebuild.

Bronze sunlight glints in Shandy's waves of black hair. "This is Angel's favorite time of day: the golden hour," he murmurs. "He says everyone looks good in this light." He pushes yellow-tinted sunglasses to the top of his head, sweeping his thick bangs back so I can see his eyes that crinkle at the corners.

Shandy looks far too hot for someone who was in a coma for days. Whenever one of us says "coma," though, he insists it wasn't that serious. The thing is, when you're not sure someone will wake up, it's serious. Though Dr. Klein was able to remove the bullet, there was no way to know if Shea was speeding recovery or death. And no one in Wellsie can bring someone back from the dead.

"Why are you scowling, Sid Spencer?" he says, smiling, though it's not quite the brilliant Shandy smile I remember. Not as wide, not as instant. Sadness lingers at the corners.

"No reason," I say, as he drapes an arm over my shoulders. "How are you feeling?"

"Healed," he says, too brightly. "Twinged for a couple days after I woke up, but that went away."

For a moment, I'm not sure what injury he's referring to. But if it's the emotional one, he's lying. When he thinks of Morrissey, he rubs the new scar on his chest, but the real wound is a couple inches right, where his heart lies.

Brian said Shandy knew Morrissey the best. It's not just Morrissey Shandy grieves, now that there's nothing but time for everything to surface. Parker. Josh, too.

*No one knows who they are until the moment presents itself.* Parker said those words to me. It'll never be okay, what Josh did, what Morrissey did. But you can still love someone who hurt you deeply.

Shandy didn't say he was shocked at Morrissey's betrayal, that he never imagined Morrissey could do such a thing. Beneath the warm exterior, Shandy thinks *everyone* could, that it takes conscious effort to care, like a muscle you have to exercise frequently or it atrophies. I also know that several years ago when Shandy's parents died, when he went through his dark period, he hot-wired a car, took it for a joy-ride without a license, and crashed it. He could have killed someone. He could have died himself. Because nothing mattered to him then. He only avoided juvie because Dr. Banerjee petitioned the judge for leniency.

I'm not supposed to know these things, things he never told me directly.

I don't know if they'll choose to forgive Morrissey, but Shandy *has* been driving his cars. Morrissey's last words probably wouldn't have held up legally, but it turns out they were in his will.

It's not like anyone would have stopped Shandy regardless.

Here in Wellsie, we're protected.

If we stay, we'll be left alone, no surveillance within town. But if we choose to leave, we have to sign a document agreeing never to use magic outside of Wellsie's borders and allowing all our movements to be tracked. That's the only way, they said. *They*, the people who came in to clean up the mess.

Most of the surviving tourists chose to go home as quickly as possible, signing whatever they had to. Hampton College dismissed its entire surviving student body.

"Some people don't have homes to go back to," Eleni said to me, when I asked her if she planned to leave. "Homes we left for a reason."

Angel has been home already, secretly, through doors they can't track. I spot him now, coasting into the parking lot on a bicycle. I'm pretty sure there's a person-sized reason he keeps coming back.

"We should make tree houses," I say. "The tourists will like that." Shandy doesn't say anything. He doesn't want to say we might never have tourists again. Considering that's how a large portion of the townspeople make their living, we need them to come back.

People in the surrounding towns saw the magic explode into the sky. They're not going to buy the story the news is reporting of the northern lights being visible in Wellsie for the first time. Wellsie is a fault-line town and they know it; everyone knows it. The rumors will spread. I think people will still come and they'll sign away rights to see for themselves if there's any magic left here. Outsiders will be allowed in and out of Wellsie, but they have to sign a pretty major nondisclosure agreement at one of the new checkpoints around the town's border and surrender all phones and cameras. I haven't looked at the document, but my father has. You'll go to jail for life if you spill, no lawyer, no trial. And they will be watching.

It'll be clear things here aren't normal. Like, it's snowing constantly in South Wellsie. But when they leave, they'll be unable to talk about what they've seen.

I don't want to be trapped in Wellsie forever, to trade a magical barrier for a man-made one. I relayed this fear to Daisy early on, but she'd looked at me with a gravity that rivaled Hyacinth's.

"Sid Spencer, we are not staying forever in a tiny white town. I have things to do. We will simply fake our own deaths."

Eleni walks up next to Shandy, wearing all black today but for her bright red lips. Her dark hair is slicked into a severe bun at the crown of her head. She sets a whitish thing on the railing in front of her.

The cat-sized Chad looks utterly miserable, but she allows Eleni to saw a smelly mat from her fur with a pocket knife. She allows it because she spends much of her time with Eleni now and I'm wondering if Matty and I should sign a joint-custody agreement.

"I drank some of Casey's Mountain Dew, so you owe me one of Morrissey's cars," she says to Shandy. "Did you think I wouldn't?"

"Sid was the one who made that bet with you," Shandy grumbles.

I shrug. "It was perhaps overly optimistic of me to assume she would not ingest human waste under any circumstances. No matter what it tastes like, it's literally pee that passed through a body, filtered through kidneys, excreted through a urethra."

"Well, I'm straight trash," she says. "But I can confirm it's legit. I swear I am not lying."

"You know what the best part is?" Shandy muses. "When zombies were coming out of the ground, he thought his pee might be magic and that he should drink it. Just in case it never occurred to you that that's what we all should've been doing." His smile is one of wonder, though, like nothing could make him lose that, not even near death. "There's a girl in there who sees the animal in you."

Eleni rolls her eyes. "How is that a useful power? Bunny ears mean you like group sex. A fox tail means you're foxy. A pig snout means you sniff for truffles and eat shit."

Shandy frowns at her. "This one girl has the heart of a manatee. You can't have something snarky to say about a manatee."

"Yeah, we've crossed paths," Eleni says. "But I don't need to know a sea cow. Later I'll pretend we've never met."

*They're too gentle. They trust everyone. They have no aggression, no defense mechanisms. Probably just float around having feelings. So easy to hurt.* That's what she thinks, anyway.

Wait, does she think *I'm* the manatee? I've changed. I'm hard now. I've seen things.

"God, save it for therapy," Eleni says under her breath.

I scowl, but make no attempt to rein in my feelings. "You don't have to like me, you know. That's fine. I don't need your approval." A frisson of pride uncurls in my chest, small, but meaningful.

She looks away sharply, facing the valley, and though her eyes narrow, the sunlight softens the color, turning them green-gold. "You remind me of her," she says.

Her sister. I know this, though she's never told me directly.

A hesitant note creeps into her voice. "She moved to California. I should call her. But we don't get along great. She thinks I'm mean."

I make my eyes all round. "Really? You're kidding."

The corners of her lips twitch, the barest hint.

We've never talked about her past. I wasn't supposed to know her life, even if on some level she wanted me to. I wouldn't have been able to do what I did otherwise.

"*I* will save that for therapy," she says, ending the conversation, but her eyes don't harden. With a flick of her gaze toward Shandy, who's been politely looking away and pretending not to hear our entire conversation, she says, "We don't need to hash this out as a group. Keep my Key hidden—don't tell me where. If any of us decide to transfer our Guardianships, the new people don't need to know, either."

With that, Eleni heads to the stairs without a backward glance, conversation over. "McRib, let's move!"

My—our—cat leaps off the railing and bounds after her.

Shandy watches her leave before tilting his head at me. "You already know my answer. It's the right thing after . . . everything."

There are five remaining Guardians. And if the world can guess what happened here, more people like Ford might come.

When the squared-jawed man sat me in an interrogation room, I wasn't inclined to trust him, given he was part of the team sent to cover this whole thing up. You can't really withhold information from a man who can detect lies, but I had nothing to give him anyway.

I don't know where the Keys are. Except for one that I kept. But Square Jaw isn't concerned with Keys that can't work.

The first thing Brian said when he woke up on the edge of the fault line was to retrieve the rest of the Keys from Daisy and hide them. Wellsie's barrier was down and the outside world was moving in.

There's a vague memory of seeing Daisy, of having Paul's/Josh's/Matty's Key in my hand, clacking against Parker's, Daisy's, and Matty's original Key. The final four.

But then there's nothing.

Some days I feel something in my mind, a shadow with hard corners, but it retreats the moment I try to grab it. I'm not sure when it'll surface fully. Maybe it never will.

Having done a thing I don't remember will never not be weird.

If Square Jaw put any of this together, he didn't reveal it to me. He had no real interest in knowing their locations as long as no one else did.

Ours is not the first fault line in the world to have opened, apparently.

We never knew—and will never know—about the others. If something goes wrong, if it affects the civilian world, these men with no names and probably no fingerprints ensure the system prevails.

It's never been true that Guardians are the only people with magic in this world, uncontrolled by outside influence. It's not true for Wellsie. And possibly countless others.

They may have kept the history vague on purpose, but Ford didn't appear out of thin air. There are people like him waiting to rise up again, waiting to wreak havoc on some other unprepared fault-line town. Square Jaw and his covert team can't find and imprison them all.

I don't know what I want to happen to men like Fireball. Or to those like Adam O'Brien, who wept when they herded him into an unmarked van. Square Jaw said they'd rehabilitate them. Rehabilitation is not something that exists in our world, only punishment. I'll never know what he meant.

As for the rest of us, we're just supposed to exist here. With magic.

I don't know if it's right, for us to have it. But it's up to us to keep each other safe now. It's up to us to decide if we want to be part of a mysterious system keeping immense power in check.

We do not. Wellsie's Keys are gone from memory now. No one, Guardian or otherwise, can open the fault line here again.

Angel joins us at the railing, and the golden-hour light kisses his cheekbones, turning his eyes to molten caramel. Paint splatters his clothes, as per usual. Shandy tries to rub a smudge from his jaw to no avail.

"Hey, whatever happened to that unicorn?" I ask Angel.

He grimaces. "Thriving. He bonded with Shandy, licks him and everything."

That doesn't sound evil to me.

"But he still has two rows of razor-sharp teeth and only eats raw meat, which could include humans," Angel says. He glances askance at Shandy. "I guess I have to keep coming back. We have a demon son together."

A smile spreads over Shandy's face. "I named him Chad the Second."

Ella is waiting in the parking lot in her white jeep. Matty sits in the front seat. It's the first time in her life she hasn't honked five cheerful, jarring times, even if I'm literally right there.

She doesn't know how to act around us.

Neither do my parents.

Our house doesn't have electricity yet, but I did go back the other day. I tried to help my parents clean, to clear the yard of debris and, like, dead bodies. By "try," I mean I stepped foot on the property for a total of five seconds, then escaped to Ella's house.

For the time being, my parents, Matty, and I are staying with their friends on the eastern side. I have a whole guest room to myself there, but every morning I wake up in the chair by my parents' bed. It turns out fear lingers even after a nightmare ends.

Some nights I stay with the Aster-Radcliffes because my parents have been letting me do whatever I want in the name of trauma, and that won't last forever. They met Brian once and they have no idea he's my . . . whatever he is. He made a pie for my mom, though, so she likes him. My dad despises him, so maybe he's guessed.

Ella and Matty are quiet in the front seat. She drives so slowly and carefully. It could be because Zora is in the car. It could be because of us.

I've never seen her cry as hard as she did when they finally let them back into town. She cried so hard she almost threw up. And thus, I almost did too.

She wasn't here, but the fear, the horror, the sleepless nights—she had those, too.

Zora, at least, is normal.

"Hey, Zo," I say to the girl currently playing with makeup out of my sister's purse.

Ella glances in the rearview mirror. "Zora, oh my God," she gasps. "You can't do that! You will trigger people."

The five-year-old next to me with the blond ponytail that matches her mother's has used some pale powder and red lipstick to zombify her face.

"Zora, what if we make a deal," I say, though my eyes are on my sister's. "I have a Key for you. It used to belong to a woman named Parker van der Kamp with hair like yours."

Zora's eyes light up. "Is it magic?"

I shake my head, making sure Ella can see. "No. I mean, technically it is. But the person with the power to use it is gone forever, which means no one can use this Key again. But if I give it to you, you have to promise not to dress like a zombie around other people. Does that sound good?"

When she nods, I drop the dead Key into her hands. It's not the only Key that belonged to Ford and is thus inactive, but Morrissey's is hidden away somewhere in the recesses of my mind.

I kept Parker's because I thought she should be remembered.

Ella relaxes visibly, but her hands grip the steering wheel so hard her knuckles turn white.

I settle back in my seat while Matty turns to look at me over his shoulder. He knows what I'm off to do. He said it was my choice. A smile touches his lips as he directs his next words to Ella. "Remember when you told Mom and Dad that Siddy had a boyfriend named Roberto just to focus their attention on someone else, and even though you were lying, they asked Siddy about him constantly for a solid year?"

As the car slows to a stop by the entrance, Ella scowls at him, a hint of her old self emerging. "Why must we bring this up?"

"Siddy has a real boyfriend now," Matty says.

"Matty," I sputter.

"OH MY GOD." Ella is swiveling in her seat at the same time I'm slipping out of the car. "SIDDY, WHAT IS HIS NAME—"

I slam the car door shut, though the sound of her muffled shrieking follows me as I hurry down a white path through a great expanse of manicured grass.

And tombstones.

I've been to many funerals this week, for people I vaguely knew, for Josh Monroe and Parker van der Camp, for Dustin Miller, and for strangers. For William James Morrissey III.

Nell stands on the path up ahead, meeting me halfway. The other night, I dyed her hair rose gold. It's not perfect because it was me, but she loves it, like, *really* loves it, all the way to the dried-out ends. Because she was never really perfect to begin with. "You're going to be nice?" she says quietly, as we walk the rest of the way together.

"You like him, right? Like, genuinely like him?"

"No," she says. "I love him."

And I knew that. There's a part of her he brings out, a side that agrees to do bold things like cliff dive and skinny-dip. Because people give you different things. And it's important to her that I fix this. "I like him," I say. "I always have."

She lets me go the rest of the way alone. When I glance back, she's lurking by a tree, pretending to examine the leaves of a maple like she's never seen one before.

The graves are covered in pungent dark soil because the grass hasn't had time to grow yet. Finn stands at the foot of one of them, shoulders slouched, hands in his pockets, staring at a white marble headstone.

Three members of the Wellsie High basketball team died the night the fault line opened.

Finn glances over his shoulder when he hears me approach. He tenses when he sees me, wary. A sadness lingers in his eyes, the way it does for all of us.

We stand quietly, looking down at the grave of Michael Keegan. I didn't know him.

"Do you remember that time, after an open mic, we went to the diner?" I begin softly. "We ate fries and talked about that one performer who was off-key the entire time, and how painful it was to sit there for two whole songs without cringing, only to realize he was sitting behind us the entire time?"

Finn winces. "Yeah, and it's not an exaggeration when I tell you it's been almost a year and I want to fall straight through the floor just thinking about that."

"Same." I slap his back awkwardly. "The point is, sometimes we hurt people we never meant to hurt."

Finn turns to face me, studying my face with the same sweet hope in his eyes that he had the night I first spoke to him, when he didn't have any friends yet. "I'm still sorry," he says.

"I'm sorry, too," I say. "Because I know you, Finn. I know you're a good person. And we have to be friends again because . . ." I jerk my chin toward Nell, who is currently shredding leaves as she watches us. "Look at the state of her." His gaze follows mine, and a tender smile touches his lips.

"Friends," he agrees, opening his arms. This time, when he hugs me, it's exactly the way I remember. "Is this why you wanted to meet?" He pulls back, perhaps sensing my tension.

"Um, well, I *do* have a favor to ask you," I say, biting my lip. I honestly think he's going to say no. "You never got a power." He's not the only one who didn't. At first it wasn't clear to me why until I went to my first funeral. Until I saw the rawest of griefs that matched the way Finn looked that day in the cafeteria. Some people were too broken for the magic to find the essence of them beyond the pain. It couldn't connect. I understand how it behaves now; I held it in my hands.

I clear my throat in his silence. "I have a Guardianship I was hoping you'd take. Matty gave it to me. It's . . . it's complicated, but he got it from a guy named Josh. He was—"

"The guy who opened the segment," Finn says slowly.

"Matty already has a Guardianship of his own and doesn't want a second one." Matty never figured out his second power, but that didn't matter to him. "He transferred Josh's to me except I don't want it either—it's not right to have more power than I already do." I'm talking too fast, but I want to get it all out before he can say no. "You'd be a Guardian and get a power, but the Key that opens the fault line is hidden. Without that Key, you'd be a Guardian in name only."

He says nothing, chewing his cheek.

I hurry on. "The only thing I know about Josh is he did what he did because he loved someone, a woman named Parker who died a couple days later. And she reminded me of Nell."

Finn looks off at Nell, who is pacing beneath the tree now. "But why me? I'm such an average guy. Frankly, it's a little weird either of you liked me to begin with."

That makes me smile. I remember something Daisy told me our first safe night when we couldn't sleep, when I told her we all probably would have died in South Wellsie if she hadn't come to find us.

With the sound of the others snoring lightly around us, she'd said, "There isn't a single person in this group who didn't save someone, and therefore all of us."

"Every person makes an impact in some way, average or not," I say. "We change one another."

He doesn't speak, swallowing hard, and his eyes shine with moisture. And after several long minutes, he gives me his hand.

The magic transfers between us, bright white.

And then there's only the soft orange embers of the sun sinking below the horizon.

It's snowing when I reach the south. But not a punishing snow, just light, fluffy, perfect snow, the kind you see in movies. The kind you imagine when you're craving peace.

They're staying in one of the rental cabins near the river. A trail of smoke slinks lazily from the chimney, pale against the darkening sky. Their fear of fire is conditional. For most, fire exists to chase the ice away, to keep you alive. Its purpose is to burn, but not to burn you. People gave it that latter function, the way magic has no bad intention unless you give it one.

The comforting scent of vanilla, sugar, and butter hangs in the air. A spread of muffins and sticky buns and round crusty loaves lay cooling on the table.

Brian's been stress-baking.

I watch them through the window. A haze of flour hovers for a moment and clears, revealing an old kitchen paneled in dark wood. At the counter, both wearing aprons, Brian and Hyacinth knead mounds of dough. Brian works his lump with the heels of his hands, a thin sheen of sweat on his forehead. Hyacinth hurls hers with vigorous slaps. Her hair is wrapped in a scarf, but flour clings to her cheeks and arms.

Hyacinth holds out her dough for inspection.

He straightens from his hunched position over the counter that's too low for him and too high for her. He rubs his brow with his elbow, leaving a smear of white dust, and a band wraps around my heart and squeezes. Bobby pins hold his bangs off his face. Bobby pins.

Brian pinches her dough between his fingers, stretching it. "Almost. One more."

Hyacinth whacks him in the stomach with the limp log of dough before he can block it.

His breath whooshes out on a laugh, and he lunges for the dough, missing, as she skirts around him, cackling. With the table between them, they eye each other in challenge.

Brian fists his hand in a mountain of flour, blowing it off his palm and enveloping her in a cloud. He gets a wad of sticky dough in the face for that.

Jack Aster lurks in the lifted corners of his mouth. Rose Aster appears in Hyacinth's cheeks that grow fuller, like apples, when she smiles back.

This was the only guardianship that ever mattered to Brian.

They used to fear CPS splitting them up, but that particular worry has evaporated. Now that Wellsie will remain relatively separate from the outside world, no one will be monitoring them. They can stay together.

"They got that from Jack," Daisy says from behind me, her voice soft. "I don't have the patience for baking."

I turn as she climbs the last porch step and stands beside me. She wears that white shearling coat again, but instead of the four cornrows, a pile of tight curls sits on top of her head, wrapped in a black-and-white scarf.

I touch one of my little pigtails, all brittle frizz.

"Every Sunday, my mom, Hyacinth, and I used to put on face masks, deep condition our hair, paint our nails, and watch episodes of *The Great British Baking Show*. We"—her voice falters, eyes smarting with fresh pain—"it was a tradition. You could do that with . . . Hyacinth and me, if you want. Brian's not allowed to watch that show. He's too judgy."

"I'd like that," I say. "No one in my family has curls, so my entire hair-care journey is self-taught."

A small smile peeks through the sadness. "It could be worse. My brother cuts his himself."

"Okay, but look at his eyelashes," I say. "He's . . . he's, uh, he's very . . ." Daisy's eyebrows rise higher with each of my attempts at words. "I saw him with his shirt off once. He's . . . he's been blessed, is what I'm saying."

"I just threw up in my mouth a little," she says brightly. Halfway through the door, she pauses. "Come in for some bread. It's not magic the way Jack's was, but when I take a bite, it's like he's still here."

Maybe everything we lose never really leaves.

I don't go in right away. I take a moment to sit on the porch swing in the cold, attempting to release the hardness of the last two weeks that's knotted into my shoulders.

When he sits next to me, the swing sways gently beneath his weight. He slips a winter coat over my shoulders and I lean against him instinctively. It feels like something I've always done. He left the door open a crack, letting out a waft of yeast and flour.

I trace the face with its sharp nose and turned-down mouth, the slashes for brows, knit together with three puckers like stitches. But his eyes are soft, and I feel them like a touch, feather light.

"Hey," Brian says softly. "I got something for you." When he produces a lump of a pillow in a familiar flowered pillowcase, a cry escapes me.

"They let us into the elementary school today," he says as I seize it. "I wanted to make sure you got this as soon as possible."

Hugging my pillow to my chest, I burrow my face into it, breathing deeply. We kissed in a tree and he rescued my pillow, so I guess we're married now. "Did you put your head on this?" I ask suspiciously, inhaling again.

"Um, no." He raises a brow. "Why?"

"No reason." *It smells like him. Woods. Mountain springs and* . . . "Snickerdoodles," I mutter into the fabric.

He tucks a fuzzy tuft of my hair behind my ear. His own hair falls over his forehead, growing faster than weeds.

Though it's probably weird, I smell his hoodie. I don't know if he really smells like evergreen, or if it's me sensing something about him, something constant, permanent.

Awkwardly, I search for his hand, and it's there without me having to try. Long, kinda knobby fingers, with calluses at the tips. Strange how a hand so large fits mine so well. And I'm not scared to say, "So it might not be a good idea since we're grieving and bonded through trauma, but maybe we could date. If you like me."

"Okay," he says, without even pausing. He places one foot on the railing in front of us, rocking the swing. "You know I like you, Spencer," he says in a low voice, sending one of those shivers down my spine. "There's something delightful about you. Like a wood sprite scampering through the trees. Or a chicken pot pie, one of those little handheld ones."

He lowers his chin, nose brushing mine, and the space between our lips fills with our breaths.

"And I know you like me," he murmurs, a hint of a smirk peeking out. "But you can tell me all about it in the letter."

This earns him an elbow in the ribs.

But his fingers tighten around mine. "Just so you know, it's not about trauma bonds for me," he says. "I remember you used to come into Sugar, Sugar every Saturday. One day, we were out of sticky buns. My father said you looked so small and hungry when you asked if there were any in the back that he went and got the one *I* put aside for *myself*. He took *my* sticky bun and gave it to *you*."

I'm unable to hide my tiny smile. "So you're saying he liked me better."

"Not just that. Because one day I was at the counter when you asked for one, and *I* gave you mine too. It was like I had no will of my own. So from that moment on, whenever he or I happened to see you at the end of the line when we were running low, we'd save you one. 'For the Spencer girl,' he'd say. 'Isidora.'"

*The Spencer girl. Isidora.*

"So you're saying you knew who I was," I whisper, as his cold cheek rubs against mine.

But his words are warm against my ear. "I knew who you were."

I left an impact. Not a footprint in the sand that washes away with a single wave, with no one knowing I existed—a mark on a heart that will always be there no matter what happens.

Out in the yard, snowflakes drift in the soft glow emanating from the windows. Every so often, I see a glimmer of pink and blue and gold rising from the ground where the glittering specks fall. All the remnants need is water to appear. The fault line must pass through here. Someday, when we die, our magic will go back there. Until then, it's here all the time. Something expands in my chest and I remember this bubble-like feeling from when I was a child. Wonder.

In fault-line towns, there are little reminders that magic used to be everywhere once.

In Wellsie, there are faint and fleeting rainbows.

And there's us.

## ACKNOWLEDGMENTS

Whenever I get an idea for a story, it always begins with the characters. I know their backstories, how they talk, their relationships to each other, and their journeys from who they are to who they'll become. The plot comes later as a means to an end. The heart of this book, for me, is human connection, empathy; how everyone we meet will change us in some way. And since my book is all about the ensemble, it makes sense that it took an ensemble to make.

To my family: this is a work of fiction. Any similarity to actual persons, living or dead, or actual events, is purely coincidental. Thank you to my parents first, who got the call in the middle of the night, who recognized me by my hair. You never thought this was a ridiculous dream. You let me stay at home in my early twenties to write books that went nowhere, and when I finally did start adulting, you still believed I would do this someday, even if it took half my life. To my siblings, Dana, Noah, and Peter: I am who I am because of you. To my nieces and nephews, Mia, Lola, Bode, Penny, and Judah: I'm so glad my siblings saved me from having to provide grandchildren. Being your aunt is one of the greatest privileges of my life.

To my editor, Alyza Liu: thank you for responding to "I didn't think anyone would want it—it's such a weird book" with "I love weird." I'm not sure if you knew this when you locked yourself in, but it was not a particularly coveted story. I am immensely grateful that you took a chance on it and that you rolled right past the four BTS references without once commenting that maybe there were too many.

I used to find it strange when authors were attached to their agents—this is a business relationship, after all. That is true, but I am attached to mine. Janine Kamouh, thank you for saying, "Okay, you have to stop telling everyone your book is weird." You're the optimistic one in this duo, the one who tells me "no" when I ask if I should quit writing forever, and the one who didn't give up on this book when I most definitely had. I couldn't have asked for a better person to have in my corner, BUT MOSTLY, THANK YOU FOR INTRODUCING ME TO BTS AND CHANGING MY LIFE.

Katy Nishimoto, you were my last query before I was gonna shelve this book, a shot in the dark after I happened to see a Twitter post of yours. You were the first person in publishing to really get this book and I remember thinking you were the only person who ever would. Thank you for finding me the best champion and proving me wrong.

A huge thank-you to the team at Simon & Schuster: publisher Justin Chanda; deputy publisher Anne Zafian; editorial director Kendra Levin; managing editors Morgan York and Kimberly Capriola; production manager Sara Berko; copyeditor Ela Schwartz; proofreader Gary Sunshine; publicist Anna Elling; and all those who helped make this a real book I can hold in my hands. To cover designer Laura Eckes; interior designer Hilary Zarycky; and cover artist Micaela Alcaino: you made my book more gorgeous than I could have possibly imagined. Thank you for taking my vague "something pretty, creepy, and cool" and creating a masterpiece.

Thank you so much to the team at WME: international rights agent James Munro; film/tv agent Olivia Burgher; and assistants Gaby Caballero and Oma Naraine, for working tirelessly behind the scenes. And to Anna Dixon (formerly WME): thank you for reading, giving feedback, and being incredibly invested in Chad's well-being.

To Rachel Johnson, my first reader: you read the draft of this that was 135,000 words and told me, "At some point, someone is going to tell you to cut the car scene to get to the action quicker. Do not under any circumstances cut the car scene." Just so you know, that's how I secretly judged whether a person loved this book or not. Thank you for supporting me for, like, twelve years.

To my soul sister, Taj McCoy, who I met while posting food pics on Twitter, which quickly morphed into me becoming your biggest fan: you are the busiest person I've ever known, but you're somehow always there to read, give feedback, and talk me down when I'm standing on the ledge. The fact that this happens ALL THE TIME makes me certain I'm getting the better end of this deal.

Writing is such a solitary experience, and I cannot express enough how lucky I am to have such an endlessly supportive writing community. To Naz Kutub, Anna Gracia, Traci-Ann Canada, Alaysia Jordan, Gates Palissery, Paul Ladipo, Pamela Delupio, Robin St. Clare, and Tana Mills of The 99 Dead: you were my first writing friends. A special shout-out to Robin and Tana for being super early readers of this story. We may all be 99 percent dead, but we are hilarious AF. Long live Paul!

My JAN FAM, Carlyn Greenwald and Carolina Flórez-Cerchiaro: thank you for navigating sub hell with me and being my venting safe space. To the Yay Squad—Graci Kim, Steph Lau, Sonora Reyes, J.Elle, and Adelle Yeung—and the 2024 Debuts: thanks for being there during this incredibly wild publishing journey. To Jared Graves: thank you for making me laugh during the dreaded author photoshoot and managing to take one I don't hate.

This book went through more drafts than I can count. To everyone who read some version of chaos, I feel so honored. Emily Miner, your comments lifted me out of post-BTS concert despair. Ariel Baker-Gibbs and Jenna Fischtrom Beacom, I am eternally grateful for your invaluable feedback. Niki Magtoto and Marie Bao, we were adults by the time there were books for us. I wrote this for the girls we were and the girls who won't have to wait. And to the many friends who've read my writing leading up to this—Meredith Adinolfi, Lummi Bae, Amir Rasoulpour, Brad Amorosino, Caitlin Buckley, and Laurin Paradise—thank you.

I can't end this without a special mention of my favorite ensemble, BTS. Sometimes I think you don't know why you mean so much to people. I can only speak for myself, but I didn't grow up seeing people who looked like me in books or movies or music. Nothing beyond a handful of racist stereotypes. So when I see you thriving, selling out stadiums, and breaking down barriers, I feel like I'm winning with you. I feel proud of you and proud of myself. By representing your authentic selves, you show me that I can too. You are in this book four times. Thank you for bringing Korea to me. Stay thriving. And to my ARMY friends—you know who you are—meeting you has been my favorite thing about being a fan. The fact that the seven of them found their way to each other, then connected so many of us, feels like actual magic.

To the adoptees out there . . . I grew up in a very white town as a Korean American adoptee within a family of adoptees, many of us transracial and transnational. My family is Korean, Mexican, Vietnamese, Cambodian, Colombian, Norwegian, Greek, Black, and random white. Within that, there are mixed people, disabled people, queer people, and I'm not entirely sure I haven't left someone out. Not every identity in my family appears in this book and vice versa, but I wanted to create a world that felt like mine, like the life I lived with the people I grew up with. While it is not a book about adoption—it does not explore the industry or many of the issues and complications with transracial/transnational adoption—being a Korean American adoptee factors into Sid's character and how she navigates the world. I wanted to write a girl who represented me, showed some small part of the many different lives Asian Americans can have. This was my Asian American experience. If it resonates with even one person, that's all I ever wanted. And to the Asian American authors who showed me it was possible for all of us to tell our stories, thank you.

And lastly, to everyone who picked up the book of my heart: there was a point in time where I didn't think this would happen. I had to make peace with the possibility that this book might just be for me. But it turns out it's for you now, and from the bottom of my heart, thank you for reading it.

# ABOUT THE AUTHOR

Robin Wasley is a YA fantasy writer with a soft spot for orphans, found families, and funny girls with no special skills who find themselves in extraordinary circumstances. She grew up in a family of adoptees, never truly seeing herself reflected in the books she devoured. As an adult, when she saw an Asian American girl on the cover of a YA book for the first time, she cried.

Robin lives in Boston and works in scientific publishing, but she writes so readers can laugh, cry, and scream, "Why are you like this?" Her favorite things are genre-mashes, bubble baths, Cheetos, and pie. When not writing, she enjoys baking and binge-watching entire seasons of TV in a single day.

Her one dream in life is to become best friends with BTS.

# ABOUT THE AUTHOR

Robin Wasley is a YA fantasy writer with a soft spot for orphans, found families, and funny girls with no special skills who find themselves in extraordinary circumstances. She grew up in a family of adoptees, never truly seeing herself reflected in the books she devoured. As an adult, when she saw an Asian American girl on the cover of a YA book for the first time, she cried.

Robin lives in Boston and works in scientific publishing, but she writes so readers can laugh, cry, and scream, "Why are you like this?" Her favorite things are genre-mashes, bubble baths, Cheetos, and pie. When not writing, she enjoys baking and binge-watching entire seasons of TV in a single day.

Her one dream in life is to become best friends with BTS.